RED DRAGON NIGHTFALL

RED DRAGON NIGHTFALL

E.A. STARK

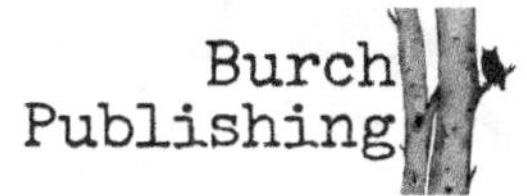

Burch
Publishing

COPYRIGHT

RED DRAGON: NIGHTFALL   Copyright © 2025 by E.A.Stark. All Rights Reserved.

No part of this book may be reproduced in any form or by any electronic or mechanical means, including information storage and retrieval systems, without permission in writing from the author. The only exception is by a reviewer, who may quote short excerpts in a review.

Printed in the United States of America
First Printing: November 22, 2025
Ingram Spark
ISBN-13 978-1-7382195-6-8 Paperback

ISBN-13 978-1-7382195-7-5 EBook

DEDICATION

For Abi, Burton, Shane, Jade, Reggie, and all the lives that crossed their paths.

May their journey remind us that every step we take is part of a greater design.

Love, loss, chance meetings, and unexplainable turns are never random.

They are the threads that weave us into who we are meant to become.

Fate is not always kind, nor is it always clear,

but it has a way of leading us exactly where we belong.

RED
DRAGON
NIGHTFALL

THE JOURNEY THROUGH

Japan

CONTINUES...

| 1 |

Bound for Osaka

Friday, December 22

Park Hyatt, Kyoto

The morning came with a crisp chill in the air, the bright light of the cold winter sun streaming through the windows of their suite at The Park Hyatt.

Packing the last of their things, Abi noticed the awkwardness had filtered into the morning. It was hard going from the closeness they'd shared only a few days prior to suddenly feeling like strangers once again. Quick to blame herself, it wasn't all about their future plans, but more so her relationship with Burton and how it affected Shane.

A knock came to the door.

Opening it, Shane found the concierge with trolleys lined up in the hallway for their bags. They'd already started gathering the luggage from everyone's rooms, hoping to load it shortly.

"Can I send your bag out with mine?" Shane asked, unsure if it was ready to go.

"Yes, I'm done. Thank you," she said.

Out in the hall, he assisted the staff and stacked their suitcases on the cart.

Amidst the chaos, their breakfast arrived right on time.

Wheeling it inside their suite, Shane announced, "The food is here."

"Okay," she said from the bathroom while applying her mascara. "I'll be one more minute."

Busying himself, the QB set their backpacks and Abi's totes by the door for their departure. Taking a gander around the room, he made sure they had everything.

As the two sat down to eat, the stress from the previous night was still present.

Desperate for conversation, he said, "I can't see how they could get our stuff dry-cleaned in such a short amount of time this afternoon. We might have to buy something to wear."

"I was afraid of that, too. I'll let Martin know. Perhaps the stylists will have extra on hand." She took out her phone and messaged her guardian. In seconds, he responded, stating he would be able to accommodate their request.

Relaying that to Shane, all he said in return was, "That sounds good."

A little frustrated, she sighed. "I know you are upset with me, and I'm sorry. But can we try and stay civil?"

He looked up from his food. Sitting back in his chair, he peered across the table. "I'm not angry." As she moved her food around the plate with her fork, he said, "Hey..." Having gotten her attention, he leaned forward and offered his hand. "I was thinking about what we discussed yesterday."

"And..."

"And," he paused. "I am determined for us to figure this out, okay?"

She slipped her hand in his and silently nodded.

"No matter what, I am devoted to you, and nothing will ever change that."

Tears streamed down her cheeks, knowing what he was alluding to. Despite Burton's constant presence, he wasn't backing down. The thought made her blot her face with her napkin.

Seeing this, he didn't need her to say anything. He felt her love.

"So, you are stuck with me." Leaning back again, he added, "For now, let's just enjoy this trip. It will be the last one for a while." Changing the subject, he asked, "So, what does one do at a symphony anyway?"

The comment stunned her.

"What?" he snickered. "I've never been to anything like that."

Abi took hold of her phone and pulled up the Osaka Symphony. Finding a video featuring conductor Takashi Asahina, she pressed play. Listening to the calming music, Abi closed her eyes.

A far cry from what they normally listened to, he said, "So, we are gonna go to that instead of the Dark Demon and Red Dragon rave?"

"I guess so."

"The two are like night and day."

"It would have been fun to see the Nightfall event, but if they don't want us there for security reasons, we need to listen."

The sound of Martin talking in the hallway signaled that it was time to leave.

Finished with breakfast, both of them quickly brushed their teeth and double-checked that they hadn't forgotten anything.

When Abi stepped out into the hall, carrying her tote bag on her shoulder, she saw Burton. He was leaning against the wall, looking exhausted but upright, dressed in his usual plain black hoodie, deep in conversation with Lorenzo and the guys.

Seeing him, Shane came up behind her and slung his backpack on one shoulder while reaching to grab and carry her bag for her. In the process, he stared the guy down.

"Please act fast and efficiently so we can be on our way," Martin instructed.

Everyone acknowledged him.

Taking the elevators down to the lower level, Martin guided them in the opposite direction from the underground parking garage. Instead, they emerged from a side door of the hotel compound. Stepping into an alcove that opened onto a narrow street, a luxury coach bus waited for them in the shadows, its dark silhouette nearly blending into the dimness of the alley. Behind it, a black SUV stood loaded with their luggage.

It was a quiet morning as they pulled away from the hotel and left Kyoto behind. Soon, the city's historical beauty slipped away in the rearview mirror. The mood on the bus remained hushed as well, a reflection of the fatigue and the personal battles simmering amidst the group.

Feeling everything they'd left unsaid, Abi turned to Shane before her eyes fell upon Burton, who sat alone a few rows ahead. Sara was noticeably absent. Her decision to leave him was like a question mark in the air.

Reg and Jade were cuddled up in their seats, jokingly referring to each other as "wife" and "husband," but the playful banter did little to break her mood.

Hoping to talk to Burton and ask how his event had gone the night before, Abi weighed her options and addressed Shane. Leaning over, she whispered, "Are you okay if I just talk to him for a minute? He seems upset. I'm sure that Sara's leaving wasn't easy, and I want to see if he's heard from her."

Shane stiffened and didn't respond at first. After a pause, he sighed. "Fine." Standing to let her leave her seat, she slipped by him and tapped his hand gently before walking down the aisle.

When she reached the front, Burton was surprised to see her and quickly shifted to make room. "Hey," he said with a small smile, peering behind them to see if the QB was watching.

"Don't worry about Shane," she whispered. "I cleared it with him first."

Not liking that, he tried to contain his anger. "You shouldn't have to..."

Interrupting, she replied while sitting down. "I know, I know. I'm trying to keep the peace. That's all."

He realized she wasn't wrong for doing that.

"I just wanted to check in with you and see how last night went."

His face brightened slightly at her concern. "It went well," he said, sounding more energized as he recalled the details. "We were at this gallery space called Yakaan. It was long and narrow. Kind of a pain for security with only one exit. But the turnout was great. We registered one hundred and fifty new vault users last night, so that's a win. Akio and Lelin were happy with how it all went."

"Akio and Lelin?" Abi asked, unfamiliar with the names.

"DJ Red Dragon and his wife," Burton explained. "They're normal people hiding behind a big name like me. Found out they have a little girl—she's two, I think they said."

Abi smiled at the revelation. It struck her how similar Burton and these other celebrities were, people hiding behind façades, characters they'd created. She asked gently, "So, you're good?"

He nodded, though his exhaustion showed through. "Yeah, a little tired, but I'm ready for tonight. It's going to be another busy one." Glancing back at Shane, he saw the guy's eyes affixed to them from across the bus. Burton cleared his throat. "You'd better head back before Coppersmith explodes."

"Burton..." Tilting her head disapprovingly, she stood up.

"Sorry..."

"I'm glad last night was a success."

"Appreciate that," he replied, giving her a grateful look.

Assuming everyone on the bus was staring, she said, "I'm just gonna..."

"It's fine. You go. We'll talk later."

As Abi made her way back to Shane, her hunch was right. Everyone was watching their interaction while she returned to her seat.

"So? How is he?" Shane asked, curious.

With a contented expression, she turned to him. "He's good. The event went well. He's just tired—it was a late night."

The road from Kyoto to Osaka stretched ahead, a ribbon of asphalt flanked by rolling hills and pockets of dense, green forests. The engine's hum was a soothing undercurrent to the rhythmic whoosh of passing cars.

Briefly catching a final glimpse of the Kamo River winding its way through the heart of the city, Abi said goodbye to the historic place.

Once they reached the outskirts, the landscape consisted only of the concrete and glass barriers lining the highway. Barely able to see the view, Abi watched the sun climb higher, casting a golden sheen over the clouds. Seeing Burton's head down and headphones over his ears, she assumed he was working.

As the bus rumbled towards Osaka, Abi shifted in her seat, the city just under an hour away. Finding Shane resting his head back with his eyes closed and one leg stretched out in the center aisle, his breath even in sleep, she took out her phone, needing something to distract her thoughts.

A quick scroll through social media revealed a flood of posts trending with #DarkDemonRave, #DarkDemonEffect, #TheUnderground, and #RedDragonXperience. Her feed was overflowing with reels, stories, and live clips from the Kyoto event. Each praised the dazzling laser tech, immersive holograms, and the hypnotic blend of music and lights pulsing through the crowd, creating a vibe that felt more like a lucid dream. Headline after headline read,

Entertainment. Upgraded. Dark Demon has officially changed the game.

Tech meets mystery—Dark Demon rave was surreal.

Red Dragon & His Queen = Couple Goals

Who is Dark Demon? I'd risk it all just to find out.

Forget Coachella. This was digital seduction in motion.

If I didn't see it with my own eyes, I'd never believe it.

Thousands of comments scrolled beneath each news article. Many commended the immersive experience. Others speculated—obsessively—about Dark Demon's identity. A surprising number of women were openly infatuated, calling him "the phantom" and "a genius wrapped in the shadows." By contrast, Red Dragon and his wife were dubbed *"Japan's hottest power couple,"* with sweet clips of the hooded DJ holding her hand, laughing together, or sharing quiet moments backstage.

Uneasy, Abi knew the truth behind it all. The more famous Burton became, the more likely it was that someone unstable would come after him. A threat, a setup, an obsessed fan—it wouldn't take much. Her fingers stilled on the screen as an intrusive thought passed: *What if the Tokuryū were watching? Waiting?*

She glanced around subtly. Yet the knot in her gut remained. The Red Dragon teens haunted her thoughts, appearing at random, their motives still unclear. Why were they targeting them? What did they want? And who was ultimately controlling them from the shadows?

Overwhelmed by it all, she dimmed her screen and slipped the phone back into her bag. Outside, every mile took an eternity. Deciding to drift off to pass the time, knowing Shane had the right idea, she rested her head against the window using her jacket as a pillow. It didn't take long before she, too, surrendered to the quiet hum of the road.

| 2 |

The Conrad

Friday, December 22

The Conrad Hotel, Osaka

A strong bump of the coach bus along the freeway jolted Abi awake, making her eyes open. Getting her bearings, it was like they'd transitioned from one world to another. The scenery changed from the serene green hills to the growing excitement of urban life.

Shane was already up. "Hey, sleepy head. How was your nap?"

"It was good? Yours?"

He laughed. "Feel like a new man."

Straightening in her seat, stretching her arms above her head, she watched the city come into view. A line of tall buildings seemed to reach the heavens as they drove deeper into the downtown core. Everything became a blur of motion. Cars crowded the streets, and motorcycles zipped through the gaps, their riders' helmets painted in bright, eye-catching colors. Billboards and neon signs flashed ads for the latest fashion, technology, and local cuisine. Street signs in both kanji and English directed them through the busy roads, pointing them toward the heart of the city. The closer they got, the more they could feel Osaka's energy: loud, bright, and full of life.

Merging from one highway to another, Abi couldn't believe how clean the streets were. Racetrack-looking, the road twisted and turned as the buildings soon closed in on either side. Upon descending below the freeway, the off-ramp narrowed. Walls towering all around them, Abi spied the river shimmering below the bridge in the afternoon sun. Leaning closer to the window, she loved the blend of nature amidst the concrete and glass structures.

As the luxury coach carried them deeper into the bustling downtown, they mingled amongst the labyrinth of tall skyscrapers, making it feel like an intricate puzzle as the group soaked in all its grandeur.

While moving along in traffic, Abi's gaze bounced between the view outside the window and Burton sitting alone near the front. She couldn't help but notice how tired he was. His face, somber. Since Sara disappeared, her heart ached for him, and though Shane sensed her worry, he didn't say anything.

Approaching the Conrad Hotel, the driver slowed down, flicked on his hazard lights, and signaled to the security guard stationed nearby. As they smoothly entered the tunnel leading to the main entrance, the concierge staff immediately swarmed around them with a flurry of activity while Martin stood tall in the aisle.

"We have arrived at our destination. Please take your baggage with you. Do not leave anything behind," he instructed before exiting to greet the woman standing by the door.

Shane got up from his seat and slipped his backpack on his shoulder. Seeing Abi about to do the same, he took it from her. "I'll carry that for you," he said firmly.

She quickly rebutted, "No, it's okay. I've got it."

Looking down at his girlfriend, Shane tilted his head to question what was going on silently.

She realized he wasn't going to give it over, so she conceded.

Gathered around the coach while the bags got unloaded onto trolleys, the men and women checked the names on the luggage tags and cross-referenced them with their guest list to ensure each piece arrived in the correct rooms.

"Welcome to the Conrad Hotel," a polished young woman greeted them at the entrance, her smile warm but professional. "My name is Yuna. I will be helping you get settled."

Martin stepped forward, bowing slightly. "Very nice to meet you, my dear."

Bowing in return, she said, "Follow me." With a gracious smile, Yuna led them through the sleek hotel lobby and divided them into groups for the long elevator ride to the fortieth floor. Stepping aboard, Shane, Abi, the newlyweds, and Abi's security team got in one elevator while Burton, Martin, Anton, and his guys went in another.

The moment the elevator doors opened high above the ground, each marveled at the awe-inspiring views - a full panoramic of the city through thirty-foot, floor-to-ceiling windows. In the lounge far below them, several guests mingled with drinks in hand.

Legs weakening, Abi stayed back. "Oh, I don't know about this..." she whispered, terrified by how high up they were above the sprawling skyline.

Shane joined her, standing close enough that their arms brushed. "Are you okay?" he asked, amazed at the large, flowing spiral staircase leading to the three-story SkyLounge below. "Feels like we're on top of the world here, doesn't it?"

Afraid, Abi backed up and stole a glance behind her, briefly noticing Burton looking her way. He had a small, pleasant smile on his face, and his eyes seemed to be asking her a question, though he remained where he was. She wanted to talk to him, but the heaviness of her situation with Shane held her back.

Yuna's instructions broke through the hum around them. "The main lobby is this way," she said, gesturing toward a set of glass walls. "We will confirm your arrival and take you to the Executive Lounge on the 39th floor, where you can enjoy a light meal before proceeding to your suites."

The walk through the luxurious hotel helped Abi settle her nerves. Passing by two white sculptures with a creature climbing among the bubbles, they entered the reception area, where sparkling crystalized drapes adorned the far end.

Everything seemed pristine, almost surreal, as they approached another set of elevators. The thought of being so high up and stepping inside when the doors opened made her stomach churn.

It's okay. Take a deep breath, she thought, trying to encourage herself despite the fear as they descended one floor.

When their group arrived in the Executive Lounge, Abi, Jade, and the guys slid into a banquette while Burton and Martin claimed a spot by the windows.

"I'm just gonna check out the buffet," Shane said, with Reg following suit.

"I'm right behind you, man."

At the table, Abi spied on the two men who were deep in conversation.

Martin had a stern expression on his face, while Burton seemed more relaxed than on the ride there, but strangely, there was still a shadow hanging over him.

"I wonder what they are talking about..." Abi whispered to herself.

"What was that?" Jade asked, having heard her say something.

"Oh, nothing. Just talking to myself."

Before long, Shane returned with two plates in hand and set one in front of Abi. "I grabbed a few things I thought you might like," he said.

Perusing what he'd selected, she replied, "Thank you," believing it was sweet of him to think of her despite the uneasiness between them.

Reggie also returned with a plate for Jade. Placing it in front of her, he instinctively bent down to kiss her cheek, but she stopped him. "Remember what Martin said—no PDA," she quietly teased, gently pressing a hand lightly to his chest.

Hating that restriction, her new husband had no choice but to refrain.

While they enjoyed the buffet, Abi's attention drifted back to her famous friend.

Yuna had returned with a leather folder. Presenting it to him, Abi watched as he flipped it open and swiped a pen across the paperwork inside, not batting an eye at the bottom line. Closing it and handing it back cordially, he added a respectful bow before the woman tucked it under her arm and offered the same gesture.

"Please, follow me," she said with a smile. "I will take you to your suites."

Both of them got up from the table.

Seeing Abi's eyes on him, he subtly raised a hand at waist level to bid her goodbye.

She offered a slight tilt of her head to acknowledge it, hoping Shane wouldn't notice. When he walked away, Abi intently focused on her friends. "I wonder what our rooms will look like?" she said.

"I think they will be pretty nice," Jade stated. "Burton's taken good care of us on this trip."

Reggie seconded that. "The hotels so far have been amazing. I'm sure this one won't be any different."

"He said it's costing two million, between private flights, security, transportation, accommodations, food…"

"And, our wedding?" Jade added, feeling a high level of guilt.

"I guess it all adds up."

Hearing her say this as they ate, Shane felt put off. He knew the guy was paying for everything, and he hadn't contributed a cent. It made him feel insignificant and more like a kid than a man. But he didn't expect it to suddenly fuel him to work harder and achieve his NFL goals. Refocusing, he straightened in his chair, knowing he hadn't trained nearly as much as he should thus far. Needing to get back into his gym routine and proper diet despite the long-awaited break, he turned to Abi, knowing she was his motivation. One day, he hoped to give her everything she could ever want. Even trips like this.

Finishing up, Yuna soon returned to escort them to their rooms. Gathered around the petite woman, she said, "Follow me," before leading the way regally.

About to leave the lounge, they spotted Sara with her laptop bag slung over her shoulder, intentionally avoiding them by walking to the opposite side of the room.

"Wow...would you look at that?"

Everyone could sense Jade's anger. They knew she was still harboring resentment about the girl who had skipped out on their big day.

"She has a lot of nerve..."

Turning to Jade, Abi said, "Don't confront her. It's not worth it."

"Yeah, Babe. It's fine. Our day was amazing, regardless," Reggie reassured, then added, "Well, despite the interruption. No need to dwell on that."

Nodding her head, she glared at the girl on their way past.

When they arrived at the private bank of elevators, descending to the 37th floor, Abi's thoughts drifted back to Burton. She couldn't help but ask Yuna, "Our friend is in the Penthouse Suite. Is it on the same floor?"

Shane hated to hear her take an interest in the guy.

The young woman hesitated, then smiled. "The Conrad Suite is on the 39th floor, where the Executive Lounge is."

Abi nodded, mentally filing the information away as Yuna exited the elevator with them and walked down the long hallway.

Handing the guys their key cards, she pointed to the doors of their suites, a mere twenty feet apart. "If you need anything, please don't hesitate to call the concierge desk. They will assist you."

With that, Shane waved the room key over the reader as the door to their executive corner suite clicked open. The sensor triggered the drapes to retract automatically on their way inside, revealing a stunning view of the city.

"Wow," Shane said, stepping toward the wall of windows. "Impressive."

Preoccupied, Abi sat down on the edge of the bed, clutching the iconic Beanie Baby bear and Ducky placed in the middle. "We're really high up," she said quietly, her eyes glued to the edge.

Not hearing her, Shane explored the space and found their luggage neatly tucked away in the closet. "They've already delivered our bags," he said, trying to lighten the mood as he walked to the other side of the room to take in the view again.

Instantly, Abi's panic rose. "Don't go so close!" she blurted out.

Frozen, Shane got concerned. "Abi… What's wrong?"

She swallowed hard, her grip on the stuffed animal tightening. "I… I'm afraid of heights," she admitted. "It feels like the floor is slanting toward the windows like I'm going to fall out."

An understanding flashed across his face. He immediately backed away and sat beside her on the bed, reaching for her hand. "Hey, it's okay," he said softly. "You're safe. We're not going to fall."

Taking a breath, she nodded, but the fear still gripped her tightly.

Gently rubbing the back of her hand, his calm presence soothed her. "We can close the drapes if that helps," he suggested.

"It's not just the windows," Abi confessed. "It's everything. We are so high up. I just…"

Shifting closer, he wrapped his arms around her, his expression softening. "You're fine. I won't let anything happen to you."

She glanced at him, her nerves slowly retreating.

"Are you sure you don't want the drapes closed?" he asked again, ready to jump up if she said yes.

"No, it's alright." Abi shook her head. "I'll be okay. Just, umm, stay close for a second."

Shane smiled, still holding her hand. "Guess I learned something new today."

"What's that?" she questioned. "That I'm afraid of heights?"

His gaze dropped briefly to their feet, then lifted to meet hers with a teasing glint. "That even you have a weakness," he said. "It's kind of like discovering your kryptonite."

She felt the knot of anxiety start to loosen in her chest. Somehow, his presence grounded her and made her feel safe.

Still perched on the edge of the bed, catching her breath after experiencing the bout of anxiety, they heard a knock echo through the room.

"You good? Can I..." Shane glanced up and pointed at the door before going to answer it.

She nodded, feeling less scared, especially when she heard it was Martin.

"Hello, Mr. Coppersmith. I hope everything is to your liking," the gentleman greeted while he spoke with Shane. "I'll be escorting you and the newlyweds to Master B's suite. The stylists have already arrived and have set out evening wear for your outing at the symphony tonight."

Joining them, she saw Martin's calm expression. Feeling her nerves shift from the earlier fear to the buzz of anticipation for the night ahead, she took Shane's hand in hers as he gave her a comforting squeeze - his presence a steadying force as he grabbed the key card from the table.

About to leave, Abi darted into the closet. "Wait one second. Sorry..." She opened her suitcase and scanned for the dressy heels she'd worn for the wedding. "I'm going to need these," she mumbled, slipping them into a tote bag.

With a content grin, Shane held out his hand to her when the door shut behind them. Following Martin down the hallway, they stopped at Jade and Reggie's room.

Their friends soon emerged.

"Oooh! I'm so excited to see what they have for us!" Jade said, bubbling over. She could tell Abi wasn't as energetic as she was when she linked her arm with her friend's. "Hey... Why the long face, girl?"

"Umm, nothing." Not wanting to divulge her fear of heights issue, she said, "Tonight should be fun."

"I hope so. It won't be as exciting as the NAKKA event would have been, but it can't be helped, so…" the girl divulged while glancing at Martin, who ignored her comment.

Their elevator ride felt lighthearted despite it.

Upon arrival on the 39th floor, a guarded, private vestibule led them to the Conrad Suite's grand double doors. Room 3901.

Walking inside, beyond the entryway, was a well-orchestrated scene awaiting them—stylists, assistants, and hotel staff moving about with efficiency, each one attending to the smallest detail in preparation for their VIP guests.

Taken by the lavish space, Abi's eyes swept the room from left to right in search of Burton. Reluctantly guided to a crescent-shaped sofa in the spacious living area, Shane remained by her side, his quiet strength steadying her as she eyed the floor-to-ceiling glass walls a few feet away. Meanwhile, Jade and Reggie were already deep in animated conversation.

A sudden flurry of movement in the adjacent bedroom caught Abi's attention. Through a crack between the doors, she saw Burton standing in front of a set of mirrors, meticulously being fitted into a custom tuxedo. The modern hooded jacket, lined with deep red silk, gave him an air of mystery. His face, partially obscured by the hood's shadow, suddenly turned as he gravitated to her briefly before paying attention to the stylists.

"Wow," Abi breathed in a whispered tone. In that moment, Burton seemed less like the friend she'd known for years and more like the famous Dark Demon—calm, composed, and exuding a quiet authority.

Reina, one of the stylists, approached the group with a welcoming smile. "Hello, ladies. We have a wide variety of gowns ready for you," she said, motioning to a rack of exquisite designer dresses.

Jade's eyes gleamed upon seeing the much-anticipated red Versace Medusa. The asymmetric draping was flawless, with Medusa '95 hardware on one shoulder shimmering in the light. Without hesitation, Jade reached for it, holding it against herself with sheer delight.

"I love it!" she announced, her excitement unbridled, while Reggie clearly admired her choice.

Abi, however, was drawn to a more understated piece—a glistening Polo Ralph Lauren metallic sweater evening gown. The dramatic scoopback and flowing train gave it an ethereal elegance, and the soft knit fabric felt luxurious against her fingertips. Loving its metallic sheen, Abi knew this was the one for her.

"That gown is stunning," Reina commented approvingly, observing Abi's reaction. "I am sure it will fit you beautifully."

With the girls excited about their selections, Reina also introduced the male stylists to Shane and Reggie after they'd finished with Burton. Each worked swiftly, taking precise measurements to ensure a perfect fit for their tuxedos. Though slightly uncomfortable at first, the guys soon eased into the process, donning crisp white shirts and tailored jackets with a newfound confidence.

With her gaze wandering back to Burton, now finished with his fitting, she heard him conversing with Martin. Discussing the final sound check details for the evening, Burton slipped out of his tuxedo jacket, revealing a sleek black shirt beneath, keeping in line with his typically dark attire.

Upon leaving, he carefully winked at Abi as he passed, his face hidden beneath his Dark Demon hoodie. Offering a subtle wave, he slung his satchel on his shoulder before exiting the suite with Martin and his security team close behind.

Flashing a partial smile after she raised a steady hand to bid him goodbye, her mind lingered on how much Burton seemed to have changed since their arrival in Osaka. A certain distance now surrounded him. The weight of his dual life as Dark Demon was beginning to show, and Abi wondered how challenging it was to carry his secret.

Soon, the stylists ushered the girls into Burton's bedroom to try on their dresses. Surrounded by the opulence of the suite, Abi slipped into the shimmering gown. The fabric hugged her figure perfectly, the metallic sheen catching the light with every movement. As she turned toward the full-length mirror, a soft gasp escaped her lips at the reflection staring back at her.

Jade, now dressed in her bold red Versace, grinned at Abi. "You look incredible," she said with delight.

"You too," Abi replied, admiring Jade's daring choice.

They both twirled in front of the mirror, their happiness overflowing as the fabric of their dresses swirled around them. For a moment, Abi felt like she belonged in this glamorous world, even though a tiny voice in the back of her mind disapproved on so many levels.

Changing again, the girls waited for the stylists to pack their gowns into garment bags carefully.

Carrying them, about to leave, Abi and Jade got stopped by Martin at the door.

"This is your itinerary for this evening," he said, emailing them a copy.

Checking her phone, Abi acknowledged it. "Thank you, Martin."

"You have free time until your departure this evening. Please keep a low profile as Master B requested."

On their way out the door, Abi replied, "Don't worry. We will."

Anticipating their outing that evening, they rode the elevator back to the 37th floor.

Dropping off Jade and Reggie first, Shane said to them, "You guys up for exploring the hotel in a bit?"

"Yeah, I guess we can't do much else," Reg replied.

Hating to hear their disappointment, Abi said, "Oh, it's fine," hoping to douse the negativity. "It's just for a few hours, and then we can have dinner and head out."

Shane agreed with her. "Absolutely."

Continuing onto their room, Abi let out a slow breath, her nerves finally settling. Everything was falling into place, and she felt more prepared for it now, almost worthy of the luxurious experience.

When he opened the door of their suite, she made a sharp left into the walk-in closet and hung up her dress.

"Are you excited about tonight?" He said gently as he placed his suit beside it.

"I'm sure it will be fun," she muttered before walking into the other room.

Able to tell there was still something not right with her, he was about to ask when he heard his phone chime.

Finding a text from Reggie, Shane paraphrased it. "He's wondering if you can get Martin's permission to walk around Osaka Castle for a bit. Apparently, it's not far. They can see it from their room."

She exhaled and agreed hesitantly. "I'll ask, but I can't promise any-thing." Deciding to text Andrew their request instead, she sent the message and waited, figuring the guy would relay it up the chain mo-mentarily.

Watching Shane walk to the window to take in the view, her stom-ach dropped again at the sight of him being so close to the edge. When she sat on the bed, her phone chimed. "Looks like we got per-mission for a one-hour excursion," she said. "Matt and Ted will have to go with us, though."

"Great. I'll let Reg know." Texting the guy, the two made plans for them to meet in the hall in five minutes.

Abi layered up for the crisp day outside, choosing yoga pants, a hoodie, and socks before stepping into her running shoes. She grabbed her lightweight down jacket and stood at the door. "Ready to go?" she asked.

Dressed in joggers and a hoodie, Shane finished re-tying his run-ners and zipped their room key securely into his coat pocket. "Yep. Ready," he said, joining her. "Let's go."

| 3 |

Osaka Castle

Friday, December 22

The Conrad Hotel, Osaka

All bundled up, eager to have her feet back on solid ground, Abi walked out the door with Shane and joined their friends in the corridor. Together, they made their way to the elevators, where they met up with Matt and Ted.

"Hi, guys," Abi greeted.

"Good afternoon, Miss." Matt stood tall with his hands fastened behind his back.

"Andrew is with Master B," Ted revealed. "Martin has us going with you."

Abi felt a sense of relief, happy to have support in case anything happened. Waiting for the elevator, she felt her stomach flutter with nerves. Feeling the guys' apprehension, along with her own, she wondered what was on their minds.

Ever the gentleman, Shane held the doors back for everyone when they parted. Stepping aboard, one by one, he released them to start their ascent to the 40th floor.

Upon arriving, the group made their way through the main reception and down the high-speed elevator to the entrance below. When the doors opened on the ground level, a woman behind the desk asked, "May I help you? Do you require transportation? Directions, perhaps?"

Reggie, holding Jade's hand, replied, "Yes, a taxi to Osaka Castle would be great."

Watching them like a hawk, Abi noticed the woman reach for her earpiece and verbally request a taxi. About to say something to Matt, she heard him intervene as he looked at his phone. "No, that's not necessary. We have a private driver waiting."

Unaware of this, Reg turned. "Sorry," he said to the woman, "Cancel that."

Catching her eyes glued to them strangely, Abi got a weird feeling, especially upon spotting a tattoo peeking out from under the cuff of the woman's suit jacket, but she couldn't make out what it was.

The valet outside let them know their luxury van had pulled up.

"Enjoy your afternoon," the lady said as they walked away.

Not thinking anything of it, Jade responded cordially. "Thank you."

Exiting through the main doors, Abi got a burst of cool air and took in a deep breath, thankful to feel her stomach settling since they'd reached the ground floor. The relief she felt calmed her nerves, but a hint of unease remained.

Maybe it's nothing, she thought as they found a seat in the luxurious black van. *You're just being paranoid.*

Finally, on their way, after packing into the vehicle, they were soon weaving through the streets of Osaka. Everyone admired the city's pristine condition—there wasn't a single piece of trash on the roads or sidewalks.

"It's so perfect here," Abi mused. "The trees, the buildings... Why can't it be like this back home?"

As they drove across the bridge overtop of the river, Reggie commented, "Doesn't it feel like we're in Chicago?"

Never having been there, Abi muttered, "I wouldn't know," while the van veered off the main street and into a park, where trees and green grass framed the road.

In the distance, they spotted a moat and the tall stone walls of the castle, with a traditional white Japanese structure perched on the corner. Slowing down, their driver turned left and pulled up to the main gates. Reggie paid the fare and arranged for the driver to return at five o'clock. After confirming their departure time, the man gave them his business card and drove off.

Matt took note of the driver's license plate, snapping a photo as they approached the Ōte-mon Gate. Walking through the iron-riveted walls of the Tamon-yagura, they followed the winding path toward the castle. At the white tent ticket office, Shane paid for everyone's ticket. Continuing along the moat toward a bridge in the distance, they crossed over to the castle grounds.

Abi couldn't help but admire the immense stones that formed the walls. Each massive rock seemed to fit flawlessly with the next, stacked meticulously without the use of mortar—an ancient technique that had endured centuries of wear.

Studying the construction, Shane shook his head in amazement. "How did they even accomplish this? It's like the pyramids of Egypt."

Some were larger than they could imagine being moved by human hands, and yet there they were, forming the solid base of the fortress.

The sheer size made Abi look small in comparison.

Rounding a corner, they followed the perimeter wall and stood at the edge to appreciate Osaka's sprawling skyline, dotted with skyscrapers and city infrastructure. The peacefulness of the castle grounds made it seem a world apart.

"Wow," Jade said in awe.

"It's hard to believe we're so close to modern society, yet it feels like we're in the countryside," Abi agreed. Taking in the beauty of their surroundings, she felt a pang of guilt wash over her, knowing Burton was missing this experience. Fully aware that his schedule was packed and he wouldn't get to see much beyond his hotel room and the event venue, she took more pictures to share with him later, hoping they might capture the essence of the place.

After getting a couple of selfies together, Matt offered to take a photo of them standing in front of the Imperial stronghold. The four friends posed for the picture with bright smiles before moving on.

Immersing in the full majesty of the castle itself, the sky above was a perfect shade of blue, except for a few wisps of clouds that drifted lazily by.

While marveling at the main tower, with its layered roofs painted a rich green atop the white stucco, Abi zeroed in on the gold trim sparkling in the light. Accenting the historic building, perched high upon the stone foundation, it gave it a magical appearance.

Walking through the vast gardens, Abi appreciated the neatly manicured shrubs in perfect harmony with the natural landscape. The cherry blossom trees, though not in season, still had a presence. Their branches framed the pathways with a promise of beauty in the spring.

Ahead, they crossed the long bridge over the moat, its wooden railings warm under their hands in the midday sun. As they walked along, the contrast between the modern skyline of Osaka in the distance and the ancient castle before them was striking—a blending of two worlds, where the past met the future seamlessly.

Once they reached the other side, they marveled at the towering walls, reinforcing the defensive design.

"Imagine trying to storm this place back in the day," Shane pondered, shaking his head in disbelief at the sheer scale of it.

Jade got lost in her thoughts. "It feels like a scene from a fantasy novel," she said, echoing Abi's sentiments. About to add a few pictures on Instagram out of habit, Reggie stopped her.

"Don't post anything," he said while confusion spread across his wife's face. Worried, he asked, "What is it, Babe?"

"That's strange. I can't log in to my account. Something's wrong. My password isn't working," she revealed in a panic. "Give me your phone. I want to check something."

Handing his phone over, she checked her profile and found two reels and three posts from the castle on her feed. She looked up, noticeably fearful. "Wait... What the hell? I didn't post these." Showing Reggie, he could see that each photo of them was taken at a distance. It caused an eeriness to seep in as he scanned the area.

"Someone took these and posted them," he said as Matt and Ted strode over, their eyes narrowing as they studied the context of the images.

Seeing the apparent *Death to her* kanji script posted amongst the other pics of them, only minutes old, Matt went on high alert.

"I think someone hacked it, Miss," Ted advised urgently. "And whoever did it is close. Real close."

"What do we do?" Abi asked, her pulse quickening.

"Remain calm," Matt ordered with protective instincts on high alert. His eyes never stopped sweeping the area. Ted stood slightly in front of Abi, his shoulders squared as if bracing for anything.

Then came the sound of laughter. Harsh and mocking. A group of teens lingering near the stone path soon became rudely disruptive. Their jeering remarks echoed through the air, but it wasn't just their obnoxious behavior that set Abi on edge. It was the way they watched.

Glances exchanged. Smirks. Every so often, their eyes flicked toward her, exuding a sinister amusement.

"I think it was them," she said, nodding in their direction.

Matt and Ted followed her line of sight, instantly locking onto one boy in particular. His posture was aggressive, with broad shoulders and his chin lifted. Without hesitation, he broke from the group and headed their way.

"We've got company," Ted commanded, his hand subtly motioning for Abi to step behind him.

Matt's voice was low. "I see him."

Shane and Reggie followed suit when they sensed the sudden shift. Their protective stance mirrored Matt's as both instinctively stepped into a guard position. The four men created a wall, towering above the advancing figure.

The young teen didn't flinch. But neither did they.

Upon witnessing this, Abi's heart rate spiked when Shane reached back to shield her.

Reggie did the same with Jade.

To their surprise, the teenager narrowly passed by without incident, but Abi caught a glimpse of something on the nape of his neck. Partially hidden under his shirt was the unmistakable image of a red dragon tattoo. Her breath escaped her lungs, and then, before she could say anything, she heard Ted intervene.

"I'm calling it," he said firmly, still tracking the teens as their group increased in size by the minute. "We're leaving. Now!"

Aware of how observant the guys were, Abi knew they were in danger.

Shane could feel her hand trembling in his as he stayed by her side, moving swiftly toward the main gate. Keeping an eye on everyone around them, he slid his arm around Abi's shoulders in case he had to protect her.

"Let's pick up the pace, please." Ted's commanding presence sparked urgency, making it clear the teens lurking nearby weren't just sightseeing.

Heads on a swivel, the men quickly shifted into response mode.

Discreetly calling Martin, Matt relayed the details of their situation. "Yes, Sir. We're heading back to the hotel," he said. "We will follow protocol."

The atmosphere changed drastically. The once peaceful tour of Osaka Castle now felt charged with hidden threats. As they neared the Ōte-mon gates to meet up with their driver, Ted and Matt got increasingly wary of using the same guy.

"I don't like this," Ted muttered under his breath, instincts surfacing. "It's too coincidental," he said to his partner.

Without hesitation, they abandoned the private car and accepted the first taxi van offered by the valets at the entrance.

Crammed in the vehicle, the ride back to the Conrad was tense. Matt had the guy drive them around the city a bit while secretly watching for anyone following them.

No one spoke a word.

Peering over her shoulder repeatedly, Abi felt her pulse racing as she tried to make sense of what they might have just escaped.

On route to the hotel, Shane said as his arms wrapped around her, "We will be fine."

Filled with worry, she blurted, "Maybe we shouldn't go out tonight."

Shocked to hear this, Jade rebutted, "What? And miss the chance to get dressed up? No way!"

"It's not worth it, Jade."

"Come on, Abs. There will be lots of civilized people there. I'm certain nothing will happen. Trust me," her friend said, hoping to create an open and shut case minutes before the taxi finally pulled into the breezeway of the Conrad.

Interrupting them, Ted spouted crisp instructions. "When he stops, we move inside quickly. No hesitation, straight to the elevators. Got it?"

Each gave him a nod to say they understood.

As Jade's hand brushed against hers, Abi looked over to see her friend's wide eyes suddenly mirror her concern. But there wasn't time to dwell on it. As soon as the car shifted into park, Matt passed the driver money for the fare and was already opening the door, ready to shield the girls.

Jumping out, one by one, every step felt like a race against time; their senses heightened as they scanned the street view on either end of the tunnel. In a tight formation, Ted flanked one side with Matt on the other, with Shane and Reggie closely following behind.

The woman concierge they'd met earlier said urgently, "Excuse me!" It made them stop a few feet from the elevators.

Matt swiveled around. "What can we do for you?"

With envelopes in hand, she replied, "A messenger left these for you."

Taking them from her, he handed them to Reggie.

Noticing each one addressed to them by name, Reg said, "Thank you," as they converged on an available lift.

"Enjoy your evening," she said as they stepped aboard and disappeared behind the doors when they slid shut.

Abi seemed clearly suspicious of the woman.

"Is there something you are not telling me?" Ted asked, leery of Abi's actions.

Unable to confirm what the tattoo was on the woman, she stopped. "Umm, no. It's nothing."

"Are you sure?" he questioned a second time, knowing her quite well.

"I'm sure."

Safely on their way to the fortieth floor, they arrived in the upper lobby to find extra security awaiting them. Still gripping Shane's waist as they walked past the check-in desk, Abi's pulse slowed. It was then she realized her fear of heights was the least of her worries.

"Martin must have alerted management that there was a problem," Ted surmised while moving past the reception area and descending in the separate hotel elevators again to the 37th floor.

When the doors opened, the men casually escorted them down the corridor toward their rooms.

About to go their separate ways, Jade said, "Can we hang out in your suite?"

Not having a problem with it, Abi nodded, "Sure. If you'd like."

Tapping their key card against the reader, Shane opened the door. Holding it back, he let Abi, Jade, and Reg enter first.

About to walk in, Abi turned to the men. "Thank you for keeping us safe."

Ted gave a thumbs-up as Matt looked on a few feet away. "No problem. If you need us, we will be just down the hall."

"Alright," she said while the door closed behind them.

After distributing the envelopes, strangely each addressed to them by name, Reg talked to Shane while simultaneously searching Jade's phone for an email from Instagram, hoping to find something to secure her account and change her password as she stood idly by.

The first to open the card, Jade shouted, "Oh my god! It's a VIP Pass to the NAKKA event tonight! Does this mean we can go?"

Analyzing hers, Abi read the ticket. Immediately, her guard went up. "Who are these from? Burton would not have left them for us."

Shane spied the Red Dragon seal on the bottom right-hand corner. "Do you think it's from the dragon DJ?"

She ran her fingers over the embossed creature. "Perhaps. But why? He doesn't know we are with Burton, let alone connected to him in any way."

"If our names aren't on the room reservations, why are they addressed to us if Burton didn't leave them?" Reggie questioned, looking up from Jade's device. "He's the only one who knows we're here."

"I'm not sure," she pondered. Taking out her phone, about to call Martin, Jade grabbed it from her.

"Abs, wait. What are you doing?" the girl asked hastily.

Put off by her abruptness, Abi replied, "Calling Martin to confirm things either way."

"No, don't do that."

"Why not?"

"This is our chance. Anyone attending is the who's who of Osaka. But if you call Martin, he will for sure say no."

"And probably for good reason." Abi was stunned. "How can you even consider this? Don't you think this is all a bit fishy?"

The girl shook her head. "You're reading too much into it."

"I'm sure he didn't invite us." Abi took out her phone again.

Frustrated, Jade got antsy. "If you alert Martin, we will be stuck at the symphony versus experiencing this once-in-a-lifetime event. Can't we just go for an hour?" she pleaded, hoping the girl would concede. "Come on, please?"

With everything that had happened that afternoon, Abi got a sinking feeling. Worried about Burton, she knew she wouldn't mind seeing him there to make sure he was okay. "Even if I said yes, there's no way we can pull that off. The guys will be watching our every move."

Dead air hung between them as Shane watched the girls battle it out while Reggie changed Jade's password and secured her account.

"I'm sure we can lose 'em for a bit," the girl mischievously suggested.

"Are you crazy?" Abi launched on her. "We are in a foreign country and have already had some scary experiences, and you want to go without security?"

"Well, it's not like you haven't lost them before."

Keenly recalling how she evaded the guys and went to Vegas, Abi said, "Yeah, and look how that turned out."

Certain she would not cave, Jade made one last-ditch effort. "Please, Abs. We will be the best-dressed there. It would be the perfect event for Reg and me to make our first social debut since the wedding."

"About that. Don't you think you should keep your marriage under wraps a while longer?"

Immediately, Jade challenged her. "Why? I'm Mrs. Reggie Wilson the third now, and I want to shout that from the rooftops."

"I get it, but at what cost?" Her instincts were screaming inside.

With hands melded together, Jade said, "Just tell me you'll think about it? Please?"

Not saying a word, the guys were secretly texting their thoughts to each other while the girls argued.

To break the conversation, Shane said, "Why don't we go and grab a bite and talk this through?"

"Yeah," Reggie agreed. "I could go for something to eat."

His wife agreed. "That way, we can think up a plan of action."

Abi knew her friend would not go down without a fight.

Handing Jade her phone, Reg said, "Here, Babe. Problem solved. I changed your password and restored your account."

"Really! Thank God!" Relieved, she perused her profile and found everything intact.

"I deleted the rogue posts. Somebody did hack it. The email was changed to some crazy-looking thing," he stated.

Hugging her husband's waist, Jade said, "Thank you!" and kissed him.

"All good."

Reminded of more than one breach today, Abi was still simmering beneath the surface. The way her friend had ganged up on her left a bitter taste. She sighed, biting back the urge to say more, knowing full well Burton would blow a fuse if he found out they'd gone against his advice—again.

"I'm just gonna change," she muttered, disappearing into the walk-in closet and closing the door behind her with a soft click.

The moment she was out of sight, Jade sprang into action.

"We need to convince her to go with us tonight or..." Her gaze snapped to Shane, finger pointed like a loaded weapon. "You'll be going solo. It's all up to you now. No pressure," she added with a sly grin creeping across her face.

Caught off guard, Shane blinked. "I can't force her," he said, lowering his voice in case Abi could hear through the door. "On top of that, she and I have been through a lot these past couple of days. The last thing I want to do is betray her trust right now."

Arching a brow, Jade was clearly unimpressed. She stepped closer, her heels silent on the plush carpet as she stared at him with quiet insistence. "Reg and I are going tonight. That's already decided. The rest—" She gave him a half-smile, the kind that said she knew more than she let on. "That's on you."

The QB's patience wore thin. "Jade. I'm not doing this."

The girl smirked as her husband looked on, knowing she often got her way.

Just then, Abi reappeared from the closet, adjusting her sweater. "Not doing what?"

Shane tensed, struggling to find a quick response. "Umm, nothing. Don't worry about it." Forcing a casual tone, he added, "Ready to head out?"

"Yep. Ready."

Opening the door for everyone, Reg escorted his wife into the hall. Shane followed, falling in step behind Abi as he shut it behind them.

The men, still on high alert, spotted them immediately.

To keep things light, Abi spoke up. "We're just heading out for a bite to eat."

Acknowledging her, the guys took their places and escorted the group to the Executive Lounge, as the restaurant wasn't open for dinner yet.

On the way up to the 39th floor, they stayed tight-lipped.

Finally reaching their destination, the bell sounded as the doors parted, allowing the girls to walk hand in hand with their guys freely while security nipped at their heels.

Passing through the entrance, the woman at the podium asked, "Table for six?"

Jade quickly interjected. "No. One table for four and the other for two."

Coming across a bit rude, Abi figured the guys could sense something was up.

Led to a table along the windows, Abi pulled Shane back. "I can't sit that close..." she whispered.

Hearing this, he suggested, "Excuse me? Can we get something more on the far side, please?"

"Certainly," the woman responded, veering toward a table on an inside wall. "How is this?"

Shane looked down at Abi for her approval. Seeing her nod, he said, "Perfect. Thanks."

The men took a seat by the window and scanned the hundred-and-eighty-degree view of the place.

Settled in their seats, their guys got up and headed over to the buffet area to see what was available that afternoon.

"So, what's with you and the windows?" her friend asked curiously.

Not wanting to share her fears, Abi conceded. "I'm afraid of heights. Being so close to the edge makes my legs feel weak."

"Why didn't you say something earlier?"

"I don't know. Embarrassment, I guess…"

"Well, if we went to the event tonight, you could spend less time high above the city. Just sayin'." Jade hoped Abi would agree solely based on that. "Are you gonna make me beg? We could even sneak out and walk there if we wanted. It's so close."

"Walk there in heels, in the dead of winter?"

Throwing out another solution, she said, "Alright, so we take a cab." Not getting a response, Jade figured she had at least gotten her considering it.

Abi glanced over at the guys sitting by the window. "Truth be told, I wouldn't mind checking out the art and…maybe spying on Dark Demon. Make sure he's okay."

Reaching her hands out across the table, she held onto Abi's. "So… Does that mean we are going?"

Before saying yes, Abi stated, "There's something I haven't told you."

"What's that?"

"The woman who handed us the envelopes had a tattoo on her wrist."

"So? Lots of people do."

"Not here. It's shunned upon."

Confused, Jade said, "Okay…" using hand gestures, hoping Abi would get to the point.

"If those tickets were from Red Dragon, how did he know our names? It makes me wonder if there is a connection between the DJ and these teenagers."

"I think you've watched too many detective shows," her friend rebutted.

Tilting her head disapprovingly, Abi analyzed, "Think about it. How is it that they all have the same red markings?"

"Honestly, who cares?"

Unable to get through to her, Abi mumbled, "You don't get it."

"You said it yourself. You want to check on Burton, right?"

"Yeah…" Abi's mind was reeling a million miles a second.

"I promise. We will go for an hour, then come back. Simple. You get to see him, and we get to mix with Osaka's elite. Everybody's happy."

"Fine."

Thinking she had heard her wrong, Jade sat up straight. "Really?"

Abi pointed her way. "On one condition."

"What's that?"

"We *all* keep a low profile. No press. No pictures." Abi put out her hand between them.

With no choice in the matter, Jade shook on it. "Deal."

"No exceptions?"

Her friend rolled her eyes. "Sure. Whatever…"

Mindful that they needed to fit into their dresses within a few hours, the girls got up from the table and made a trip to the buffet, but were careful not to overindulge.

Upon returning, Jade took a seat and began strategizing on how to outmaneuver Matt and Ted that evening.

Words floating in the air, Abi barely listened while moving the food around her plate with her fork, not feeling right about what they were about to do. Recalling everything that had happened at the last Nightfall event, a chill rolled down her spine while thinking of Eastwood. Thankful, he was no longer a threat, she put down her fork.

"So, do you think that will work?" Not paying attention, Jade waved her hand in front of the girl.

Breaking from her daze, Abi said, "Sorry. What did you say? I missed that."

A bit frustrated, Jade sighed. "Look. Are we gonna do this or not?"

Shane and Reggie returned with a second plate of food.

"Is what gonna work?" Reg questioned, unsure what they were referring to.

His wife quietly divulged, "We are planning how to ditch the guys this evening to get to the NAKKA event."

Taking a bite of his pastry, the big QB stated, "Why don't we just ask them?"

"Because they will never agree to it."

"I think we should just head downstairs and grab a cab quickly. I'm sure it can be done." Reg smiled at his wife.

"But we need a plan B, just in case."

Hearing them conspire against Matt and Ted, Abi remembered a promise she made to herself after the Vegas event. *You told them you wouldn't put them in that position ever again,* she thought to herself.

"Let's just play it by ear and see what happens," Shane suggested. Finishing off his second plate, he reached for a full glass of water. "I'm sure it'll work out."

Appreciating his attempt to ease the tension, Abi still couldn't sway from the gut feeling she had.

While wrapping up their meal, Reggie signed the bill and stood up. Ready to be on their way, they saw Matt and Ted do the same, and soon, everyone was on the move.

Stepping aboard the elevator, the gentle hum of the descent somehow amplified Abi's unease. She clenched Shane's hand tightly, trying to ignore the persistent thought of plummeting to the ground.

Noticing her discomfort, he slipped his arm around her waist and pressed a reassuring kiss to her temple.

Exiting on their floor, Ted remained on high alert and accompanied Abi and Shane back to their room while Matt escorted Jade and Reggie to theirs.

"We'll meet you in the hallway at exactly 7:00," Ted instructed them. "We need to arrive at the music hall before eight."

"We will be ready," Shane confirmed, pushing open the door for her as they entered their suite.

"See you shortly then," she said quietly, waving to the guy.

His ever-steady demeanor sparked a sense of calm in her when he said, "Don't worry, Miss. Everything will be fine."

As the door clicked shut behind them, Abi took a deep breath, trying to focus on getting ready. She knew tonight could be a pivotal moment for Burton, but couldn't shake the sinking feeling that something bad might happen.

| 4 |

Trust Me

Friday, December 22

The Conrad Hotel, Osaka

Within the hour, the rustle of fabric accompanied Abi's curls as they cascaded over her shoulders, her makeup enhancing the evening look. Finally able to step into her shimmering Ralph Lauren gown, the metallic threads caught the light as she crossed the room, the dress clinging elegantly to her figure.

Shane stood by the window, fastening a few lower buttons with his dress shirt still open. The sharp contours of his chest were clearly visible.

Catching sight of her, he froze. His eyes widened with admiration. "Wow," he said in a low, almost reverent whisper.

Humble, she lowered her head. The one-word compliment spoke volumes.

"You look beautiful."

"Thank you for that." What he said quickly made her smile as she slid her feet into her shoes.

Unable to veer away from her, he steadily finished buttoning his shirt and tucked it in neatly before threading the belt through the loops. A brief struggle with the collar made him pause, his neck just slightly too broad for the top button. "Do I really need the tie?" His reflection frowned at the thought, clearly uncomfortable with the formal attire despite the evening's vibe.

Approaching, she reached up to help him fix it. "Maybe just for the entrance," she suggested. "You can always take it off later."

"Maybe I'll do that." The knot in the tie felt stiff between his fingers as he adjusted it, clearly resigning to the minor discomfort for the time being. His gaze shifted, catching hers in the mirror. A flicker of emotion passed between them, one that went beyond the simple act of getting dressed. "So, is this what it would be like?"

Confusion knitted her brow. "What do you mean?"

Slowly turning to face her, his thoughts surfaced. "Being together. Married. Getting ready for big things like this." Tinged with uncertainty, he revealed a rare, vulnerable side.

The closeness between them grew as he stepped closer, hands resting gently on her arms. "I want us to work, Abs. I don't want the distance between us to ruin what we have." His forehead lowered to hers as a quiet kiss pressed into her skin. "I don't want to lose you."

The sincerity hit like a wave. Her heart caught in her throat. It was a moment she'd feared and longed for all at once, the reality of their futures suddenly feeling far too real. His lips brushed against hers gently, the softness of the kiss a strong plea. "I love you."

The confession caused a wild flutter in her chest as it stirred a storm of emotions she hadn't expected tonight. For the first time, the thought of not going to Harvard seemed like a possibility, even if it terrified her. Could she really follow him to Alabama? The idea left her conflicted, yet the possibility lingered in the back of her mind, tempting her in ways she'd never anticipated. But then Burton's face appeared in her thoughts, reminding her of the ties that kept her rooted in California.

With less-than-perfect timing, a sudden knock on the door shattered the intimate moment.

Shane moved quickly. Upon opening it, he found Andrew standing there, his imposing frame filling the doorway.

"Given what happened today, I'll be escorting you downstairs before passing you over to Ted and Matt. I must join Master B later at the event," he remarked in an overly serious way.

Hearing this, Abi knew they were in trouble. "You'll have an exciting evening then, versus babysitting us."

The guy released a deep, comforting chuckle. "I'm fine with it either way." Glancing at his watch, he offered a casual nod. "Ready to head out? Jade and Reg are waiting down the hall."

"Give me one more minute." Abi disappeared into their closet. "I'll just put on my necklace."

Andrew stepped into the vestibule. Pulling Shane aside, he said, "Make sure she is never alone tonight."

"Will do," the football player confirmed.

The big guy nodded before latching his hands behind his back.

Opening the box holding the delicate diamond necklace and matching earrings from Burton, she asked Shane, "Can you help me?"

Not fully happy with her request, he slipped the necklace around her neck to fasten it, the cool metal a sharp contrast to the warmth of her skin. A fleeting look passed between her and Shane, his eyes tracing the jewelry with a flicker of unease.

"Are you alright with me wearing these?" she asked, searching his face for any sign of disgruntled feelings.

Hesitating, only for a second, he muttered, "Of course I am. Why wouldn't I be okay with it?" he said, his smile more genuine this time. "They're perfect for tonight."

With one final glance in the mirror, the reflection of two poised figures ready for a questionable night out, Abi grabbed her evening bag and slipped her phone inside with their VIP passes. Spreading her cape over her shoulders to conceal her dress, she elegantly hid under the hood.

Together, they left the room and followed Andrew. Seeing their friends, Jade immediately shot Abi the eye, assuming the guy would be tough to fool.

Hanging back, Jade slowed their pace, put her hood over her head, and tucked in behind the guys so Andrew wouldn't hear what she was about to say. Leaning in, she whispered, "What do we do now?"

"Go to the symphony, I guess."

Not willing to accept defeat, Jade stood tall.

Her brain noticeably scheming, Abi got worried. "Jade?"

Eyes glued to the corridor in front of her, she said, "What?"

Abi whispered in her ear. "It's over. We are not going to the NAKKA event."

She turned to her and glared. "Oh, we're going. Trust me."

| 5 |

NAKKA

Friday, December 22

Conrad Hotel, Osaka

Nakanoshima Museum of Art

When they reached the ground floor and rounded the corner from the elevators, they noticed the woman who had manned the desk was no longer there. Another gentleman had taken her place.

"Your private car is waiting," he said to Andrew on the way past.

Acknowledging him with a nod, nothing more, Andrew swung open the door and scanned the area. Head on a swivel, he got the guys to get in the van first while Jade and Abi followed. Facing one another in the luxury vehicle, Jade suddenly glanced over her shoulder.

Her friend looked a bit suspicious as she locked the sliding door beside her.

As Andrew was about to get in the front passenger side, Jade said, "Sorry! I forgot something upstairs. Can you go with me, Andrew?"

Not having settled in yet, he got out and shut the door. When he did, Jade reached ahead, locked it, and said to the driver, "Go!"

Heart pumping a mile a minute, Abi gasped upon seeing Andrew's face. "Jade! No!"

"Do not stop," she ordered, showing the man the NAKKA Museum pass. Pointing to it, she said, "We go here."

The man agreed and said, "Hai!"

Instantly, the SUV jerked forward.

Abi's eyes flicked to Andrew, who stood frozen on the pavement. His expression hardened, a flash of disbelief mingling with frustration as his brow furrowed in a sharp, commanding glare. Rushing toward the vehicle, his hand slammed against the side as the driver sped away.

Shocked, Abi twisted in her seat, breath quickening the second she saw Andrew's mouth move, shouting something she couldn't hear through the closed windows. His phone was already in his hand, fingers gripping it with intent. She knew exactly what he was doing.

"We can't do this!" Abi cracked, but it was too late.

Jade flashed a devious smirk while she crossed her legs. "That wasn't so hard. Now, was it?" The city blurred past, Osaka's bright lights streaking through the glass. She didn't bother to look back.

Chest heaving, Abi's mind started spinning. The sharp vibration of her phone from inside her purse sent a jolt through her. With trembling fingers, she took it out. Andrew's name flashed across the screen.

"Don't you dare?" The edge in her low tone was impossible to ignore.

"Sorry, Jade," Abi whispered, guilt gnawing at her. The call had already gone to voicemail, but a text appeared almost immediately after.

What the hell was that? Where are you going? The security guard questioned.

With fingers hovering over the screen, frozen with indecision, Abi's stomach twisted - her lungs barely able to pull in air.

"Hey..." Shane leaned forward in his seat across from her. Not scolding—he tried to remain calm. "You don't owe anyone an explanation right now. We're not kids. We're just living a little."

"But the look Andrew gave me..." Stumbling on her words, she knew it wasn't just anger. It was worry and panic. "He wasn't just mad, Shane." The thought of it crushed her.

"It'll be fine, Abs. Don't give it a second thought."

She stayed silent, wishing she had never agreed to any of this. On top of that, there would be no escape from the consequences now. Without delay, her thumbs moved quickly across the screen.

Jade wants to go to NAKKA, she typed. The moment she hit send, the phone buzzed again.

Please tell me you're joking.

Sorry, Andrew is all she sent in return.

Maneuvering the one-way street, they saw a massive red dragon flying through the air above the black cube. When they pulled up to the entrance, the girls jumped out as the guys joined them. It was then, they realized the dragon in the air was a series of small drones programmed to fly in formation.

Amazed by the sheer size of it, Shane said, "That's impressive."

On task, Jade said, "Come on. Quickly."

Hoods over their heads, they blended amongst the crowds flowing up the tall staircase into the venue. Showing their passes to security at the door, Jade kept an eye out for Martin and the guys, knowing Andrew had most likely alerted everyone there. Passing through without incident, they walked into the lobby. It was an architectural masterpiece.

Hit by a wave of sensory overload, Abi panicked slightly. Holding onto Shane, the last thing she wanted was to get separated from him.

The high ceilings seemed to stretch on forever as they walked toward the escalators. Pulsing dance music echoed through every level, vibrating through her chest and making it hard to think straight. Some of the art on display seemed quite controversial. But it suited the theme.

Crowds of people swarmed everywhere, their excitement mixing with the beats until it felt like one loud, never-ending buzz. They moved in clusters, disappearing into a maze of lights, art, and sound. Even the bright, modern art on the walls seemed to move with the shifting strobes, making everything blur together.

Abi's pulse quickened as she tried to get her bearings, her eyes darting from face to face, expecting to see Martin at any moment.

How will I ever find Burton here? She thought. The place was huge, and with so many people, it felt like trying to locate a needle in a haystack. Even the cloakroom was surrounded by a noisy group, the staff barely visible behind a wall of people.

She took a deep breath, trying to calm herself, but the music thumped in her ears, adding to the whirlwind in her mind.

Without warning, Jade pulled back her hood and swept off her long black cape with an air of theatrical precision. The effect was immediate: her red Medusa dress, with its striking, timeless design, caught the attention of those around them. Flashes erupted as people gawked and cameras clicked, capturing the commanding presence of Reggie, who effortlessly posed beside his new wife, exuding unrivaled confidence.

"So much for keeping a low profile," Abi muttered, watching the growing wave of attention. Onlookers buzzed with excitement, and whispers of recognition spread like wildfire.

Not wanting to be swept up in the frenzy, Abi grabbed Shane's arm and pulled him forward.

"Hey," he called out, surprised. "Aren't we waiting for them?"

Not missing a beat, Abi responded, "If we do, we won't be staying long."

Shane followed her, his curiosity piqued. He wasn't entirely sure where she was headed, but the urgency in her movements kept him close. They wove their way through the sea of people until they reached the stage flanked by towering LED screens, each depicting a crimson dragon in mesmerizing 4D. Its scales glistened with a life-like sheen. The DJ, silhouetted against a backdrop of pulsing lights, bobbed to the beat, dressed in a deep red tux, fueling the energy of the crowd while swaying and moving in sync. To his left was a striking woman dressed in a crimson satin gown adorned with an intricate silver dragon. The embroidery shimmered as she danced rhythmically.

"That's Lelin," Abi whispered to herself, recalling what the woman looked like as she walked down the hallway at the Kyoto hotel.

Taking a moment to absorb the scene, realizing just how electrifying the event truly was, Abi noticed most of the attendees were in their late twenties to late thirties and exuded a sophisticated yet rebellious energy. There were a few younger too, barely old enough to be there. Her eyes widened as a spotlight panned the people in front of them.

"No way!" A young man shouted to another in English, carrying just enough for Abi and Shane to catch it, as he ended the conversation with a snicker. "This is a competition! I'm not helping you! You're on your own!"

"Well, I'm gonna win!" Another said in broken English.

Overhearing them, Abi fearfully nudged Shane.

"What competition?" he said loudly in Abi's ear.

Instantly, the living sea of people scattered as if a pistol had sounded to start a race.

Big kanji letters flashed on the LED screens.

Death to Her.

Abi read and shuddered at the sight of it. Eyes darting in every direction, she watched the crowd's movements, highly synchronized, like being choreographed by some unseen hand. The air grew thick, almost suffocating, charged with the kind of menace that turned every pulse of light into a jolt of fear. Amidst it all, Abi spotted it. A red dragon tattoo. Then, another. And, another—until terror seeped into her veins as she could no longer keep count.

"Oh my god," she whispered. Pulling Shane down to her level, she shouted in his ear, "They're everywhere!"

He took notice right away. "What the hell is this?"

Abi pointed to the DJ on stage. "It's him. I think he's the Kingpin," she said. "Maybe the mark shows their loyalty? He's their boss."

Feeling like they were surrounded by sharks, experiencing a familiar fight or flight response again, Abi scanned from left to right.

"That's why Burton didn't want us here…" Feeling trapped, she repeated, "He knew… He knew."

"I take it the guy is still working for that four-letter agency by day…DJ by night?"

Suddenly, as if reading the room, Lelin stepped forward. The dance floor seemed to pulse harder under the beat as her crimson-clad figure paused, casting a watchful, sinister gaze.

Standing amongst a group of mischievous teenagers, Shane and Abi noticed that their phones lit up simultaneously. One after the other showed a recent picture of Jade and Reggie, taken only moments ago. The word GO! Highlighted right after that.

"Go? What does that mean? What are they doing?" She knew their friends were being targeted. But how?

Holding Abi's trembling hand, Shane pulled her toward the glass balcony as they peered down at Jade and Reg, surrounded by photographers on the lower level. "There!" Shane pointed as the flash of cameras caused a slow-motion spectacle.

But before they could do something, a group of teens shoved them out of the way. "Move!" they shouted, making Shane's back go up.

Pushing two of the guys and pinning them to the railing, the teen turned and shot an evil glare his way.

Scared the kid might pull a weapon, Abi frantically grabbed his arm. "Let it go, Shane! Let it go!"

He immediately backed off on her command and got another glimpse of a phone screen in the process. But this time, it wasn't a picture of Jade and Reggie. It was Abi.

"We gotta hide, Abs!" he yelled, flipping the hood of her cape over her head. "Now! This way!" He didn't hesitate. Guarding her, he carved a path through the masses, holding her hand tight behind him as they pushed onward.

The music thumped harder, the bass sending shivers up Abi's spine as they inched to the next level, step by step. Eyes sharp, they saw their friends on the move and stayed alert.

The two stopped dead in their tracks upon seeing Andrew standing at the entrance to another large room. Shane was secretly relieved, but Abi yelled, "No! Don't!"

"Don't what?" Confused, he stated, "We need to go to him!"

She shook her head. "Not yet! One minute!"

Veering to the left, Abi dragged Shane behind her and slipped through an overlap in the black velvet drapes lining the walls. Tucked in the shadows, it gave her a moment to breathe as she peeked between the panels - the fabric muffling the beats emanating from across the hall. Hearing Burton's signature sound seep through it unexpectedly sparked a half-smile.

Staying on task, she read the sign at the start of the long line of guests waiting on a red carpet between the lux stanchion posts.

"Nightfall. Private Party. Members Only," she said aloud. "That's his venue."

"What is the objective here, Abs?" Shane asked, his eyes searching hers. "Do you know something I don't?" The determination in Abi's expression made him pause.

She glanced around the dimly lit space.

He stepped closer and shouted over the noise around them. "What's going on? Tell me!" He rested his hands along his beltline almost angrily.

"I came to see if my hunch is right!"

"What hunch?" he pressed.

Abi's resolve wavered. "Something's wrong!"

When the doors to the Nightfall event parted, Abi's eyes darted to the stage beyond the security stationed outside the door. She could faintly make out Burton standing behind the deck, the red lining of his hooded tux giving away his location.

Seeing this, Shane stared intensely at her, not happy.

"Based on what we just witnessed, it's not DJ Red Dragon who is the mastermind leading these kids... It's his wife! She is connected to those gangs, following us everywhere. But why are they targeting us and nobody else? We need to know!" She found it hard to breathe as a faint chill brushed the back of her neck, bringing with it a hint of doubt. "Maybe I'm completely off base here… But… I don't think I am."

"At this point, I don't care about any of this! I just want to get you to safety! We need to leave!"

Her mind reeling, she said to him, "Give me a minute to think."

"No! Abs, I saw your picture on a guy's phone! You're targeted, too!"

Not flinching upon hearing that, she ignored him and analyzed those entering the Nightfall room. She knew these people were only there for the crypto vault. Mostly thirty-something couples dripping in designer labels and expensive jewelry, she looked closely for any sign of dragon tattoos. Not seeing ink on anyone, a well-dressed young man walked past with a laptop in hand. She spotted it immediately. "That's random…" she muttered as he evaded the crowds and casually sat on the floor a distance away before resting his back against the wall.

"Hiding in plain sight," she mumbled.

"What?" Shane questioned.

Abi pointed to the guy as the light from the screen lit his face. "Look!"

Confused, Shane said, "Why would someone bring a laptop here?"

She interjected. "Exactly… Unless they planned to hack into something…"

"So, what's the target?"

Knowing she'd have to tell Shane the truth, she turned to him and said, "What I am about to tell you is between you and me. You don't breathe a word of this to anyone, is that clear?"

Taken by her seriousness, he replied, "Fine. I promise. What is it?"

"Nightfall events are not just upscale elite raves. They harbor a secret society."

"Wait? What do you mean, secret society?"

"Burton designed an impenetrable crypto vault. Apparently, it's the most sophisticated system in the world. The attendees of his events are there to make ultra-secure cryptocurrency transactions using his system. Some people are above board, and some are not – if you know what I mean."

Fully comprehending the scope of what she said, he turned and looked out at the line of people going into the private party. Recalling what happened in Vegas, he questioned, "Who is he working for? Really?"

Not elaborating, she replied, "Don't ask me anything more on that."

He silently acknowledged. "What do we do, then?"

She took out her phone, hoping to text Martin and warn him, but, in true rave fashion, she had no signal. It was jammed.

"We need to get inside…" She zeroed in on the Nightfall entrance. "Martin is in there. He can shut down the system." Intent on keeping an eye on the guy with the laptop, she noticed three more doing the exact same thing. "Holy crap…" Pointing to the young men with their fingers flying across the keyboards, Abi said, "Look, I see five more!" Seeing this sparked a sense of urgency.

Shane grabbed Abi's arm. "Umm, Abs…" Following his line of sight, they found their friends arriving on the red carpet a few feet away, attracting a slew of unwanted attention.

"Want me to get them?"

About to answer, a group of teens marked with vivid red dragon tattoos emerged from the far corners of the venue and converged, crashing like a wave without warning. Encircling their friends with intensity and purpose, Abi and Shane witnessed their synchronized, almost hypnotic motion, causing them to fear for the newlyweds.

"Oh, my god!" Abi panicked. "Shane! What are they doing!"

Jade's enamored smile faltered as the black-clad teens closed in all around them.

Reggie instinctively wrapped his arm around her and pushed back the crowd with the other, but realized his protective actions were useless. "What the hell-" he started before it got drowned out by the swell of verbal malice. "Hey! Back off!" He shouted as the first wave reached them, knocking them off balance. Hands and elbows jostling, the line blurred as the group attempted to separate the two of them.

Ready to intervene, Shane was biting at the bit. His stance, prepared to fight.

"Reg!!" Jade yelled while trying to find a gap, an exit—anything.

One of the taller tattooed teens, with multiple facial piercings, pushed his way through and leaned in closer than the others. Making it to Jade's ear, he roared, "Ahh, American! We found you!"

Jade's breath hitched. The gravity in his tone anchored her in place, even as adrenaline urged her to run.

Pulling on the curtain, Shane was about to step out of the shadows.

That's when Abi saw Andrew, Ethan, and Bray appear with a flood of security. Yanking the football player back, she said, "No, wait!"

One finger pressing on his earpiece, Andrew spoke low while scanning the chaos. She assumed he was talking to Martin. As they surrounded their friends, additional security guards flanked them, increasing their presence by twenty.

"Reg, follow me," Andrew instructed.

Nodding, Reggie pulled Jade close, shielding her as they shadowed Andrew through the crowd, thankful to escape the escalating mob.

Just when Abi thought the worst was over, everything surged again. Screams and shouting erupted as the delinquent teens reached into their suit jackets and beneath their dresses. Terror gripping her, her mind jumped to the worst-case scenario and braced for an impending bloodbath.

"Get down!" Shane growled, wrapping himself around her and pushing her to the floor. "If they fire, lie flat!"

Abi's heart pounded, but she managed a shaky nod.

But instead of gunfire, the teens unrolled long banners of fabric. Like a pack of hyenas, they moved in unison, corralling people into chaotic clusters. They worked fast — stripping bags, jewelry, wallets, even expensive shoes — tossing the stolen goods into large totes held by others. It was a well-orchestrated smash-and-grab.

Abi instinctively clutched her necklace. Shane noticed immediately. "Give it to me," he urged. "I'll keep it safe."

Fingers trembling, she turned, allowing him to unclasp the delicate chain. He slid the diamonds into his jacket's deep interior pocket.

Then, the piercing wail of sirens converged as police swarmed the scene, and panic set in.

A loud whistle cut through the commotion. On cue, many of the thieves spun on a dime, vanishing like ghosts. Some leaped over barriers, while others slid down the steel panel between the escalators, making a break for the main doors.

In the chaos, Abi spotted an opportunity. The entrance to *Nightfall* was wide open and unguarded.

"This way!" she grabbed Shane's hand, her pulse racing. "Come on!"

Whipping open the drapes and weaving through the crowd, they slipped inside. The pounding bass reverberated through the massive space, swallowing the noise from outside. Yet, despite the turmoil, dozens of people near the back remained transfixed on their screens, engrossed in whatever transactions they were completing. In contrast, those closer to the stage swayed and jumped to the pulsing beat.

Burton was at the far end, commanding his elaborate station with multiple laptops spread out along the DJ deck. Even from a distance, his presence loomed. But it wasn't the music that caught Abi's eye.

A colossal LED screen flared to life to the left of the platform, the crimson countdown timer illuminating the numbers: **00:11:00.**

"They only have eleven minutes left to make their transactions," Abi murmured, the realization hitting her. "Then the vault closes and goes offline."

Shane nodded, his protective stance unwavering as the music strangely changed mid-stream. It wasn't Burton's usual beat. As they moved closer, navigating the throng of people, they spotted Martin hurrying across the stage about thirty feet away. He looked slightly panicked. Leaning in, the two exchanged words quickly, making Burton's head snap toward the main entrance.

Even though Abi couldn't fully see his face, she could tell he'd found them amidst the crowd.

Subtly pointing at her so as not to bring unwanted attention, he motioned for them to move to the right side of the room.

"He wants us to go over there," she pointed, already heading in that direction.

Maintaining the rhythm of the unknown set, Burton seamlessly adjusted the tempo and added his own flair while the crowd roared in approval, none the wiser to the mayhem unfolding behind the scenes. When they reached the stage door, it swung open. Martin stood there, stepping aside to usher them in.

Defensively raising her hands, Abi blurted, "Before you say anything, this wasn't my idea. Hear me out!"

Preoccupied, Martin nodded. "One moment, Miss. Our systems have been compromised." With his attention split, Abi found Burton's tech crew battling against a relentless cyberattack. Fingers flying across the keyboards, the hum of machines echoed as streams of code cascaded down the screens while the massive clock ticked down, every second heightening the pressure.

"We must remain active for another minute and a half! Trace their IPs! Isolate their systems!" Martin barked. "If they are cycling proxies, launch WAFs!"

"They're shifting locations faster than we can trace," a tech replied, panic edging his voice. "I need thirty seconds!"

"You've got less than fifteen!" Martin snapped before turning to Abi and giving her his undivided attention. "What is it, Miss Abi? What did you see?"

Reminded of the teens with laptops in the building, Abi recounted every unsettling detail while Martin listened intently. Sharpening his focus, his eyes darkening, he stared at each screen. "Redirect suspicious IPs to the sandbox to buy us time! Almost there!"

A shrill warning bell pierced the room.

"They're trying to hijack the vault," one of the techs muttered grimly.

Without missing a beat, the music shifted once more. The hackers' exclusive mix was gone, replaced by one of Burton's generic backup tracks. A clear signal that the attackers had been cut off — for now.

Then, from the shadows, the hooded DJ emerged. Burton's presence demanded attention, his movements swift and controlled.

Martin stepped aside as his boss slid into the chair, fingers flying over the keys. Data cascaded in columns, each corrupted file a mark of the hackers' intrusion as the countdown burned in the corner.

"Seven seconds…" Abi held her breath.

With unwavering focus, Burton executed the final command. "Cut it!" The moment the clock struck zero, the screens went dark.

Silence.

Then, with a decisive snap, Burton slammed his laptops closed.

"Secure tech!" he ordered, low but commanding. "Now. Move out!"

The crew rushed to comply, tearing cables free and handing over laptops. Every movement was seamless — they had practiced for this. Three additional laptops were shoved into Burton's bag as he slung it over his shoulder.

"We gotta go," he said, not waiting for further discussion.

Shane stayed close to Abi, ensuring she was protected as Martin and Burton led the way. Down an industrial steel staircase, they moved swiftly. Every second remained tinged with lingering adrenaline. The back door opened to reveal a line of black SUVs.

Already waiting in the front vehicle, Lorenzo nodded in acknowledgment.

Shane helped Abi into the third row, taking his place beside her. Burton and Martin settled into the middle seats, tension hanging thick. As the convoy pulled away, Dark Demon lowered his hood and turned toward Abi, his eyes sharp.

"What were you doing here, Abs?"

"It's a long story…" Abi cowered in her seat.

"There were Red Dragons everywhere," Shane interjected protectively. "Some had laptops."

Burton's jaw tightened. "Tell me what you saw."

| 6 |

Debrief

Saturday, December 23

The Conrad Hotel, Osaka

Under the cover of night, they returned to The Conrad just before two in the morning and took the elevator to the main lobby in the sky before descending again using the interior hotel lifts. Arriving on the thirty-ninth floor, Martin instructed them to stay with Burton while he went to get Reggie and Jade.

Escorted to the Conrad Suite, he opened the door and walked in.

"Take a seat. I'll be back in a second." Ducking into his bedroom, he disappeared.

"Something's up," Abi whispered, hoping to know more.

"What do you think it is?" Shane asked, clutching his fist inside the opposite hand.

"Not sure... Guess we will soon find out."

Emerging again, now dressed in joggers and a t-shirt, he grabbed a bottle of water. "You guys want anything to drink?"

After turning to Abi, Shane replied, "We are good for now."

"The bar fridge is fully stocked. Just help yourself."

Abi nodded her head. "Thanks," before adding, "So… Are you going to tell us what's wrong?"

When she said that, Martin walked in with Jade and Reggie, already changed out of their good clothes.

"Please have a seat with your friends," Martin instructed.

Each was quite sheepish.

Burton stood before them. "I thought I told you not to attend my event."

"What do you mean? We got invited," Jade defended.

"By who?"

The girl spoke up. "By Red Dragon. He left us tickets at the front desk. We just assumed…"

Burton turned to Martin. "Is this true?"

"I was not aware of any tickets left for them, Sir."

Opening her bag, Abi took out the VIP pass and handed it to Burton. "Each was addressed to us personally, so we just assumed it came from you. Otherwise, how would anyone know our names?"

Puzzled, he inspected it, then passed it along to Martin. Concerned by that bit of information, he said to him, "Find out where these came from."

About to step away, he replied, "Absolutely, Sir," and walked into the bedroom, his iPad in hand.

Needing to know more, Burton asked, "So, you received these passes and didn't think to let Martin or the guys know? Why?"

Lowering her head, Jade knew the reason.

He read their minds. "Because you wanted to go and knew if you told us, we would have still declined. Am I right?"

Abi nodded, "Yes, that is right."

Prepared to take the blame, Jade piped up. "It was me. It's my fault. I'm the one who pressured them into going. I'm the one who tricked Andrew."

"Perhaps, but…"

"In all fairness, Abi was against it the whole time…" Jade revealed.

Angry, he stated the obvious. "That's because she knows ditching security isn't smart."

About to speak, Jade saw Burton raise his hand to stop her.

"Once again, I can't stress enough. These guys are here to keep you safe – to keep you alive." Finding all their eyes on him, he sighed. "What's done is done. We can't do anything about it now." Pacing the floor with his hands in his pockets, he looked out over the city before returning to lock eyes with Reg and Jade. "From what I'm told, you two had a rough night."

Agreeing, Jade lowered her head again, recalling the fear. "You could say that…"

Martin reentered the room.

"What's the verdict?" Burton asked.

A seriousness flashed across the gentleman's face. "The passes weren't from him."

Abi's heart dropped upon hearing that. Immediately, her sight moved to Jade.

Not given a choice, Burton made an executive decision. "Because none of you heard me the first time, I will repeat - from here on out, everyone is keeping a low profile. No exceptions! Is that understood?"

Each of them nodded.

Giving Martin the eye, he said to them, "Return to your rooms and pack up. We leave for Tokyo in three hours."

Exhausted and mentally drained, Jade was about to complain, but stopped herself when Burton glimpsed her way. "For the record," he said, "This trip was never supposed to turn out like this. Full disclosure. From what my sources are gathering, we've gotten roped into some kind of recruiting scheme. It's a competition for the Tokuryū – a group of young people with exceptional skills who do the grunt work these days for the Yakuza."

"What kind of skills?" Abi asked.

"The kind you never advertise, if you know what I mean." Burton had a seat in the chair across from them. Leaning forward, resting his elbows on his knees, he said, "These recruits have specific tasks."

Unsure if he should be divulging this, Burton raised his hand and counted fingers to nail down his point. "First is to TARGET. The second is to TRACK. Next are THREATEN, HACK, MAIM, and STEAL. Then there's KIDNAP and finally…" he hesitated before adding, "KILL."

In shock, Reggie got up. "Wait… What are you saying?"

"I'm saying there is a dangerous game taking place, and we are the pawns."

"Tell me you're joking…" In disbelief, the guy turned to his wife.

"Wish I was," he paused. "Thus far, we have been targeted, tracked, threatened, and hacked." Pointing at Jade, he said, "I hear you had an Instagram issue, right?"

"Umm, yes," the girl confirmed.

In conjunction with what was said, Martin added, "And tonight, we had multiple attempts on our systems at the event."

"And before we ran into the Nightfall venue, the Red Dragons gathered a bunch of people and stripped them of their jewelry and belongings before evading the police," Abi divulged.

That bit of information Burton and Martin weren't aware of. Beyond concerned, the two looked at each other.

"The first tasks are bad but trivial compared to the last few. From now on, you need to be smart. Aware and always alert. We believe they operate in Kyoto, Osaka, and Tokyo, but for some reason, they steer clear of Niseko. Once we head north, the threat level should die down."

Martin nodded to back up his statement.

"That said, while we are in Tokyo, I have multiple appearances. Please help me do my job by keeping out of trouble for one day. Can you do that?"

Hesitant, they each nodded their heads.

"If not, I can't guarantee your safety." Hoping he'd gotten through to them, Burton stood tall. "Alright. Go and gather your things. We leave at five for Kansai airport. From there, wheels are up at quarter after six." Before leaving them, he eyed up Abi while her friends and

Shane made their way towards the doors. Getting close, he gently took hold of her arm and pulled her back. "Are you okay?"

She silently nodded. "Yes. I'm fine. A bit shaken, but I'm good."

"I'll have Andrew come to your room to escort you downstairs. Do not leave without him."

"Alright."

"Don't worry about breakfast. Martin ordered some for the plane."

Not saying much, they parted ways as Abi joined her friends in the hall alongside Andrew and Lorenzo.

Burton offered a subtle wave before locking the doors.

On their way to the elevators, they bypassed the Executive Lounge.

Noticeably thinking, Jade questioned, "He never did reveal who left the passes for us. Do you think it was that gang?"

Looking back at them, Andrew turned, "He didn't say because we don't know yet. And to be honest, it's not good."

Upon hearing that from him, Abi got scared. Needing to apologize, she said, "I'm really sorry for, umm…"

He could see the regret written all over her face. Leaning in, he quietly replied, "I know. Don't worry about it. I promise I will keep you safe, Miss."

Hearing this, she felt even more guilty.

The ride to their floor was a silent one. Everyone was showing signs of exhaustion, but their day wasn't over yet. It was just beginning.

Moving down the hallway, Lorenzo said, "Nobody leaves their rooms without an escort. Got it?"

Feeling like caged cats, they appeased the men and gave them a thumbs-up before disappearing to gather their things.

| 7 |

Early Departure

Saturday, December 23

The Conrad Hotel, Osaka

Kansai Airport, Tamayura Gate

Abi walked into their room and dropped onto the bed, her legs aching. Kicking off her shoes, she began to rub her feet, while Shane grabbed their suitcases from the closet. Appearing from around the corner, he set them on the side table and unzipped them as a rigid expression appeared on his face.

"Well, that was an eye-opening evening." He nervously chuckled in disbelief.

"No kidding." Reaching for her phone, she searched up the Tokuryū and found an article. Her eyes skimmed the text, then she read aloud, "The Guardian reports, the term *Tokuryū* refers to ad hoc groups formed to commit crimes, where members often don't know each other or those planning and directing their activities. They are distinct from the Yakuza and less hierarchical." Her breath hitched as she read the paragraph aloud. "These crimes range from robberies and fraud to assaults and…umm…murders."

A sharp turn of Shane's head brought his wide-eyed stare to hers. "Are you serious?"

"It says authorities have only been aware of the group's activities for less than a year, and they have become a growing threat since then."

Moving toward the floor-to-ceiling windows, he pressed his hands to the glass, taking in the glittering cityscape. "So, now we're in the middle of some recruitment game for a crime syndicate." Tense, he rubbed his temple. "And you're okay with that?"

"Of course not," Abi said matter-of-factly. "None of us asked for this, Shane. Burton included."

He exhaled sharply and walked toward the window again, resting his hands on the frame as if searching for answers in the twinkling city lights. "I'm just saying... The guy's not innocent here. He's playing both sides, Abi. And we're the collateral damage."

She got off the bed. Their reflections were ghostlike in the glass. "I get it," she admitted. "But do you really think he'd put us in harm's way intentionally?"

Shane turned to her. "Maybe not. But that doesn't change the fact that people are technically hunting us. You heard what he said. Target, track, hack, maim, steal, kidnap, and kill... They are doing this for sport."

"I believe Burton and Martin know what they are doing."

"And do you trust them?" he paused, mid-motion, leveling a piercing gaze her way.

Her hands froze on the zipper. "Do I what?"

"Trust them."

A long exhale passed her lips. "Of course I do." She thought for a second. "They've given me no reason to otherwise. That said, there is still a lot I don't know – a lot I am not privy to." She resumed packing, folding her clothes with jerky, hurried movements.

Shane did the same. "So, we just pack up and hope for the best in Tokyo?"

"I guess so."

Stepping away from the window, Shane said, "From here on out, we stick together, like Burton suggested. No sneaking off, no trusting strangers, and definitely no taking any more mysterious VIP passes." He shot her a pointed look with a hint of humor.

She rolled her eyes. "Noted. But for the record, that was Jade. Not me."

He grabbed a pair of sneakers from the closet and added, "Hey, you went along with it, too." He knew that comment didn't fare well with her. Needing to make amends, he walked over. "I'm just as guilty. It's not like I didn't follow suit, also."

Happy to hear he admitted it, Abi kept gathering her things.

They both fell into a rhythm while they got changed, the silence this time more focused than tense.

As Shane zipped his suitcase shut, he glanced at her. "You good?"

Abi nodded again, meeting his eyes.

A knock on the door reminded them of the ticking clock. With a final glance around the room, they wheeled their bags to the entrance and prepared to leave.

"Ready?" Shane asked her as she made a final sweep of the place.

Joining him, she said, "Yeah. Ready."

Peering through the peephole to see who it was, Shane found Andrew leaning casually against the wall with a tactical bag slung over one shoulder. Monitoring the hall from left to right, when Shane opened the door, the guy stood tall as Abi exited the room.

Not saying a word, Andrew gestured for them to follow. "Let's move," he said curtly, his eyes locking briefly with Abi's before he turned and strode down the corridor.

She exchanged looks with Shane, as he shrugged and grabbed the handle of each suitcase. Trailing behind Andrew, their footsteps muffled on the plush carpet while their bags rolled along quietly.

About to round the corner, familiar faces came into view—Jade, Reggie, Matt, and Ted were waiting near the elevators, their bags piled around them. No one was in the mood for small talk.

"Everyone here?" Andrew asked, taking a body count. A few nods answered him. Without waiting, he hit the button while everyone stood in silence until the first elevator dinged its arrival.

Having to break into two groups, Abi and Shane squeezed with Andrew and Matt until there was barely room to breathe.

To try and lighten the mood, Matt muttered something about sardines, earning a faint smile from Abi, but no one laughed.

Smoothly, the elevator ascended to the fortieth floor. When the doors opened to the expansive lobby of the Conrad Hotel, Andrew took the lead again. Waiting for the others to join them, the second elevator opened. Guiding everyone past the sleek furniture and soft, glowing lights, they moved toward the main elevators that would take them to the ground floor.

Descending to the lower lobby, it wasn't long until they exited and rounded the corner.

In an instant, Abi's gaze landed on Burton, slouched in a chair near the main desk. A hood shadowed his features, but his exhaustion was unmistakable. She hesitated, her feet faltering for a split second. Every instinct urged her to approach him, to ask if he was okay, but she held back.

When the sliding glass doors opened, the cold air bit at her cheeks, a stark contrast to the warmth of the hotel. Martin got his boss in the first truck waiting near the curb and orchestrated the loading of their bags into the back of each sleek Blacklane SUV.

"Let's go, people," the gentleman called out, waving them toward the waiting vehicles, hoping to stay on schedule.

Abi ducked into the second truck after Jade and Reggie cozily got settled in the third row. Seated near the window, Shane climbed in beside her, his jaw tight as he gazed out at the still-dark streets of the city.

Once everyone had piled in and the doors shut with a soft thud, one by one, the trucks pulled away from the hotel, the headlights cutting through the predawn gloom.

The city of Osaka began to blur past the windows, its neon signs and empty streets giving way to the busy industrial ports to their right. The horizon lightened with each passing moment, but the sun had yet to crest.

Thoughts tangled, she watched as they merged onto the highway. Abi leaned her head against the cool glass. Driving across the long bridge leading to Kansai Airport, she stared at the dark water below. Gazing at the endless expanse, broken only by distant city lights and the bustling airport filled with planes, the rhythmic hum of the SUV's engine filled the quiet space. Taking a deep breath, the thought of leaving their troubles behind offered a fleeting sense of relief.

As the convoy reached the Tamayura Premium Gate, the vehicles slowed to a stop along the curb. A group of baggage handlers, quick and efficient, descended on them immediately, stacking their luggage onto carts with ease. Searching the area discreetly, she kept an eye out for the Red Dragon-tattooed young man who had helped them on arrival, but he was nowhere to be seen.

"Everybody out," Andrew announced from the front seat, snapping everyone into motion as he signaled for the group to follow him.

Entering the lobby of the private FBO, without hesitation, they navigated the modern corridors toward security - their VIP treatment making the process feel almost routine.

Burton and Martin were in front of them. But Sara was nowhere to be seen.

A striking woman dressed formally in black awaited them beyond security, her polished demeanor radiating authority. With a smile as flawless as her tailored suit, she gestured for them to follow her toward the private plane.

The sliding glass doors opened to the tarmac, and a gust of icy wind whipped through the group once again, sending shivers down their spines.

Abi wrapped her coat tightly around herself, bracing against the chill, while the others quickened their pace toward the waiting jet.

Climbing the steps into the cabin, they slowly warmed themselves as everyone took their seats.

Facing the rear of the plane, Abi sat down while Shane settled into the one across from her without saying a word. Eyes fixed on Burton at the back of the cabin, she found him hunched over while sitting on the bed, his hood hiding his exhaustion. Not once did he glance in her direction.

Martin appeared moments later, sliding the pocket door partially closed.

Through the narrow gap, Abi caught a glimpse of her childhood friend collapsing onto the bed. Her chest tightened as she stared his way. Alone, desperate to check on him, she pulled out her phone. About to send him a text, she stopped. Believing he needed to sleep, she quickly put the device away.

A gentle nudge of her foot broke her train of thought.

"You okay?" Shane's quiet question pulled her attention back.

"Yeah," she replied. "Just tired."

As the staff secured the door, the engines began to hum. Soon, the plane shuddered as it began to taxi toward the runway. Resting her head against the seat, Abi let her eyes drift shut, trying not to think about flying at thirty thousand feet.

| 8 |

Tokyo

Saturday, December 23

Aman Hotel, Tokyo

The flight to Tokyo seemed to pass in the blink of an eye. Abi barely had time to register the steady cruising altitude before the captain's voice announced their approach to Haneda Airport. Peering out the window, she watched the runway come into view, the sprawling airfield perched on yet another man-made island surrounded by shimmering water. Her fingers tightened instinctively around the armrests as the plane descended with the ground rushing toward them.

When the wheels touched down with a soft thud, she let out a breath she hadn't realized she was holding, relief washing over her.

Shane's voice broke through her focus. "Well, we made it."

Turning to him, she said, "Yes, we did," while managing a faint smile.

Within minutes, the cabin doors opened, and the group filed out into the FBO. The Universal Aviation lounge was modern and comfortable, but the atmosphere among them was anything but relaxed. Burton sat silently in a chair near the wall, his hood still drawn over his head. His posture, slouched and heavy, seemed to show that he was more than tired. Had something happened? Was something wrong?

Jade and Reggie leaned into each other, their hands tightly clasped as if holding on to the only source of energy they had left. Unusually quiet, neither spoke.

Glancing at the others, Abi noted the murmurs of agreement when Martin assured them they'd soon be on their way to the hotel.

Pushing through the glass doors of the International Business Gate, a brisk morning breeze swirled around them. A string of identical SUVs lined the circular curb, their Blacklane logos gleaming under the morning sun, trying to peek through the clouds. Confusion flickered across her face as she mentally counted the vehicles and attempted to reconcile the small size of their group with the number of cars waiting for them.

Martin noticed her hesitation. "I threw in a few decoys, just for good measure," he said regally, just enough for her to hear.

The girl nodded. Standing idly by, she turned to her guardian. "How is he?"

Straightening his posture, he replied evenly, "He's tired. But doing fine."

Her eyes lingered on Burton for a moment, noting the faint dark circles under his eyes and the weight of whatever thoughts he carried.

The first SUV's doors opened, and the concierge began loading their luggage into the back while Martin directed the group to their assigned vehicles, despite each of them being in a daze.

Climbing into the second car, the four of them quickly found their seats before the trucks left the gated area and merged with the city, blurring past her window.

As their convoy navigated deeper into the heart of the metropolis, everywhere she looked, Tokyo seemed endless. Slowly venturing further into the downtown core, the city's sheer density became undeniable. Buildings seemingly piled one atop another, their terraces crammed with neon signs, antennas, and rooftop gardens. Overpasses twisted above intersections, while pedestrian bridges climbed even higher, casting elongated shadows below. The city felt almost alive, its pulse evident in the multitude of vehicles, trains, and people moving within this stacked urban jungle.

When they finally reached the Otemachi Building in Tokyo's financial epicenter, Abi searched for a hint of signage to indicate where they were staying. But there was nothing. Just a modern building touching the clouds above. She knew, then, the level of secrecy surrounding this hotel. With it, her stomach dropped at the thought of sleeping inside the far-reaching floors of this sleek, modern monolith.

Surveying their surroundings, Shane said, "Guess this is the same setup as the last place."

"Suppose so." Abi watched as they pulled into the dark underground breezeway.

Staying to the left, the SUVs stopped outside a set of sliding doors, where uniformed staff stood waiting, their bows impeccable as they greeted them.

"Kon'nichiwa. Hello. Welcome to Aman," the well-dressed gentleman said to her.

"Arigatō," Abi replied, bowing slightly out of respect as the cold air blew through the tunnel and brushed against her skin.

Seeing her, Burton smiled before following her example and doing the same. Amidst it, he noticed Shane glancing at him. He wasn't happy.

Stepping through the clear sliding doors when they parted with a swoosh, Abi felt oddly significant, like crossing an invisible line into a different world. The air seemed quieter, softer, almost sacred, as faint music effortlessly created a sense of peace. Intent on keeping an eye on her friend, she waited for him to enter the room framed by light wooden panels, reminding her of Kyoto's torii gates. The design was subtle, hinting at a transition from the city outside to something more exclusive within the walls.

As the hotel's ambiance washed over her, she knew they would soon be making their ascent to the lobby high above the city, promising the serenity and rest they all desperately needed after not getting a stitch of sleep.

The polished floors reflected the overhead lights as Martin checked in with the hotel's security at the desk before they were authorized to move onto the private elevators. Ensuring the group stayed together, Martin pressed the button for their ascent to the thirty-third-floor lobby in stages.

Shane, Abi, Jade, and Reggie were left to ride up together, along with Andrew, Ted, and Matt. The small space felt cramped as they settled in, and Abi's pulse quickened the moment the elevator glided upward.

She gripped the railing tightly, her stomach doing uneasy flips. The higher they went, the more her nerves buzzed, especially upon hearing her ears popping. Being suspended so far above the ground made her palms sweat. *Was the elevator swaying?* She thought. It probably wasn't, but the sensation sent her heart racing.

Her eyes flicked over to Shane, who was still fixated on his phone. There was a time she would've slipped her hand into his, letting his quiet strength settle her nerves. But now, she hesitated as the thought crossed her mind.

Chest tightening, the elevator's gentle hum seemed louder than it should as she tried to focus on anything else, but the sight of the floor numbers ticking higher made her grip the railing harder.

"You okay, Abi?" Jade asked, her concern breaking the silence.

She forced a small smile as Shane briefly looked her way.

"Yeah...umm, I'm good," she said as his attention returned to his screen.

Jade gave her an encouraging nod, but Abi could tell she was not convinced.

Before anyone could say more, the elevator dinged, and the doors slid open to reveal the incredible lobby.

Stepping out quickly, taking a shaky breath, Abi was thankful that the floor beneath her feet felt solid despite knowing how high up they were. An audible gasp escaped the girls while their eyes flowed upward, admiring the breathtaking thirty-foot cathedral ceiling resembling a massive shoji lantern. Strategically placed plush seating offered cozy spots to take in the view of Tokyo's skyline. On either end of the vast lobby, a restaurant and the lounge buzzed with life.

Corralling the group near the front desk, Martin and Burton stepped forward to handle the room arrangements at check-in. The rest of them sank into buttery leather chairs, their conversations quiet but excited as they took in the view. Alert while getting their bearings, their security stood in the shadows and kept a low profile.

With a stack of sleek cards nestled in leather pouches, Martin passed along Burton's key and issued his guys' room assignments. In seconds, they were leading him away. As they passed her by, she noticed his hand raise subtly before disappearing around the corner.

Distributing everyone else's room information, Martin got them to follow him to the hotel's private lifts.

Intent on helping Abi with her bag, Shane attempted to slip it off her shoulder.

"No, it's okay. I got it," she said, making him stop in his tracks.

As they moved with the group to the far end of the lobby, the stone walls dressed in dark gray slate to match the floors were in stark contrast to the light wood trim accents.

Upon hearing a subtle bell, the doors opened when they arrived.

Anton and the guys loaded up while Martin and Andrew stayed behind with the young group to wait for the next one. In seconds, the doors parted on the right.

Andrew stepped inside and pressed the very top button on the panel as everyone piled in.

"Top floor?" Shane remarked, having seen the gentleman hit number thirty-eight.

Abi's stomach fluttered as they began their ascent. The numbers on the panel blinked steadily upward, her nerves rising. Thankfully, it was a short trip.

Hearing the chime, Shane stepped aside and gestured for her to lead the way.

The soft carpeted hallway muffled their footsteps as they followed the signs. When Abi glanced down another corridor, she caught sight of Burton's broad shoulders before he disappeared into a room with double doors.

"Here is where I leave you," Martin announced.

Lifting her hand, she waved to him as he dipped his chin slightly.

When they found their room, Shane tapped their key on the lock and held it open for her.

She hesitated for a moment, peering back down the hall, only to see that Burton was gone.

Inside their suite, Abi gasped. In the center of the room, a luxurious bed awaited, flanked by elegant, minimalist furnishings. Beyond that was a sunken seating area showcasing a panoramic view of Tokyo, the vast city stretching endlessly below.

Silently dropping his bag, Shane stepped toward the windows to take in the view as Abi sat on the edge of the bed, hating that they were up so high.

Exhausted, Shane walked over and took a seat beside her, then flopped backward. Closing his eyes, hands folded on top of his chest, he figured they'd relax a little until their luggage arrived.

While scooching backward and resting her head against the pillow, Abi debated whether she should try to talk to him, but just as she opened her mouth to say something, a knock at the door interrupted.

In seconds, Shane got up and went to answer it. Helping to wheel in their suitcases, he slipped the man a tip and said, "Thank you. Appreciate it." The moment the door fell closed behind him, he unzipped his suitcase and pulled out gym clothes without another word.

Watching him head into the bathroom to change, she hesitated because she could tell he was upset about something, and she figured it was best to give him space.

When he returned, dressed for a workout, he said coldly, "Reg and I arranged to check out the gym. I'll be back in an hour."

Abi nodded quietly. "Okay."

Shane didn't look back as he walked out.

The door slid shut with a soft click.

Now alone, Abi sat in the middle of the room, unsure of what to do. She realized she might have been cold to him that morning and had caused friction between them despite his efforts to smooth things over.

In need of a distraction, she turned on the television to the hotel channel and watched as most of the advertisements focused on the holiday season and Tokyo's famous attractions. Pulling out her phone, she texted Jade to chat, only to get a quick reply saying she was about to take a nap while Reggie was out, before promising to catch up later.

Casually scrolling through her contacts, her eyes purposefully landed on Burton's name. Not wanting to bother him, she thought she'd inquire with one of the guys before texting.

Opening the door to peek out into the hallway, she found Andrew not far from her. "Is it okay if I go and check on Burton?"

Andrew spoke quietly into his earpiece. "I've got Abi wanting to speak to the boss. Is he available?"

"Don't bother him if he's busy."

Waiting for a second, he soon got confirmation. "He will see you," he said. "Follow me."

Moving down the corridor to the opposite end, he knocked on room 403. In seconds, Burton opened the door.

"Thanks, Andrew," he said to the man as he stepped aside to allow the girl to enter. "Come on in, Abs."

"I thought you'd be sleeping."

"No, I've got too much to do." Leading her to the left-hand side of the large room, she walked into a kitchen, living, and dining area with three laptops open on the table. "I did rest on the plane, though."

The door shut behind her. "Glad to hear that...you...umm, got to sleep."

Picking up on her nervousness, he asked, "Hey. Are you doing okay? What's up?"

"Nothing," she shrugged.

With a tilt of his head, he was unconvinced.

"I don't know. It's the day before Christmas, but it doesn't feel like it." She checked her phone. "I searched up some of the holiday-themed attractions here, hoping it would help spark a bit of festive spirit." She smiled. "Did you know they have all these light festivals everywhere? Whole streets are lit up."

"Yes, from what I know, it's pretty impressive."

As their conversation dropped off there, she could tell Burton was preoccupied. "What are you working on?" she asked curiously.

He walked over and perused the screens. "I'm running diagnostics on the vault. I'm concerned about the breach attempts on the system last night." His tone seemed flat.

"You were pretty quiet on the flight here." She sat across from him. "Are you still mad about last night?"

Looking up from one laptop, he locked his eyes with hers. "I'm not mad. Just concerned and kinda exhausted. After all, we have been up all night."

Fully aware of what he meant, she lowered her head. "I know. I'm sorry…"

"How could you let someone dictate to you, knowing it's going against your better judgment?"

Understanding that she let Jade lead her astray, Abi replied, "I don't know…" With a sigh, she added, "Guess I wanted to make sure you were okay. That was the main reason for me agreeing."

Focused on his screen, he typed and said simultaneously, "I realize. But evading the guys again after what happened in Vegas? Didn't you learn your lesson then?"

"It was a bad decision."

"No, Abi. It was a dangerous one…" he paused. "You know I hate being the buzz kill here, but this trip has not turned out the way I thought it would. We've discovered some things are not as they seem. I'm on high alert, and I need you to be, too."

She nodded tentatively.

"These Tokuryū recruits are unpredictable. And, as I said, they will execute those tasks given to them. No questions asked." He could see a fearful expression creep across her face. "They get together for one job only and then split up without a trace – like ghosts. That's why we are having a hard time tracking them, let alone identifying them. They are far from stupid," he paused. "We could see the interference they were creating with the system last night. Thankfully, my fail-safes worked, and the algorithms adapted to the emerging threats." Running lines of code with his fingers flying over the keys, Burton stopped. "Tonight, I have three public appearances and two private vault access events. For me to do my job, I need you guys to keep a low profile – and I mean it. I want us to get out of this city unscathed. Tokyo is prime territory. So, if something is going to happen, it'll be here."

"Are you with Red Dragon tonight?"

He nodded. "We are performing at Ce La Vie, Womb, and his home base, T2 Shinjuku."

"So, do you think he is involved in this Tokuryū thing?"

"I can't see that he is. Despite still collecting intel on him, we did conduct a deep dive into the guy and his past. He was squeaky clean – no priors – not even a traffic ticket. To me, if he is involved, I'm sure they are threatening him if he doesn't comply."

"Are there going to be more of those Red Dragons showing up tonight?"

"If they do, I can't stop them from attending the public events, but the members-only stuff will be hard for them to trace." He chuckled humorously. "Guess I'll have to wait and find out." After saying that, he stopped and realized what he said scared her. "Don't worry. Everything will be fine. Martin and the guys are on top of it, and we have some others lurking in the shadows, just in case."

"How do guests find the private locations? Is it like Black Lyon raves or Dark Demon's?"

"The elites are using the usual Black Lyon protocol." He leaned back in his chair while perusing all three screens. "It's kind of ingenious, actually. On the International Nightfall App, an address pops up for members. It provides the coordinates for a vintage phone booth that we had installed in an obscure location. But it's not just any phone booth."

"How so?"

"Well, for one, there's no phone. Upon scanning their QR code with the red light, a token is dispensed, and a receipt is then printed. It gives the member the address of the event's secret location. I'm interested in seeing how the masses respond to the process. We installed surveillance cameras around it so we could observe them from every angle and obtain biometrics to identify attendees. For whatever reason, I can't understand why they love the thrill of the chase and the threat of being excluded. It's bizarre."

"Guess they want what they want."

He leaned forward and typed something before adding, "Since we had issues last night, I'm limiting attendance at both of these events. Those who aren't fast on their feet get locked out. Because of this, I'm sure the exclusivity will cause pandemonium."

"It sounds complicated," she said.

"The demographic of most of the clientele here is between the ages of twenty-two and thirty-five. Bored rich kids in search of a challenge. Martin says it's trending already. I find it interesting how their social posts are so cryptic, yet if you are in the know, you understand. Anyone else would simply be in the dark."

Worried about him, she asked, "So, are you working for the agency tonight or yourself?"

A seriousness crossed his face. "Both. It's not like I have a choice."

"Please be careful," she pleaded quietly.

Burton stopped, his eyes gravitated to hers. "Don't worry. We know what we're doing."

She nodded wearingly. "I know."

He rubbed her arm. "I'll be fine." About to close one laptop, he said, hoping to lighten the mood, "Just think, by this time tomorrow, we will be spending Christmas in Niseko. I hear they've gotten two feet of snow already. Can't wait."

"Me too." Fidgeting with her fingers below the table line, she asked, "Do me a favor?"

"What's that?"

"Text me between appearances and let me know you're good."

Wanting to do that for her, he was leery of one thing. "I'm certain Coppersmith won't appreciate it."

"I don't care at this point. I need to know you're okay."

He tilted his head sympathetically. "Martin and the guys will be with me. I think we are leaving Matt or Ted behind to watch over you with added hotel security."

"Alright." Checking the time, knowing Shane would be back from the gym soon, she said, "Umm, I should go and let you get back to work."

He got up from his seat when she did. Walking her to the door, he offered open arms. "I'll text you," he said as he hugged her.

"Make sure you do," she pointed accusingly.

"I will. I promise."

Opening the door, they found Lorenzo and Bray on duty.

Abi smiled at them, then turned to Burton and said, "Bye."

Fanning out his hand, holding the edge of the door, he replied, "Bye."

With Bray not far behind, Abi walked back to her room at the other end of the hall. Ensuring she got back okay, he stood there as she tapped her black door key to the reader. Swinging it open a crack, she said, "Thanks. I'll see you later."

"Very well, Miss."

When she walked in, she found Shane had already returned. Hearing the water running in the shower, she assumed he would question where she had been earlier and tried to prepare for that. In the meantime, she took out her phone and checked the venues Burton would be at that evening. One by one, she was surprised at the scope of each location. They were massive clubs in upscale areas frequented by the young elite. Not worried about them, given the number of guests that would be in attendance, she was mostly concerned about the secret locations. She mumbled to herself, "Less than a hundred people…" After saying that, she heard the shower turn off. Exhaling, she whispered, "Guess I've gotta be honest with him."

In seconds, the paper screen slid along its tracks. Shane emerged from the bathroom with a towel around his waist and a second around his neck.

"Do I dare ask where you've been?" He could not look her in the eye.

"I just went to apologize to him for last night. I got the impression he was mad since he didn't talk much on the flight here. Guess he's got a lot going on tonight, too."

"I bet he does," Shane replied while rifling through his open suitcase on the luggage shelf.

Immediately sensing a jealous vibe, she sighed.

Hearing it, about to go and get changed, he said, "I'm sorry. It's none of my business what you do."

Those words cut like a knife. "Shane… With everything going on, I'm just concerned – for all of us. Burton said, if anything goes wrong, it will be here."

Watching him disappear into the bathroom, she could hear him getting dressed. Able to take a minute to calm down, he soon emerged again.

"When you asked me to come on this trip, I didn't realize I'd become a target in some crazy mob game. This is more than I signed up for."

"How do you think I feel?"

"I don't know, Abs… How do you feel?" he paused and awaited her answer almost accusingly.

Certain he meant him in contrast to Burton, her sight gravitated to the floor. "Don't do that… Please…"

Shane's phone chimed. Checking it, he said, "It's Reg and Jade. They're bored already. They're wondering if we can get a private tour guide to show us around the Ginza shopping district? Apparently," he read, "It's not far from here."

"I don't know... We will have to pass it by Martin first."

When she said that, Shane sent a reply and read Reggie's in return. "They're coming to our suite. What number are we again?"

"We are 411."

Moments later, Shane got to the door when they knocked. Abi stayed on the bed, suddenly feeling the floor slant towards the window again when she recalled how high up they were.

"Hey, girl," Jade said on the way past.

"Hi."

"Our rooms are exactly the same." Jade analyzed. "Except our bathroom is on the opposite side."

Realizing Abi wasn't overly talkative, she asked, "All settled in?" Upon moving to the sunken seating area, she peered out at the view.

"As settled in as we can be for one night."

Sensing the tension, Jade tested the waters again. "Did you have a nap?"

"Umm, no. Not exactly..." she replied coldly as the guys joined them.

"Okay, girlfriend. What's with the attitude?" Jade questioned while Reg sat down beside her.

Abi subtly snapped. "Nothing."

"You're still mad at me for last night?"

Knowing it wasn't the girl's fault fully, Abi exhaled to calm her nerves. "No. I'm not mad. It's just this whole situation is getting to me."

Shane put in his two cents. "This trip is getting to all of us at this point. We literally have no freedom to do anything."

"About that. Do we know what we are allowed to do and not allowed to do?" Jade asked, sprawled on the sofa with Reg.

Answering her friend, she said, "Low profile, remember?"

"But what does that mean? Can we go out? Text Martin. See what he says."

Reluctantly doing as Jade asked, Abi stated, "I sent him a message. There are no guarantees we will get authorization given the circumstances."

"Well, we didn't come all this way to sit around and look at the skyline," Reg divulged sternly.

The comment scared Abi. "Even if it's not safe?"

"Fourteen million people live in Tokyo. I'm sure that would make us hard to find." The Wilson family heir sat up. "If you guys can't go out, we will just have to leave without you."

Leaning against the pillow, Abi gripped her phone tightly, frustration etched across her face.

"Still no reply from Martin?" her friend asked.

Abi shook her head. "No."

A scoff came from the couch, accompanied by the sound of someone shifting to a more relaxed position. "Well, Jade and I want to go exploring. We saw an enormous tower from our room." He scanned the horizon and pointed at it. "See. There it is."

Both Shane and Abi spotted the attraction towering above the city.

Excitement flickered on Jade. "We could hire our own security and get a private driver. That way, we wouldn't have to worry about anyone else's schedule – or drama."

Not in favor of what she said, Abi knew her friend had forgotten what happened last night all too quickly.

"I just want to go shopping. If you don't want to go, it's fine. You can stay here," Jade said point-blank. "No pressure, either way."

A hint of friction tainted the air, threatening to escalate things further between them.

"She has a point," Shane said calmly. Seeing Abi's reaction to what he said, he pulled back. "Can't we just stick together and do something fun?"

A quiet moment passed as his suggestion lingered.

Jade shrugged and tapped Reggie's knee as he agreed with his friend. "Shane's right," he said. "We are in Tokyo! Don't you want to explore the city, Abs?"

Searching for solutions, Shane's fingers moved quickly across his phone screen. Sourcing out a tour guide, Shane confirmed the locations the guy frequented. Showing a vibrant street lined with colorful stalls, he said, "What about this?" and presented the image of Nakamise-dori. "It's not far, and looks pretty unique. We could do some trinket shopping and visit the temple before heading over to that tower."

Reluctance softening, Jade knew it wasn't the Ginza Six shopping excursion she was expecting. "If you want to do that, it's fine. I'll go."

A grin spread across Reggie's face. Nudging Jade playfully, he stated, "It'll be fun, Babe," secretly thankful she wouldn't be blowing thousands of dollars in the luxury shopping mall.

With that decided, Shane booked the guide and waited for confirmation. "Since he's a local, I'm sure he can show us some hidden gems off the beaten path. The best part is, he'll know the streets like the back of his hand, so we won't get lost."

With a plan forming, Abi got a message from Martin. Reading his reply out loud, she announced, "He sent his apologies and told us to stay within the confines of the hotel."

"Well, I'm sorry, Abs. We're heading out. You can stay or come with us. That is up to you," Jade stated, giving her an ultimatum of sorts.

While her friend continued planning their afternoon, a pang of guilt settled in the pit of Abi's stomach as she turned off her device and set it aside. "There is no way you will evade the guys after what happened."

Reg got up from the sofa and walked to the front door. On the back of it was a fire escape map. Pointing to it, he said, "There is a staircase at the end of the hall, right there." Head for that staircase. We will use the one at our end. Go down one floor and meet at the elevators. From there, we will head to the lobby before moving to the ground floor." He stepped back into the room. "Got it?"

"Got it." Shane gave him a thumbs-up.

"We're just gonna grab our coats and stuff," Jade said on the way out.

Seeing Abi sitting on the bed, deep in thought, Shane asked, "So, are you coming with us or what?"

Seemingly not given a choice, she gave a faint nod. "I guess."

"Good. Let's get a move on." He put on his coat. "We won't be out long. Possibly two hours. Nothing's gonna happen? I promise."

Dressed in warm layers, Abi slipped on her jacket. Meeting at the door, shoes tied and her bag slung across her body, they tucked their passports inside their clothes for safekeeping.

About to leave, Shane stood in front of the door. "I don't want to fight," he said, his eyes locked on hers. "I'm sorry."

"Me, too," she whispered.

"You don't need to be. Just me..." Hugging her, he added, "I'm still working on this jealousy thing."

"There's no reason to be..."

He suddenly kissed her lips. "I know."

| 9 |

Sneak Out

Saturday, December 23

Aman, Tokyo / Sensō-ji Temple / Skytree

Shane peeked out through the narrow crack of their hotel room door and swept the dimly lit corridor, scanning for any sign of their security.

Seeing Andrew pacing near the elevators, posture alert, they waited for him to round the corner.

Double-checking the hotel's emergency evacuation map one last time, tapping a finger against it, Shane said, "The stairs should be three doors down, on the right. You go. I'll follow."

Hesitant, hating herself for what she was about to do, Abi nodded.

Exhaling, he whispered, "Ready on three…"

Andrew was about to disappear from view.

"One…"

She prepared and shifted her weight, ready to run.

"Two…"

The moment the guy vanished, Shane whispered, "Three. Go, go, go."

Slipping out, moving swiftly and silently down the hallway. Shane made sure their door latched shut with the softest *click* before sprinting toward the stairwell. Abi held the door open, her pulse hammering.

The second Shane was inside, he eased it shut, muffling the sound of the heavy steel before taking hold of Abi's hand. "Let's go."

Quickly descending the stairs, stopping on the next floor, Shane cracked open the door, checking both directions, leery to step out into the hallway. At the far end, Reggie and Jade emerged from another staircase.

Shane raised a hand as they hurried toward each other.

"We made it," Jade whispered on the edge of celebration.

"We're not out of the woods yet." Reggie's expression darkened as he glanced around. "We still have to get through the lobby and to the remaining elevators without being seen."

Abi swallowed, her stomach twisting. A part of her hoped somewhere along the line that they'd get caught.

Moving in silence, they headed towards the main lobby. As they neared the soaring atrium, Shane and Reggie paused, scanning the expansive hall.

A few guests milled about. Hotel security was visible near the entrance, but no one seemed to be paying attention to them.

"Hoods up," Shane signaled.

Jade and Abi did the same, tilting their heads downward as they slipped through the grand space with measured strides. Each step felt heavy.

When they reached the main elevator bank, Shane pressed the button on the wall.

The doors slid open. It was empty. Quickly getting inside, each released the breath they had been holding as they agonizingly descended to ground level.

"Almost there," Reggie muttered.

When the elevator finally opened on the bottom floor, Jade checked her phone. "Our ride's here."

They moved quickly toward the exit. A dark-colored van idled at the curb. One by one, they climbed inside.

"Nakamise-Dori Street, please." Jade held up a picture of the place on her screen.

The driver nodded.

When the black van eased away from the sleek entrance of Aman Tokyo, they soon merged onto the street. Amidst towering skyscrapers, with their reflective glass facades shimmering under the midday sun, the traffic moved in an orderly flow.

Inside the vehicle, the group sat in silence, their eyes flicking between their phones, the driver, and the scenery passing by. The stress of their escape from the hotel still clung to them, but for now, they had blended into the moving city.

The roads twisted between a maze of high-rises before spilling onto Chuo-dori, a broad avenue cutting through the heart of Tokyo's shopping and business districts. Pedestrians filled the sidewalks, darting in and out of high-end boutiques, neon-lit cafes, and towering department stores. Digital billboards flashed bright advertisements, their colors bouncing off the glass windows of the surrounding buildings.

As they moved deeper into the city, the ultra-modern skyline slowly gave way to the older charm of Asakusa. The towering glass and steel softened into lower, more traditional structures. Narrow alleyways stretched between wooden storefronts, their entrances adorned with noren curtains swaying gently in the cool breeze. Small izakayas and tea houses sat nestled between the more contemporary buildings, a testament to Tokyo's seamless blend of past and present.

The Sumida River came into view, its surface shimmering as sunlight reflected off the gentle waves. Beyond it, the Tokyo Skytree loomed in the distance, an unmistakable beacon against the blue sky.

Finally, the van slowed as they approached Kaminari Mon—the grand entrance to Sensō-ji Temple. The massive gate stood proud, its wooden pillars supporting a colossal red paper lantern adorned with bold black kanji. The golden statues of the wind and thunder gods flanked the entrance, their fierce expressions watching over the steady flow of visitors passing beneath them.

As the van pulled to a stop, the driver glanced back. "We're here."

The moment they stepped out into the pulsating energy of the tourist location, the crowd buzzed with excitement. Locals and tourists alike filled the street as a symphony of different languages surrounded them.

Jade handed the driver a generous tip and leaned in. "Meet us at Nitenmon Gate in one hour," she instructed, showing him the location on the map.

Referring to it, the driver, a middle-aged man with kind eyes, nodded and repeated her words in broken English. "Nitenmon Gate. One hour." His accent was thick, but his intent was clear—he understood. As he tucked the tip into his pocket, he smiled and repeated their plan once more for good measure. "Hai. I be there."

Jade offered a quick nod in return before stepping back. The van's tires rolled over the asphalt, easing away from the curb and disappearing into the steady pulse of Tokyo's traffic.

The air was thick with the mingling scents of incense, sizzling street food, and a faint chill carried on the wind. Small vendor stalls lined the path beyond the gate, their owners calling out to passing tourists, their voices blending into the hum of the crowd.

Many eyes found them almost instantly. Their polished appearance made them stand out in the sea of shoppers and vendors.

Abi felt the weight of their stares bearing down on her, tightening around her chest like a vise. She wanted to reach for Shane's hand—to anchor herself—but he kept them shoved deep in his jacket pockets.

A man approached them at the corner, his dark hair combed neatly, a warm smile upon his face. "Are you the Coppersmith group?"

Shane stepped forward, glancing at his phone. "Are you Ken Kamachi?"

The man bowed respectfully. "That is me. I will be your tour guide today."

Ken's presence brought a sense of relief to Abi, though she didn't relax entirely knowing the guys weren't hovering close by.

"We will start here by entering the Kaminari Mon Gate. You can peruse the shops on our way to Sensō-Ji temple."

"Sounds good," Jade said, taking hold of Reggie's hand.

Surveying the crowd as they passed the red and gold structure, Abi's paranoia increased with every young man who turned his head. Fearfully, scanning the napes of their necks for the distinctive Red Dragon tattoo, her chest loosened just a little every time she saw unmarked skin.

With their friends wandering ahead with Ken, Shane's shoulders squared, and in an instant, he offered his hand.

Grateful, she took hold and held tight as he gave it a reassuring, gentle squeeze. "Thank you," she muttered.

"No problem."

Ken gestured to the colorful stalls lining Nakamise-dori, their wares displayed in an enticing array of fabrics, trinkets, and traditional crafts. "Should you wish to shop at any of the stores, I can translate for you. Please note, most vendors only take cash."

Enthralled, Jade tugged on Reggie's arm. "Cash isn't an issue. Right, babe?"

Pulling his wallet from his back pocket, Reg smirked. "I've got sixty-two thousand Yen on me. Sorry, but that's your limit."

She rolled her eyes, snickering. "Please. I've got over two hundred thousand Yen on me. That should cover it."

Tilting her head, Abi did a quick calculation. "You're really planning to spend over a thousand dollars here?"

Already scanning the storefronts, deciding where to stop first, Jade replied, "You bet."

Watching her friend gravitate to a shop specializing in hand-painted chopsticks, Jade picked up a pair, admiring the intricate floral designs etched into the wood. Selecting eight sets, she approached the counter and handed over the cash as the elderly woman behind the register smiled appreciatively and wrapped her purchase with care.

The group pressed on, weaving through the masses, filling the narrow street. Vendors called out cheerfully in Japanese, enticing them with paper fans, silk kimonos, and sweet-smelling snacks. Abi tensed each time someone glanced their way. Every face seemed suspicious, every movement startling.

Shane picked up on it. "Abi. Relax. We're good."

When he said that, her gaze flicked to the back of a young man's neck as he bent to restock a shelf. Relief washed over her when she saw nothing. Turning back to Shane, she whispered, "I'm just nervous."

He leaned in and said reassuringly, "I've got you. Just stick close."

Though her heart continued to beat a little too quickly, the colorful chaos of Nakamise-dori dazzled her friends as Ken Kamachi helped translate while Jade haggled over the price of a set of handcrafted hairpins.

With his hands in his pockets, Reg grinned as his wife flashed a victorious smirk, having made an impressive deal with the vendor.

Leaving the small shop, they soon reached the end of the marketplace and the towering Sensō-ji pagoda.

In the open space, the brisk chill was enough to redden cheeks and quicken their steps. Admiring the temple grounds, they snapped a few pictures and read various plaques amidst all the visitors exploring its many wonders.

Suddenly, a noticeable hum filled the air, causing a shift in the crowd. A ripple of motion followed as people began tilting their heads back and shielding their eyes from the low-hanging winter sun.

"What is that?" she said, hearing a high-pitched buzzing.

"I think it's a drone," Shane said, spotting it.

Sleek. Black. Hovering. At first, they brushed it off as a tourist getting aerial shots of the historic district. But as they moved through the towering Hozomon Gate, it didn't drift away. It dipped lower and stayed close. Too close.

Anxiety cloaked Abi as her fingers tightened around Shane's. "Look," she murmured, nodding toward the sky. "Is it just me, or is that thing watching us?"

He followed her line of sight, eyes narrowing. "Umm… guys?" he called out.

Still caught up in their selfies, Jade and Reg barely noticed.

"Hey!" Abi's tone sharpened. "Guys!"

When they flung around, confusion crossed their faces—until they saw Shane's eyes glued upward.

The drone loomed above them, a mechanical shadow against the pale sky.

Freaked out, their tour guide said, "Oh, wow!" before ducking for cover at the edge of the building.

Checking the time on her phone, Jade shouted, "Our driver should be there! Let's move!"

One by one, they nodded with a sense of urgency and started in that direction, stealing glances as the drone followed.

Abi's pulse quickened.

Then, to their right, not far from it, they spotted another one.

It was bigger. Faster.

Jade gasped. Breathing erratically, panic set in. Soon, she ran.

"Jade, wait—!" Reg lunged after her.

Veering towards them as the second swooped in just above the trees, Ken took cover fearfully and yelled, "Hey!" About to chase them down, the drone swooped again, making him cower. "You didn't pay!"

Hearing this, Shane stopped abruptly and went back while pulling a number of bills from his wallet. "Here! Take this! I'm so sorry. We need to go!"

The poor guy stood there dumbfounded as the group fled.

In seconds, Shane caught up. "Come on! Go! Go!" he prompted as they ran.

When they disappeared, the drones followed. Eyes on the sky, Ken peeked out from under the roof of the building. Thankful the coast was clear, he peered down at the cash in his hand, shocked to find six 10,000 Yen notes. "Oh..." he muttered, slapping his hand to his head. "That's too much..." Knowing he could never find them now, he shrugged and went about his day.

Approaching Nitenmon Gate, they bolted past many startled tourists and spotted their driver in the black van idling along the curb.

The buzzing drones ascended over the sloped roof, engines whirling.

"Almost there!" Shane shouted.

Abi ducked as one dived at them, so close she swore she could *feel* the force of its blades.

When they reached the vehicle, Shane knocked on the window.

Seeing them, the man opened the sliding door remotely.

"Inside! Hurry!" Scrambling to find their seats, the QB got in last and slammed it shut behind them.

Panting. Hearts hammering, Reggie barked, "Take us to the SkyTree, please!"

The driver didn't hesitate. The tires screeched against the pavement as they lurched into motion, weaving into the chaotic Tokyo traffic.

Everyone's eyes darted to the sky as they crossed the bridge.

"I think they're gone," Abi said, but her fear hadn't faded.

"Do you think it was a hobbyist just screwin' around?" The QB tried to defuse the situation with eyes still peeled.

Still scanning the sky through the sunroof, she replied, "Maybe. But somehow, I don't think so..."

As the van crossed the bridge, the towering silhouette of Tokyo Skytree loomed ahead, its spire piercing the sky. Slowly, their driver navigated through the busy streets before pulling up beneath the colossal structure.

"Where do we go to get in?" Jade asked, her eyes scanning the base of the tower.

"Up staircase to entrance," the driver replied in broken English, gesturing toward a nearby set of stairs.

Offered another tip, Jade instructed, "You come back? One hour?"

He accepted the money with a nod. "Hai. One hour. I be here."

"Thank you," she said as they slid the side door open and stepped out, their eyes instinctively scanning for any sign of the drones.

Seeing nothing, Reg took Jade's hand. "Come on," he urged. "Let's get inside." Assuming they weren't targeted, he figured the incident was simply coincidental.

Shane wrapped his arm around Abi as they ascended the staircase to the main entrance. The glass panels slid open, welcoming them into the expansive lobby.

Inside, the atmosphere was a blend of modern design and bustling energy. Visitors milled about, and the ambient hum of conversations filled the air. Approaching the ticket counter, they requested passes for the Tembo Deck.

Feeling a sense of excitement, the guys pooled their cash and paid the admission fees. A grin spread across Shane's face as he handed over the payment.

"This only gets us partway?" Reg asked the attendant.

"Ticket for 350-meter level," the woman explained in fairly clear English. "You want Tembo Galleria at 450 meter? You buy ticket at Tembo Deck."

Shane said to his friend. "There's no way Abs will go that high. Let's just get these tickets first. See how she does. If she's feeling adventurous, maybe we can convince her to go higher."

He gave the QB a thumbs-up. "Sounds like a plan."

Reluctantly, Abi hung back, arms crossed tightly over her chest while watching the video of the whole experience on the screen. Her body fluttered nervously as a sense of dread crept in at the thought of being up so high.

Tickets in hand, nudging her reassuringly, Shane asked, "Hey, you okay?"

Uncertainty looming, she confessed, glancing at the elevator in front of them, "I don't know if I can do this."

"I bet you'll love it," Shane said calmingly, though concern still lingered.

"You'll be fine, girl," Jade encouraged. "Don't worry. It'll be fun."

Shane flashed a teasing wink. "And if you faint, I've got you covered."

With her heart racing as they queued for the ride. The thought of ascending to such heights made her palms sweat.

Giving in, she sighed, allowing him to take her hand as they stepped into the elevator. While they began their rapid ascent, Abi felt her ears pop, a reminder of the altitude they were gaining. The ride up was smooth despite it all, though a slight tension built in her chest with every passing second. Eyes affixed to the floor, both hands clutching Shane's tighter, the doors suddenly opened to the Sky Lounge. She closed her eyes for a brief moment before inhaling and stepping out into the glass-encased corridor.

On the Tembo Deck, Abi was surprised by the spaciousness. The floor-to-ceiling windows offered a 360-degree panoramic view of Tokyo, stretching as far as the eye could see.

"This is insane!" Jade's excitement broke through the awe. "Look at that!"

Despite her nervousness, her eyes slowly lifted to see the view. It was nothing short of magnificent. "It's… beautiful," she muttered.

Pointing at the shimmering canal below, Jade said to Reg, "We need to check that out before we leave. It'd make the perfect backdrop for a social post."

Her friends eagerly approached the windows, marveling at the city's expanse below, but Abi hung back, her fear anchoring her feet to the floor.

"Come on, Abs! You need to see this!" Jade called out, waving her over.

Shaking her head, she just couldn't move closer to the edge.

Suddenly, a familiar buzzing sound reached her ears. She looked past Jade and Reg and saw it—a drone hovering just outside the glass, its lens seemingly fixed on them.

"Shane!" she shouted, panic rising.

He turned to her, concern etched into his features.

"We need to go!" Fearfully pointing at it, she immediately reached for him and saw Reggie staring at something on the street below.

Spotting a caravan of black trucks pulling up in unison, he saw men in dark clothing spill out of each and move with eerie coordination. "Umm, guys..." Reggie swallowed hard. "I think we might have a problem."

His wife saw it also. Her face paled as she gripped his arm. "Wait... Are they here for us?"

"I'm pretty sure they're not tourists, babe," Reggie confirmed grimly.

Not hesitating, Shane seized Abi's hand. "We gotta go. Come on."

Heart pounding, Abi shadowed him to the elevator.

Finding the attendant, a petite woman in a crisp uniform, she greeted them with a polite smile.

Assuming she didn't speak very good English, Shane said, using hand gestures, "We go down elevator? Now? Fast."

She shook her head meanly and said, "No. Must wait."

Abi's stomach twisted as she heard the mechanical hum of a second drone hovering outside the glass. Around them, the other tourists began to notice and point. Some even took pictures of it.

Military-grade, Reg figured this was more than someone's hobby.

"Those men. Are they coming up here?" Jade was a little slow in processing the seriousness of it.

Upon hearing that, Abi's panic spiked. She squeezed her eyes shut. "I wish Andrew were here. He'd know what to do," she whispered a desperate prayer under her breath.

The soft chime of an elevator arriving made her snap her eyes open.

Like an answer to her spoken plea, familiar faces stepped out and locked onto their group in seconds.

Andrew quickly assessed the situation. "Follow me," he commanded. "This way!"

"How did you…?" Abi said before he interrupted.

"Not now! Move!"

Swiftly doing what they were told, they trailed Andrew, with Ted keeping watch behind them.

The drone dipped lower and zeroed in on their group.

Abi's pulse roared in her ears.

"Aren't we taking the elevator back down?" Jade asked, anxiety surfacing as Andrew led them away.

His sharp eyes scanned the employees lingering nearby. Without hesitation, he snagged one by the arm. "Emergency staircase? Where?"

The man smirked. "You not permitted—"

Pulling back his jacket just enough to flash the grip of his gun, Andrew threatened, "Do we have a problem?"

The employee's smirk vanished. His eyes widened. "No, sir. This way." Hurrying to a black security door, he swiped his access badge against the reader.

When the lock clicked open, Andrew ripped the badge off him and tossed it to Ted before shoving the man aside.

"Go! Go! Go!" Andrew barked as the group rushed through. Then, he warned the employee. "You no see us here."

Hands up, the man nodded submissively. "I see nothing."

"Good." Andrew slammed the door shut and followed the others into the stairwell.

The air inside was stale and cold. The sound of their footsteps echoed eerily, swallowed by the seemingly endless spiral of steps stretching downward.

"Oh my god," Jade trembled, gripping the railing as her legs wobbled beneath her. She didn't dare look down. Just knowing how high up they were made her stomach twist.

"Keep moving! Be careful! Do not fall!" Andrew commanded sharply.

Their gaps came quicker, feet slamming against the concrete as they descended. Each level was the same; the monotonous pattern of steps was disorienting and messed with their depth perception. The winding stairwell felt like an optical illusion, as if the stairs kept going for infinity, and they had yet to make any headway.

Lungs burning. Breath shallow. Abi's vision slowly blurred.

Shane noticed her wavering and steadied her immediately.

"Breathe slower," he instructed calmly. "In through your nose, out through your mouth. You're doing great."

Staying close to Jade, Reg placed one of her hands on the cold steel railing and the other on his shoulder. "Just focus on me," he said. "One step at a time."

Then—suddenly—the lights cut out.

Jade screamed when the stairwell went dark.

"Shit!" Andrew swore, reaching for his penlight when the dim red emergency lights flickered on, casting long, shifting shadows.

"They cut the power," Ted snapped before Andrew added, "Keep moving. Watch your step!"

Pulse pounding, Abi inhaled slowly. "You need to focus," she muttered before she continued on.

The stairwell itself was a tower within the tower, yet at this moment, it felt like a never-ending maze.

Spotting CCTV cameras mounted along the stairwell walls, Ted said under his breath before shouting to Andrew, "With the power out, at least the cameras aren't working. Maybe they won't see us."

His colleague didn't look convinced. "Or maybe they already did."

A wave of dizziness washed over Abi as the red lines marking each tread blurred. The constant spiraling, the dim lighting, the sheer exhaustion—it was making her lightheaded. The never-ending flights of stairs, all stacked one after another in an endless sequence, each landing providing a brief pause before the pattern repeated as the sharp turns added to her growing nausea.

She immediately sat down.

"Abi!" Shane's grip tightened around her.

"I need a minute," she said, though she wasn't sure how much longer she could keep going. Every muscle in her legs screamed, and her knees wobbled.

Just ahead of them, Jade's breathing was shallow and erratic.

"I can't—" the girl gasped.

"Yes, you can," Reggie said firmly. "You're doing amazing, babe."

Andrew stood beside them. "We gotta keep moving. You can't stop. If we do, they will find us."

Hearing that, Abi said, "Okay, okay," and took a breath.

Jade did, too.

Floor after floor, they continued their descent. The world outside the narrow stairwell felt impossibly far away. The only thing that existed now was the relentless downward climb, the echo of their footsteps, and the creeping exhaustion threatening to overtake them all.

Then—a noise from above.

A metallic clanking sound echoed down the stairwell. Someone was knocking on the steel rails.

"Move! Move!" Andrew commanded. "Now!"

Fear stripped away their exhaustion, and they bolted down the steps, knowing someone was following them. Ted kept a steady pace, his eyes flicking to the floor markers as they passed. Approaching the bottom, he began counting down to maintain morale. "Ten!" he shouted.

Barely able to breathe, all Abi could hear was Shane encouraging her.

"Focus. Stay with me. You're doing good, Abs."

"Nine!"

Andrew's earpiece crackled to life. "Did you get that, Ted?"

His friend confirmed what they heard on the radio. "Yep! Matt. Redirect! Bravo-One-Charlie-Four-Seven!"

"Roger that!" Andrew verified.

Step by step, they kept counting down. "Eight!" Ted shouted.

The flights blended, each landing only a fleeting moment before turning the corner and finding the next.

Joining in, Andrew said, "Seven!"

Passing the last four flights, Abi's legs felt like lead. They had been descending for over twenty-five minutes. Her body was reaching its breaking point. But then—finally—the basement level door loomed ahead.

"Two!"

Everyone could see the light at the end of the tunnel. Had they made it?

"One!" Andrew pulled the door marked with kanji letters. Holding it for everyone, they surfaced from the staircase and into the entrance foyer of the parking garage. Emergency lighting cast a dimness.

"Which way?" Shane questioned.

"Wait," Andrew said while corralling everyone to the left.

Hearts hammering, they took a moment to catch their breath, unsure what would be waiting for them on the other side of the steel door.

"Matt. Bravo One Charlie Four Seven. Ready for evac," Andrew said into his comms.

There was a moment of silence before they heard the screech of tires beyond the door.

Gun drawn, Andrew cracked the door open while Shane and Reggie shielded the girls.

Outside, a black SUV idled, its windows tinted.

"Let's move!" Matt shouted from the driver's side.

Andrew didn't hesitate. He flung the door open and ushered everyone out. Each scrambled to the vehicle and took their seats.

"Drive!" Ted said while jumping in last.

As Matt peeled away with precision, weaving into the flow of traffic, he kept a low profile. No sudden movements. No reckless speeding. Just a calculated blend into the Tokyo streets.

As they passed the SkyTree's front drop-off area, they ducked down upon spotting the cluster of Tokuryū teens standing near the entrance, eyes scanning the crowds. On the ground beside them, two drones sat idle, their lights flickering.

Andrew turned to Abi. "What were you thinking?" The words came out like a punch. "I expect this from them, but not you."

Quickly snapping back, Reggie's frustration spilled over. "What the hell, man?"

He pointed toward the group of teens swarming the attraction. "Does that look like a joke to you?"

They all went quiet, knowing he was right, even if they didn't want to admit it.

"How did you find us?" she asked him.

The big guy pointed to her jacket. "Check your pocket."

Slipping her hand inside, Abi pulled out a small black tracker with a blinking red light. The guy held up his phone, showing her the signal.

"This is closed-circuit," he explained. "Only my phone can trace it. No one else." Andrew stared at her sharply. "Do you have any idea what could've happened up there? What if we hadn't gotten to you in time?"

A cold wave of realization hit Abi. She didn't need to look at him to feel his disappointment. Once again, they had risked their lives to save hers.

| 10 |

Change of Plans

Saturday, December 23

Aman, Tokyo

The ride back to the Aman was cloaked in silence, but Abi's mind churned. The chaos at Skytree kept replaying—shouts, shadows, the rush of adrenaline—each moment a reminder of how close they had come to disaster. Fear lingered sharp in her chest, not just of the Tokuryū hunting them, but of what waited at the hotel. Facing Martin felt unbearable, but it was Burton she dreaded most. How would he look at her now—angry, disappointed, or worse, seeing her as the weakness their enemies meant to exploit?

Now, close to five o'clock, the city was coming alive with festive illuminations along various routes. As the van approached the large building, Abi saw a nearby street completely lit up, stretching as far as the eye could see. A good distraction from her thoughts.

Andrew happened to look back at the same time and saw the amazement on her face.

Taking it all in, she spotted the security guard staring her way. Despite wanting to explore the pretty streets at night, she knew enough not to ask him about it.

By the time they arrived at the hotel, extra security and police officers had already taken action. With danger still lurking, Matt drove through the breezeway under the Otemari building. When they stopped, everyone got out.

Inside the foyer, Abi spotted Burton, dressed as Dark Demon, surrounded by his men. His head remained lowered to hide his identity. But there was no Martin.

On their way inside, Andrew leaned in quietly. "Walk past. Do not engage," he advised all of them.

Burton saw Abi. Having been kept up to speed by Martin on what had happened, he wanted to speak with her but knew he couldn't—not without drawing attention.

While they walked by the entourage, Abi noticed Burton subtly raise a few fingers alongside his thigh to acknowledge her. She mirrored the gesture as they passed.

After Burton left, they waited for the elevator to arrive.

Her phone chimed. Checking it, she saw a secure message come through from him. Waving the phone over her fob, it opened to the encrypted screen.

Are you alright? It read.

She typed quickly: *Yes, we're okay. Don't worry. Focus on your events tonight. Be safe. I'll be thinking of you. Don't forget to text me your location changes. Okay?*

His thinking bubbles rambled, and the word *okay* popped up. Knowing he had to go, Abi responded with a thumbs up, hoping it would fuel him to get through the long night.

"Is that him?" Shane asked with a roll of his eyes.

"He's got a lot going on, and he's worried about us," Abi said. "I told him to stay focused. That we were okay."

When the elevator doors parted, they soon sped toward the 33rd floor. In the main lobby in the sky, they walked through the atrium on their way to the second set of interior lifts.

Andrew's tone was as hard as stone. "No one leaves the premises tonight. Got it?"

They all nodded, keeping quiet, knowing there was no room for debate.

Grateful for what he'd done, Abi glanced at Andrew. "Thank you for coming after us..." The weight of her guilt pressed down.

He replied sternly, "It's our job to keep you safe, but you're making it harder and harder to do that."

Darting away sheepishly, Abi felt the sting of his disappointment.

The second the elevator arrived, Reggie prompted Jade to step in first. Then, just as Shane was about to do the same for Abi, Andrew suddenly shot his hand out to block her path.

"No, Miss. You're coming with me," he said ominously. "Martin wants to have a word."

She flashed Shane a fearful look, but the security guard held the QB back when he was about to join them. "No, Coppersmith. Just her. Nobody else."

Shane zeroed in on her. "You good?" he asked quietly.

Nodding at him, she replied, "Yeah. I'll be fine," regardless of the knot developing in her stomach.

As the doors closed, Ted hesitated a second before pressing the button again. When the second set of doors opened, Andrew prompted Abi to get in, and Ted followed behind with a sense of unease.

The elevator ride was silent, the tension thick between the three of them.

Able to sense Andrew's dismay, she muttered again, "I'm truly sorry for everything today..."

He didn't answer right away, his jaw clenched. "You keep apologizing," he said. "But you keep making the same mistakes."

She bit her lip, knowing he was right, but was unable to change the feeling gnawing at her.

When they reached the 38th floor, Andrew led her down the hallway to Burton's suite. Knocking on the door, Martin opened it. They could see he wasn't happy.

"Come in," the gentleman said curtly, walking away without a second glance.

Abi hesitated and followed.

Returning to his chair with a steeped tea awaiting him, Martin took a sip and looked at her above the rim of the cup, his eyes narrowing. "I hear you had a close call."

"Umm, yeah." She shifted uncomfortably. "You could say that..."

Martin set his cup down with an intentional clink. "This stunt could've cost you."

Silence stretched between them, thick and uncomfortable. Then Martin's iPad pinged. He read the notification before standing up.

"Follow me," he ordered, not leaving any room for argument.

Unsure what to expect, she walked alongside the men down the hall, assuming they were taking her to her room to meet Shane. But instead, he pressed the button for the lobby floor.

"Wait... Where are we going?" she asked, slightly worried.

Neither of the men answered.

When the doors parted, they stepped aboard and descended to the thirty-third floor again before passing the reception.

Standing by the elevators, Martin pressed the button and clasped his hands behind his back regally. His face was like stone.

"I'm sorry, Martin," she said again, panic creeping in. "What's happening? Are you sending me home?"

Getting in when the empty lift arrived, the ride to the ground floor was almost unbearable. Nobody said a word. Upon reaching the lobby, Martin silently prompted her to follow him while Andrew stayed close.

The cold air hit her as the glass doors slid open to the breezeway tunnel. Upon seeing them emerge, the men scoured their surroundings.

A sleek Mercedes SUV was waiting, flanked by two black trucks.

Martin opened the back door and gestured for her to get in.

"Please, Martin," Abi pleaded, her voice shaking. "Please. I want to stay. Don't send me home."

Suddenly, a shadow appeared from behind a pillar. Then another and another.

Scared, Abi fell back behind Andrew.

"It's okay, Miss. You've got company," he whispered.

As the figure slowly moved into the light, she froze. Her heart racing, she saw Burton. "What are you doing here? I thought you had appearances tonight?"

"Change of plans." He paused and smiled. "I heard you wanted to see the illumination displays. Figured I'd join you." Hands in his jacket pockets, he offered a bent elbow for her to hold.

Surprised, she linked her arm with his.

"Shall we?" he said.

Martin held open the door to the Mercedes-Maybach EQS for Abi while Burton rounded the vehicle and got in on the opposite side. Sliding into the plush, contoured seats, the light gray interior exuded sophistication with smooth, quilted leather and a faint new-car scent. The cabin's LED light shone an ambient blue, creating a cool luminescence along the sleek door panels and across the hyperscreen dashboard.

Shifting in her seat, Abi ran her fingers lightly over the leather armrest, taking in the quiet hum of the electric vehicle. The doors closed with a soft, airtight thud, sealing them in luxury.

Burton adjusted his seat with the intuitive touch controls, the heated seats engaging as he rested his elbow on the console between them.

With the driver ready to depart, a woman from the hotel appeared. She had hot drinks secured in a tray and a small white box in her hand.

Intervening, Lorenzo received the order. "Thank you, Ma'am," he said in a low voice. "I'll take it from here."

She bowed and said, "Arigato."

Giving her the same respect, he waited for her to get a safe distance away before Burton rolled down his window.

"Thanks, Lorenz." Taking the drinks and the box from him, he said, "An evening like this is not complete without hot chocolate, whipped cream, and something to munch on." Placing one hot drink in her cup holder, he did the same with his. Meanwhile, Lorenzo got into the front beside the driver, and the others loaded into the vehicles around them.

Leaving the hotel, Abi unzipped her jacket.

Handing her an Aman-logoed napkin, Burton opened the two-tiered box of elegant chocolates. "Which one would you like?" he asked, offering for her to pick from them first.

Intrigued by everything inside, she selected a delightful little powdered sugar truffle ball.

He tried the same one. Raising it between them as if to offer a toast, he said, "Merry Christmas, Abs."

She giggled and tapped his chocolate with hers. "Yes! Merry Christmas."

Silently moving down Marunouchi Dori, Lorenzo paired his phone with the sound system. Soon, holiday music filled the vehicle, adding to the festive spirit.

The avenue stretched ahead, flanked by towering trees adorned with strands of champagne-colored LEDs. The twinkling lights were like a cascade of stars, illuminating the streets, making them look enchanting.

Abi leaned closer to the window, her breath fogging the glass as she admired the rows of lights. Meticulously wrapped from root to branch, each tree's soft brilliance contrasted with the sleek, dark silhouettes of the luxury office buildings behind them. Peering through the glass roof, she watched the lights go past.

"This is incredible. Don't you think?" she said over the subtle piano notes streaming from the speakers.

"This city doesn't do anything halfway." Leaning on the armrest between them, Burton glanced at her with a faint smile. "Even their holidays are next-level."

Ahead, the Tokyo Station building came into view, its red brick fa-cade standing proudly against the golden backdrop. Pedestrians bun-dled in coats strolled along the sidewalks, their laughter and chatter weaving into the festive atmosphere.

As they paused for a red light at the intersection, Abi spotted a small group of children pointing excitedly at a beautifully decorated tree while their parents snapped photos. The sight brought back memories.

"Imagine how long it takes to set all this up," she said, marveling at the artistry and effort.

"Months, probably," he stated. "But with crowds like this, it makes it all worth the trouble."

Her cheeks warmed as he smiled, and she broke away, turning back to the window to watch Marunouchi Dori stretch on, each golden tree extending the dazzling tunnel of light that seemed endless. For a moment, her world felt perfect.

"So…about today?" he said out of nowhere.

Abi shamefully lowered her head. "Please, don't remind me."

"I'm sure I don't need to reiterate what Martin said. But, this could have…"

"Cost me? Yeah, I realize. You're sounding more and more like him."

"Is that a bad thing?"

"No…"

"You could've been hurt, kidnapped, or worse. I'm sure you under-stand."

She nodded as reality set in.

"These people are dangerous. I don't think your friends get it?"

"After today, I believe they do now."

He looked at her for a long moment, then spoke more gently. "Just a bit of advice, Abs. You've got good instincts—but you've got to learn to trust them. Don't let others lead you astray, especially when the stakes are this high. Make your own calls. Own them. Don't be led—take the lead."

Sipping his hot chocolate, not wanting the conversation to become long and drawn out, he held up his cup. "Try yours. It's pretty good."

She took what he said to heart and then tried her drink. "Hmm. It's yummy."

"I hope you know my main concern is to keep you safe on this trip. That's all."

"I know…"

"But in order for me to do that, you need to adhere to our advice."

She stayed silent, knowing she'd screwed up again.

"If anything had happened to you…" Not elaborating, he paused, hating the thought. Upon seeing her regret, he ended the talk and tapped her hand with his. "So, are we good?"

Turning to him, she said, "Always."

Having already circled the festive district for an hour, Abi noticed Burton checking his phone.

"Do you need to go?" she asked, hating the thought of their evening ending.

"Sorry to say, but I do."

Hearing this, Lorenzo instructed the driver to head back to the hotel.

"Thank you for doing this with me."

"You're welcome," he smiled, just as Abi went in for a hug and wrapped her arms around his neck.

As expected, he embraced her back.

The quiet moment between them felt intimate, the kind that made the world outside fade.

"I guess you enjoyed the lights," he chuckled, unable to retreat from her.

Captivated by him, she noticed the intensity in his eyes. "Yes, very much." Her tone was softer than she intended.

"I'm glad."

Not knowing what to say, her lips parted just as his blue eyes searched hers, believing she was about to say something.

Abi's heart thudded loudly in her chest as her gaze unknowingly dropped to his lips as she leaned back. Realizing what she did, he seemed to notice at the same time.

Clearing his throat to break them from the moment, he sat upright. "You're going to love Niseko," he intervened, forcing a more casual tone. "I promise, when we get there, I'm all yours for a couple of days. Martin has some exciting things planned for all of us."

Hearing this, Abi blinked. Her cheeks now warm, she turned back toward the window, trying to focus on the sparkling trees outside instead of the electric charge she still felt in the air. "That sounds like fun."

"I'll make sure of it."

About to arrive at the hotel, they both fell silent. It wasn't uncomfortable, but it wasn't easy either.

Burton tapped his fingers lightly on the center console as they entered the tunnel under the enormous building. Stealing one last glance at her before the driver stopped, he pointed out, "We didn't get a chance to finish our drinks."

Trying to calm the flutter in her chest, she took the cup from the holder and said, "That's okay. I'll take it with me and finish it on the way up."

He handed her the little white box. "Here. These are for you."

"Are you sure?" she asked.

"Absolutely," he replied, seeing Martin waiting for him inside the lobby with a duffel and his laptop bags in hand. "I've gotta get to work."

"Be safe," she said.

Exuding a strong presence, he replied, "Always."

The driver came around to open her side door.

Getting out, Burton handed her the white box and her hot chocolate. "I'll see you in the morning. Sweet dreams."

"Yes, you too..." Realizing what she said, she giggled. "Well, you know what I mean."

"Hope you're ready to race me down the slopes this week."

"Oh, I was born ready," she taunted before adding, "Don't forget to text me your locations tonight."

He offered a thumbs-up. "Will do."

And just like that, the moment passed.

Stepping onto the curb, she smiled and waved at Burton while Martin joined them. Moving with his usual efficiency, loading Burton's duffel and laptop bags into the sleek black SUV, the man took her place in the back seat while Burton glimpsed her way one last time, his confidence making the brief look feel significant.

The vehicle's quiet hum faded into the distance, leaving Abi standing outside the lobby. Clutching the little white box and the cup of hot chocolate, she savored the unexpected sweetness of the evening. But it wasn't the food that she would remember. It was the guy who gave it to her.

Matt appeared by her side. "Ready, Miss?" he asked.

Nodding, she watched as Burton's caravan drove away. Hit by a cold breeze, breaking her from the moment, she stepped through the doors as they opened with a swoosh.

Escorted to the elevator, the two stayed quiet as Abi took inventory of her evening out. Her thoughts were swirling. The tunnel of golden lights on Marunouchi Dori, Burton's gentle smile, and the stolen glances they shared replayed vividly in her mind. The first elevator ride barely registered. Not fearful of ascending to the thirty-third floor, the soft music and gentle hum faded into the background. By the time they reached the top, she was still lost in the perfection of everything, sipping her hot chocolate absentmindedly.

Noticing how distracted she was, Matt refrained from interrupting her train of thought.

While walking through the lobby toward the interior lifts, she caught a glimpse of her friends out of the corner of her eye. Jade and Reggie were seated in the lounge area, clearly deep in conversation. Her heart raced as she passed at a distance. The last thing she wanted to do was explain where she'd been or the emotions she was wrestling with.

"Don't look at them," she said quietly to Matt, keeping her pace steady. "I want to go to my room."

The big guy gave her a slight nod. "Will do, Miss," and blocked their view of her as they moved forward.

With a short elevator ride, she soon reached her suite without further interruptions.

Matt stepped back and offered a polite, "Goodnight, Miss."

She turned. "Goodnight. I'll see you in the morning."

"I'll be in the hall for another hour before Ethan and I change shifts," he replied, professional yet kind. "In case you need anything."

"Good to know." Managing a small smile, she added, "Can you pass along a message to Andrew?"

"Yes, Miss."

"Thank you for everything you did today. I hope you know how grateful I am. Like beyond words..."

He silently gave a strong single nod. "Sure thing. I'll pass that along. We're just doin' our job, Miss."

Bidding him goodnight one last time, she opened the door and slipped into her room before hearing the soft click of it closing behind her.

Exhaustion settling in, she leaned against the wall to remove her boots. Sighing, her grip on the white box tightening, she set it and the hot chocolate on the nearby table. Allowing herself a brief moment to savor her thoughts, there was so much she couldn't articulate. Once again, she'd gotten sucked into Burton's world, causing a blend of joy, confusion, and longing. Despite his bluntness while addressing the incident that day, she knew he said it out of concern because he cared, nothing more. Still feeling his strong presence as it lingered, she peered out the window at Tokyo's glittering skyline and quietly asked that it keep her friend safe that night. With her mind a muddle, she walked into the closet and got ready for bed, thankful to be alone in the room.

| 11 |

A Quiet Goodnight

Saturday, December 23

Aman, Tokyo

Moving methodically, Abi took a shower, her thoughts still mulling over the evening. It seemed whenever she was with Burton, things just seemed easy. Unable to put her finger on the reason why, she exhaled.

Drying herself off and slipping on a soft nightgown, she gathered her comfortable clothes for their travel day and laid them neatly on a nearby chair. The rest of her belongings got packed away. Tucking the white box into her tote bag, she sipped the last of her hot chocolate—lukewarm now but still sweet.

Enjoying the peacefulness, she grasped hold of the covers and turned off the light before climbing into bed. The faint glimmer of the city outside filtered through the drapes, casting a soft, ambient light across the room. Propped against the pillows, she let her head sink into their comfort. Reaching for her phone, she unlocked the screen to check her messages, noticing immediately the cycling bubbles indicating Burton was typing.

Good timing, she thought, glancing at the clock. It was nine-forty. His message came through a moment later:

Just sitting in the talent Green Room at Ce La Vie. Then, off to Womb at eleven.

Curious, Abi opened Instagram and searched for the club's feed. As expected, there was only a pre-taped announcement about Dark Demon and Red Dragon's appearances—nothing live or specific yet. Letting the phone fall onto her chest, she sighed, knowing it was only a matter of time before someone posted something about him. She was determined to find it when they did.

The sound of the door opening snapped her out of her thoughts. Her body tensed as Shane entered, his presence disturbing the quiet.

His voice spread across the room. "Abs? Are you here?"

"Yes," she answered, sitting up slightly against the pillows. When he reached the edge of the bed, she asked, "Where did you guys go?"

"We ended up going for a walk to see the lights," Shane said, shrugging. "I wish you could have joined us. We were fine. Nothing happened."

"No Red Dragons?"

"Nope, none that I could see," he replied confidently, though she couldn't help but wonder if he'd actually been looking. There was a casualness to his response that made her uneasy, as if he didn't quite grasp the potential danger.

"What happened with Martin?"

"I'd rather not talk about it..."

Spotting the hot chocolate cup on the table, he asked, "Did you go somewhere?" His eyes narrowed as he studied her.

Caught between telling the truth and hiding her omission, she replied, "I went to see the lights, too."

"By yourself?" he fished as he stood up and walked toward the bathroom.

"No. I went with..." Afraid to say his name, she finally said, "Umm...Burton."

His back to her, Shane stopped in the doorway, his posture stiffening. "Is that right?" he said disapprovingly.

Hoping to make light of it, she replied, "The streets looked so pretty..."

Feeling the air between them suddenly get heavy, without a word, Shane slid the pocket door closed and started the shower.

Deflated, Abi rolled onto her side and placed her phone on the nightstand. Struggling to breathe, she closed her eyes and allowed her thoughts to drift back to her evening out. Without warning, the warmth of Burton's laugh, the quiet intensity in his gaze, the way he'd said *sweet dreams*—all mulled in her mind, vivid and impossible to ignore. For a moment, she let herself wonder what it would be like if things weren't so complicated, but the thought only deepened her confusion.

Slowly pulling the blanket higher, she hugged it close. The sound of the shower became a background hum as her eyes remained shut. Thankfully, nothing more was said between them that night.

| 12 |

Christmas Eve Morning

Sunday, December 24

Aman, Tokyo

The morning of Christmas Eve, Abi woke up early, determined to push through the unease of sharing a room with Shane. Showering quickly, she got dressed and packed her toiletries before emerging from the bathroom.

Catching his eye as he sat on the edge of the bed, she said bluntly, "All yours."

Able to tell from her clipped tone and quick movements that she was upset, he replied, "Thanks," before making his way to the bathroom, giving her the space he assumed they both needed.

To her, his actions just added fuel to the fire.

By the time he came out, freshly showered and dressed, Abi had zipped and wheeled her suitcase into the foyer. Slipping on her boots, she stayed silent.

"Abs?" Shane said, a note of frustration in his voice. "We need to talk about this."

She didn't stop. With her bag trailing behind her, the door clicked shut as she continued down the corridor, her heart racing. Unsure what she was doing, feeling conflicted, her eyes welled up.

Near the elevator, she spotted Lorenzo and Andrew standing on duty.

"Morning, Miss," Lorenzo greeted warmly, though his expression shifted the moment he saw her glistening eyes and trembling lips. "Everything okay?"

Shaking her head, a tear slipped down her cheek, betraying the attempt to keep it together.

Concerned about her, Andrew pulled out his phone and sent a quick message to his boss.

Within moments, Burton emerged from his suite just down the hall. "Abs? What's wrong?" When his eyes landed on hers, he reached out. "Hey? Hey…." he said kindly. "Come inside."

She hesitated but eventually stepped over the threshold, allowing him to take the suitcase from her hand and her backpack and tote from the other. Leaving it in the foyer, he followed as she walked into the living area and sank onto the plush couch at the far end, oddly unafraid of the view, thirty-eight floors up.

Sitting down across from her, he clasped his hands together in front of him. "What happened?" he asked, his tone low.

Abi stared at the floor, her silence stretching out.

Taking a seat beside her, his protective nature flared as a spark of anger ignited. "What did he do?" he asked sharply, assuming Shane had hurt her.

"Just the usual," Abi muttered quietly.

"And that would be?" he questioned, afraid of what she would reveal.

"He wanted to talk this out," she admitted. "But that would entail a conversation surrounding me and you. He hates us spending together."

He straightened up, heavily exhaling as he ran a hand through his hair. "Let me guess. You told him about our drive last night?"

"He saw the hot chocolate cup on my side table and put two and two together."

"Honestly, you should just save yourself all the heartache and not say anything. We've been over this before."

"No. I can't do that because it's the truth," she said with certainty. "I wouldn't want him hiding anything from me either."

Respecting her honesty, Burton nodded slowly. "Fair enough. But come on, he's gotta know nothing is going on here. You and I—we've known each other forever. After all this time, he needs to get over it."

Her heart sank upon hearing him say that. Believing what she felt last night wasn't the same for him, Abi felt naïve. "No matter how you see it, I'm still stuck in the middle. I literally can't even breathe without upsetting one of you."

He frowned, leaning forward. "You shouldn't have to feel like that. You're not a piece of property, Abs. You're free to do what you want, be with whoever you want—whether that's spending time with me or anyone else. He needs to trust you, and if he doesn't, that's on him."

With throat tightening as she listened, his words hit closer to home than she wanted to admit. "It's not just about trust, Burton. It's about respect, too. Shane feels like I'm choosing you over him sometimes."

"You know that's not true."

Abi shook her head, her fingers fidgeting with the hem of her sleeve. "It's just exhausting trying to keep the peace. I just want to enjoy the holidays without feeling like I have to tiptoe around everyone."

Reaching out, he hesitated as his hand hovered over hers before he took hold of it. "Look, Abs. I don't know what's going on in his head, but you deserve better than this. If you ever need space, my door's always open."

A faint smile tugged at her lips.

"Just FYI. When we get to Niseko, things might get complicated."

"Why?"

"We will all be living under the same roof - and I mean that literally."

"Same roof?"

"A large vacation home at the base of the mountain."

"Can I have my own room?"

He froze upon hearing her request. "Of course. Whatever you want. I'll let Martin know."

A few tears slipped down her cheeks. "I think that would be best."

Desperate to comfort her, he opened his arms. "Maybe it's time to take a step back and spend the rest of the vacation on your own," he said gently, though he could almost hear her silent protest.

Clinging to him, she murmured, "Maybe so…"

Holding her tightly, his chin resting atop her head, he tried to offer reassurance. "Everything's going to be okay. I promise."

Silent, she let go as he leaned back. Tapping her knee, he said, "How about I order you some food? You need to eat before we fly out."

The tension easing slightly, she silently nodded.

As Burton stepped away to call for room service, Abi leaned back against the couch. For the first time that morning, she allowed herself to breathe.

Meanwhile, out in the hall, Shane left their suite, frustrated and worried. He hadn't seen Abi since she stormed out earlier, and it was starting to eat away at him. Believing he should have gone after her, the thought crossed his mind: *She probably hates me because I let her go.*

Spotting Lorenzo and Andrew near the elevator, he approached with a casual nod. "Hey, morning, guys. Have you seen Abs?"

The two exchanged glances, their expressions cold.

Lorenzo, ever diplomatic, replied smoothly, "I believe she went to have breakfast," which was not entirely out of line.

Shane sensed something, but didn't push them. "Thanks," he said with a forced smile. "I'm just going to grab my stuff. If you see her, let her know I'm looking for her, okay?"

"Will do," Lorenzo said, giving him a thumbs-up.

As Shane turned to head back to his room, the men shared a subtle look, silently agreeing not to betray Abi's whereabouts. Whatever had happened, their loyalty was to her. Nobody else.

| 13 |

Tokyo Skyline

Sunday, December 24

Aman, Tokyo

The morning sun filtered through the sleek floor-to-ceiling windows of Burton's suite when their breakfast arrived. With the city sprawled out below, a mesmerizing blend of ancient tradition and modern architecture, Abi stayed firmly focused on the dining table, away from the vertigo-inducing edge, as the concierge placed their food in front of them.

Sitting opposite Burton as they ate, she angled her chair slightly away from the glass. A half-eaten croissant rested on her plate while her hands wrapped around a warm mug of coffee, the faint aroma waking her senses.

"Suppose I should take one last look at this skyline since we're leaving today," she stated, taking in the view from a distance.

Burton leaned back in his chair and took a bite of his toast. "It's pretty impressive, but you're missing out by sitting back here. The best view is from the corner over there." He pointed to the far side of the room. "You can practically see the whole city."

Abi shook her head quickly, her grip tightening on her coffee mug. "No, thanks. It's bad enough being on the upper floors of a building like this—I don't need to be right next to the edge."

"The day we went to Tahoe, you didn't seem afraid of being in the helicopter?" he teased.

"You're kidding, right?" she replied. "I was terrified. Just didn't show it."

Burton felt bad. "Sorry, I didn't know."

"It's fine. I survived," she chuckled to herself.

"So you'll be okay in the gondolas when we go skiing?"

"That's different." Her eyes narrowed. "We are closer to the ground. Besides, on the slopes, I'm in my element. Well, unless I'm staring down a sheer drop."

Burton raised an eyebrow, his smirk widening. "I was hoping to ski some backcountry. Up for that? Maybe tackle a few black diamonds."

Groaning, she squinted and pointed his way. "Are you challenging me?"

"Maybe." A playfulness flashed across his face, knowing how competitive she was.

Her fingers drummed lightly against the mug, then stilled. She looked out the window, her posture growing quieter. It was clear her thoughts were elsewhere.

Able to see the change in her demeanor, he debated whether to back off, but didn't. "What's on your mind?"

"It's been a rough couple of days," she said, her voice weighted. "And, as for the others. I'm still upset at myself for going along with everything yesterday."

"At least nothing came of it in the end."

With a sharp exhale, Abi crossed her arms. "I know it was dangerous. Once again, the guys put their lives on the line for me. I hate myself for that. All Jade and Reg cared about was doing whatever they wanted, no matter the consequences."

"And Shane?"

"I believe he should've been the one to shut it down, not join in," she surmised. "But, that said, I'm as much to blame. I let them pressure me, and I stupidly went along with it."

Leaning forward, Burton placed his coffee mug on the table and shook his head. "Don't beat yourself up. It's over and done with now. Time to learn from it and move on - hopefully, not make the same mistake twice."

Her frustration came down a notch. "I guess...."

"Because you walked out on him this morning, I feel you left things unsaid. If you don't talk to him about it, you're going to let this simmer, and it will hover over you the rest of the trip."

The croissant on her plate suddenly seemed unappealing. "I know. I just... I don't even know where to start. After last night, things have gotten so uncomfortable between us..."

"Calmly get your point across. Just tell him why you're upset and why it matters. He'll listen because he cares."

"You really think so?" She hoped it would be that simple.

"Absolutely," he said without hesitation. "Shane's not a bad guy. He just needs a nudge in the right direction every now and then."

A faint smile crept onto her face as she let out a breath she hadn't realized she'd been holding. "Thanks. You always know how to make sense of things."

Burton shrugged, the corner of his mouth quirking up. "It's a gift."

Taking another sip of her coffee, Abi braced herself for the conversation ahead. It wasn't going to be easy, but she knew he was right. Both of them needed to clear the air.

| 14 |

Niseko Bound

Sunday, December 24

Aman, Tokyo to Haneda Airport

Burton placed his laptops into a sleek black satchel and set it down beside his luggage, neatly adjacent to Abi's in the foyer. Wearing a gray sweater layered over a white shirt, he paired it with dark jeans and sturdy black boots before throwing on his designer down jacket and looping a gray scarf around his neck.

She spotted a few creases on his sweater, hinting at the hurried way he'd pulled his outfit together, giving him a rugged charm that said he hadn't tried too hard. Leaning against the wall, watching him with an amused smile, she said, "I have yet to see you wear the same outfit twice on this trip."

"Abi..." He gave her a knowing look. "You've seen my closet. I couldn't wear everything in there in a year if I tried. Stuff keeps arriving, and I keep wearing it. Simple."

"Must be nice," she teased.

He studied her for a moment, one brow arching suspiciously. "Wait—is this your roundabout way of saying you need new clothes? Because if it is, just say the word, and I'll make it happen."

Hands raised in mock surrender, she quickly shook her head. "No, no, nothing like that. I have plenty, trust me. It was just an observation." She tilted her head, admiring his outfit one last time. "This combo, though? I like it."

Peering into the mirror mounted behind the door, Burton gave his reflection a casual once-over.

A firm knock interrupted their banter. Burton crossed the room and opened the door to find a uniformed bellhop standing with a luggage cart.

"Good morning, sir," the young man greeted with a polite nod.

"Morning." Burton handed over the bags stacked in the foyer, his movements unhurried. He kept the satchel slung over his shoulder as the bellhop began loading everything onto the cart.

"Ready to head out?"

She gave him a small nod. "As ready as I'll ever be."

With a final glance around the room, he held the door open for her.

Flanked by Lorenzo, Andrew, Bray, and Rob, Abi walked steadily with Burton toward the elevators. Her eyes scanned the corridors, expecting to see her friends, but there was nobody in sight. She assumed they might already be downstairs in the lobby.

When the bell chimed, they got in with the guys.

The doors parted on the 33rd floor. Exiting, they rounded the corner.

Abi spotted the rest of their group immediately. A knot tightened in her stomach as she muttered under her breath, "Oh, here we go."

Burton turned his head slightly, his tone calm yet firm. "Stay composed."

"I'll try…"

Ahead of them, her friends stood near a cluster of their security and staff, with Martin seated at a desk, appearing every bit his regal, professional self. He saw them approach and met Burton halfway. "We need to settle the bill," he informed him.

"No problem." Burton's tone remained casual when he said, "Give me a second. I'll be right back."

Not ready to face her friends just yet, she hesitated. "Mind if I stick close?"

"Sure," he replied with a shrug. "Whatever you want."

At the desk, the man slid the bill across to him. Adjusting his glasses, Martin meticulously scanned the charges before showing them to Burton.

Able to see the total owed, she couldn't help but mentally convert the numbers: almost seven million yen. Her quick math told her it was about $47,000.

"Good," Burton said with a simple nod, unfazed.

Martin handed over a sleek Black Amex card while Abi pretended to be engrossed in a random lobby detail, feeling a little out of place among such extravagance.

When the payment was complete, Burton reached for her. "Come on. Let's head downstairs."

They walked toward the elevators, and though Abi didn't look back, she could feel her friends staring. Andrew pushed the button, and the group surrounded them protectively again as they waited. She was surprised to notice Shane didn't make any attempts to approach her.

Once the elevator arrived, she and Burton managed to step in first, leaving the others behind. The moment the doors closed, Abi let out a small exhale.

"You okay?" he asked.

Unable to speak, she simply nodded.

On the ground floor, they waited briefly in the lobby before Burton pointed toward the entrance. "Our ride's here," he said, motioning toward a sleek luxury sprinter van pulling up.

Joining them, Martin ushered everyone toward the vehicle. "This way. Our chariot awaits."

Inside, Abi chose a seat near the front, settling into one of the comfortable chairs with a small table. Burton slid into the seat beside her while Martin and Lorenzo sat opposite them.

Noticing someone's absence, Abi frowned. "Still no Sara?"

Burton stared straight ahead. "No, she's already in Niseko, prepping for the event there."

Disappointment weighed her down. Knowing Sara was still involved, even at a distance, was unsettling.

A shuffle of movement down the aisle caught her attention. Shane had boarded, followed closely by Jade and Reg. His gaze met hers, then moved on.

"Remember, don't let this thing between you linger," Burton said quietly, leaning closer. Lighting a fire under her, he added, "I believe you should clear the air or send him home."

His tone was even, but the straightforwardness caught her by surprise.

Abi's head snapped toward him. "Wait... What?"

"No sense keeping him here if you don't want him around."

She opened her mouth to argue, but realized he wasn't wrong. Still, admitting that aloud was another matter entirely. "I'll deal with it once we're on the road," she muttered.

Having glanced at his phone, he said, "You've got forty minutes or so until we reach the airport. That's your window."

Nerves starting to creep in, she rubbed her palms together. Taking a deep breath, she tried to steady herself.

Burton gave her a reassuring nudge. "Don't worry. I'll be listening if you need backup."

"That won't be necessary."

His smirk returned. "Fine."

With a small sigh, she mentally braced for the inevitable conversation.

As they got underway, the bus rolled through the quiet streets.

Burton rose from his seat and stepped aside to let Abi pass when she was ready. He exchanged a look with Shane, the unspoken tension simmering between them.

Steadying herself, holding onto the headrests, Abi moved carefully down the aisle and stopped beside the big QB. "Can we talk?" she asked.

Guarded yet curious, not making eye contact, he shifted over and allowed her to sit.

Taking a seat, she sighed, gripping the edge of the armrest. "It's the night of Christmas Eve." Cautiously venting, everything suddenly unraveled like a spool of thread. "I hate that my Dad is marrying that woman tonight." Not getting a response, she added, "And Mom being gone...umm, yeah... Even now, after all this time, it still doesn't feel real." He gave her his full attention, letting her finish what she had to say. "The truth is, I'm struggling on so many levels." Her voice cracked, but she kept going. "And what happened yesterday didn't help matters."

A flicker of guilt crossed his face. "I get it," he admitted.

Her fingers twisted together in her lap as she continued. "Last night, I took the heat for our excursion gone bad."

Upon hearing this, he asked, "What did Martin say?"

"He obviously wasn't happy."

"I'm sorry for that. But he shouldn't have singled you out."

"It is what it is... But, I'm his responsibility. He's my guardian. It's his job."

"Can I ask you something?"

Hearing him say this, Abi's stomach churned. "Sure..." she said hesitantly.

"Why did you sneak off with him and not tell me?"

"He arranged for us to see the lights. I'm not sorry I went because it was his way of checking in after everything that had happened. He wanted to make sure I was okay." Shane opened his mouth to speak, but she lifted a hand to stop him. "Wait. I need you to hear me out." Pondering the rest, Abi exhaled. "Yesterday, I went along with all of you despite knowing I shouldn't. That's on me. But, in hindsight, you knew what Burton and Martin said about keeping a low profile, and I feel you should have backed me up. Instead, you made me feel like I was the problem." She paused a second, knowing it wasn't all their fault. "Regardless, I stupidly went along with it, and it could have cost us…like a lot."

He nodded, knowing she was right.

"Burton, Martin, and the guys have risked so much to keep me safe. From here on out, I can't betray their trust anymore. My loyalty will be to them, not you."

Shame etched lines into his features. "I'm sorry," he muttered. "I shouldn't have put you in that position."

She could feel his regret. "I should've said something instead of shutting down." Her gaze locked with his, unwavering. "As for Burton. I've told you this before—he'll always be in my life. If that's still an issue, I won't force you to stay. Martin can have you on a plane to the States tonight."

Shane's head snapped up, his eyes wide. "What are you saying? You want me to leave?"

She shook her head. "No, not exactly. It's Christmas Eve. I want to spend it with the people I care about—and that includes you."

Relief calmed his expression.

"And for the next five days, I need you to cut Burton some slack. He's carrying enough stress without us adding to it."

"Fine."

From behind them, Jade peeked over the seat, her curious eyes betraying her guilt. "We heard everything," she said tentatively. "Are you mad at us, too?"

Facing her, about to explode, she divulged, "Honestly, I'm not happy. Everyone here worked hard to make sure you had the wedding of your dreams. The guys put themselves on the line to keep you safe from that man with the cane, sent by your father-in-law. And how did you thank them? By plotting against them so you could attend the NAKKA event. That wasn't just inconsiderate—it was selfish. Childish, even. That said, I guess I'm no better. But like Martin pointed out, this pattern of behavior is becoming a trend, and personally, I hate it."

Reg shifted uncomfortably, his mouth opening as if to argue, but Abi's glare silenced him.

"I'm not done," she said abruptly. "Instead of wasting time with petty games, you should be strategizing a hostile takeover of your family's company, and figuring out how to survive it."

For a moment, the air in the bus felt as thick as fog.

Then Reggie's shoulders slumped. "You're right. We owe you an apology."

Jade nodded in agreement.

"But you got one thing wrong," he added.

As the guy straightened his posture, Abi arched an eyebrow. "And what's that?"

"Martin, Lorenzo, and Andrew have been working with me after hours," he explained confidently. "We've already got a plan in motion to deal with my father. They have people preparing to arrest him on charges. That's set to happen in a few days." His fingers entwined with Jade's as he glanced down at her. "Yesterday, I just needed to blow off steam before I cracked under the pressure. That's all. Nobody needs to tell me what's at stake. I'm painfully aware."

Jade leaned against him. "We were going to tell you later, but we're leaving for an undisclosed location tomorrow, set up by Martin. Loren and her husband are meeting us there to finalize the merger. Thankfully, her father's already on board. Now, it's up to Reg to convince the Wilson Corp executives he's the right man to lead the company. For our safety, we are doing this remotely. Hopefully, everything goes according to plan."

"And if they don't back him?"

"They'll lose billions in revenue," Jade replied confidently. "Loren's already taken over as CEO of her family business, thanks to her Mom getting her Dad to step down. What we didn't know is that Loren's Mom is the true heir of the company. Her father married into the family. She says what goes. Now it's Reg's turn to do the same, either amicably or by force."

Reg tightened his grip on Jade's hand. "I've been groomed for this my whole life. That doesn't make it easier, but it's the reality. And yeah, Burton's not the only one under stress."

As that sank in, Abi leaned back. "I'm sorry," she said quietly. "I didn't know."

"Well," the wealthy heir replied with a faint smile. "Now, you do."

Realizing he'd be left alone with Abi and Burton for the rest of the trip, Shane felt unsettled but attempted to keep the peace. "Hey. Enough of this talk. It's Christmas. I think we need to put this incident aside and refocus. You know. Start fresh."

The four friends looked at each other before engaging in a group hug.

Spotting Martin smiling at them, she offered a thumbs-up while Burton did the same.

Having cleared the air just in time, the group arrived at the private FBO at Haneda Airport. Slowly entering the secure hub, the vehicle stopped at the covered entrance as the baggage handlers converged to unload their luggage, while all of them moved indoors with their carry-ons in hand.

One by one, they passed through security without issue and prepared for the ninety-minute flight to the new Chitose airport.

While boarding the sleek private plane, the ambient lighting felt warm and cozy despite the cold.

Burton grabbed a window seat at the back and set his laptop bag at his feet. Knowing Abi much preferred the aisle, he figured she would sit beside him. Seeing her and her friends take seats near the front, he was disappointed but knew he had to work anyway.

As everyone found their places, Shane was glad Abi opted to stay with him.

Ready to leave, the co-pilot stepped into the cabin, offering a friendly nod before sealing the door and securing it for takeoff.

Soon, the engines roared to life, and the plane began its slow taxi down the runway. Through the windows, frost-lined edges of the tarmac blurred as the jet picked up speed, lifting smoothly into the air. Japan's winter wonderland awaited, and excitement buzzed quietly in the cabin.

As the plane ascended above Tokyo, the sprawling city sparkled like a jeweled mosaic before fading into the distance as the jet leveled off and began to soar northward.

Martin took that opportunity to make an announcement. "Quick update now that I have your undivided attention," he began, standing in the aisle with his iPad in hand. "When we land at Chitose Airport, we'll split into groups for the two-and-a-half-hour drive to Niseko. Unfortunately, there is no private airport nearby. Once we arrive, I'll assign your rooms. We have two luxury homes: Seasons Niseko and Song Saa." He continued, "Tonight, we'll have a traditional Christmas dinner. Afterward, the main house offers a private pool, sauna, spa, and fire pit for your enjoyment. Tomorrow, those interested in skiing Annupuri can get fitted for gear by the Niseko Black team before heading to Grand Hirafu Resort. On Tuesday, we've got a snowmobile excursion planned."

Jade raised her hand slightly.

With a small gesture, he preemptively addressed her unspoken question. "Yes, Miss Jade, I'm aware of you and Mr. Wilson departing. I have made all the necessary arrangements."

Satisfied, Jade gave the gentleman a casual thumbs-up.

Martin concluded, "Any questions? If not, please check the itinerary sent to your email or come see me."

When no one spoke up, he returned to his seat beside Burton. The two were immediately engrossed in quiet conversation. Meanwhile, Abi leaned her head back, earbuds playing gentle instrumental music as she drifted into a light rest. Around her, soft murmurs of conversation filled the cabin, though some of the group were already dozing off.

At cruising altitude, Shane got up and went to speak to Martin and Burton, who were discussing business with the guys.

Without looking his way, Burton muttered, "What is it, Coppersmith?"

"Just asking for a little space," Shane replied steadily. "When we get there, I want time with Abi."

Burton's fingers tapped the table. "That's a bold ask."

"I'm just trying to make things right," Shane said, frustration creeping into his tone.

Barely glancing up from his laptop, the famous DJ surmised, "Seems like you're always trying to fix things." Impactfully leaving it at that, he added, "Apologies, but we're kinda busy, so…"

Angry that he'd made no progress, Shane turned away and swore under his breath as he returned to his seat.

Earbuds still in place, Abi remained blissfully unaware of the tension, her head leaning against a small pillow in quiet rest.

Phone in hand, Shane searched Niseko's attractions and scrolled past crowded group tours and ski excursions, instead bookmarking quiet spa experiences, private snowshoe trails, and small tucked-away cafés with a view of Mount Yotei. He wanted time alone with her—just the two of them, away from the chaos and noise of their group—somewhere she could breathe, laugh, and maybe forget everything else for a while.

Forty minutes went by in a blink as the plane began its descent. Snow-covered mountains appeared through the windows as they approached Chitose's private FBO. The landing was seamless, the jet gliding onto the tarmac before rolling to a stop near a quaint, sleek, snow-dusted terminal.

Disembarking, the group stepped into the icy air. It hit them sharply when the doors opened. As snowflakes drifted lazily from the overcast sky, they gathered inside the private hub while the baggage staff delivered and packed the SUVs awaiting them.

Assembled by the doors, Martin divided them into groups for the drive to Niseko and gave final instructions. "I strongly recommend a bathroom break before we head out," he advised. His tone was firm. "It's a long trip, and Andrew and Lorenzo would prefer not to make stops along the way."

The girls didn't waste any time and disappeared in search of a washroom.

Spotting an opening, Burton seized the chance to address Shane. He approached quietly, his voice low. "Just so you know, Abi's riding with me."

Shane glanced over his shoulder. Showing restraint, he fired back, "I think that decision is up to her, don't you think?"

When the girls returned moments later, Burton wasted no time. Flashing a pleasant look, he stepped toward Abi. "Hey, want to keep me company?"

Her eyes found Shane, whose tense posture and fixed stare spoke volumes.

"What do you say?" her famous friend prompted.

Unable to ignore how little time she'd spent with Burton thus far, she replied, "Sure. That sounds good."

Shane watched as Burton picked her bag up off the chair and slung it over his shoulder with ease.

As the two of them walked behind Lorenzo to the first SUV, Reggie saw his friend lock onto them. "Something wrong?" he asked the QB.

"I'm pretty sure Burton just declared war."

"On who?"

"Me," he concretely said while getting into the middle truck with him and Jade.

Spying on them, watching Lorenzo open the door for Burton and Abi to load everything into the vehicle, Jade said, "Don't jump to conclusions, Shane. You may be getting bent out of shape for nothing. The guy and Sara broke up. He probably needs to vent. That's all."

He stared intently. "Hope you're right."

Ahead of them, Abi looked back, wondering what her friends were thinking as she got settled in.

Burton did the same.

In seconds, Lorenzo closed the door and got in the front.

As the convoy prepared to depart, the DJ noticed a hint of doubt crossing her face. "Having second thoughts?"

"About what?"

"Driving with me," he paused. "It's not too late to change your mind, you know."

Their eyes met when she shook her head. "No, I'm good. We can talk and enjoy the scenery. Other than last night, I haven't really seen much of you. How did your appearances go?"

Upon hearing that, his expression relaxed, and for the first time that day, his guarded demeanor came down a notch.

Giving Burton her full attention, Abi turned in her seat.

"It didn't let up," he said, running a hand through his hair. "Back-to-back venues for seven hours. We had a full house everywhere. Red Dragon started things off, and I wrapped them up. The energy was solid—people really responded to the cultural vibes I mixed in."

"Any Red Dragons in the audience?" She hoped he'd say no.

"Not that I noticed. But I was pretty busy. Martin and the guys kept watch."

"So, a success then?"

Lowering his head humbly, he said, "Yeah, I'd say so. I have yet to check the numbers this morning, though."

"Numbers?" she asked, tilting her head slightly.

"The list of people registered to use the vault and how many transactions that took place," he explained.

"Interesting." Her gaze flicked toward the driver, realizing Burton couldn't elaborate further.

After a beat of silence, he could tell she was off. "Still trouble in paradise despite making amends with everyone?"

Her shoulders slumped while her fingers toyed with the zipper of her jacket. "Lately, it feels like there's a lot of noise around me."

"Noise?" he echoed with a small chuckle. "Hopefully not my music."

She shook her head quickly. "No, not that."

Seeing her turn to stare out the window, he spoke gently. "Are you going to explain what you mean, or do I need to pull it out of you?"

A sadness settled upon her face. "Since Mom died, my life's just been...noisy. You know - overwhelming. It feels like everything's coming at me all at once. School, friends, drama, stress—"

He finished another thought for her. "Eastwood."

Without hesitation, she flashed him a wary look. Her expression darkened upon hearing the name.

"I've probably added to that noise," he admitted apologetically.

"Not gonna lie. You've created some..."

"But?"

"But," she continued, "You've given me peaceful moments too."

A faint smile played across his face. "I'm glad."

"Like your place in Tahoe," she said softly. "Despite everything, somehow, that trip felt like an escape. I loved it there."

"Well," he offered, "If you ever feel the need to go back, just say the word. We can go anytime."

Her smile brightened. "I'd love that."

As if on cue, Lorenzo paired his phone with the sound system, and the soft strains of *Have Yourself a Merry Little Christmas* filled the SUV. Outside, the snow began to fall heavier, blanketing the landscape in white.

Burton leaned back and quietly said, "I hope this Christmas will be memorable despite all this noise in your life."

Their eyes met.

"So far, so good," she said. "We're in Japan. It's snowing, and we are going skiing. I don't think it gets much better than this."

"I agree," he chuckled. "Wait until you see what Martin has in store. You're gonna love it."

| 15 |

Arrival in Niseko

Sunday, December 24

Seasons Niseko

Driving through the small town, they noticed the lights in Annupuri before continuing along a private road that led to a set of stone gates.

"So, what do you think of the house?" Burton asked as Abi looked out at the beautiful snow-covered home. "Will this do?"

Two feet of snow cloaked the roof, and the banks around the circular driveway were almost five feet high.

To Abi, it was a beautiful place to celebrate Christmas. "Oh, Burton. It's perfect," she said as one of the other SUVs pulled in next door.

"Even though we have two places, this will be the main hub for meals and socializing, from what I understand."

"It's like being in New England," she said quietly, unable to keep her thoughts to herself.

When they stopped and got out, Shane, Jade, and Reggie arrived not long after.

"Come on," he said, ushering her quickly. "Let's go inside." Wanting a moment alone with Abi, he quietly motioned to Lorenzo as his eyes drifted to her friends. "Stall them."

"Will do, Sir."

The chalet's door closed behind them as Abi and Burton entered, shaking off the cold. Their boots thudded one by one as they removed them and placed them on the tray. Burton took her coat from her and hung it in the closet beside his. Anticipation building, he couldn't wait to see her reaction - a secret thrill building within him as they ascended the staircase to the upper level.

Abi's breath caught as they reached the top. The space unfolded before her like a holiday dream—a harmonious blend of traditional Christmas décor and the cozy luxury of the modern alpine retreat. She panned the room, her eyes soaking in every detail, from the twinkling fairy lights nestled amongst the greenery to the festive floral centerpieces adorning the table. Abi was in awe.

Behind the kitchen island, the Chef offered a quick wave before returning to his preparations.

Abi acknowledged him with a timid smile as her focus drifted to Burton, who was watching her soak up every ounce of the room. That is when she spotted it. Amidst the festive flowers, she found red and green plaid napkins with silver napkin rings adorning every plate.

Her fingers brushed over the familiar fabric. "It looks just like..." Her voice trailed off, overcome by emotion.

"I showed Martin a picture of your Mom's Christmas tablecloth," Burton explained quietly, stepping closer. "He found something similar."

Astonished by what he did for her, she noticed the delicate scent of turkey roasting in the oven as she placed the napkin back on the plate. Her hands moved instinctively, fanning it out in a way that mirrored her Mother's touch.

A glint from the corner of the room caught her attention. The tree stood tall and elegant, its branches decorated with intricate hand-blown ornaments. Her steps faltered, and her hand flew to her mouth.

"Are these..." Her question hung in the air, unfinished.

"They're not hers," Burton admitted, "but they're close."

A tear slipped down her cheek before she turned abruptly and pulled him into a tight embrace. "This is so wonderful." She could barely speak. "I can't believe you did all of this for me."

"Merry Christmas, Abs." He leaned down, his lips hovering near her forehead.

The two heard everyone filing inside below them. The sound of footsteps nearing the staircase cut the moment short. Straightening quickly, he stepped back just as Shane reached the top—his expression hardening the instant he saw them.

Conversation filled the house as the rest of the group arrived, their chatter breaking through the quiet intimacy. A tray of warm cider appeared, carried by the Chef, each glass topped with cranberries, an orange slice, and a cinnamon stick.

Stepping into the room, Shane lingered near the edge, keeping his distance from the rest of the group.

A bright smile bloomed across Abi's face as she approached. "Look at the ornaments," she said, holding a delicate Christmas wreath attached to the branch. "They resemble my Mother's. We used to hang ones just like this every year."

Only a clipped "It's nice" followed. Immediately, Shane's focus drifted elsewhere. The sight of Burton across the room made him curl his hands into fists.

"Just nice?" Staring forward, she was in disbelief.

He answered with a shrug, aware of something happening between her and Burton.

"Don't do this," she whispered. "Not today."

"I'm not doing anything. Just observing," he mumbled before blurting, "I need some air." In seconds, he'd turned on a dime and b-lined it for the door.

She watched him leave. Her fingers still curled around the tiny ornament as that all-too-familiar ache returned to her chest.

Amidst the drama, Mr. Alexander, the chalet's host, stepped forward and raised his glass high. "Welcome to Seasons Niseko," he announced warmly. "We aim to give you a holiday to remember. Enjoy your Christmas Eve celebration this evening. Kanpai! Cheers!"

"Kanpai!" the group echoed, their glasses clinking together as snowflakes drifted lazily outside the windows.

With his ever-present iPad in hand, Martin approached, efficient yet friendly. "You and Mr. Coppersmith will be staying in the second primary suite downstairs on the right," he said, gesturing toward the lower level before moving on to Jade and Reggie, then the men.

Her lips pressed into a thin line. Burton hadn't reminded Martin about her request for separate rooms. Clearing her throat, she quietly took him aside and asked, "Martin, excuse me—could we change that? I prefer my own room if that's okay."

Hearing this made Martin pause mid-step. With eyebrows lifting, he glanced back at her discreetly. "Of course. If that's what you'd like, Miss, I'll adjust that right away."

A small nod of appreciation followed. "Sorry about that. I didn't mean to disrupt everything." Feeling a need to explain, she whispered, "I just need a little space right now."

Concern flashed across his face. "That's quite alright, my dear." With a sharp eye, he offered, "Please know I am always available if you need to talk."

"Thank you. I appreciate that."

Still looking mildly puzzled, Martin walked away, leaving her to scan the room. The absence of Shane tugged at Abi's thoughts. Turning to Jade, her friend said bluntly, "I think you should go and talk to him."

Not exactly wanting to, Abi sighed. "Where did he go?"

"Downstairs, I think," Jade replied, silently prompting Reg for confirmation.

"Yeah. I saw him go that way," he pointed with a nod.

Uncertainty swirling, she stood there a second, building up the courage to go and find him. Setting her glass down, Abi quietly excused herself and navigated the staircase, the warmth of the upper level fading as she descended. The lower floor was quieter, a calm stillness replacing the festive energy above her.

Turning the corner as Martin had indicated, her steps slowed when she spotted him. Shane lay stretched out on the bed, one arm draped above his head, the other resting on his chest. With eyes closed, it gave away the turmoil he didn't bother hiding.

Abi knocked on the doorframe.

His arm moved, eyes narrowing as they met hers.

"Hey," she said, trying to stay lighthearted.

Silence stretched between them.

"How was your trip?" she asked, nerves swirling.

"I'm sure it wasn't as exciting as yours," he said flatly, his eyes still avoiding her.

The words stung, but she pressed on. "You should come back upstairs. The decorations all remind me so much of home. Her voice carried a warmth she hoped might ease his mood.

A humorless laugh escaped him. "Of course. It's perfect—just like everything he does."

Caught off guard, she didn't know what to say.

"The guys said you requested your own room."

She fidgeted.

He sat up. "I'm sorry about last night. I'm sorry, I'm not perfect. I'm sorry I never had the chance to meet your Mom or spend Christmas with your family..."

When he said it, she realized why he was acting this way. "First of all, this is not a competition. Second. Of all people, I thought you'd understand how difficult this Christmas would be. Guess I was wrong."

About to walk out, he jumped off the bed and quickly grasped her hand to stop her. "Wait," he said. "Don't go."

Upset by their conversation, she divulged, "When we got here, I was happy for all of fifteen minutes. You just couldn't let me have that moment of peace."

"What do you want me to say?"

The disappointment was etched all over her face. "Nothing." Letting go of his hand, she left the room.

Before he could state the obvious, she was gone. He felt her slipping away and knew he was about to lose her. Not knowing how to embrace the celebrations upstairs, given what just happened, he stared at his reflection in the mirror and fixed his Alabama hat. "You have no choice. Suck it up."

Climbing the stairs, following the sound of laughter and Christmas music, he made it to the party. With an apple cider in hand, he kept his distance from Abi, who was now standing and talking with Burton and the guys.

Forever on top of things, Martin approached. "So, Mr. Coppersmith. I apologize, but I've had to change your..."

"Yeah, umm, I heard." Knowing that would come up, Shane took a sip of the warm drink. He could tell the man was analyzing his behavior. Somehow, he had a wise Yoda-like quality to him. "Where do you want me?"

"Bunk room, lower level. It's on the right-hand side."

"Great..." He took another sip of his drink, hating the thought of being shut out.

"Don't be upset with Miss Abi," he stated. "She is still grieving, and her Father's marriage doesn't help matters. That said, Beth Ann was like a mother to Master B also..."

Focused straight ahead, Shane replied, "Yes, I get it. He has a piece of her past. It's something I can never share with her."

"You are not meant to," he paused and crossed his arms in front of him. "Your job, young man, is to be present and supportive. Let her grieve and reminisce. Listen intently to the stories that help her remember the life she once had. Soon, you will know her past as if you lived it alongside her."

Realizing, by far, the man was one hundred percent right, he felt like an idiot. Once again, he let his ego overshadow his love for her. Humbly turning to the man, he presented his hand. "Appreciate the talk."

Noticing the Chef ready to make his announcement, Martin said, "Anytime," before clinking his glass to get everyone's attention.

Their host picked up on the cue. "Dinner is served. Please find your seats."

Abi scanned the room. "Where is Sara?" she asked Burton.

Not prepared to answer that, he said, "I believe she is staying in the other house."

"I may be overstepping my bounds here, but no matter how angry you are at one another, it's Christmas Eve. Are you really gonna make her spend it alone?"

Torn, Burton struggled with the idea, especially given the circumstances, some of which Abi was not aware of. Stepping aside, he texted the girl to come by and have dinner with them. Pressing send, he left it at that.

Sitting down next to Burton at the head of the table, she watched as Shane was about to sit opposite her. Making eye contact with him, she pulled back the chair beside her to silently offer it.

Obliging, he walked over and had a seat, thankful for the olive branch.

And just like that, the conversation around the table almost drowned out the holiday music playing softly as everyone enjoyed the festive dinner.

| 16 |

Gift Giving

Sunday, December 24

Seasons Niseko

Everyone gathered together by the fire after their Christmas Eve feast with all the trimmings. Laughter and conversation filled the space while Burton's curated holiday playlist filled the air. Snowflakes drifted lazily outside the window, painting the world beyond in a blanket of white.

After a while, Burton got everyone's attention by clapping his hands with a mischievous grin. "Alright! Time for a little surprise."

One by one, they all descended the stairs. Standing beside the second Christmas tree on the lower level, the twinkling lights set the stage as everyone took a seat. Stacks of beautifully wrapped presents, each adorned with satin bows and festive designs, were arranged at its base. With a knowing smirk, Burton reached for the first set of gifts.

"Ladies first," he said, his attention shifting to the girls. Handing them square, silver-wrapped boxes with pretty ribbons and bows, he watched as they opened them and found the booklets inside. "Abi and Jade. I figured you could use some relaxation. So, I booked you a luxurious spa weekend getaway at the Ritz in Laguna Niguel."

A gasp of excitement followed as their faces brightened.

"Are you serious?" Jade questioned.

"Hope you like it?" he said.

"I'm so excited," Abi smiled appreciatively. "Thank you so much, B."

"We have to plan everything—facials, massages, the whole works," Jade bubbled.

While the girls perused the spa service menu, Burton tossed long, thin envelope boxes to each of his men, Martin, Anton, Reg, and Shane, announcing, "This is for all the guys here."

The moment they spied the golden Super Bowl tickets inside, chaos erupted.

"No way!" came the booming exclamation as Reg held the ticket aloft like a championship trophy. At the same time, the security guards all grinned happily at the opportunity to take in the game from a private stadium box.

Glancing down at it, Shane realized the cost of the ticket as his reaction remained far more subdued. "Thanks," he said before slipping it back into the sleeve for safekeeping.

With his eye on Shane, Burton simply ignored the QB's reaction.

Getting involved in the gift-giving, Abi passed around her packages, placing them into the eager hands of their security team. Each opened the gifts to find hi-tech smart sunglasses. It didn't take long for them to test them out.

"These are awesome, Miss Abi," Matt said, bowing his head slightly, impressed by the gadget. "Thank you."

"You're welcome," she said, beaming as the others quickly followed suit while watching Martin open the leather, monogram-embossed journal, and a Mont Blanc pen she got him. "Something to record your thoughts," she explained warmly. "I figured you'd like something classic."

Brows raised in appreciation, Martin's fingers traced over the fine leather cover with his initials. "This is beautiful, my dear. Thank you."

The Christmas lights danced across the room as Abi handed Jade her elegantly wrapped box.

The girl lit up with curiosity as she peeled back the wrapping to reveal a Van Cleef & Arpels Sweet Alhambra pendant in a velvet case. "Oh, Abs. It's stunning," she whispered while running her fingers over the delicate gold clover.

A warm smile followed. "I thought it would be perfect for you," Abi stated joyfully. "I hope you like it."

"Are you kidding? I love it." Arms reaching out to her friend, she clung to her tightly. "Thank you so much. Can you help me put it on?"

With a smile, Abi replied, "Absolutely," and gently fastened the necklace around her neck.

Seeing her reflection in the window, Jade saw the pendant sparkling against her skin. "Thank you," she said happily before saying, "Okay! Now, here's yours!" Jade tucked her clenched hands under her chin after handing Abi a sleek white leather booklet tied with a satin bow.

Untying it, Abi flipped open the folder. Her eyes widened upon reading the elegant invitation inside—a custom fragrance experience with Maison Francis Kurkdjian, which included a luxurious trip to Paris. Speechless for a moment, words finally came out. "Oh my... Jade. This is too much..."

Her hand reached out, squeezing Abi's gently. "I wanted us to share something special. We are going to have a signature scent created that nobody else has, and the place just so happens to be in Paris, so pack your bags, Abi Acardi. We are going to France!"

Her heart swelling with gratitude, overwhelmed by the luxurious gift, Abi hugged her friend and said, "I'm so excited. Thank you! This is amazing!"

"I knew you'd like it."

At the same time, Shane and Reg exchanged gifts.

In the quiet corner, Reggie held a small, matte black gift. "Since you kept stealing mine all season," he said, tossing it lightly to Shane. "This is for you."

Having an inkling of what it was, just based on the clue, Shane caught the box mid-air. Unwrapping it, he let out a short laugh. "Yeah! McLaren Edition buds!" He pulled one of the Bowers & Wilkins earbuds from its case and inspected the sleek black and orange finish. "Yours always sounded better than mine. That's why I borrowed them all the time," he grinned. "Thanks, man."

Fully aware of Shane's inability to keep earbuds longer than one month, Reg laughed. "Yeah, well," and waved him off before adding, "Just don't lose these."

"I won't." Shane handed Reg a heavy box. Excited for his friend, he'd waited a month for this moment.

As the girls looked on, his best friend slowly opened it and then froze. "Dude…"

Inside sat his Gilderson championship jewel-encrusted ring, but it wasn't the standard issue. This one had his number, the team crest, and on the side, two letters engraved in bold silver: *AC.* Assistant Captain.

"Check inside," Shane said quietly.

Reggie carefully twisted off the ring's top, revealing a hidden compartment with a carbon replica of the Rose Bowl stadium where they'd sealed their championship win. Every detail, down to the field markings and tunnel, was etched in. For a second, Reggie just stared. "Bro… this… This is unreal."

"I asked Coach if we could get ours customized. I tossed in a little extra cash, and he agreed." Shane flashed his ring finally. "Figured, since we're graduating and all, we should have something to show for all the hard work."

Reg stood up and offered open arms. "Thanks, man."

Knowing his billionaire friend appreciated nostalgia, he obliged and offered him a strong pat on the back. "Sure thing."

Seeing Anton watching everyone, Abi grinned as she handed him his present next. "This is for you," she said, eyes shining. "A little thank you for everything you do for us."

Surprised, he flashed a curious expression. When he opened it, he stared for a second. Inside was a crisp white Japanese chef coat with his name stitched in shimmering gold thread on the left chest. But the real showstopper was on the back—an intricate golden dragon embroidered in incredible detail, its body twisting like it was ready to take flight.

Running his fingers over the stitching, his usual seriousness softened.

Abi smiled. "I know you've been studying the art of Japanese cuisine while you've been here. I thought you should have something to remember the trip."

With noticeable appreciation, a smile appeared on his face. "I've cooked for some of the most important people in the world, but no one has ever given me something like this." With genuine gratitude, he hugged her. "Thank you. I will wear it with pride."

Amidst the happiness, Shane tried to catch Abi's attention, hoping to steal her away and share a private moment. "Do you mind if we..." he gestured quietly toward the door of the room they no longer shared.

Agreeing, she walked alongside him as he led the way.

Burton watched as they disappeared around the corner.

Once alone, the door clicked shut behind them, and they sat on the bed.

Handing her a small box, Shane said, "I saw these and thought of you."

Uncertainty cast a shadow over her as the package exchanged hands. It was as light as a feather.

The ribbon fell away easily, revealing a red Cartier box. Inside, two Trinity cord bracelets lay neatly nestled, their elegant charms intertwined in yellow, white, and rose gold with matching black bands.

A sharp inhale followed. "Oh, Shane... They're beautiful."

"At the store, they told me the design represents fidelity, friendship, and love," he explained. "I thought it fit...umm, what we have. Or at least, what I hope we still do."

Her fingers froze momentarily. What he said was significant. So much so that the charm's symbolism felt heavier than its small size suggested.

Breaking the silence, he said unnervingly, "Hey. Are we okay?"

The question lingered between them. Reaching for his hand, she offered reassurance. "Yes, we are okay."

"So, if that's true, Abs, why are we at odds?"

A deep sigh escaped as she searched for the right thing to say. "There's just a lot on my mind. Honestly, I just needed some space to feel, well… Sad." The bracelet dangled in her fingers as she spoke, its charm twisting aimlessly. "These past few days have been stressful, and I was at my limit."

"I'm sorry if I've made that worse," he said with regret.

She lifted the bracelet. "Can you help me put it on?"

He took it from her and fastened it around her wrist. "Now, no matter where life takes us, we will always be connected."

Tears developed in the corners of Abi's eyes, making her quickly blink with a smile. "It's so pretty. I love it."

Pulling back his sleeve, he slipped his on. "So does this mean I get to stay here with you instead of bunking in with the guys?"

After a brief pause, an amused sigh signaled her surrender. "I guess that can be arranged."

He hugged her. "I love you."

"I love you, too," she replied, despite, deep down, a list of questions still lingering. Not skipping a beat, she handed him a black box wrapped in silver ribbon. "This is for you."

Shane took hold of it and unwrapped the paper. Inside, he found a Garmin FĒNIX multisport watch.

"It's rugged and has a lot of features. I figured it would be good to have when you train."

He happily admired the tech attached to the striking orange band. "This is awesome."

A wave of relief softened her expression. "I wasn't sure what to get you."

"Well, it's perfect."

"Later, you can look at all the features it mentions in the booklet. I believe you can also store your training data. If you go for a run, it will track your route, heart rate, miles, and more."

Reaching out, he hugged her tightly. "Thank you."

Amidst the tension between them, still rearing its ugly head, they heard a commotion in the other room.

Pointing, she said, "We probably should, umm, get back to the…"

"Party? Yeah. Guess so."

The two rounded the corner and returned to the tree as a sudden shriek of laughter erupted when Jade pulled many pieces of delicate, lace-trimmed lingerie from an unwrapped box.

"Reggie!" she screeched, half-scolding, though her blushing couldn't hide the excitement. "What did you do?" A playful pose followed as she held up each piece for all to see. "Guess I know what I'm wearing for the next few nights!"

Reg's wicked grin answered back. "Yeah, that was the plan," he taunted as he opened his gift from her – a set of bespoke, custom, hand-crafted leather journals with his initials embossed on the cover. "Wow, Jade. Made in England," he muttered.

"Every powerful businessman needs to record his thoughts and analyze his every move while learning from the experiences along the way. I remember you talking a while back about recording your life every night, reflecting on each day, hoping to have enough material years later to publish your memoirs like you planned."

Hearing this, he hugged her tightly. "Thanks, babe. I love you so much."

"Love you, too."

A quiet moment passed as an unnoticed figure slipped into the house. Having dished out a plate of food, Sara calmly sat on the stairs, overlooking the party. Laughter and cheerful chatter floated past her, but she intentionally kept her distance.

A sharp glance from Burton acknowledged her presence, but his focus remained on the joyful scene below.

Two final gifts were left under the tree unclaimed, but only Abi noticed.

As the evening settled into a cozy rhythm, the group bundled up to make their way outside to gather around the bonfire. Snow fell lightly, sparkling in the firelight, while s'mores got passed around and stories were freely shared.

Amid the warmth and laughter, Burton leaned toward Abi, his voice low and just for her. "Come with me for a moment," he asked.

She followed Burton quietly, curiosity lighting her features as they slipped upstairs to his guest room. On the bed sat the two exquisitely wrapped gifts that had been left under the tree, each adorned with shimmering ribbon and glittering paper that caught the light like tiny stars.

She sat on the corner of the bed opposite him. Tilting her head with a smile, she asked, "What is this?"

Burton's expression brightened as he gestured toward the presents. "I wanted to give you something a little more personal."

"But you already gave me the spa weekend."

"I know. This is just a little something extra."

Reminded of his gift, she said, "One second," before disappearing from the room. When she returned, he saw her holding a black box with a silver ribbon.

Taking a seat again, placing the gift for him beside her, she unwrapped his first present. Inside was a leather-bound photo album. Flipping it open, she gasped upon finding photos from their childhood. She raised a hand to her mouth. "Are these..." she paused, carefully turning the pages. "How many do you have?"

As she continued flipping through the album, her fingertips stopped on a five-by-seven picture of her Mother. Wearing a white sweater with hair cascading over her shoulders, her smile was bright enough to light the world. Tears welled in Abi's eyes while lingering on the photo.

"She looks so good here," she said, a little weepy. "This was before she got sick—before life fell apart."

Burton watched her with quiet affection. "My mother always took a lot of pictures of us," he explained.

Letting out a tearful laugh, she brushed the droplets away. "That's what happens when you're an..."

"Only child?" Burton finished, grinning happily.

She giggled. "Exactly." Leaning forward, she wrapped him in a warm hug. "This means the world to me."

"I'm glad you like it," he replied gently.

Pulling away, Abi held the album close as Burton handed her the second, smaller box.

"One more."

"Wait," she said. "Open yours first."

The masculine-themed wrapping rested in Abi's hands as she extended it toward Burton. Intrigued, with a spark of wonder, he took hold of it. Tugging at the ribbon, he tore away the crisp paper to reveal the contents inside.

Nestled within the packaging was a Garmin FĒNIX watch, its charcoal-black design sleek and modern. The moment he laid eyes on it, a grin appeared.

"I figured you could use a lot of the features it has," Abi said, watching as he lifted the watch from its holder.

Immediately, he fastened it to his wrist and examined the details, running his fingers over the wearable tech design. "I don't have anything like this. It's great."

With slight hesitation, she stammered, "There's, umm, just one thing..."

His gaze lifted to meet hers. "What's that?"

A sheepish smile played on her lips as she admitted, "Please don't read into this, but I got you and Shane the same thing. I figured he could use his to track his training, and you could use it to stay connected."

Instead of the reaction she feared, he noticeably felt flattered.

"I don't have a problem with that." A trace of satisfaction crossed his face as he flexed his wrist, testing the feel of the watch. "Thanks, Abs."

Before she could respond, he pulled her into a quick hug, solid and reassuring, then pushed the wrapped gift into her hands. "Okay. Last one," he said while perusing the watch's manual to familiarize himself with it.

Shaking the box, hearing something hit the sides, her eyes flickered up to meet his, searching for any hint of what lay inside. "You didn't have to do this, you know."

"But I wanted to," he admitted with a small shrug. "This one's a little more selfish of me."

"Selfish, huh?" she repeated, unsure what he meant. While her fingers slipped beneath the wrapping, careful yet eager, soon, the paper peeled away. Opening the box, she gasped as she pulled out two tickets. Her eyes widened. "No way... Are you serious? Heli-skiing?"

He laughed. "Remember how we used to watch Warren Miller films and talk about doing this one day?"

Recalling the memory as it rushed back, she replied, "Yes, I remember."

"Well, this gift is selfish because it's just for you and me. No distractions. What do you say?"

She smiled brightly, holding the tickets close to her heart. "Are you kidding? Of course, I'm up for that."

Her gaze fell to the watch on his wrist. "And here I was, thinking a watch would be enough."

"What do you mean? It's perfect." His face brightened. "I'm sure Martin's already paired it with his iPad to monitor me."

Abi laughed. "I racked my brain trying to figure out what to get you. But what do you give the man who has everything?"

"I wouldn't say I have everything I ever wanted," he confessed. "Not yet, at least."

Their moment was interrupted by a burst of laughter echoing through the house. It was Jade shouting something about Reggie tackling her into a snowbank.

Abi shook her head with a laugh. "I guess we should get back to the group."

"Yeah, I'm sure Coppersmith will wonder where you disappeared to."

As they stood, she reached up and wrapped her arms around his neck. "Thank you for everything. This trip, these gifts—but most of all, your love and support. It's meant everything to me."

As he held her, his sincerity was clear. "I'm glad," he said. "Merry Christmas, Abs."

"Yes," she said as they parted ways. "Merry Christmas."

Slipping out of the room undetected, they moved carefully, ensuring no one noticed. Downstairs, paths diverged as she headed to her room, her heart still warm from the exchange. As she tucked the gifts in her luggage, the zipper pulled closed with a quiet resolve before she made her way back upstairs.

Upon finding her, Shane asked, "Everything okay?"

"Yeah, all good," she replied, adjusting her composure. "I just grabbed another layer—it's freezing outside."

A loud thud unexpectedly hit the window as a snowball splattered across the glass, the laughter outside unmistakably Reggie's.

Having instinctively shielded herself, she flinched at the noise.

A groan escaped him as he shot his friend a look. "I'm going to kill him," he muttered, though a faint grin betrayed his amusement.

"Come on," she said, grabbing hold of his arm. "Let's join the snowball fight."

Taking her coat, they stepped into the crisp night air where the bonfire crackled low. Laughter and warmth surrounded them as the group savored the last moments of the evening.

One by one, the flames faded to embers, signaling the end of their Christmas Eve festivities. A night Abi knew she'd fondly remember for years to come.

| 17 |

Night One

Sunday, December 24

Seasons Niseko

As everyone went their separate ways, Matt and Ted were on duty and began making the rounds, checking the doors to ensure each was locked.

Abi hugged Jade and Reg goodnight as they ascended the stairs.

About to do the same, Burton waited his turn with his hand resting on the banister. "Night, Abs," he called out, carrying a note of hesitation.

Pausing, she moved closer as he leaned in for a quick side hug. "Merry Christmas," she said before he bid her the same.

"Merry Christmas to you, as well." His gaze briefly shifted past her, landing on Shane. "Hope you have a good sleep."

"You too," she replied with a small smile. "I'll see you in the morning."

"Sounds good." Stepping aside as she walked away, he noticed Shane wheeling his luggage down the hall and wasn't happy when he followed Abi into her room. Unable to do anything about it, he ascended the stairs and tried to let it go.

On the lower level, Abi settled in for the night. Watching Shane move to the opposite side of the bed, he opened his bag on the floor. The sound of the zipper broke through the silence as he pulled out a pair of pajama bottoms and a T-shirt before glancing over his shoulder to find her entering the ensuite.

"I'm just going to get ready for bed." Her tone was light but somber.

"Sure, no problem. Take your time."

Alone, she turned on the faucet to warm the shower. When she stepped in, the rush of water filled the small space as she stood under the cascading droplets. But the warmth of the stream failed to ease the weight pressing on her mind. Thoughts of Shane, his expectations, and the complications of the night circled relentlessly. She knew he cared, but her heart still wasn't ready for more.

Drying off, she slipped into soft cotton pajamas, brushing through her damp hair before partially blow-drying it. After brushing her teeth, she lingered at the door, her hand resting on the handle. With a deep breath, she whispered, "Okay, Abs. Just go."

When she emerged, his eyes darted toward her. "All done?" he asked, already on his feet.

"Yep. It's all yours," she replied.

Without hesitation, he gathered his things and disappeared into the ensuite. Alone in the dimly lit room, she shut off the bedside lamp and slid under the plush covers. Exhausted, her thoughts made her feel restless.

Shane returned sooner than expected, his steps quiet as he approached the bed. Trying not to disturb her, he inched closer and noticed Abi move.

Feeling his fingers brush lightly against her arm, she saw him lean in and press his lips gently against her cheek. An unease surged within her, and in an instant, she tilted her head slightly. "Goodnight," she muttered, despite it carrying a certain finality.

His arm retracted, understanding she needed space. "Night," he said respectfully, leaving her be.

Outside, the winter storm raged, and the wind howled like ghosts rattling the windows. Snow piled up fast, covering everything in white.

With him beside her and Burton just a floor above, she felt safe, even as her mind reeled. Pulled in too many directions, struggling to settle at first, sleep finally found her somewhere between the flicker of doubt, the confusion, and the hush of falling snow. As a calm washed over her, she closed her eyes and thought about what tomorrow might bring.

| 18 |

Christmas Day

Monday, December 25

Seasons Niseko

The morning light filtered through the drapes as the heavenly aroma of breakfast wafted through the air.

"I smell bacon and eggs," the big QB said, rolling over onto his side, his voice still thick with sleep.

Abi sat upright, her back resting against the headboard, clutching her phone. "Yeah, smells good," she replied, her tone light but distant.

The tension from yesterday was still present and felt heavier than the blankets they shared. Neither of them moved. Neither of them spoke.

Staring at the wall with her back to Shane, Abi counted the seconds between each breath as she remembered his initial reaction to everything Burton had planned last night to make her Christmas Eve special. As she scrolled through her social media, her fingers gripping the edge of the comforter now and then, she debated what to say, but nothing felt right. Some words that came to mind seemed harsh, while others were too soft to get her point across firmly.

Shane shifted beside her, the mattress dipping slightly with his weight. He opened his mouth, then shut it. The silence stretched, awkward and loud.

Hearing activity upstairs and footsteps walking across the floor, she glanced up just as Shane did the same. Their eyes almost met, but not quite.

He cleared his throat. "Were you going to say something?"

"No..." she said quietly, not turning around. "Were you?"

Sighing, Shane lay back and exhaled. "Tell me what you need me to do," he said finally, sounding desperate. "I want to fix things between us."

Her gaze dropped to her hands, fingers fidgeting with the corner of the comforter.

Sitting up, he leaned against the headboard. "For the record, yesterday I felt kinda helpless. I don't know what to say to help you navigate the issues with your Dad and the loss of your Mom. That said, I'm trying my best..."

"I know you are, and I haven't been making it easy for you. I'm sorry. But it's been hard to accept this as my new reality. It seems I no longer have a mother and a father. It all happened so fast." She paused, trying to swallow the lump forming in her throat. "And the stress of this trip has compounded on all that. I thought I'd be okay, but I'm not."

Reaching for her hand, he clasped it gently, his thumb brushing over her knuckles. "I completely get that. But I just... I want to understand why you're shutting me out." He thought for a minute. "I know you were angry at how I acted yesterday."

When he said that, she once again relived every aching moment.

"I want to apologize." His brows furrowed. "But in my defense, you taking off with him again wasn't easy for me either."

What he said stabbed the silence.

"Look, Burton knew I wanted to see the lights. With everything that happened at the SkyTree, he also felt the need to make sure I was okay. He wanted to be there for me..."

"When I wasn't?" Shane finished her sentence with what came to mind.

"To a degree, yes."

In hindsight, given how the day transpired, Shane could understand that.

"And, as for the drive here, he caught me off guard, so I said yes. We mostly talked about his relationship ending with Sara and how I was feeling with everything going on with my Dad and missing my Mom, being Christmas and all."

"About that." He interrupted and rolled over when she said it. "To take your mind off things, I thought we could grab a hotel in the village for a couple of days to spend time alone together. Just you and me. Maybe go shopping? Explore the restaurants. What do you say?"

Unsure how to respond, her first instinct was to say, "No."

"Why not? We are halfway through this trip. I've compromised and done everything you wanted. I've even tried to do a few special things along the way. And, I have to say, dealing with Burton hasn't been easy. But I've done it for you."

"With everything going on, I don't want to be away from the guys."

"Away from them? Or him?"

She shot him a look. "I mentally... I can't do this right now..."

"I've given you space, haven't I?" There was a hurt in his eyes.

She didn't respond.

"Is this about spending the night with me, away from everyone? Are you afraid?"

Panic flashed across her face. "No, that's not what I'm saying."

His voice dropped, raw and quiet. "What is it then? You don't want to be with me at all? Is that it?"

Tears welling at the thought, she stopped and forced herself to breathe. "How are you so sure of us? Of me?"

He slowly ran a hand through his hair. "Because I am. I've told you. You're unlike anyone I've ever met. A once-in-a-lifetime kind of girl. The one you don't let get away - the kind of girl you marry."

She saw such certainty in his eyes.

"I need to know you want this…" He motioned between them with a pointed finger. "Us. To work." He paused sincerely. "We've been together for months, Abs. You do realize that loving each other—really loving each other—is part of a normal, healthy relationship."

"I know. I'm sorry, but—"

"This is the thing - I don't want you to be sorry." He leaned back, eyes fixed on the ceiling. "I just need you to love me as much as I love you and want to share that."

Hit with a guilt trip, Abi felt her chest tighten. "That's not fair," she stated, gaze dropping to the floor. "You know you're the only guy I've ever been this close to."

"I know you love me. You say you do… But intimacy is part of life."

She searched for something to say but came up empty.

"We've had the perfect chance on this trip," he continued. "All this time alone, just us. I've tried my best to be patient and give you space."

"Why do we keep fighting about this?" She blinked back tears. "It's not how it's supposed to be."

"No, it's not," he agreed. "It's supposed to be two people who care so much, they want to show it—completely." He hesitated before adding, "And once we're back in California, moments like this won't happen often. Well, unless you move to Huntington Beach with me."

Her throat went bone dry. "And what happens to us if I don't?"

The question landed hard. He looked at her, pain flickering behind his eyes. "Then I guess we find out how strong we really are." He exhaled, frustrated.

The way he said it—it felt like a challenge, like a line drawn. Abi flinched inwardly.

He tried to analyze her silence. "On top of that, I don't want to stay at this house all week with him here. We need to break away from everyone. All I want is to spend time with you and you alone. Nobody else."

"No. We are guests on this trip. I can't do that to him."

He shook his head. "Well, I'm sorry. I can't do this anymore. I need to be upfront and tell you where I stand. We need time alone so we can figure some things out, and I feel we can't do that here." When she said nothing, he reached for his sweatshirt at the edge of the bed. "I'll give you a minute to decide." About to leave the room, he said, "I'll see you upstairs."

Heart aching, she watched him go. It sparked this unbridled need to run away. Now alone, she got out of bed and slipped into a pair of pants before hastily ascending the stairs, smelling the aroma of breakfast. Reaching the foyer and swinging open the closet door, she grabbed her parka, hoping nobody would see her. Taking the hat and mitts from inside the sleeve, one by one, she threaded her arms into the coat and slipped her bare feet into her boots. In seconds, she was out the door.

Zipping her jacket haphazardly, she breathed in the icy air.

It wasn't long before Andrew appeared. On duty, he stood nearby, his breath puffing out in clouds. "Morning, Miss," he greeted jovially. "Going for a walk?"

"Something like that," Abi replied, avoiding his gaze.

His cheerful demeanor faltered as he spotted her red, puffy eyes. "Need some company then?"

Stomach tightening at the suggestion, she shook her head quickly. "No, I'm good, thanks. I won't go far. Just down to the end of the lane and back."

"Very well," Andrew hesitated before nodding. "I'll watch from a distance, then."

She gave a small nod, pulled her hat snugly over her ears, and walked toward the stone gates. As she passed through them, Andrew lifted his radio.

"Martin. Miss Abi's gone for a walk. She seems pretty upset."

The gentleman's reply crackled back almost instantly. "Keep your eyes on her. I'll alert the boss."

By the time she'd made it halfway down the snow-covered lane, Abi heard the crunch of footsteps. Glancing over her shoulder, she froze when she saw Burton striding toward her.

He'd dressed hastily, his coat barely zipped, with hair a bit disheveled. "Abs!" he called out.

Turning around, she said, "You didn't have to..."

"Yes, I did." Closing the distance between them, his eyes swept across her face. In an instant, his expression darkened when he noticed the tears streaking down her cheeks. "What happened? Why are you crying?"

She tried to make light of the morning's events, pressing heavily upon her. "It's nothing," she muttered, turning away.

"Don't do that." He blocked her path. "Talk to me. What did he do?"

Abi swallowed, her lips trembling as she finally looked up at him. Like a torrent, she sang like a canary. "We had a fight... It started with you and me seeing the Christmas lights. He didn't like it. Then yesterday, he hated that I drove here with you and not him." She lowered her head, then blurted haphazardly, "After that, he asked me to get a hotel. Spend the night alone with him, and..I...umm...yeah..."

Burton's jaw clenched, his hands curling into fists at his sides. "He what?"

Realizing she'd said more than she should have, she raised her hand to her forehead as a rash of emotions took over.

"I don't think he meant to pressure me. He's just...umm... he's struggling. He feels like I'm holding back, and it's hurting him. He's not a bad guy—"

"Not a bad guy?" Burton interrupted, his tone sharp. "Abi, he's making you feel guilty for not being ready. That's not love—it's manipulation, even if he doesn't realize it."

"He's not manipulating me," she argued with a hint of doubt.

He changed his approach and softened his tone. "Maybe he doesn't mean to, but it's still not okay. You've been through hell this past year—losing your Mom, dealing with your dad, and everything else. He should be supporting you, not making things more difficult."

She looked down. "I don't think he meant to make me feel this way..."

"Maybe not," Burton said firmly. "But it doesn't change the fact that he did."

Hesitating, she could feel the tears threatening to spill again. "I just...I don't know why I'm waiting. What's the big deal? Really? Maybe I should just go. See what happens. But..."

"Is that what you want?"

Pausing, she shook her head. "No."

"Then, that's settled. You stay. If he wants to go, he can go."

"But I don't want that either." Unable to hold back any longer, her emotions got the better of her, and she broke down.

With a deep breath, he reached out with open arms as she fell into them. "If you need me to deal with this, I will."

Seeing him waiting intently for an answer, she blinked. "I don't know what to do."

"I think it's best if you stick with me today," he said, leaving no room for argument. "If I'm around, he won't overstep his bounds. Agreed?"

She opened her mouth to protest, but the determination in his eyes stopped her. Instead, she nodded slowly, her chest aching with a mix of relief and uncertainty.

"Good," Burton said, his lips curving into a faint, reassuring smile. "Come on. Let's go back before you freeze out here."

Taking her hand, he turned and led her back toward the house, his grip steady and warm despite the cold breeze swirling past them.

As the snow-packed road crunched beneath their boots, they soon made it back. Just then, the heavy wooden door creaked open, revealing a figure silhouetted against the lit entryway. Tension rippled in the air as Shane's piercing gaze locked onto the two, walking hand in hand, his jaw visibly straining. "What's going on here?" The question cut through the chilly morning like a blade, sharp and accusing.

Feeling her hand start to slip, Burton tightened his grip as her fingers grabbed onto his. He stepped forward, standing steady and firm. "It was just a walk," he said flat out, "You have a problem with that?"

Arms crossed, Shane's shoulders squared, his glare darting between the two. "Yeah, I do," he stated bluntly. "Funny how she didn't want to talk to me earlier, but suddenly she's fine wandering off with you."

How he said it made Abi flinch. As her lips parted to respond, Burton interrupted. "Enough. This isn't the time—or the place—for whatever this is."

A humorless laugh echoed off the stone walls. "Oh, I think it's exactly the time. Let's not pretend you're just a *concerned friend*, Burton. Everyone here knows better."

"Watch your tone, Shane." Another step closer brought the two men face to face, anger crackling between them. "Abi doesn't owe you an explanation for every choice she makes. And frankly, you need to step back and give her some space."

Shane's laughter was bitter. "Space? That's rich coming from the guy who's been smothering her since day one. Bossing her around like you own her!"

Almost suffocating, Abi spoke up, her body trembling. "Guys!"

Burton raised his hand to ward her off. "This stops now!" he said sternly. "If you can't respect her boundaries, maybe it's time you packed your bags!"

A shocked silence followed, landing like a slap. Shane's eyes widened for a fraction of a second before narrowing again. "Are you serious?"

"This is not up for debate!" he shouted without hesitation. "Martin will set you up at a hotel nearby."

Abi's heart thudded painfully in her chest.

With a deep breath, the big QB turned to her. "If you want me to stay, I'll stay. Just say the word. But if he's right—if my being here is making this harder for you—then I'll go."

What he said hit like waves, pulling her under. She opened her mouth, searching for something to say, but no sound came out.

"Don't worry. I get the hint." His shoulders slumped, resignation evident in his expression. "You know, not like it's any of your business…" He locked eyes with Burton. "All I wanted was to spend time with her – be alone with her. Connect with her. How on Earth could loving someone that much be considered wrong?" That said, he turned and disappeared inside.

The quiet that followed was deafening. Frost biting at her cheeks, Abi stared at the empty doorway, her breath clouding before her.

"To me, this break is about letting you find clarity. You need a minute to breathe and think about what feels right and what doesn't. You're entitled to that."

Crying, she nodded while the ache in her chest spread like wildfire. No matter how hard she tried, she couldn't escape the weight of her heart pulling her in two directions.

Amidst it all, the Niseko Black company van pulled up.

"Let's get you inside. You can stay in my room until he leaves."

Burton guided her through the front door as Martin passed them by to greet the concierge service.

He hung up her coat while she placed her boots on the mat. Peering downstairs, feeling the need to talk to Shane, Abi felt conflicted. She knew being an adult meant facing your problems head-on and not running away, but for whatever reason, she couldn't bring herself to do that.

Ascending to the upper level with Burton, they threaded through the living area, his hand resting lightly on her back. The murmur of whispers faded as they passed. She could feel the guys staring. The argument had been loud enough for everyone to hear, and to Abi, the aftermath was almost louder.

At the door to his suite, Burton pushed it open and ushered her inside. Jade's hurried footsteps followed before she incessantly knocked. "Abi? Hey, can I come in?"

Burton answered instead, borderline dismissive. "Just give her a minute."

Hearing this, Abi could hear Jade sigh outside the door. Needing to see her friend, she nodded to Burton. "It's okay. Let her in," she said, sinking onto the edge of the bed with hands twisting nervously in her lap.

Moments later, the door creaked open, and Burton stepped aside to let Jade enter. "I'll be out here if you need me," he said before closing it behind him.

Jade crossed the room, concern sparking in her eyes as she sat beside her friend. "What's going on, Abs? What was all that about?"

Her voice cracked as she answered, "Shane and I had another fight."

"About what this time?"

"It's always the same thing." Abi's gaze dropped to her lap.

Jade didn't need her to elaborate. "What is it with guys and sex?" she said, exasperation creeping in. "Honestly, it makes them crazy, and we couldn't care less..." she shrugged. "- well, most days."

"What do I do?" Trembling, she divulged, "He feels like it's a bonding thing, a way to connect. After all this time together, he says he needs that from me."

Her friend chose her words carefully. "I'm probably not the best person to talk to about this, but... that's just how they are. Guys feel loved that way. We, on the other hand, feel loved when they do nice things for us. I get his point, Abs. It *has* been four months."

The reminder hit hard. Abi stared down at her hands, her fingers fidgeting. "I know... What's wrong with me, Jade? What am I waiting for?"

With a gentle tap on her shoulder, she offered a faint smile. "Only you can answer that, girlfriend."

A knock interrupted the moment. Reggie's voice filtered through the door. "Hey, babe, we gotta get moving if we're gonna make that flight."

The girl stood up, her reluctance clear as her hands melded to her hips. "You gonna be okay?" she asked, reaching out to rub Abi's arm. "I hate leaving you with all this going on."

Drawing in a deep breath, Abi wiped her eyes. "I'll be fine. Go. You can't be late."

"I'll call you, okay? Promise." Jade nodded and stopped in the doorway. "And if you need to talk, please don't hesitate, day or night."

"I might have to take you up on that."

Listening to muffled voices as Jade and Reggie exchanged goodbyes with Shane, she also overheard him saying something about going with them before hearing the sound of the front door closing. Then, there was only quiet.

The stillness pressed in and only broke when Burton reappeared.

"Is he gone?"

"Yeah," he said, devoid of any facial expression.

Not responding to that, she looked out the window.

Making his way over, he offered his hand. "Come with me. You need to eat something."

Even though she wasn't at all hungry, she tagged along just to appease him.

| 19 |

Freedom

Monday, December 25

Seasons Niseko

Exiting his suite, they made their way toward the dining room, where the men had gathered around the table in quiet conversation as they ate. Martin kept a close eye on the two as they approached. The clatter of cutlery against the stone plates and the occasional laugh, combined with the banter from the Chef and Anton in the kitchen, added to the busy atmosphere.

Below in the mudroom, they could hear the Niseko Black team working efficiently. Ready to suit everyone up for the week of adventure, they offered a wide selection of snowboard and skiing equipment for every type of skier.

With arms crossed tightly over her chest, Abi caught the smell of freshly made waffles drifting her way, but sadly, it did little to soothe the knot in her stomach.

Standing beside her, Burton rested his hand lightly on her back, urging her forward. "You need to eat," he said gently.

"I'm not really hungry."

He tilted his head toward the table where a plate of her favorite blueberry pancakes waited, still steaming. "Humor me. One bite, and if you still don't want it, I'll leave you alone."

A few heads turned as they hovered, but the men continued to focus on their food.

With a neutral but watchful expression, Martin offered a brief nod before resuming his conversation with Andrew.

Sighing reluctantly, she allowed Burton to escort her over. Pulling out a chair and sliding it across the custom rug, Abi had a seat. Once settled, he leaned down, speaking low enough that only she could hear.

"Let's try this," he said, nodding toward the plate.

Abi picked up her fork and poked at the pancakes, her appetite still nowhere to be found. But the first bite was warm and sweet, a small comfort against the pain in her heart. Had she made a mistake? Was it too late to bring him back? She took another bite and then another, the knot loosening ever so slightly. Then, without warning, she felt a sense of freedom with everyone gone, almost as if she hadn't a care in the world.

Sipping his cup of coffee, Burton remained beside her. Not rushing, he didn't push for conversation either. He just stayed, his quiet presence steady and grounding.

As the room buzzed around them, the Niseko Black team emerged, ready to begin distributing ski gear. Soon, they could hear the clipping of boot buckles.

Abi's eyes drifted toward the activity, her mind briefly wandering to the slopes in the distance. The thought of fresh powder and the crisp mountain air stirred something inside her—a longing for peace, for quiet, for escape. "I want to go," she said.

"Where?" he asked.

"Skiing. Is that okay?"

Surprised, he leaned back. "I think hitting the slopes and getting some fresh air would be good."

Her lips twitched, almost forming a smile. "You know me too well."

"Yes, I do."

That made her pause. She set down her fork and looked at him - really looked at him. The sincerity in his eyes was impossible to ignore.

"How do you do that?" she said at last.

"Do what?"

"Know what I need before I do."

"I told you. It's a gift," he light-heartedly chuckled.

She nudged him. "No. Really…"

"What…" he paused. "It's just easy when you care about someone."

Hearing that warmed her heart.

Standing up, he offered his hand and guided her down the steps to the lower level, where an attendant outfitted them for the day. Within minutes, she had everything she needed.

After breakfast, about to leave the table, she said, "I'll be right back."

Descending the stairs, she walked into her room. About to go and brush her teeth, she noticed a note on her side table. Her name was on the tented card. Picking it up, she opened it.

Dearest Abs, I'm sorry things turned out the way they did. But I will not apologize for loving you. Shane

Gently setting it back on the table, she walked into her ensuite as her thoughts gravitated to him. Guilt followed. Overwhelmed, she wondered if she'd blown this all out of proportion.

"Abs? You ready?" Burton called out from the foyer.

With a deep breath, she sighed and refocused on hearing him. Peeking her head out the door, she shouted, "I'll be right there!"

Warm socks in hand, she returned to the landing by the front door, where Martin handed out their ski passes. Attaching it to her jacket, she got dressed alongside Burton. Having put on her cozy socks, she slipped her feet into her ski boots and followed the others out the door and down the steps.

The crisp morning air woke her senses as the snow crunched beneath their feet. Loading into the SUV, the sky above was a soft slate gray with hints of sunlight breaking through the clouds.

All the way to the ski hill, nobody spoke, which was fine with her. She needed time to think. The fight with Shane and the importance of her decisions weighed heavily, but as they pulled up to the gondola, she was more than ready to experience the scenic ride to the top. Thinking about being immersed in nature all day, she thought, *Maybe, just maybe, I'll finally find the clarity I need.*

| 20 |

Hitting the Slopes

Monday, December 25

Mount Annupuri, Niseko

That afternoon, on the slopes of Grand Hirafu, the guys joined their boss and Abi as they skied over to the gondola. One by one, they piled into the cable car, chatting excitedly before slowly leaving the building. Moving high above the ground, they traveled steadily up the mountain, the glass windows revealing a stunning panorama — endless fields of deep powder, tree-covered ridges, and the jagged spine of Mount Annupuri basking in the winter light.

Abi pressed her nose closer to the window, her breath fogging the glass.

Watching her reaction to it all, Burton smiled to himself. He'd seen incredible landscapes all over the world, but somehow, none compared to seeing this reflected in her eyes as they sparkled with wonder. "You don't see views like this every day," he pointed out.

"It almost doesn't feel real," she whispered as she took it all in.

With a keen eye on the crowds below, Lorenzo instructed, "When we reach the top, the two of you are skiing between us. We'll have two in front and two behind. I'll make sure to give you a buffer."

"Bodyguards on skis," Abi chuckled. "Imagine that."

"No solo stunts. Got it?" Lorenzo added with a wink.

She gave a thumbs-up and adjusted her gloves. "Stick to the formation. No heroics."

Her comment sparked a silent flicker of amusement from Burton as the corner of his mouth lifted. He liked the way she'd said it—like maybe she knew just how serious things could get, but still chose to taunt the big guy a bit anyway.

When the gondola crested the final ridge, the station came into view. Disembarking into a blast of crisp mountain air, the group snapped into their skis and boards before shuffling toward the King Hooded Lift, snow crunching beneath them. Ahead, the summit loomed in the distance, kissed by sunlight.

Burton reached for Abi's arm, pulling her gently toward him. "You're with me."

She didn't hesitate. Just nodded like it was the most natural thing in the world.

The guys fell into formation, two ahead and two behind. When the chairlift rolled up, Burton and Abi took the middle seats, leaving no room for anyone else. As the lift jerked upward, Burton pulled the cover down, and in seconds, they were gliding into the sky.

The mountain stretched wide on all sides, snow catching the light like powdered diamonds. The air was sharp and clean, and the silence between them strangely didn't feel awkward.

Burton leaned back, exhaling slowly. "Pretty sure this beats Christmas back home."

Her head swiveled around. "Yes...hands down."

Something in the way she said it made him glance over. Maybe it was her smile or the pinkness of her cheeks, but for a second, something shifted. The usual calm in his chest faltered as he looked away.

But Abi noticed. She waved a gloved hand in front of his face. "Earth to B?"

He blinked and turned back to her. "Yeah?"

"What's going on in that head of yours?"

"Just thinking," he said, recovering fast. "Last year, I spent Christmas alone. So, umm.. I'm just glad you're here."

She bumped her shoulder into his, laughing, and for a moment, the whole world felt quiet. "I'm glad too."

The chair jostled as they approached the top. Sliding off with ease, they veered left, following the others down a freshly groomed trail. Burton snapped his boot into his board, and Abi dropped into motion beside him, skis carving clean lines into the snow.

After regrouping, the crew slid into a short line for Ace Pair Lift 4—the last stretch to the summit. This one was smaller, just two seats per bench, and Abi eyed it with hesitation.

As their turn came up, Burton nudged her forward. "After you."

When Abi scooted into place, Burton slid in right beside her in one smooth move. The bench was tighter than the others, and his broad frame pressed close. She tucked her poles to her chest, laughing lightly as her knee bumped his.

"This one's way smaller," she said, adjusting her balance.

"Not exactly built for guys my size," Burton replied with a grin, bracing the bar across them as the chair began its slow climb.

Below, the slope fell away while the wind whipped across the mountain, stinging their cheeks. It made Abi tug her ski mask over her nose and squint into the bright, cloudless sky. Above them, the sun drifted lower, casting long shadows over the snow.

Glancing over with a flicker of concern, he asked with a hint of humor, "Hey. You're not getting cold already, are you?"

A small shake of her head answered him, her voice muffled by the fabric. "No, I'm good. Once we get moving, I'll be fine."

Turning around, he peered behind them. "Wow, look at that."

Following his line of sight, Abi twisted and found herself staring at the towering silhouette of Mount Yōtei, its perfect, snow-draped cone stretching toward the pale winter sky. "That's incredible," she breathed, full of wonder.

At the top of the lift, her skis scraped the icy platform as they slid off and coasted to a stop. The view begged for more than just memory. Without a word, Abi pulled out her phone, framing the volcano in the shot.

Burton captured a few pics of his own— some of the mountain and one of her, mid-laugh, with eyes shining.

When he wandered toward a trail map bolted to a wooden post, he scanned the intricate web of lines and lifts. A dotted route caught his eye. This narrow path extended beyond the standard trails. Next to it, a small icon for a single chairlift and a note: *Hike to Summit (30 minutes)*

"Hey!" he called out, nodding toward the map. "There's another lift up here. We can take it partway, then hike the last stretch to the very top."

Skis sifting through fresh powder, Abi joined him, studying the trail markings. Her mitt-enclosed fingers brushed a bit of frost from the sign as she leaned closer.

"Maybe we should save it for the end of the day," Burton suggested. "Climb up, then ski down the opposite side toward the house."

A moment's hesitation crossed her face — not from fear, but from weighing the challenge. Tugging her gloves tighter, she straightened, determination flashing in her eyes. "I'd be up for that. Sure."

"Great." Beneath the layers of gear and confidence, he felt a deeper, quieter bond developing between them. With a teasing glint in his eyes, he surveyed the trail. "You sure you're ready for this? No backing out once we drop in."

Squaring her shoulders, Abi shot him a playful look, her cheeks smiling beneath her ski mask. "Absolutely," she challenged. "Try and keep up."

A laugh rumbled out of him, low and genuine. "I was about to say the same thing to you."

She gave a mock salute with her ski pole, then pushed off without warning, a blur of motion against the white slope.

Their descent was swift and wild, carving clean lines, hitting a few small jumps along the way, and throwing up sprays of powder with every tight turn.

But Abi, ever adventurous, spotted a gap in the trees—the out-of-bounds powder beyond gate G4, and without hesitation, she veered off the main trail and into the forest.

Burton gave a low, mischievous groan and shot after her.

Not impressed, two of the guys instinctively followed while the others kept an eye on them from the adjacent groomed run.

The snow was knee-deep, untouched, and exhilarating, but dodging narrow trees while trying to maintain their tight protective formation around Abi was nearly impossible.

"They've gone rogue," Rob spoke into his comms while bearly dodging a low branch.

Andrew swerved to avoid a tree, shouting, "Stay close! Eyes on them!"

As they zigzagged down the narrow trail, the thrill of the run outweighed everything else. Abi whooped with laughter as she led the way, with Burton right behind her, carving his path through the glittering maze.

Unaware of the chaos they caused, the two made it through in one piece, spilling out onto an open glade below, breathless and laughing.

Eventually, making it all the way to the bottom, Abi knew the men weren't happy with her. When they stopped to take off their skis and boards to jump on the gondola again, they piled into the cabin and took a seat.

Andrew zeroed in on her.

"I know, I know," she apologized. "I'm sorry. I just couldn't resist."

Coming to her rescue, Burton quickly defused the situation. "It's fine. Right, guys?" Knowing they didn't want a repeat of that move again.

For the rest of the afternoon, Abi adhered to the rules. Despite the tight constraints, she still had a great time.

Ready to make their final run, they prepared for the trek from King Lift 4 to the summit of Mount Niseko Annupuri. The only way up was the solo *meat hook* chair - a single-person lift dangling high above the steep slope.

Abi's nerves prickled down her spine at the sight of the thin chairs swinging in the wind. But when she caught Burton's encouraging smile, something inside her steadied. She wasn't about to back down—not in front of him. Tugging her gloves tighter, she took a deep breath and shuffled forward, determined to prove she could handle it.

Sliding into her single seat, without a safety bar, she clung to the metal and concentrated on not falling out.

Burton was in the one behind her and waved. "You okay there, Abs?"

"Yep!" she quickly replied before a solemnness settled in. Left with her thoughts, she peered down at the town below while the wind whistled past. She felt guilty as Shane crossed her mind. "Here I'm out having fun, and he's all alone, probably beating himself up after what happened this morning." Captivated by the sky, she asked quietly, "Tell me what I need to do, Mom. Give me a sign. Something to guide me in the right direction." Just then, the lift jerked and swayed as it carried her higher over the barren, snow-swept ridge.

Able to see she was bothered by something, Burton kept an eye on her. "Still good?" he called out, raising his voice over the gusts.

"Living the dream!" she shouted back, not to let on that anything was wrong.

Rare and quiet, a short, breathless laugh escaped his lips. It disappeared as fast as it came. He didn't say much. Never did. But the way he looked at her and held his gaze a beat longer than usual spoke volumes.

She was incredible. Fearless. Always game for whatever came next. Most people disappointed him. But not her. There she was, ahead of him on the narrow lift, fifty feet in the air, legs dangling like she didn't have a care in the world.

He adjusted his gloves. "You amaze me," he muttered to himself.

At that moment, Abi happened to turn around. Grinning from ear to ear, she bravely threw him a thumbs-up.

He did the same.

At the top, the chairs dumped them off into a swirl of sparkling snow. Shoulders brushing, they paused for a moment to take it all in. Mount Yōtei rose before them like a painting come to life. But when they approached the ridge, reality set in. The true summit loomed even higher, reachable only by a steep hike.

Burton turned to her, his eyes zeroed in behind his goggles. "Give me your skis," he said, already reaching for them. "You just take your poles."

Without protest, Abi handed them over, thankful for how he naturally looked after her without making a big deal of it.

Their group joined a loose line of skiers and snowboarders slowly making their way up the snowy incline. Skis and boards slung over their shoulders, boots crunching and slipping slightly against the packed trail, they trudged upward. The crisp air was biting at their cheeks, every breath swirling in misty curls, while faint laughter and shouts from the distant lower slopes drifted up on the wind.

Spirits soaring with every step, the climb added to the collection of memories Abi would forever treasure. Grateful for Burton by her side, carrying her skis and his board effortlessly, she knew how fortunate she was to have him in her life. Experiences like this were unheard of for most, but he always made the extraordinary feel almost normal, like magic was just part of his world.

"This better be worth it," Andrew grumbled, adjusting the strap of his goggles.

Rob smirked. "This coming from the guy who's climbed Everest."

"I was a lot younger then," the big guy revealed.

"It doesn't look far, but man, it feels like we've barely made a dent in the distance," Matt chimed in as he huffed with every step.

"Where's a helicopter when you need one?"

Hearing Lorenzo muttering to himself, Burton chuckled. "That's on Wednesday!" he said, knowing his head of security would be on that trip.

Upon hearing their banter, Abi laughed as they complained, but was happy it was light and genuine. Wanting to light a fire under them, she taunted, "You guys are such babies. It's only what? Another fifteen more minutes at the most?"

"That's easy for you to say," Andrew shot back humorously. "You're not carrying tree trunks for legs."

With his snowboard under his arm and Abi's skis on his shoulder, Burton walked just ahead of her and glanced back. "Ignore them. They're just mad you're handling this better than they are."

She giggled and used her poles to climb steadily to the top. Seeing the clouds drift by, she said, "You know, I feel like up here, I'm that much closer to my Mom."

Hearing that, Burton waited for her to catch up. Bumping her shoulder, he said, "Are you doing okay?"

She genuinely beamed. "Yeah. I'm good."

As they crested the summit, the banter subsided. It was replaced by a collective silence as each of them took in the breathtaking 360-degree view. Surrounded by mountains with a front-row seat to Mount Yōtei standing majestically in the distance, the valleys below stretched out like a postcard for miles. Dusted in frost, forests of trees lined the powdery slopes along the horizon.

"Okay," Andrew admitted, dropping his skis into the snow. "This was definitely worth it."

Burton pulled his phone from his jacket pocket and snapped some pictures.

The group gathered together, playfully jostling while Burton held the phone up. "Alright, everyone say...Summit!"

"Summit!" they chorused, laughing as the camera clicked.

"Let me see," Abi said, leaning over to look at his screen.

Burton showed her his phone. "Looks good, right?"

She studied the photo, a smile tugging at her lips. "It's perfect."

"How about one with just you and me?"

"Sure," she said while inching closer, his arm wrapping around her tightly.

Snapping the pic, he checked it out. "Doesn't get any better than that." Zipping the device back into his inside pocket, he said, "I think we should make this a Christmas Day tradition. What do you say?"

"What? You mean this hike?"

"No. You and I - skiing somewhere in the world. Maybe next year we can go to Austria, Switzerland, or France."

Unsure how to answer him, she paused. "I'll be at school. Not exactly sure how that will go, but I guess I'll need a break by Christmas."

"Well, we've got lots of time to make plans."

She nodded. The comment reminded her of everything she would have to endure when they returned home to LA. And for a minute, it cast a shadow. Determined to live in the moment, she straightened her posture. "So, which way to the house?"

"We need to traverse the mountain and ski down the far left side. Lorenzo seems to think he knows the way."

"Okay, I'll follow your lead." When she snapped into her bindings, she took a second to appreciate the view one last time. It felt like she was on top of the world.

While the crowd slowly dispersed, Burton stayed close. Boarding alongside her, a few feet apart, he could see her cheeks were pink from the cold, but her eyes sparkled with a carefree light he hadn't seen in days.

Arms out at her sides as if she were flying, Abi happily shouted, "This whole afternoon has been absolutely amazing!" It sparked a sudden burst of energy. Tucking into position, she challenged, "Race you to the bottom!"

"You're on!" Burton shouted.

Speeding down the hillside, the men tried to keep up while scanning their surroundings for any threats.

Quickly approaching a fork in the road, she stood up straight to slow down. "Which way?" she shouted, pointing her ski pole left and then right.

"Follow me!" Burton laughed while trailing behind Lorenzo, who took the lead.

Heading down the mountainside, Abi felt a lightness she hadn't expected. Perhaps it was the crisp mountain air, the view, or the company that made that day special. Whatever it was, for the first time in a while, she felt happy and carefree. Despite the way the day started, she was thankful it was ending on a high note.

| 21 |

Après Ski

Monday, December 25

Seasons Niseko

Descending to the foothills of Niseko's Northern Annupuri, the group spotted Ted waiting alongside the SUVs at the bottom. Having radioed Martin to let him know they'd finished for the day, Lorenzo guided everyone toward their destination with ease.

When they stopped at the rear of the second truck, Burton grabbed Abi's skis and handed them off, one by one, for Ted to stow them efficiently.

Collapsed in the middle row, Abi slouched in the seat with a tired but contented sigh. When Burton joined her moments later, his gaze flicked in her direction. He could see how happy she was from their first day on the slopes.

"So," he began, leaning slightly toward her, "What did you think of that?"

"Loved it," she replied, awestruck. "Definitely a bucket list item."

"Just wait until Wednesday. Heli-skiing will be even better."

Abi turned to him, her expression a mix of excitement and apprehension. "I'll be honest, I'm a bit nervous about it. But still up for the challenge."

"Good to hear," he said reassuringly.

On the short drive back to the house, the rhythmic hum of the tires on the snow lulled everyone into a contented state of mind. As they pulled into the driveway, Abi's thoughts drifted to the phone she had left behind. Uncertainty crept in. Had Shane left any messages?

The change in her demeanor didn't go unnoticed. Burton caught it immediately. Not knowing what was wrong, he watched her shoulders stiffen. Hoping to draw her away from the spiral, he broke the silence. "Want to watch a movie tonight after dinner? I think we'll need to rest our legs after today."

Her eyes lit up faintly. "Sure, we can do that."

"As for tomorrow, Martin's got a snowmobile excursion lined up for us."

"That sounds fun," she said, perking up a little more. "I've never done that before."

Driving through the stone gates, Ted pulled up to the front door.

When Burton got out and offered his hand, she slid across to his side.

Stepping onto the crunchy snow, the slippery surface beneath her ski boots betrayed her balance. With her arms flailing, she suddenly felt a firm grasp steady her before she hit the ground.

"Whoa, easy there," he said as he caught her around the waist.

"Not exactly graceful off the slopes, am I?" she pointed out with a self-conscious laugh, slightly embarrassed.

"Don't worry. I got you. You're fine," he assured, hands lingering just long enough to keep her upright.

She adjusted her hat nervously. "Thanks."

"No problem."

The warmth of the equipment room greeted them as they stepped inside, the heaters humming while they shed their gear. Snow clung stubbornly to the edges of their jackets and pants, but it quickly melted away.

Abi eased off her ski boots with a groan, rubbing her lower calves. "I think my shins got bruised," recalling the same feeling she got years ago after a full day on the slopes.

"To enjoy the sport, sacrifices must be made," he replied humorously, leaning his board against the rack.

She shot him a look, half amused. "Sounds like a line you tell yourself to justify the torture."

"Wasn't the view and the powder all worth it?"

Sliding her feet into a pair of soft slippers from a nearby cubby, she replied, "Without a doubt. Yes."

"Well, then. Case closed," he said with a wink, hanging up both their jackets.

The banter between them remained light as they exchanged a few more playful remarks. While stepping into the main house, the aroma of dinner wafted through the air, promising a satisfying end to the day's adventures.

About to head upstairs, he stopped. "I'm just gonna shower and change."

She smiled. "Then, I'll do the same."

"Meet you back here in fifteen?"

"Sure."

Parting ways, they headed to their rooms.

Finally able to collapse, Abi flopped backward on the bed, the adrenaline from their exciting afternoon still lingering in her limbs. Not wasting another minute, she reached for her phone on the nightstand and checked the screen.

"No new messages," she mumbled.

A flicker of relief passed through her, but it didn't last. Thoughts of Shane quickly followed the familiar ache she'd been trying to ignore all day. Their fight mulled in her mind, sharp and raw, no matter how much she wanted to push it away. Because he'd left and she hadn't said goodbye, Abi didn't know if he'd flown home or just checked into some hotel in town to cool off.

Thumb hovering over Martin's name in her contact list, she was tempted to ask if he'd heard anything. About to press send, she paused, knowing he had enough on his plate without getting dragged into her mess. Besides, what would she even say? Have you seen him? Is he okay? Is he still angry? She thought. Instead, she switched off the phone and dropped it face down on the bed.

Recalling their experiences from that afternoon, she focused on the rush of wind against her skin, the laughter, and the way Burton had made her forget all the negative for a while, at least. Her body felt calmer now, like she could breathe a little more freely. But her heart? It kept drifting back to Shane and pulling her in a direction she couldn't control.

Entering the bathroom and turning on the shower, she watched the steam bloom against the mirror. Warmth crept over her skin as she stepped in and let the hot water wash away the cold. For a few minutes, it all faded, but soon a number of questions burned inside. *Had he left? Was that it? Had she lost him?* Panic set in.

"What have I done?" she whispered.

Wrapped in a soft white towel, she tried not to overthink it. Selecting the coziest clothes she had, Abi got dressed. Leaving her room, she climbed the stairs, holding onto the laughter shared hours before. She hoped, just for tonight, that feeling could last a little longer and help her forget the mess waiting on the other side of tomorrow.

| 22 |

Outnumbered

Monday, December 25

Seasons Niseko

Already seated at the dining table, the men were deep in conversation, discussing business as they often did. The air carried a sense of routine, yet the undertones hinted at something more pressing.

Abi held back on the landing and listened for a minute.

"She mentioned the layout," Burton said to the gentleman, his brow furrowed. "It doesn't align with the schematics we approved. If they can't adapt the set-up by tomorrow, it's going to derail the entire flow."

Martin nodded, his tone clipped. "And what about the lighting? That was another issue she flagged."

"It's being addressed, but the staging needs a final decision. She's still waiting on input."

Outnumbered, now the only girl in the house, Abi proceeded up the stairs and approached slowly. Not wanting to interrupt, the mention of the word "she" unmistakably piqued her interest. Sara's name came up moments later, confirming her curiosity. The girl had yet to surface since yesterday's brief appearance, a fact that only deepened Abi's unease.

Burton glanced up, his expression brightening as he noticed her. Standing, he pulled out the chair beside him, motioning for her to sit.

Sliding into her seat, she asked lightly, "Is something wrong? It sounds like there's a problem."

"Yes. A few..." Burton replied. "We are having issues with the private Andaru rave location."

Knowing he still had events to attend made her feel uneasy.

Before she could dwell on it, his tone shifted. "Maybe you want to sneak in? You know, hide backstage and watch on Friday night?"

Her brows lifted at the unexpected offer. "I seem to recall asking about backstage passes before, and you flat-out refused. What sparked the change of heart?"

"Well, I kinda like the idea of you being there."

The contented smile that crept onto her lips was impossible to hide. "Then, yes. I'd love to."

"Perfect." Burton's reply carried an air of confidence as he turned back to Martin, though the older man's expression stayed firm, clearly not thrilled with how things were shaping up.

Before the mood could get awkward, the guys took their seats just as the chef stepped in with their food - the delicious smell of stone-baked pizzas filled the room. Each one was piled with toppings that looked as good as they smelled. Burton grabbed his napkin and tossed it onto his lap just as the plates got set in front of them. It was exactly what they all needed after such a long, active day.

| 23 |

Movie Moment

Monday, December 25

Seasons Niseko

With full stomachs and heavy eyelids, Burton pushed back her chair, offering a hand to help her up. "Ready for that movie now?" he asked, hoping she'd say yes.

"Absolutely," she replied with a tired smile, covering up a yawn. "But I can't promise I'll make it through the whole thing."

They walked downstairs, passing by the men and Martin, who exchanged knowing looks. Abi couldn't help but feel their silent acknowledgment of the connection between her and Burton, something she hadn't fully allowed herself to process. For a fleeting second, thoughts of Shane crept into her mind, only to vanish the moment Burton powered up the screen and the surround sound filled the room.

"So," he said, scrolling through the options, "Are we thinking something recent, a vintage classic, or maybe an international gem with subtitles?"

"Since it's Christmas, I always rewatch *The Holiday* with Cameron Diaz. Up for that?"

"I've never seen it," he admitted point-blank.

"What? Are you serious?"

"You know I rarely watch TV. That shouldn't come as a surprise."

Shrugging, she knew he was right.

When he selected the movie, he disappeared for a moment. Returning with two bags of popcorn, they settled into the plush gray chairs, as he grabbed a fuzzy black blanket and handed it to her.

She wrapped herself up as the movie began, the room cocooned in warmth.

While the story quickly unfolded, Burton's curiosity surfaced. "Wait," he asked during one of the early scenes, leaning toward her, "These women actually just switch homes? Like, with total strangers? Do people actually do that?"

Abi chuckled. "You know… I'm not entirely sure. I think this movie was made prior to VRBOs becoming a thing."

He smirked. "Otherwise, it kinda seems risky."

As the film continued, he watched her reactions, noticing how her face lit up at the romantic scenes. The part where Iris and Miles sat by the piano caught his attention. "That's a good line," he remarked at what Miles said.

Abi laughed. "Isn't it? Sometimes corny is exactly what you need."

Agreeing, a thoughtful look passed over him.

The more the movie progressed, the more her head bobbed, and eventually, she curled up in her chair with the blanket tucked under her chin. By the time Graham kissed Amanda, Abi was fast asleep.

Burton stayed awake, surprisingly invested in how the story played out. When the credits finally rolled, he turned off the screen and the surround sound as quietly as possible. The room fell into stillness, broken only by the faint hum of the heaters and the muffled sound of the wind outside. With the room dark, he walked into her bedroom and pulled back the covers. Returning to Abi, looking at her sleeping figure, he hesitated for a moment before carefully scooping her up, blanket and all. She stirred slightly but didn't wake as he carried her through the doorway and over to her bed. Upon setting her down, head gently cradled in the pillow, he tucked her in, making sure she'd be warm enough. Standing there, Burton couldn't help but linger, studying her peaceful expression. Once again, he saw her differently—not just as a friend or someone to protect, but as a person whose presence had quietly become essential to his world. True to his nature, his thoughts spiraled, analyzing every detail of their relationship, every shared moment. That's when the realization hit him even harder. The feelings he was developing were growing exponentially, and there was no stopping it.

Breaking free from his daze, he stepped back and closed her door before heading upstairs. Hands plunged in his pockets, he walked into his room and stood near the wall of windows, staring out at the snow falling heavily outside. Thoughts of Abi filled his mind: her laughter, her smile, the way she leaned into him without realizing it.

Getting into bed, resting his head on the pillow, he exhaled, his mind racing. Sleep wouldn't come easily that night, not with her occupying every corner of his heart.

| 24 |

Tag Along

Tuesday, December 26

Andaru, Niseko

Beyond tired, Abi blinked against the soft morning light filtering through the drapes. For a moment, she lay still. Alone in the quiet room, without Shane there, she smelt the aroma of breakfast as it spread through the air.

"Wait..." she mumbled, getting her bearings.

The last thing she remembered was watching a movie with Burton in the theater across the hall. Everything was a blur. But now, she was tucked in bed, warm and safe, with no memory of how she'd gotten there. Sitting up slowly, groggy and aching, she felt like she'd been hit by a truck in her sleep.

"What the heck..." she muttered to herself, rubbing her forehead, body stiff and sore. "Oh, boy...today is going to be a rough one." Forcing herself to stretch her arms and legs, every muscle hurt. Wishing she had a bathtub to soak in, she wondered if one of the other rooms might have one.

Upon pulling her hair into a messy bun and changing into soft loungewear, she layered a chunky knit sweater over it for warmth.

The cozy fabric gave her a small sense of comfort as she opened her door and stepped out of her room.

Heading for the stairs, she paused upon hearing someone call out, "Good morning, sleepy head."

Sitting on the sectional sofa, Burton removed one headphone from his ear and veered from his laptop screen.

"Morning," she replied, walking over. Her mind drifted back to the movie last night. "So...quick question. How did I get from the theater to my bed?"

He chuckled while continuing to work. "Hope you don't mind that I carried you."

Surprised, she blinked. "Oh. Well, thank you."

"No problem. I just couldn't leave you there, so..." As he resumed typing, he asked, "How'd you sleep?"

"Good, but..." Her sentence trailed off.

He immediately looked up while his fingers stilled on the keyboard, waiting for her to continue.

"Is there a bathtub in the house? One I could use? My body's stiff, and I need to soak, or I'll be moving like a grandma all day."

"There is," he chuckled at her dramatics. "I have one in my room. Feel free to use it. I don't mind."

Her eyes widened. "Are you sure?"

"Absolutely," he said, intently focused on his screen. "It's all yours."

"Is something wrong?" she asked, noticing the faint furrow in his brow.

He sighed. "Unfortunately, I'll have to stop by the Andaru venue to check on a few things." While pondering that thought, their eyes met. "Perhaps you want to tag along?"

Her face lit up. "Wow, really? I'd like that."

"You'll have to cover up and wear sunglasses to stay incognito, but it'll only take about forty minutes," he added with a grin. "I was also thinking—since I feel just as tired as you do—maybe we could take a drive afterward. There's this volcanic lake called Lake Tōya, not too far from here. Apparently, there's a restaurant perched above it with incredible views. Up for it?"

"Sounds fun," she said.

"Perfect." He leaned back, stretching. "Go ahead and take your bath. I'll see you in a little while for breakfast."

Abi nodded, her steps still ginger as she headed up the stairs. Once inside Burton's room, she rounded the corner into the spacious bathroom and closed the door. The sight of the large tub immediately made her relax. Turning on the water, she perused the spa products lining the nearby shelf before pouring in some lavender foaming bubble bath. As the air filled with its calming scent, she looked around at how neatly Burton kept his vanity. Everything had its place. His toothpaste and toothbrush lay on a folded face cloth. The glass was centered at the top, and his shaving gear was to the left. Careful not to touch anything, she backed away, impressed.

Sinking into the luxurious bubbles, Abi closed her eyes and let the tension in her body melt away, the fragrance weaving a calming spell over her senses. The warmth eased the stiffness in her muscles, but it couldn't quiet the conflicting thoughts swirling in her mind.

Thoughts of Shane surfaced first. They'd been through so much together, as she recalled his laughter and the feel of how his hand always found hers in a crowd. Yet, those memories, while vivid, felt like echoes compared to the magnetic pull she'd been experiencing around Burton.

Conflicted, she rolled her eyes and let out a huff. Unsure what to think, her thoughts shifted unexpectedly to the night before. Not awake to witness it, Abi imagined the way Burton might have carried her to bed, certain he'd done so with such quiet care, his strength and gentleness forever present. There was something about him—attentive and undeniably loving. It was different from what she had with Shane, and that left her feeling curious.

Sighing, Abi sank deeper into the water, the foam grazing her chin. Shane loved her; she knew that without question. But was that enough? What would happen when they returned home? She knew she couldn't just leave Burton and move to Huntington Beach. And what would happen when she left for Harvard? Analyzing the situation between them, she whispered aloud, "Is it admiration? Friendship or something more?"

She pressed a hand to her forehead, trying to quell the thoughts, but they only persisted. At the wedding, Burton had looked at her as if she were the only person in the room. Memories of that night lingered longer than she wanted to admit.

"Urghh," Abi muttered, sinking further beneath the bubbles as if they might drown out her swirling emotions. "What am I doing?" she whispered, unable to comprehend how two people could occupy her heart at once. Closing her eyes, she tried to let her mind rest.

When the water began to cool, still at odds with her heart, she finally got out and wrapped herself in a plush towel before borrowing one of B's robes, realizing she'd forgotten to bring one with her.

Leaving the bathroom, she thought the house seemed overly quiet as she emerged. Tiptoeing towards the stairs, her hair still damp from the bath, the scent of lavender clung to her skin as the morning light streamed in through the tall windows, casting golden patches across the polished floors.

Immediately spotting Burton's laptop open on the side table with a mug of coffee resting beside it, still steaming slightly, she glanced around, curious about his whereabouts. Then, almost on cue, she heard the sound of footsteps coming from the kitchen.

"There you are," Burton said, his headphones encircling his neck with a plate of food in hand. A strange look developed on his face. "Hey, umm…is that my robe?"

Looking down at it, she replied, "Yes. Hope you don't mind. I forgot to bring one upstairs with me."

"It's all good. No worries." Looking at his plate, he added, "Breakfast is ready. Would you like some?"

"Sure," she said as he handed her his plate. Surprised, she replied politely, "No, no. You go ahead."

Prompting her to take his, he insisted, "No, really. It's fine."

Believing the gesture was overly thoughtful, she took the plate as he escorted her to the table. Pulling out a chair, she had a seat.

It wasn't long before he returned. Setting another plate down across from her, they started eating.

Abi noticed him tapping his fingers on the table absently, clearly mulling something over. With a raised eyebrow, she pointed to his hand.

Seeing this, he said, "Just thinking about our plans for today," he admitted. "That, and making sure the Andaru venue is ready. A lot is riding on this event."

"You're always juggling so much. How do you do it?"

A hint of amusement appeared on his face. "You get used to it. Comes with the territory. But hey, I meant what I said earlier about you joining me today. I'm interested to see what you think of the setup."

"I'm excited," she replied, brushing away the conflicting thoughts parading through her mind.

"Great. Wear something comfortable but warm. After the venue, we'll hit Lake Tōya."

Upon hearing this, Abi couldn't help but smile. He always seemed to have a plan, a way of taking the reins that was both reassuring and, admittedly, a little unnerving at the same time.

After finishing her breakfast, Abi went to her room to pull on a pair of dark jeans. Adding a cozy sweater, she tied her hair in a loose braid and grabbed her sunglasses and a scarf to complete the incognito look.

When she came back upstairs, Burton was already standing by the door with his Dark Demon hoodie under his coat and a messenger bag on one shoulder. Behind him, four of the guys were waiting.

"Sorry about that. Guess I'm holding you up?"

"Not at all," Burton replied calmly, holding her jacket so she could put on her boots.

Standing straight, she slipped her arms into each sleeve as he held it for her. "Thank you," she said before zipping it and wrapping her scarf securely around her neck.

Dressed to meet the cold, everyone headed outside.

The crisp air bit at her cheeks and made her breath visible.

As they approached the sleek black SUV, Lorenzo stepped forward and opened the back door for them. Abi climbed in while Burton slid in beside her.

Watching the men take their seats in the front while two more got in the second truck, their keen eyes systematically scanned the perimeter as the convoy began to move. For the first few minutes, the only sound was of tires crunching against the snow.

Immediately opening his laptop and balancing it on his lap, Burton started typing, his focus unshakable as he worked on the fly.

Stealing a glance at him, her thoughts drifted to how effortless it felt to be in his company. It seemed the time spent together was always easy. Too easy, she thought, her heart heavy. It seemed every glimpse exchanged meant more than it should have recently. Thoughts of Shane interrupted all that. A sense of guilt was not far behind. She wondered where he was and what he was doing. Had he accompanied Jade and Reg to Europe? She wished she knew.

Abi cleared her throat. "I was just wondering…"

He turned to her. "About what?"

"Will Sara be there?"

"Possibly." He could tell she wasn't happy to hear that. "It'll be fine. Don't worry." He paused a second and said, "When we get back to the States, she will no longer be part of the team."

"Does she know?"

"Not yet. I want the Andaru event to be over first."

Quickly returning to his work, Abi could feel his occasional glances as if he were silently deciphering her thoughts.

Rounding the long corner along Hokkaido Road 343, the sleek SUVs approached the Andaru resort. A structured flagstone wall framed the entrance as they passed the two modern barn-like buildings blanketed in snow and ventured to the back of the property. What caught Abi's eye wasn't the impressive architecture of the Clubhouses but rather the enormous inflatable structure behind it—a set of two massive white domes connected in a figure-eight shape.

"Wow, is this it?" Abi asked, pressing closer to the window to get a better look.

"Yep," Burton replied, his shadowed face turning briefly to the site. "They call it a fluid scarab dome."

As they pulled closer, the sheer scale of it became evident. Each resembled colossal igloos. The glossy material reflected the sky above, making the structures look otherworldly. The entrance tunnel—a sleek red carpet leading to spinning glass doors—seemed both futuristic and luxurious. Through the faint translucent material, she caught a glimpse of the dazzling lights inside, hints of the magic waiting within.

His features concealed by his Dark Demon hood, he removed his coat before stepping out when Lorenzo opened the door. Head covered, Abi followed suit with Andrew and Ethan in front and Matt close behind. A rush of warmth quickly replaced the brisk air as they stepped through the rotating doors.

Inside, the space was like stepping into a dream. The LED-lit walls shimmered and changed colors, creating a dynamic backdrop for the props and elaborate technology installed everywhere. Lit bars curved gracefully along the sides, and steel scaffolding secured the rows of intricate lighting rigs, which were pointed strategically toward the ceiling and main stage. The design reminded her of Burton's famed *Vegas Nightfall Club,* although this one had a distinctly futuristic vibe.

Ushering her alongside him, the famous DJ greeted Yasuhiso, his sound engineer. The two exchanged handshakes, Yasuhiso bowing slightly before speaking in rapid Japanese. A translator aided their conversation about the acoustics, the dome's soundproofing, and the optimal placement of the equipment.

Abi watched as Burton intensely nodded. Then, out of the corner of her eye, she spotted Sara.

The woman stood near the far end of the venue, speaking with a technician. The second Sara laid eyes on Abi, she froze, her expression darkening. Slowly, her piercing eyes gravitated to Burton.

If looks could kill, Abi thought, she'd be six feet under.

Able to see Sara's jaw tighten, her glare shifted back to Abi before she began striding purposefully toward them. Her body language radiated anger, and even at a distance, she could sense the hostility between her and Burton.

"I'll be right back," he said to Abi while signaling for Andrew to stand by.

The guy gave his boss a sharp nod before flanking her on the left side.

Floodlights painted the venue in shades of blue and white while she wandered through the place with Andrew. Not trying to be too obvious, she eventually found Sara standing stiffly in front of Burton, arms locked in that familiar fortress-like stance. Words flew from her lips, abrupt and heated, though he barely reacted.

Feet anchored sturdily in place, Andrew divulged, "Thought she was gone for good," he said under his breath. "Guess we're not that lucky."

"You didn't know she was here?"

A frustrated sigh followed as he shook his head. "She disappeared after Christmas Eve. To my knowledge, she is no longer staying at the second vacation house. She must have gotten a hotel room instead. That was probably best. The guys had grown tired of her."

Blinking, Abi's curiosity grew. "I'm surprised to hear you say that."

"It's because, when she's around, things get messy," he replied with a dark look. "She likes being in control."

The mood seemed to intensify as Abi noticed another daggered stare from Sara.

Shutting down her behavior, Burton remained stoic, his replies calm and collected. This restraint fueled Sara's anger, and before she could say another word, he raised his hand and shouted, "Stop!"

"Here we go again. I'm telling you. She's trouble," Andrew continued, eyes narrowing toward the woman trying to command the space once more. "Her behavior gets worse when she feels excluded. And trust me, right now, she definitely feels pushed out."

A tightness in Abi's chest matched the frosty air outside, her thoughts still circling Andrew's warning. The sudden clash between Sara and Burton was like a storm threatening to break.

Finally, Burton stepped away, leaving the ticked-off woman behind with a scowl that could melt glass. Returning to Abi, he said, "We are just gonna do a quick sound check, and then we can head out." His mood was surprisingly light, as if the earlier confrontation had never happened.

Nodding, Abi let him go about his duties as he stepped onto the stage. The room transformed as the music filled the space, starting with a low hum that built into a pulsing rhythm. The LED panels flared to life, colors dancing across the room in sync with the beat.

Abi stood where the audience would be, letting the vibrations run through her. Now, under the lights, Burton seemed larger than life, and he gave Abi a thumbs-up followed by a sexy wink.

She smiled brightly at his reaction to it all, but soon noticed Sara watching the two of them.

As his fingers moved across the deck, he gestured to Yasuhiso and the crew near the back. Every adjustment made added more magic to the atmosphere.

Breaking Abi's spell for a moment, Andrew leaned closer. "See what I mean? She's furious. Sorry, Miss, but she doesn't like that you're here."

The woman paced along the edge of the dome and bit back several comments.

Andrew was right—Sara was clearly fuming, but Burton was completely in control.

Unsure if she should mention it, Abi said, "Between you and me, it sounds like she won't be around much longer."

"Good to know."

As the music swelled, Abi's eyes drifted back to Burton on stage. There was something about him in moments like this—focused, driven, and confident. He was in his element and loved what he was doing despite the ulterior motive. It was a side of him that drew her in, making her heart skip in ways she didn't expect.

When the sound check was complete, Burton left the stage and moved on to a group of tech guys seated at two tables, each hiding behind a number of laptops. Leaning over their shoulders, pointing at the screens, he spoke, perhaps explaining a few things in detail before giving off a positive expression, followed by a smile.

Suddenly turning, he made his way toward her, and she was surprised to see him offer his hand. "We are all done here. What did you think? Looks good, huh?"

"It sounds amazing. I love the imagery on the screens. Are you using holograms here, too?"

"Absolutely. They will test those later tonight when it's dark."

Feeling the warmth of his hand in hers, she caught sight of Sara at the far end of the dome. She could see the hate in her eyes.

"Ready to go, then?" He asked her, quickly moving out of his ex-girlfriend's view.

"Yes. Ready," Abi replied, following him.

Walking through the turnstile doors, they found Matt already warming the SUV and Lorenzo scanning their surroundings with eyes peeled. When the big guy opened the door for Abi and Burton, the two ducked inside and once again got comfortable.

Sliding back his Dark Demon hood from his head, he said, "Looks like we have a forty-minute drive south to Lake Tōya. We will grab something to eat when we get there."

"Sounds good," she said, secretly happy to finally leave the venue.

| 25 |

Lake Tōya

Tuesday, December 26

The Windsor Hotel

The drive from Niseko to Lake Tōya unfurled like a dream carved through the wilderness. Towering snowbanks, some higher than the SUV itself, flanked both sides of the winding mountain road. Evergreens sagged under the weight of fresh powder, their branches bowing like silent monks in prayer.

Abi pressed her gloved hand to the window, breath fogging the glass. It felt like driving through a snow globe. "This is insane," she said, eyes wide with wonder. "The amount of snow they get here… It's surreal, isn't it?"

Beside her, he nodded. "Pretty incredible," he said, leaning on the armrest between them. "And it's still early in the season. From what I hear, they get four times this by midwinter," he paused. "During the summer, people like to hike up to this volcano observatory. Gorgeous views, apparently. But today? With all this snow and wind, I thought we'd do something, umm, better." His head tilted slightly.

Eyebrow raised, curiosity flickered in her eyes. "Are you going to give me a hint?"

A slow, playful grin pulled at his mouth. "Don't worry. You'll see soon enough."

When he said it, she was both intrigued and somewhat scared at the same time.

Eventually ascending the mountainside to the Windsor Hotel, they reached the summit as the SUVs rolled into a long tunnel that led to the main lobby.

"Here we are," B said, quickly removing his signature hoodie and slipping his jacket back on. Beating Matt to the punch by opening the SUV door himself, he stood there and held out his hand for her.

Taking hold, she stepped out onto the deep red monogrammed carpet. In his gentlemanly way, he tucked her hand inside his bent arm and pressed his free hand flat against his chest to escort her toward the entrance.

The concierge, dressed in a formal uniform, greeted them with a bow and opened the heavy wooden doors to welcome them inside.

Walking into the lobby toward a massive wall of windows, the elegant and tranquil atmosphere was mixed with the soft instrumental music drifting from the marble floors up to the soaring ceilings.

"Give me a second," he said, leaving her briefly with Andrew by her side. "I'll be right back."

Watching Burton move to the reception desk and speak to the woman there, she noticed him take a key card from her.

When he returned, she said, "This view is incredible."

He smiled. "It is, but..."

"But what?" Her legs weakened at the sight below them - the waters of Lake Tōya stretching out like a shimmering, deep blue canvas, a stark contrast to the snow-covered island in the middle.

"You'll see. Follow me." Burton's hand returned near her lower back, his presence both comforting and almost electric. "This way," he stated confidently while guiding her toward the elevators.

Getting inside, when the doors parted, he pressed the top floor button. Immediately, her heart raced.

"I know you hate heights, but this hotel is a third of what the other hotels were. I think you'll be fine."

She flashed an uncertain look.

"Do you trust me?" he asked.

Unable to say she didn't, she simply nodded as they ascended to the tenth floor.

When the doors opened, they walked the long, quiet hallway to a set of double doors. Passing the card key over the top of the lock, it clicked, allowing them access to something special beyond them.

"After you," he said with a small smile, gesturing for her to walk in first.

Abi stepped into the room, her heart skipping a beat with anticipation.

The G8 Summit Suite at the Windsor Hotel was nothing short of breathtaking. As the two walked into the living room, the vast waters of the lake lay anchored before them. In the middle was a table for two, set elegantly, draped in pristine white linens, accented by fine dinnerware and festive flowers.

Leaving Lorenzo and Andrew in the hallway to stand guard, Burton casually shed his coat and draped it over the arm of the sofa before strolling toward the window. His darkened silhouette stood tall. "You can see the entire crater from here," he remarked before turning to her. "Thought we could have a private lunch so we wouldn't be bothered by anyone in the restaurant. Hope that's okay?"

"It's, umm, perfect," she replied, keeping her distance from the edge.

Seeing this, he inched closer, realizing she was afraid. Holding out his hand, he said, "It's okay. I've got you."

Hesitant, she looked into his eyes and, hypnotically, took one step forward, then another. Reaching for his hand, feeling its warmth in hers, he guided her closer but stayed far enough away for Abi to remain comfortable.

A knock at the door broke the quiet.

Peeking his head in, Andrew addressed, "Room service is here, Sir," before allowing the concierge to wheel the beautifully arranged cart inside.

The scent of freshly brewed tea mingled with the sweet aroma of delicacies, each catching Abi's attention. Her eyes lit up at the sight of the three-tiered tray stacked with dainty pastries, scones, and sandwiches. Teapots in delicate patterns sat beside fluted glasses while crystal pitchers of sparkling juice completed the charming afternoon spread.

Burton stepped forward, passing the concierge a cash tip before offering a polite bow. "Hontō ni arigatō gozaimasu," he said with a respectful nod, his demeanor calm yet commanding.

Returning the bow, the woman curiously glanced at the security stationed outside the door. "Tanoshinde kudasai," she said with another nod before turning and departing.

Andrew quietly followed her with the take-out containers of food for the guys.

When the door shut behind them, for the first time in what felt like ages, they were alone again. The quiet hum of the suite wrapped around them like a protective cocoon.

He moved to the table, pulling out a chair with a slight gesture. "Shall we?" he asked, warm and inviting.

Abi took a seat, the elegant setting and rare moment of solitude making the experience feel even more special.

A gentle warmth spread through the room while they savored a variety of flavors. Burton poured her a cup of tea and handed it over with quiet care. She did the same for him.

"Thank you," he said, somewhat guarded. Setting his cup down, he looked at her, the silence between them charged. "At the start of this trip, I didn't expect this," he admitted, honesty threading through.

She tilted her head, intrigued. "Didn't expect what? The chance to explore?"

"No..." he hesitated before opening up a little more. "The chance to spend time together without everyone else around."

A shy smile flickered across her face, surprised by the quiet confession.

The moment deepened.

"Look…" Eyes on the saucer under his cup, he kept rotating it in a circle. "I know Coppersmith, and I don't see eye to eye. But that doesn't change one thing— you are my priority. I'll always have your best interest at heart."

Touched to hear that, she replied, "I know. And I appreciate that so much."

A pause stretched between them. Then, gently, he asked, "Have you decided what you're going to do?"

She blinked. "About what?"

"Him."

The question hung in the air while Abi tried to think of the answer. When she peered across the table, she found a sincere expression, not at all angry or resentful.

"I don't know yet," she answered finally. Letting the words settle, she straightened in her chair. "Can we change the subject, please?"

His expression shifted to something more lighthearted. "Of course," he replied respectfully, lifting his cup again.

Peering out at the view, she asked, "So, I'm assuming we won't see any Red Dragons around here – well, other than the DJ?"

"I'm confident we are out of harm's way. Niseko is not part of their territory, to our knowledge."

Relieved to hear that, she exhaled. "And the recruiting games?"

"Martin assured me we are off the radar now."

Because he said it so casually, she was convinced this was true. "Thank God."

"Don't worry. The guys and Martin have been on top of everything since the moment we arrived here."

"Okay. I trust you."

Hearing that a second time meant everything.

"So what is special about Lake Tōya anyway?"

Burton set his cup down and leaned back in his chair, glancing out the window. "From what I read, it's a caldera lake formed by volcanic activity ages ago. They say it never freezes, no matter how cold it gets."

She fixated on the deep blue waters below. "Never freezes? That's kind of wild."

"Yeah, something about the geothermal activity beneath it. The same thing that keeps the lake warm powers all those hot springs around here."

"It's so peaceful. I didn't expect it to feel like this. Maybe it is the limited commercialism." She tapped her fingers lightly on the edge of the table, soaking in the serene landscape.

"That's part of Niseko's uniqueness," he said quietly.

"It feels timeless. Like another world." Her eyes locked with his, catching something reflective in his tone. "Thank you for bringing me here," she said sincerely. "I needed to take a minute and breathe."

"That was the idea. However, I can't let you get too comfortable." He squinted one eye.

"Why's that?" A laugh escaped her, light and genuine.

"Because we still need to take our snowmobile ride, remember?"

"Oh, right," she pointed his way. "But you're driving."

"Hope you like speed," he smirked, finishing the last bite of a macaron from the tray before glancing at the time on his new watch. "We should probably get moving if we want to make it back in time."

Offering his hand, he pulled out her chair and helped her slip on her coat.

"Thank you," she whispered.

The way she said it sparked something in his chest. Having put on his jacket, he asked, "Ready to head out?"

With a smile to light the room, she replied, "Ready."

Reaching out, she rehooked her arm with his. Looking at the lakeview one last time, she felt a quiet sense of gratitude for the moment they'd shared—a nice break before diving back into the whirlwind awaiting them back at the house.

| 26 |

A Snowmobile Ride

Tuesday, December 26

Annupuri, Niseko

Walking back through the lobby and into the underground breeze-way, Burton spotted Matt and Ethan already waiting by the SUVs. He reached for the door handle and opened it for her in the most gentle-manly way. Abi stepped in with a grateful nod and took her seat.

Sliding in beside her, Burton leaned casually on the armrest between them. To his surprise, she placed her arm there too. When hers brushed against him, it was subtle—intentional, maybe. He quietly cleared his throat as the vehicle pulled out into the daylight.

With impeccable timing, his phone chimed.

"Sorry—I've gotta take this. It's Martin," he said, already reaching for the device. Instead of answering, he opted to text, tapping out a message with quick precision.

Abi, watching the slight furrow in his brow, sensed something was off. "Everything okay?" she asked.

He glanced at her, pausing just long enough to mask the weight of the message. "Yeah. He's just confirming our heli-ski excursion to-morrow. Excited?"

She exhaled a nervous breath. "Yes and no."

Aware of her apprehension, Burton tapped her forearm. "It'll be fun. I promise," he said earnestly. "You've got nothing to fear. I'll be by your side the whole time."

She smiled faintly, reassured by his words.

They settled into a comfortable silence as the SUV cruised along the winding mountain roads. Outside, the snow-draped trees blurred past, their branches etched against the sunset sky. While Burton continued texting with Martin, Abi listened to the tires cutting through the slush below them.

As the road curved closer to Niseko, the conversation returned in gentle waves—about the view from the summit earlier, the taste of the tea, and how unproportionate Matt's snow boots looked against his large frame. Laughter came more easily, their earlier tension dissolving into lightness.

By the time they passed through the village and began the final stretch toward the chalet, twilight had begun to settle in, painting the snow in hues of lavender and rose.

As the car rolled to a gentle stop in front of the house, Abi sat upright, watching Burton as he got out to help her.

"Thank you," she said, sliding over. Stepping down, she adjusted her coat as her boots crunched against the icy driveway.

Ahead of them, two sleek snowmobiles sat parked, their black and red designs contrasting with the white surroundings. A guide stood nearby, bundled in layers and wearing a friendly smile.

Burton gave him a polite nod. "We'll just be a minute," he said with his usual calm authority.

"Certainly, Sir. No problem," the guide replied with a small bow, his tone respectful.

Inside the foyer, the heat from the fireplace wrapped around them, a stark contrast to the crisp air outside. Burton slipped off his coat and turned to Abi. "I strongly suggest you dress in layers and grab your warm mitts. Meet you back here in ten?"

She nodded, her eyes alight with excitement. "Okay."

Abi disappeared down the stairs as Burton headed to the upper floor. Passing through the hallway, he entered the living room, where Martin was seated in his usual spot, a steaming cup of tea on the side table and an open book in his hands.

Peering over his reading glasses, the man greeted him. "Hello, Master B. How is the day going?"

Burton paused, his rugged composure softening slightly. "It's been good," he said, noticeably holding back.

His book falling gently to his lap, Martin's expression remained pleasant. "Happy to hear that, my boy."

The corners of Burton's mouth curved into the faintest grin before he excused himself to prepare for their ride. Layering up, he made sure he was ready for the cold night ahead.

By the time Abi returned to the foyer, dressed in a puffy jacket, thermal pants, and thick gloves with a hat pulled snugly over her ears, Burton was already waiting.

Taking her mittens from her, he slipped in a pair of HotShots, already warmed after a quick shake. "These will keep your hands toasty," he said, then announced, "We should go. We are running late," while swinging open the door wide.

Following him outside, unsure of the urgency, she watched him put a Thinsulate layer on his head before slipping on his helmet and turning to help her do the same.

With it securely on her head, he fastened the strap under her chin. "How is that?" he asked.

Hearing his muffled voice, she replied, "It's good."

Getting on the machine, he started the engine. "Well, jump on!" he shouted over the noise. "You're riding with me, right?"

Not arguing, she nodded and quickly sat on the sled behind him. Wrapping her arms securely around his waist, she leaned in close. "You're up to something, aren't you?"

"You know me too well." Unable to see his face hidden beneath the helmet, she had a sneaky suspicion he'd flashed a half-smirk.

With a low rumble, the snowmobiles roared to life. Gliding off into the snowy woods, cold air whipping past, the day's last light faded into starlight as they followed their guide with their security behind them.

As they climbed the mountainside, the low-lying clouds took on a faint pink hue, remnants of the sunset bleeding into the dark blue.

Eyes fixed on the horizon, Abi was slightly disappointed they'd missed the setting sun, but the beauty of the moment wasn't lost on her.

Upon reaching a landing partway up Mount Annupuri, their guide slowed to a stop and cut the engine. Burton parked beside him, angling the snowmobile slightly.

Sliding off the machine, Abi felt her boots sink into the almost knee-deep snow. "I bet we missed a nice sunset tonight."

Scanning the faint colors, Burton walked up beside her. "I believe we did," he agreed, then added with a playfulness, "But..."

"But, what?" she questioned.

A bright light appeared behind them.

Noticing this, she turned. Her eyes widened.

"We're just in time for the full moon," he said, watching as the luminous orb cast a silvery light while it steadily crested behind the snow-covered peaks.

Her mouth dropped open at the sight of it. "Oh, wow! Look at that," she whispered in awe, her mouth partially open.

Burton didn't respond immediately. He was too captivated by her reaction to speak, so he let the moment stretch.

At first, just a glow behind the ridge, soon the round, silver face appeared, bright and clear against the darkening sky. Its light spread over the snow, making the slopes sparkle as if dusted with tiny crystals. In the distance, Mount Yōtei looked small in comparison. One by one, stars began to appear, adding to the quiet beauty of the night.

As the moon lofted higher, they snapped a few pictures and took a couple of selfies while enjoying the miraculous experience. It was as if they could reach out and touch it.

But when Abi shivered, Burton noticed her cheeks flushed from the cold and got concerned.

"We should probably head back," he said, signaling to their guide. "It's getting late."

The machines roared back to life, and they descended the mountain, the moonlight illuminating the trail as it filtered through the trees.

Arms tightening around Burton's waist, the steady rhythm of the ride, and the chill in the air made her hyper-aware of every shared breath between them.

She rested her cheek lightly against his back, surprised by the calm that settled over her. Since they'd left the house, she barely thought of Shane once, and strangely, she didn't feel guilty. This caught her off guard. It was as if her heart had stopped pulling in so many directions and was finally leaning toward something new. Part of her was still hurting, given what she was leaving behind, but the other was beginning to see what was right in front of her. Burton had been attentive, kind, and present. He made her feel like she wasn't just part of the moment but the reason for it. With him, her guard had finally slipped. For once, she wasn't walking on pins and needles, trying to watch what she said or analyzing every word. Today, she could just enjoy every unfiltered moment—and through it all, he made her feel safe.

By the time they reached the house, Abi was half frozen.

Shutting off the machine, Burton helped her up before going to shake the guide's hand. "Thank you very much," he said sincerely as the man acknowledged him.

"Enjoy your night, Sir."

Leading Abi toward the side door, they walked inside the boot room and shed their winter layers. Burton hung their jackets while Abi slid their gloves on the warm dryers. Slipping into a pair of soft house slippers, she followed Burton upstairs, the aroma of something delicious wafting through the air.

Drawn to the fireplace, standing close to the flames, her hands caught the warmth.

Burton joined her, the orangey glow reflecting in his eyes just as Martin appeared, a book still in hand.

"Dinner is ready when you are, Sir," he announced.

"What are we having?" Abi asked, turning toward him.

"Master B requested pasta Bolognese, Miss," the man replied with a smile.

Abi turned to B. "Really?" she said in a whimsical tone, recalling years past.

Casually shrugging, he nodded, happy to see her reaction. He knew how much the dish meant to her. It was a childhood favorite that her Mother always made after long days on the slopes.

"I can't believe you remembered." The gesture touched her heart.

"Of course I did," he said, raising a hand to let her lead the way to the table.

As they sat down, she tilted her head playfully. "You've spoiled me too much today."

"That's okay," he replied with a warm glint in his eyes. "I don't mind if you don't."

| 27 |

Lost in Thought

Tuesday, December 26

Seasons Niseko

After dinner, the two retired to the living room to sit by the fireplace. Abi wrapped herself in a fur blanket and curled up on one end of the sectional, a steaming cup of tea cradled in her hands. The subtle crackling of the fire filled the cozy space.

Sitting down not far away, Burton joined her.

Feeling the warmth radiating from the blowers, he leaned back with a contented sigh. "So? Did you have a good day?" he asked, glancing at her.

She shook her head. "No."

Concerned, his expression paled.

Breaking into a smile, she revealed, "It wasn't just good. It was *great.*"

Relief washed over him. "I'm glad."

"But I'm pretty tired."

"Me too," he admitted. Pulling out his phone, he checked their itinerary for the following day. "I'm told we've got to be up by seven and out the door by eight. They want us on the hill no later than nine-thirty."

Her hand drifted along the edge of the blanket, her gaze dropping as a hint of worry crossed her face. "I don't know why I'm so nervous about tomorrow."

"You don't need to be," he reassured, his tone calm and steady. "You're a great skier. We'll take it slow if that's what you want. No pressure. I might even forgo the board and join you on skis."

"Like old times."

"Yeah." He stared into her eyes as things got awkward. "On that note, we should probably get some sleep."

A soft yawn escaped as she nodded. "That's a good idea," she said while stretching before finishing the last few sips of her tea. Taking the cup to the kitchen, she returned. "Guess I'm off to bed then."

"Same."

Following her down the stairs, she noticed him walking her to her room. When he stopped outside the door, she turned and slowly leaned into his waiting arms.

"Thank you again for today," she whispered.

"You're welcome," came the reply, his embrace lingering a little longer.

A light kiss brushed his cheek before she pulled away. "Good night, B," she said, her expression gentle.

"Night," he answered, watching her disappear into the room, the blanket trailing behind her.

About to head upstairs, the sound of footsteps made him turn around.

Martin appeared with an empty glass in hand. "I must refill my water," he said while following Burton up the staircase.

He could tell his advisor had something to say.

"If I may, Sir," the fatherly figure stated, "You need to tell her. Time is running out."

Silence followed as he glanced toward the floor, the pressure settling heavily. "We still have tomorrow," he said quietly.

The man gave a single nod and headed to the kitchen. "Don't let the moment slip away."

"I know." With that, Burton retreated to his room.

Lost in thought, he dimmed the living room lights, then walked into this suite, mind mulling over what tomorrow might hold.

Meanwhile, downstairs, Abi headed into the adjoining bathroom. Twisting the shower knobs, she let the water heat up while retrieving a clean pair of pajamas from her suitcase. Her phone sat untouched on the nightstand, and curiosity finally got the better of her. Checking it for the first time all day, she found no messages from Shane.

"Figures," she muttered, debating whether to reach out. After a moment, she shook her head. "If he isn't making an effort, why should I?"

Steam filled the small space as she stepped into the warm cascade of water. The heat worked its way through her chilled fingers and toes, melting away the lingering cold from their snowmobile adventure. With muscles relaxed and her mind clearer, she finished up and slipped into bed, the covers soft and welcoming.

Setting her alarm for the early morning start, she let out a sigh of relief. The constant fear of the Red Dragons and their recruiting games felt like a distant memory now, left behind in the city's shadows. Yet, her thoughts moved on to the Andaru event, only two days away.

Excitement mingled with a touch of unease about the upcoming performance. Knowing how unpredictable the world around Burton could be, she reminded herself to stay vigilant.

"You just never know," she whispered, placing her phone face down on the side table.

Snuggling deeper into the blankets, she tucked them under her chin, her eyelids growing heavy. Reaching across to the empty space beside her, she wished she weren't alone. Outside, fresh snow blanketed the hills of Niseko, muffling the night with its peaceful quiet as she slowly drifted into a safe and dreamless sleep.

| 28 |

Heli-Ski

Wednesday, December 27

Seasons Niseko / Mount Shiribetsu

Waking to the intrusive sound of her alarm, she fumbled around and finally switched it off. At the same time, she caught the same faint buzzing above her, followed by the thud of footsteps moving across the floor. A grin spread across her face as she sat up. "A race to breakfast it is," she whispered, a playful challenge lighting her eyes.

Tossing back the covers, she straightened the bed in record time, fluffing the pillows before heading to the bathroom. After brushing her teeth and layering up in thermals and polar fleece, she dashed out of her room.

Bounding up the stairs, the aroma of breakfast greeted her. At the table, Lorenzo, Andrew, and Ethan were already halfway through their meals. She glanced around, hoping she'd made it first, but a familiar voice called out as she rounded the corner.

"Morning, Abs. Sleep well?" Burton said, pouring a glass of juice.

"Like a log," she replied, grabbing a plate. "I don't think I moved all night."

"Same here. My covers were almost too perfect this morning."

"Mine too," she laughed while scooping some eggs and placing three strips of bacon and a waffle onto her plate.

Around the table, the conversation buzzed with excitement over the day's heli-skiing adventure. Fresh powder from overnight snow had everyone eager to hit the slopes. As the group swapped tips and plans, she made a mental note to take her rosy mirrored goggles since the sun was so bright this morning. The last thing she wanted was to risk snow blindness in such challenging conditions.

The hour passed in a blur, and soon, everyone gathered in the equipment room to bundle up before heading outside. A van from Niseko Backcountry idled in the driveway, their gear already stowed neatly in the back.

Approaching the vehicle, a flutter of apprehension stirred in her stomach. The air felt colder than before, sharper against her skin. A hand touched her arm through the layers of her jacket—firm, grounding.

"Hey?" His quiet concern cut through the noise. "How are you holding up there, Abs? Excited?"

A quick nod came without much thought. "Yes, very excited," she replied, forcing a small smile she hoped was convincing.

Gloved fingers rubbed her arm again, this time with more focus. "You don't have to pretend. I know that look."

A soft breath escaped her lips, fogging the air between them. "It's just the helicopter. The unknown. I'm excited but a little on edge."

His eyes never left hers. "That's normal. We're about to fly to the top of a mountain. But we've got this. I'm not going to let anything happen to you."

What he said brought a warmth that eased her nerves. Strangely changing her tune to one that was more upbeat, she flashed him a quick grin and added, "Let's go. I'm ready."

With a nod, he stepped back to open the van door, ushering her inside as the two settled in.

The vehicle rumbled to life and rolled onto the snow-covered highway. Frosty trees blurred past, interspersed with powdery fields stretching toward the horizon.

As the van turned into the heli-ski hanger, a white helicopter came into view. Her skin prickled with both anticipation and unease as they stepped out, ready for the adventure ahead.

The Backcountry Guides meticulously transferred their gear into the baskets along the helicopter skids before ushering the group into the lodge for a safety briefing.

Inside, the mood grew serious as they were walked through the potential dangers, strict rules, and survival techniques needed to ski this untouched terrain. Each person double-checked their survival backpack, testing straps and memorizing the locations of key items—avalanche beacons, shovels, and probes—before latching their boot buckles and heading back outside.

Prepared for departure, their group filed toward the helicopter, the cold biting at their faces as they got in and found their seats. Tension crackled in the cabin as the propellers whirled to life, sending vibrations through the machine.

Burton glanced her way. "Here we go!" The words cut through the noise.

She flashed a confident smile. "Yep!"

With a jolt, the helicopter lifted off, climbing steadily into the sky. The tree line fell away beneath them, revealing the Hokkaido wilderness blanketed in pristine white snow. Mount Shiribatsu stood ominously before them, bathed in golden sunlight. The chatter in the cabin quieted as everyone took in the beauty of it.

Reaching their drop zone, the helicopter descended to a snow-covered ridge. Their guides unloaded the gear as the group jumped out and huddled together a safe distance away. The roar of the rotors grew deafening as the helicopter took off, whipping snow into a swirling vortex around them.

Crouched low, Burton shielded their faces until the storm of snowflakes settled and silence descended, broken only by the faint rustle of the wind.

"That was awesome," he said, standing straight to help Abi to her feet. "Doing okay?"

"Stop asking me that!" she laughed while getting her bearings. "I'm not a little girl anymore. I can handle this."

He stopped dead. "Oh, I know you can. I don't doubt it for a second."

Giving a single nod, she smiled from ear to ear. "Come on," she said, "Let's get suited up."

"Right behind you."

Their group gathered as the first run beckoned—a steep, powder field calling their name.

Burton and Abi surveyed their line. They noticed that the trees at this altitude were encased in snow and ice, their twisted shapes resembling creatures from another planet. Flash frozen, the limbs curled and hunched, each casting an eerie silhouette across the mountain. As the sun peeked out from behind the clouds, ribbons of light glinted off the surface, making everything shimmer.

Slipping her goggles over her eyes, she snapped into her bindings and secured the backpack safety strap across her chest. To not show fear, she made the first move and glided a few feet to test out the depth of the powder. Realizing she would have to keep on top of her turns, Abi noticed Burton do the same before their guides, and the security team followed suit.

To start them off, the first guide broke trail ahead of them.

"Once we drop in..." Burton announced.

"There's no going back!" Abi shouted, following the trail that had been left for them.

Effortlessly sifting through the powder, Abi's adrenaline surged as they wove through the open canvas before heading into the trees. The whoosh of movement and the occasional laugh echoed through the wilderness as they carved their way down.

As the mountain steepened, the descent demanded total focus. Every muscle worked to stay balanced as her skis threatened to sink with each shift in weight. Deep powder clung to her shins, resisting movement like wet cement, but the steep pitch made it harder to slow down. Her breathing grew sharper, more intentional, knowing one wrong move could send her tumbling. Each bend of the trail revealed a true winter wonderland painted with thrill and danger as they tackled the unforgiving terrain.

When they finally reached the base of the mountain, their grins were infectious. Burton gave her a playful nudge. "Not bad for a first run, huh?"

"Not bad? That was incredible!" she replied, her cheeks flushed from the pure exhilaration.

Climbing back into the helicopter, the pilot lifted them to a new drop zone. This time, they landed on a lofty peak known as the Northwest Gully, where the clouds hung below them, their misty tops brushing the valleys far beneath. The view was otherworldly, like standing on the edge of heaven itself.

She paused, the vastness of the scene stealing her breath. For a fleeting moment, it felt as though her Mom was close. The sensation brought an ache to her chest, bittersweet and comforting all at once.

Seeing her lost in thought, Burton bumped her shoulder. "Hey..."

Blinking back to the present, she could see he was concerned. "Stop worrying about me," she laughed, her eyes gravitating toward the view again. "This is just so beautiful. I want to take it all in."

He looked over the landscape below. "Pretty amazing, for sure."

Silently, she agreed, her heart full of gratitude for this moment, this place, and the people sharing it with her.

Ahead, they watched their guide begin to break another trail, his skis cutting clean lines through the snow as he plotted a safe, sweeping descent. Burton nudged her arm gently, a silent cue. It was time. With a deep breath, she adjusted her goggles, leaned into her poles, and followed as the group dropped into the gully.

Making it down the first section, they stopped for a brief rest before continuing. The guide went first, carving an effortless path through the pristine powder. Abi followed close behind, her movements fluid and confident.

Wanting to capture it, Burton pulled out his phone and started recording as he watched her expertly weave back and forth across the steep slope.

All at once, a series of loud explosions popped off—sharp, concussive blasts that echoed off the mountains like distant thunder.

Unsure of what was happening, Burton ducked.

Shouts erupted from the group.

In seconds, Burton's head snapped up. His gut clenched.

The guide closest to him yelled, "AVALANCHE!" But it was already too late.

Adrenaline roared in his ears. "Abi!!" he shouted in disbelief, his voice swallowed by the sound just as the ground beneath him let out a deep, unnatural groan. It was the kind of sound that didn't belong to the Earth—a low, trembling that sparked the shuddering crack.

Then everything shifted.

A deep fracture suddenly split across the slope like a fault line, swallowing the world. In seconds, the massive slab sheared off and surged downward. The air filled with the thunderous roar of moving snow, fast, unstoppable, and deafening.

Burton twisted to locate Abi and caught a glimpse of her pink lenses looking his way as she tried to avoid the slide. But the snow beneath her feet gave way. One moment, she was upright. Then, gone the next, vanishing under a crashing wall of white. "Abi!!!" he shouted, knowing he'd lost her.

Shoving his phone into his pocket, he charged down the slope toward the last spot he'd seen her, despite the danger still lurking, his skis buried in the loose snow. Panic surged through him upon overhearing their second guide calling for emergency help on the radio. Eyes peeled, he yanked his sleeve up and started the timer on his stopwatch, his voice raw as he shouted, "Abs! Abi!"

The race against time had begun.

Frantic, his heart hammering in his chest, Burton tried to listen for the faintest of sounds as his guys scanned the area for any sign of her.

Fumbling with the radio strapped to his chest, gloves slick with snow and shaking from adrenaline, their second guide turned his back to the wind and pressed the transmit button. "Mayday, mayday, this is Shiribetsu backcountry team, Gully Northwest—avalanche incident! We have a slide—repeat, we have a slide! At least two buried! Coordinates incoming!" He paused to check his GPS. "Approximate location: 42.7749 north, 140.9126 east! Request immediate medivac ASAP! Over."

Static crackled in response, followed by a calm but urgent reply from base command. "Copy that, Shiribetsu team. Helo en route. ETA twelve minutes. This channel remains open." The guide's breath came in clouds as he clipped the radio back to his vest, eyes scanning the slope. "Spread out!" he yelled. "Help's coming!"

Burton listened to the faint beep on the guide's beacon device, narrowing the search radius, but time was slipping away as everyone searched for signs of life.

"Abi!!!" His voice cracked as he shouted her name into the silence, the snow glistening under the sun, hiding its deadly secret.

Around him, the others joined in, their shouts echoing against the jagged peaks before they went silent, waiting to hear something-anything. The weight of it was almost unbearable.

"Abi!!!!" Burton's thoughts raced as he pleaded under his breath, "Oh God, please, give me something..." Images of her laughing over breakfast, her lighting up at the sight of fresh snow – all of it flashed before his eyes.

"I got one!" the guide broke the silence, sending a jolt through Burton.

"Where?" he shouted before racing toward where the guide was pointing, his boots slipping as he reached the spot where the man had started digging furiously into the compacted snow. Seeing the black ski glove punching through, Burton shouted, "It's not her!" Pointing at Ethan and Andrew, he said, "You help them! We'll keep looking!" His security guards got out their shovels and started digging while Lorenzo helped Burton and the others search for Abi.

"Eleven minutes!" Burton alerted them, panic rising again. His eyes scanned the area, his mind recalling her last position. "She was near here. Not far!"

The guide's GPS beeped again, pinpointing another signal a few meters away, and he shouted to them, "Here! Check here!"

Burton trudged toward the spot, dropping to his knees, and removed the shovel from his backpack. Frantic, he shouted her name again and again.

Afraid to hit her, he flung off his gloves and started digging with his bare hands. Ignoring the sting of the ice biting into his skin, he called out, "Abi! Abi! Say something!" The stopwatch on his wrist ticked louder in his mind. Not finding anything, he shouted, "She's not here!"

Another shout pierced the air. "There!"

One of the men near Burton motioned to the tip of a white glove, rising through the snow like a corpse waking from the dead.

Lunging toward it, he grasped hold with furious determination. "Hold on, Abs! We've got you!" he said as her fingers weakly clung to his. The others joined in tandem, their hands and shovels working in sync, exhuming her as carefully and quickly as they could while the other guide got resurrected.

Then suddenly, there she was. An arm. A leg. A ski.

Gingerly removing the snow, soon, he saw her, pale and still, one hand cupping the beacon. Panic clawed at his throat. She wasn't moving now.

"Abs!" he said, digging her out.

The guide pushed past him with an oxygen mask and placed it over her face while Burton and the guys continued to free her from the icy tomb.

In seconds, her eyes flickered faintly.

"Abs? I'm here. We're gonna get you out!"

The sound of the approaching helicopter sent a gust of relief through the group, but time was still of the essence. When it landed, teams of rescuers raced toward the two victims.

"Her beacon led us here just in time," the guide briefed. "She's hypothermic. Get the blankets ready!"

The guys could see the fear in Burton's eyes.

"Come on, Abi," he pleaded, his forehead pressing against hers. "Don't you dare leave me? Not now," he said as they pulled her from the snow.

At last, her chest rose in a shallow breath, and a weak cough escaped her lips before her teeth began to chatter uncontrollably.

"She's breathing!" one of the medics shouted, but the severity of her condition muted the victory. "Lips blue! Skin pale and cold!"

The medivac team cautiously secured her on a stretcher, wrapping her in thermal metallic sheets as a second helicopter and a third landed in open spaces.

Refusing to let go of her lifeless hand, he had no choice in the end as they made their way to the medivac.

The paramedic radioed ahead to the emergency center. "Victim two - buried minimum of twenty minutes! Hypothermic! Possible oxygen deprivation! We need to move fast!"

Spotting the other guide loaded simultaneously on the other helicopter, Burton nodded, his eyes now locked onto her. "She's strong. She'll make it," he whispered, more to himself than anyone else.

Lorenzo went with him, leaving his two colleagues behind. When they were seated in the chopper, he took out his phone to call Martin. The second the man picked up, he said, "Sir, we have a situation. There's been an avalanche. They're airlifting Abi out."

Martin asked, "What hospital?"

Turning to talk to the attendant, Lorenzo shouted, "Hey! What hospital?"

"Kutchan!" he yelled to him as the blades whirled overhead.

"He says, Kutchan!" Lorenzo shouted.

"We are on our way!"

Hearing that, Lorenzo ended the call and rested his hand on Burton's shoulder. He could see his boss's jaw clenched as he stared at Abi—still in and out of consciousness, strapped to a stretcher, an oxygen mask over her face.

"You got her out, Sir," Lorenzo said confidently below the thrum of the rotors. "She's alive. Focus on that. Must stay positive."

He didn't answer him, but his fingers curled tighter around Abi's glove, his eyes not leaving hers.

"She's tough," Lorenzo added. "She'll make it."

| 29 |

The News

Wednesday, December 27

Seasons Niseko

Back at the house, Martin scurried around after getting the news. Still in shock, he gathered everything he needed and tried to calmly coordinate with his men for updates on their group's location and Abi's status. Outside, the familiar hum of the Range Rover's engine reached his ears. He glanced up to see the vehicle pulling into the driveway. Before he could step out, a van arrived unexpectedly.

To his surprise, Shane emerged, suitcase in hand.

Spotting the stress etched on Martin's face, Shane's expression changed. "What is it? What's going on?"

Keeping a level head, not wanting to cause alarm, Martin instructed firmly, "Leave your bag inside. Quickly. It's Abi. There's been an accident."

Shane froze for a moment as the color drained from him. In seconds, he tossed his suitcase inside the house and sprinted over to the SUV, sliding into the seat beside Martin. "What happened?" he asked with a hint of dread.

"Avalanche," he grimly said as they turned onto the main road while Matt and Ted followed.

Shane tilted his head back against the headrest, trying to process it all. "How bad?"

Not knowing for certain, Martin shook his head. "I don't have any details other than they had to medivac her out. That's all I know so far."

Leaning forward, Shane rested his elbows on his knees as he buried his face in his hands. His thoughts spiraled into the worst-case scenarios as images of her flashed through his mind, only to be replaced by the crushing fear of losing her.

"She has to be okay," he muttered under his breath, body trembling. Suddenly, the arguments they'd had didn't seem important. None of it was as the SUV sped toward the hospital.

| 30 |

Airlifted

Wednesday, December 27

Mount Shiribatsu / Kutchan Hospital

Slicing through the mountain air, Burton felt his heart thudding painfully in his chest, a rhythmic ache that almost ended him. Stressed, his body remained rigid, but with every beep of the heart monitor, a flicker of hope rekindled. Abi was alive, and no matter what happened, he would do everything in his power to ensure that she stayed that way.

The helicopter began its descent, the whirling of the blades growing louder as they approached the helipad. Burton squeezed her hand a few more times, his fingers trembling as if trying to transfer all his strength to her.

"Hold on, Abs. Hold on," he whispered, barely audible over the noise of the chopper.

A flutter of movement from Abi caught his attention. Her eyelids twitched slightly. Then, as if the sound of his voice reached her, they opened just a fraction.

Burton's breath caught in his throat.

She blinked slowly, the movement hesitant, as if caught between worlds. For a moment, he feared she wouldn't come back to him. But then, in a flicker of clarity, her gaze locked onto his. Time narrowed. The sounds, the cold, everything around them disappeared. In that suspended heartbeat, he saw it—the trace of recognition in her eyes. That is when he knew she was still with them.

"Abs..." Overwhelmed with emotion, he encouraged, "I'm here. We got you." He leaned in closer, his words gentle but filled with urgency and relief. Caressing her forehead, cold and clammy, he said, "Stay with me."

Her chest rose with a shallow breath, a faint glimmer of hope present, though exhaustion and confusion still clouded her features.

As the skids made contact with the platform, Burton couldn't tear his eyes away from her. Speaking softly, he whispered in her ear. "We're here. They are gonna help you. Stay with me, Abs. Be strong."

Forced to release her hand, the medical crew was already moving quickly, unloading her from the helicopter with practiced precision.

He watched, powerless, as they wheeled her toward the hospital doors, his legs becoming heavy, almost refusing to move.

Lorenzo, ever loyal and steady, stood by Burton and guided him along, offering support.

"She's gonna be okay," the guy reassured his boss, but he could see the agony Burton was in.

Ushered into a waiting room, the sterile walls were cold and unforgiving. The sounds of doctors and nurses in action echoed down the hall.

Pacing the floor with hands clenched, Burton leaned forward as he stared at the doors where Abi had been taken. The uncertainty gnawed at him. "I shouldn't have taken her there..." he whispered, thick with guilt, while his mind replayed every moment, every decision that led to this.

With strength and reassurance, Lorenzo placed a hand on his back. "You couldn't have known, Sir," he said. "It's not your fault."

Letting out a shaky breath, he pressed his hands against his knees as he looked down at the floor. His mind raced, the flood of "what-ifs" overwhelming.

"Come on," Lorenzo said gently, guiding him to sit down. "We gotta stay positive. For her."

Recalling the minutes prior to the ledge giving way, he mumbled, "There was a series of explosions."

Lorenzo sat beside his boss.

"Did you hear it? Feel it?" he asked him.

"Yes, Sir. I did. At least five explosions."

"Someone did this...intentionally."

Lorenzo confirmed, "That's my thought, too."

"Call it in. We need evidence of that. Camera footage. Seismic. Anything."

"Will do, Sir." His head of security pulled his phone from his pocket and walked a few feet away to make the call.

The world around him muffled as Burton sat alone. Straightening his posture, he knew he couldn't fall apart. Not while Abi was still fighting for her life.

| 31 |

Blame

Wednesday, December 27

Kutchan Hospital

Martin, Shane, and the guys arrived at the same time as Andrew and Ethan. Entering the emergency room together, Martin wasted no time in taking charge, his mind already whirling with a number of things that needed his immediate attention. Quickly locating a translator, he began navigating the mountains of paperwork, his hands steady despite the turmoil twisting in his gut.

Meanwhile, Andrew, phone in hand, texted Lorenzo and Burton to await updates.

With arms tightly crossed, Shane stood to the side, his jaw clenched. Watching the activity around them, he suddenly demanded, "Where is she? I need to see her."

Relaying a heads-up text to Lorenzo, Andrew got his reply with the grim news. "They're still working on her," he announced solemnly as everyone went quiet.

A rush of frustration and anger surged through Shane. He started pacing, his fingers balling into fists at his sides. *This is Burton's fault.*

He's the one who put her in danger. He should never have taken her up that mountain.

Things grew more intense when the men moved into the enclosed waiting space. There, they all came face-to-face with Burton.

The moment their eyes met, Shane's fury erupted with a mix of panic and rage. "She'd better be okay, or I swear I will kill you!"

That cut through the air like a knife.

Martin instinctively stepped in between them, his hands outstretched, trying to keep the peace. The men backed him up.

But Shane was beyond reason now as he moved toward Burton with a force that made the others fall into line.

"Get him out of here!" Burton barked, pointing at the QB, his tone dark and threatening.

"I'm not going anywhere!" Shane shot back. With bloodshot eyes and his body tinged with adrenaline and worry, the football player's mission was clear.

"Your actions aren't helping her, so decide! Shut up or get out!" Burton's words were cold and final.

He countered, standing his ground. "But she needs me!"

"Fine! Then we agree on something!" Burton calmed down. "She needs all of us right now!"

Able to put their differences aside, not allowing the situation to escalate further, a doctor finally appeared with news. Thankfully, he spoke English.

Having heard the two men arguing, he stared the group down. "I'm going to have all of you removed if you don't act accordingly," he warned.

Martin exchanged glances with both men, his calm demeanor forcing a moment of pause. He extended his hands, gesturing for everyone to take a step back and breathe. "We need to stay calm. Focus on her."

However, Burton could hardly contain himself. Pushing forward, standing with everyone behind him, he asked, "Is she okay?" and held his breath.

The man in the white coat paused, offering a moment of measured silence before answering. "It seems Ms. Acardi was pretty lucky. A few more minutes, and that might not have been the case. She's stable now."

Those words hit Burton like a wave. The relief was overwhelming, yet the fear still gripped his chest as he bent forward, taken by emotion. Doing his best to compose himself, he took a few deep breaths, his eyes welling with tears. In need of a minute, he walked away from the group.

Martin followed. "You okay, my boy?"

Looking up at the ceiling in silent prayer, he muttered, "Yeah," as his lip quivered slightly. Quickly drying his tears with a sweep of his hands, he addressed his most trusted friend. "Yeah, I'm good."

With a strong, positive pat on the back, the man smiled.

Reality settled in. She was going to be okay.

Before the doctor walked away, Burton asked, "Can I see her?"

"Only one at a time. Come with me," the man said as Burton followed.

Shane's fury simmered, but the anger didn't dissipate despite the flicker of relief. About to request permission to go along, Martin reached out his hand and stopped him.

"No. Give him a moment," he said in a commanding tone. "We will all get a turn."

"Fine," Shane said respectfully.

"We must all be strong and united so that we get her through this - together."

Each one of them took those words to heart.

| 32 |

Relief

Wednesday, December 27

Kutchan Hospital

Following the doctor to the intensive care unit, they stopped outside the door.

"You have ten minutes," he stated. "She needs to rest."

Burton nodded as the man left him to go about his duties. Afraid of what he'd find, he reached for the handle but stopped and took a breath before going into the dimly lit room. Finding her surrounded by nurses monitoring her condition, he caught the faint antiseptic smell mingling with the hum of machines. The rhythmic beeping of Abi's heart monitor filled the air, a steady reassurance in the otherwise somber space. Covered in heating blankets, managing her body temperature to ward off the chill of her ordeal, an IV line ran to a saline bag hanging to her left. For a moment, the reality of seeing her like this hit him harder than expected. She looked so small, her usual vibrance dimmed by the horror of the day's events. Swallowing the lump in his throat, Burton moved closer.

Giving him privacy, the nurses left the room.

His fingers hovered over the edge of the bed, hesitating, before sliding under the blankets to find her hand. Her fingers were cool against his, and he gave them a gentle squeeze.

Her head turned slowly in his direction, her eyes fluttering open. They were clouded but brightened slightly when they found him.

"Hey, Abs..." he said quietly, his strength slowly increasing as he pulled up a chair beside her.

"B?" Her voice was faint as she traced the ceiling before locking onto his face.

"How are you doing?" he asked, leaning closer.

Still shivering under the blankets, she forced a flat smile. "Good..." Her brows furrowed as the confusion deepened. "What happened?"

He lowered his head. "There was an avalanche."

Shock rippled as the memory of it began to stir.

"We found you. Got you out." His opposite hand rose to her forehead. Resting there gently, his warmth seemed to soothe her, and she closed her eyes briefly, leaning into him.

When she opened them again, she noticed something she rarely saw from Burton. Tears. His red-rimmed eyes betrayed the strength he usually exuded.

"Don't be sad," she mumbled, her concern breaking through the haze.

He shook his head. "Typical...always thinking of others before yourself."

Lips twitching, she could see how this had deeply shaken him to the core. "Are you hurt?"

"No... I'm fine," he added, his fingers running through her hair. "I'm more worried about you."

Leaning down, he pressed a lingering kiss to her forehead, his lips warm against her cool skin. When he pulled back, he rested his cheek against her a moment, letting the quiet comfort between them speak louder than words.

"Everyone's here," he said after a pause. "Including Shane."

The mention of his name sparked a nervousness. "He is?"

"Yeah, umm," Burton hesitated. "He wants to see you."

Abi nodded weakly, unsure of how she felt about that.

He squeezed her hand again. "I'll just be outside the door if you need me."

"Don't go far," she whispered.

"I won't. I promise." About to leave, she called after him, "Burton?" He stopped and glanced back. "Yeah?"

"Thank you for saving me."

He gave a shaky nod. "I'd do it a million times over if I have to."

Immersed in the moment, he waited a second before opening the door and walking into the hallway. There, Burton found Shane pacing, his shoulders tense. Sighting the QB, he said civilly, "Go ahead in. Keep it calm."

Shane silently nodded and walked past him. After building up the courage, he pushed the door open and stepped inside. The sight of Abi surrounded by machines caused the guilt and frustration to intensify within him.

When he approached slowly, he said, "Hey, you…"

Abi leaned to the right with chattering teeth.

The silence between them felt heavy. Finally, Shane broke through. "You gave us a fright."

"I'm sorry," she said, teeth chattering a little less.

"I'm the one who should be sorry." His lips twitched. There was so much he wanted to say, but the sight of her like this held him back.

As he stood there, something within her quietly gave way. The bond she'd once held onto with him felt dim now. The truth of it hit her with startling clarity as her brain fog began to lift.

Then, with perfect timing, the nurses returned.

"I'm sorry," one woman said gently. "She needs to rest now."

Not wanting to leave her, Shane looked down at Abi as if trying to memorize her face. "I'll be back," he said, quiet but certain.

Abi managed a small nod as she drifted off.

When he turned and walked toward the door, his thoughts were heavy as it clicked shut behind him.

Over the next hour, after napping, she had a visit from Martin and the men, each offering an overwhelming sense of love and support. Despite the cold, her body aching, and the absolute exhaustion, their presence brought her comfort. She clung to their reassurances, as though they were lifelines tethering her.

As the hours passed, her condition improved dramatically. The machines around her became less intimidating as the numbers on the monitors stabilized. The warmth of the fluids she sipped seemed to chase away the chill from her terrifying ordeal. By ten o'clock that night, Abi slowly sat up, her strength returning in small, steady increments.

Through it all, Burton had returned and never left her side. The staff allowed it since he'd submitted a huge donation to that wing of the hospital. Vigilantly sitting in the chair beside her, his hand resting on hers whenever she drifted into a restless sleep, his quiet presence spoke volumes.

The rest of their group, at the doctor's insistence, were told to go home.

Shane lingered longer than the others, pacing the hall with a frustrated energy. His fists opening and closing as if to physically contain his emotions, he surprisingly didn't argue with the doctor, but the decision to leave stung. Seeing her inside the room, there was a mixture of worry and reluctance in his eyes before he finally followed the men and left without question, despite Burton being authorized to stay.

About to join them, Martin went to bid his boss goodnight and rested a hand on Burton's shoulder. "If you need anything, my boy, just ask."

"I will." Casting a sharp glance, he said to the man, "Keep an eye on Coppersmith."

"Don't worry. He will be fine."

Watching the group leave, Burton waved before turning his attention back to Abi, who was now looking at him with heavy-lidded eyes. "They'll be back tomorrow," he said while adjusting the blanket over her shoulders.

"Thank you..." she said sleepily, "...for staying."

"You don't have to thank me, Abs. There's nowhere I'd rather be." Knowing it needed to be said, he muttered, "I'm so sorry. This happened because of me."

Shock flooded her face, and a spark of energy ignited her. "You could not have known. It's not your fault. Accidents happen."

"But if we hadn't been on that mountain..."

"I would not have felt closer to my Mother and seen where Heaven and Earth collide..." she exhaled. "Please don't... Don't blame yourself..."

He nodded but still felt the guilt mingling as the room grew quiet again, the rhythmic beeping of the heart monitor blending with the noise of the warming blanket.

Abi felt the trauma of the ordeal begin to lift. That day, the people who cared for her so deeply surrounded her with the love of family. As her eyes shut, she held onto the feeling of Burton's hand in hers. It was a steady anchor, a quiet reminder that she wasn't alone.

| 33 |

Recovery

Thursday, December 28

Kutchan Hospital

The following morning, the doctor arrived with Abi's release papers in hand. Seeing her sitting up, her cheeks tinged with a faint pink hue, he offered a smile. "You're making quite the recovery, Miss Acardi. I want you to rest for the next few days—no strenuous activity, just sleep, small meals, and plenty of fluids."

Burton listened intently, nodding as the doctor spoke. "I'll make sure of it," he stated with a firm, determined tone.

The doctor chuckled lightly. "Best of luck to you, although I dare say you already have that in spades."

Shortly after, Martin arrived with a bag of warm clothes for Abi to change into. Burton noticed her hesitance as she glanced at the excessive bundle. Weak and unsteady, she shifted slightly under the blankets.

"Need me to, umm…?" Burton started before faltering at the awkwardness of the offer.

Abi blushed, shaking her head. "Umm, no… I'll manage. Thanks, though."

He nodded quickly. "Okay. I'll be outside. Just call me if you need anything."

"Alright," she replied as he pulled the privacy curtain.

Stepping out, Burton closed the door behind him and leaned against the wall.

Martin remained nearby, his arms crossed, studying him. "How was the night?" he asked. "Did you get any sleep?"

"A little," Burton replied, though the weariness in his eyes told a different story. Running his hands over his face, he needed to know - "Any news on those explosions? I'm convinced this wasn't an accident."

Not wanting to discuss the sensitive subject so early in the morning, he replied, "We have reason to believe that to be true."

Crossing his arms over his chest, B stood tall.

"We got reports of a helicopter pilot who got jumped yesterday, then gagged and bound."

"I don't understand. The guy we had?"

"No, the one you were supposed to have but didn't." Martin watched as Burton quickly put two and two together. "So, the pilot we had was a setup?"

"That is the consensus, my boy."

"The guy dropped us there, knowing the ridge was loaded with charges?"

"It seems so. Our sources say there was a rash of seismic activity reported at the same time on that side of the mountain, each listed as a mining explosion."

"And there were no controlled avalanche detonations scheduled?"

"None."

Burton ran his hand through his hair. "So this means it was..."

"An attempt on your life, Sir?" Sadly, Martin nodded. "Yes, the men, and I believe it was."

"And Abs got caught in the crosshairs." He buried his hands in his pockets and looked to the ceiling, anger boiling over.

"Unfortunately."

"I assume the recruiting games have migrated to Niseko?"

"We are still trying to confirm this." Having no choice but to bring it up, Martin added, "There is one more thing."

"What's that?"

"Just a reminder—we need to attend the Red Dragon pre-event party this evening." He kept his voice low. "And from what we hear, some Tokuryū may be embedded in the crowd. This isn't going to be just another social stop, Master B. The men think it could be pre-planned."

Burton's jaw tightened. "If they followed us here, I can't leave her."

"I understand, Sir, but..." Martin said sympathetically. "We must make an appearance. If we don't, it will look suspicious, not to mention certain, umm, people are depending on this."

He exhaled sharply, his shoulders stiffening.

"Don't worry. I'll make sure the guys keep her safe. We can always send her to an undisclosed location until the coast is clear."

"Might have to do that." Burton's thoughts gravitated to the QB. "And what do we do about Coppersmith?"

His advisor raised an eyebrow. "He stayed at the house last night. Hasn't been much trouble. Do you want him to stay with her while we're out?"

Burton paused, his mind reeling. "I guess that's up to him."

Before his trusted friend could respond, Abi called out from inside the room.

"Burton!"

Startled, he turned on a dime and immediately flung the door open to find her tangled in her hoodie, her arms caught awkwardly in the sleeves.

"A little help... please?" she asked sheepishly.

Chuckling with a hint of relief, Burton gently guided her arms through the sleeves and adjusted the hood around her neck. "How's that?"

"Better. Thank you," she said before reaching for her jacket.

He took it from her and held it up so she could easily slip it on. While zipping it closed, she suddenly got a little woozy. "Easy there," he said, wrapping his arm around her waist to carefully sit her on the bed.

Eyes a bit glassy, she muttered, "I'm okay."

A nurse entered with a wheelchair and handed Burton a set of aftercare instructions. Tucking the papers into his pocket, he helped Abi with her hat, ensuring she was bundled up against the cold. Wheeling the chair close to her, he scooped her up effortlessly and placed her in it.

"I can walk, you know," she whispered, though she didn't protest.

"I'm sure you can. Just not today," he said firmly while wheeling her out of the room and down the hall.

Lorenzo waited by the SUV outside the main doors as Martin held it open for them. "Looking good there, Miss," the head of security called from the driver's seat.

"Thanks to all of you," Abi replied warmly as Burton lifted her into the vehicle.

Inside, he made sure she was bundled in a thermal sleeping bag before climbing in beside her.

The thirty-minute drive back to their Seasons Niseko vacation home passed quietly, with Burton's watchful eye never leaving her.

When they arrived, he carried Abi in before setting her carefully on the sofa near the fireplace. Removing her coat and adjusting the blankets around her, he hung them up and noticed Shane approaching with a steaming cup of tea and a plate of scrambled eggs and waffles.

"Hey... You seem much better this morning," Shane said, kneeling beside her and handing her the food.

"Yes, I feel better," Abi replied, still a little shaky. "Thank you. I am kinda hungry."

From across the room, Burton watched Shane's careful attention. Seeing this, he made his decision to walk over and address them both.

"Tonight, I have to make an appearance at the Red Dragon event. Investors are expecting me, and I can't avoid it." He turned to Shane. "Would you stay with her?"

Surprised by the request, Shane nodded. "Of course. Don't worry. Do what you have to. She'll be fine."

With everyone settled in, Martin reappeared. "I suggest you get some sleep. It will be a long night if you don't, Sir."

He nodded silently.

"I'll just be in my room," Burton said. "Shane, if she needs anything, wake me up."

"Sure," Shane replied to keep the peace, knowing he'd never do as he asked.

Leaving her on the couch, Shane sitting at her feet, B slipped into his room to shower. Before trying to get some rest, he pressed the blackout shades button to rid the room of any light. Setting his alarm, he braced himself for the short nap before he would have to step back into the role of Dark Demon, ready to face the demands of the night ahead.

| 34 |

The Confrontation

Thursday, December 28

Seasons Niseko

When Burton woke, he found Abi and Shane sitting by the fireplace, talking quietly. The glow from the flickering flames gave the room a calmness that contrasted sharply with the tension simmering beneath the surface.

"Did you get some rest?" Burton asked, eyeing Shane and wondering if he had stayed up talking the entire time.

"She slept a little," Shane replied.

Abi hesitated. "Burton, do you mind if I use your washroom?"

"Of course not. Go ahead."

Shane rose to help her, gently wrapping an arm around her waist as he guided her to the bedroom. Burton watched them disappear, a strange unease settling over him. Before he could think too much, the sound of the front door opening drew his attention.

Sara appeared wearing her messy boots as she ascended the stairs. Her smirk was enough to sour his mood further.

"What are you doing here?" Burton asked, his tone sharp.

"I heard there was an accident," she said with mock concern. "Thought I'd check on your little damsel."

"She's fine," he replied abruptly.

"Good to hear." Sara's gaze flicked toward the bedroom door just as Shane emerged. Her smirk widened. "Well, isn't this cozy? The two of you are getting along. Surprising, really, considering you're both pining after the same girl."

"I highly doubt Burton can steal her from me," Shane smirked confidently.

"Oh, Shane…so naïve…" Her voice slithered. "Don't you know? He already has."

As the statement sank in, Shane's brow furrowed as his attention flicked to Burton. "What's she talking about?"

"Sara. Don't…" The DJ shot her a warning look before his eyes veered toward the flames.

But she ignored him. "I take it you haven't heard what happened in Tahoe?"

Hearing the subject surface again after all this time, Shane's blood boiled.

"Since Burton isn't talking, let me enlighten you." Sara's expression spun cruel and cold. "Hmm, where should I start? Holding hands? The kiss? Sharing pajamas? Or sharing the same bed…"

That landed like a grenade.

"You never even had a chance…"

Shane's expression darkened as Sara sauntered out of the room, clearly satisfied with the chaos she'd unleashed. "Is that true?" he asked, barely restraining his anger.

"It's not what you think," Burton began, but he offered no further explanation.

The QB pointed at him as his right hand balled into a fist.

Before Burton could respond, Abi reappeared, moving carefully into the room.

She immediately sensed the charged atmosphere. "What's going on?" she asked.

Unable to contain himself, Shane launched at B and sent him stumbling backward into the wall with a loud thud. A framed art piece crashed to the floor, shattering the glass.

Abi shouted and covered her ears, but neither of them flinched.

Shane continued charging, throwing the first punch—fast, angry, and dead-on. Grunting as it landed, Burton didn't hesitate. He fired back, catching Shane in the ribs with a solid hit that knocked the wind out of him. And just like that, it exploded. Within seconds, fists were flying, and the two were beating each other to a pulp on the floor.

"HELP! Someone, help!" she cried as the sound of footsteps thundered from the lower level.

Lorenzo and the others rushed in, pulling Burton off while Shane struggled to break free.

"Stop it!" Abi shouted as tears streamed down her face. "Stop!"

The men held Shane back as he seethed, his chest heaving. Turning to her, he asked, "Is it true? Did you sleep with him?"

Abi froze in shock. "No! How dare you even ask me that?"

"She's telling the truth," Burton said, stepping forward. "Nothing happened."

The quarterback's glare darted between the two of them. "Don't speak, or I swear I'll—"

"Shane, that's enough!" Stepping between them, she pleaded for him to calm down, but the pain on his face was undeniable.

"I don't want to hear it," Shane muttered. Feeling utterly betrayed, he stormed out, slamming the front door behind him.

Tears streaming down her face, Abi turned to Burton, voice trembling. "What just happened?"

"Sara..." he replied bitterly.

About to collapse, her body wavering, Burton reached out and sat her down on the sofa.

"I'm sorry, Abs. I never wanted this to come out."

She wiped at her tears. "It doesn't matter now. He will never come back from this. It's over."

| 35 |

The Mission

Thursday, December 28

Seasons Niseko

Having spent the last couple of hours icing his face and hand, Burton made sure Abi was comfortable while Andrew entered the room and took a seat, ready to take over.

Going to get ready, Burton reappeared within a short time and emerged from his room, fully transformed into Dark Demon - the sleek black hoodie giving him that air of commanding mystery.

In the foyer below, Martin waited, checking his watch.

Making eye contact with all his guys, Burton gave them a sharp nod. "Don't leave her side. Not for a second."

"Don't worry, Sir," Andrew replied, his posture confident.

Satisfied, their boss stepped into the dimly lit living room, where Abi was curled up on the couch.

Her demeanor softened when their eyes met.

As he moved closer and wrapped his arms around her, he held onto her a little longer. "I'll be back soon," he said quietly. "Try to get some rest."

"Please tell me why all the guys are guarding me tonight and not going with you. Don't you need them?"

Not wanting to alarm her, he replied, "It's just a precaution."

She zeroed in. "What are you not telling me?"

Avoiding the question, he looked away. "It's complicated."

"Burton?"

"It's not a big deal. Lorenzo will be with me and quite a few, umm, shadows if you know what I mean. It'll be fine."

Upon hearing that, she seemed to relax a bit.

"I won't be long. Promise. Just rest, okay?"

"You shouldn't worry about me so much."

He chuckled while gently brushing a strand of hair from her face. "You know I can't help it."

She patted his chest lightly. "Now go. I assume you've got work to do?"

Reluctantly, he nodded. "Yeah…something like that."

A part of her wished she knew the real reason.

As Burton descended the stairs, he heard Andrew ask Abi if she wanted to watch a movie. He glanced back briefly, wishing he could stay, but tonight was too important to postpone. Steeling himself, he met Martin by the door.

"Ready, Sir?" Martin said, nodding gravely.

About to walk out into the crisp night air, Burton replied, "Yeah…"

The two men slid into the back of a sleek Bentley SUV idling in the driveway, its tinted windows blurring the outside world.

Burton pulled his hood up and leaned into the leather seat, brushing snow from his knee. His mind had already shifted to the mission ahead.

"Okay," he muttered. "Get me up to speed."

Martin straightened. "Our objective is unchanged. We must identify who's bankrolling Red Dragon. We're keeping a close eye on his wife; her family is deeply tied to the Yakuza. But we're convinced someone higher is pulling the strings."

He rested his elbow on the window ledge as his eyes narrowed. "And the intel from Osaka and Tokyo? The tattooed recruits?"

"Confirmed," Martin nodded. "Several Tokuryū operatives arrived in Niseko this week. It's only a matter of time before they surface. And they're not just here to snoop. They're likely planning to take you out—either tonight or at the rave. This isn't just about the vault anymore. This runs deeper. For them, there's a lot at stake. This is a blood business. If they're here, it's kill or be killed."

"Do you think Red Dragon's behind it all? Is he the mastermind?"

Martin shook his head. "No. He's too clean, too polished, too strategic. That said, he's not totally innocent. He lured you here, believing you'd be outside our jurisdiction. But what they don't know is we've had agents embedded in the country for over two months."

Recalling this, he nodded.

"The one organizing the Tokuryū is our true target."

From the front seat, Lorenzo said nothing. He simply reached into the glove compartment and handed over the concealed weapon.

Burton unzipped his hoodie just enough to slip it into the holster beneath his arm. The cold metal pressed against his ribs—a quiet, chilling reminder that this was no ordinary party.

"Tonight's invite-only. Mostly Investors," Martin continued. "All of them are here to protect their crypto transactions and conceal the identities of their partners. Over two hundred will be in attendance. At tomorrow's event, over a thousand are expected, and close to eight hundred will use the vault. If there's ever a time to strike, this is it."

"And the tech team?" Burton asked.

"They're ready. They've doubled encryption protocols and set up a tripwire system. Any breach attempt will trigger an automatic lockdown. If someone even sniffs too close to the core code, they'll be flagged, traced, and locked out before they know what hit them. But we can't assume we're untouchable. If the Tokuryū are involved, they'll probably bring more than muscle and malware."

"And our main targets?" Burton's brow furrowed.

"The top five, high-level users. Deep pockets. Maximum influence. Your job is simple—get in, observe, ID them, and get out. Whatever happens, protect your cover."

"Got it."

The SUV pulled out onto the icy road, headlights slicing through the snow-veiled dark. No one spoke. The silence was heavy.

Burton thought as his hands balled into fists. *All you've gotta do is stay on task. Survive the night and get back to Abi. Nothing else.*

| 36 |

Their Return

Thursday, December 28

Seasons Niseko

Nearing two in the morning, the snow was falling heavily when Burton and Martin returned. Arriving in a smaller, unassuming car, the driver dropped them off discreetly at a house down the street. From there, they walked through the path from the backyard to the main house, their footsteps muffled by the freshly fallen snow. Certain they weren't followed, the two stealthily made their way toward the side door amongst the shadows.

The guys had kept a tight perimeter. Inside, Andrew met them and unlocked the final bolt.

Peeling back his hood, Burton stepped inside first and crossed the threshold. "How is she?" he asked quietly.

"Sleeping soundly for the past four hours," Andrew replied.

He nodded as his shoulders relaxed while ascending the stairs.

Andrew leaned in slightly. "How'd it go for you guys?"

He kept his reply short. "Got what we needed."

Martin continued downstairs and headed directly to his room. There was a report to file and encrypted updates to send back to HQ. Burton, however, paused at the top of the stairs, his gaze fixed on the flickering flames from the fireplace in the living room.

Still curled up on the sectional, the blanket bunched underneath her chin, Abi's soft, even breaths were the only sound in the room.

Approaching slowly, he moved around the couch to sit beside her. For a moment, Burton watched, the faint lines of worry on her face no longer evident. The sight stirred something protective in him. Leaning back, he crossed his arms over his chest and propped his feet up on the coffee table.

"Just a little while longer," he whispered. "Then, I'm free."

Andrew reappeared briefly, checking in before making his rounds outside. "I'll let you know when the others arrive," he said, referring to more reinforcements.

Burton acknowledged him with a small nod but didn't move as he closed his eyes. Exhaling deeply, he finally let himself relax. Within minutes, he'd drifted off, his breathing syncing with hers.

| 37 |

Secrets

Friday, December 29

Seasons Niseko

The faint rustling of movement stirred Burton awake. Startled, he jolted upright, his eyes locking onto Abi's. Finding her bright-faced with eyes open, looking more alert, he said, "Hey, good morning." He sounded rough, almost growly.

"Morning," she replied. "You must have come back really late. I didn't hear you."

"Umm, yeah," he replied.

"How was the party?"

He smirked slightly, closing his eyes again for a moment. "Nothing special." Reaching his arms over his head, Burton stretched, his muscles aching as he sat up fully and rubbed his hands across his face. "How are you feeling?"

"Pretty good. Still warm. Not so tired."

He tapped her hand lightly. "Do you need anything? Water? Food? A cup of tea, maybe?"

"No, that's okay. You stay. I'll get it," she said, noticing he was drained.

Not about to let her do that, Burton gently stopped her from getting up. "No," he insisted, a groan escaping as he stretched his arms straight out in front of his body. "What will it be?"

Abi squinted. "I should probably have a cup of tea."

"The doctor said plenty of warm fluids." Pushing himself to his feet, he added, "Coming right up." On the way to the kitchen, he tugged at the neck of his hoodie, realizing he was still wearing his Dark Demon gear. With a quick motion, he pulled it over his head and tossed it onto the couch.

The shift in Abi's expression was immediate. She went pale, her eyes wide as they locked on the holster strapped to his side.

"What is it?" he asked, noticing her reaction.

She pointed at him. "Why are you wearing a gun?"

Burton froze as his eyes locked onto the weapon still strapped beneath his arm. He'd meant to stow it away before she woke up. "Abi..." he began, his voice low and measured, as if speaking too loudly might make it worse.

Her response wavering, it didn't stop her from challenging him. "Tell me."

He shook his head, forcing a small, calm smile as he stood. Sidestepping their conversation, he walked toward the kitchen to get that cup of tea.

She wasn't having it. Throwing off the blanket, Abi followed him.

Her soft footsteps on the hardwood made his shoulders tense. "Abs, no," he said firmly, while filling the kettle with water. "Don't ask..."

"Please..." she pushed, beyond insistent. "Were you in danger? Is that why you have it?"

Gripping the handle of the kettle tightly, his knuckles turned white.

"I thought you said we would be okay here - that those people would not travel north."

After a long beat, he let out a sigh, keeping his back to her. "I don't want you worrying about this."

Her voice cracked slightly, the fear creeping in despite her effort to sound steady. "Tell me the truth. Why did you need it?"

The burden of his double life surfaced yet again, making him feel conflicted. "Abs…" He shook his head. "You know I can't—" and looked at her straight on for a long moment, the concern on her face hanging in the air. With a quiet exhale, he reached to remove the loaded holster and placed it on a far table. His fingers lingered for a moment on the cold steel before he walked back to the kitchen, taking a mug from the cupboard and a tea bag from the chest.

Abi stayed still, her arms crossed tightly, her eyes locked on him. "I just…" she mumbled, shaking with a mixture of frustration and terror. "I don't want anything to happen to you…"

Hearing that, he stopped what he was doing but did not turn around. "I promise. I'll be fine. Always am."

Somehow, what he said seemed hollow. She wasn't convinced. The memories of the mob families and the safehouse in Newport Beach, where he'd hidden her away, flooded back in an instant. She felt the same panic creep in as it had that night. Before she could stop herself, tears began to fall.

Upon hearing her sobbing, Burton's heart ached. He crossed the room quickly, opening his arms, as Abi quickly collapsed into them. Tightening their embrace, his hand moved to the back of her head as he held her close.

"Abs, don't cry. Everything is fine. I'm good. You gotta trust me."

She nodded against his chest, but the sobs still came, her body trembling in his arms.

Catching Martin emerging from the lower level, he gave a simple wave of his hand, hoping to veer the man off. Thankfully, the guy got the hint and quietly retreated downstairs to give them a moment alone.

As she calmed down, Burton gently pulled back to look into her eyes, wiping away the tear stains on her cheeks. His voice softened. "So… think you're still up for the rave event tonight? I have a backstage pass with your name on it."

"Really?" Abi brightened as her interest piqued. "I can still go?"

"If you feel you're up to it." Grateful for the change in her expression, he answered, "You'll be surrounded by Martin and the guys. They'll keep an eye on you while I'm on stage."

Her smile faltered slightly. "But is it safe for me to be there? I mean…"

He didn't flinch. "Yes," he said firmly. "You'll be fine. I promise."

She studied him for a moment longer, then gave a small nod. "I'm excited."

It made her smile. "I really wanted to go and see you perform."

He didn't mention that he couldn't risk her being anywhere else. Not tonight. If something went wrong, they couldn't be separated. "Afterward, we'll head back to the States early, maybe make a stop in Tahoe before continuing home. How does that sound?"

Her eyes lit up before a dimness surfaced.

He knew what she was thinking. "From what I hear, Shane went home."

Releasing a long-winded sigh, she nodded, acceptance creeping in. Not wanting to dredge it up, she quickly changed the subject. "Will it be snowy in Tahoe?'

"Yes, I'm pretty sure it will be the same as what we have here."

When he handed her the hot tea, she took it. Instantly, all her worries were momentarily forgotten.

Somehow, Burton had managed to pull her away from the darker thoughts, if only for a second. And now, all he wanted was to focus on sharing the peaceful morning alone with her.

| 38 |

Risk

Friday, December 29

Seasons Niseko

That afternoon, while Abi slept, Burton and Martin sat at the dining table, papers and laptops spread out in front of them. Their voices were low, but the urgency in their conversation was unmistakable.

Abi remained wrapped in a blanket, her body still heavy with exhaustion as her ears caught fragments of their discussion.

"You should never have told her she could attend. You know the rules," Martin said firmly.

Her eyes opened, but she didn't move a muscle.

Burton knew Martin was right, but at the time, he couldn't help himself. His protective instincts always steered his heart when it came to Abi. "Look, I still think it's best if she stays with me regardless, especially given what happened. That was another warning shot, and you know it."

"But at this point, with the intel we got, we don't know what we're walking into tonight. There is a chance that things might not go as smoothly as planned."

The DJ's brow furrowed as he met the man's gaze, his fingers drumming the table. "Then, we will deal with it when the time comes."

Putting down his pen with his elbow resting on the armrest, Martin propped up his head with his hand. "This could be a huge risk."

"If I see any sign that things are going sideways, I'll send her to safety with Andrew, Ted, and Matt, then we'll follow." He could see Martin's brain smoldering as it moved a mile a minute, analyzing every possible scenario. "If she's with us, we can control the environment."

"Fine," Martin agreed, sitting up straight as a pin. "The guys will flank her backstage, and the others must be with the SUV waiting in the wings. But if I call it, she goes. You have no say in the matter. Understood?"

There was a pause, the kind that made Abi feel like they were checking to see if she was listening. Keeping her breathing slow and quiet, she buried herself in the blanket.

Under his breath, Burton muttered, "Agreed. Tonight, we get what we need, and afterward, we cut this trip short and get out of here."

Chest tightening upon hearing the sketchy details, she wondered what kind of event they were walking into. Was it different from the others, or was this the norm? Stirring more noticeably, she shifted positions on the couch as if just waking up. In seconds, she heard Burton walking over.

When he approached, he glanced down to see if she was awake. "Hey… Doing okay here?" he asked quietly, moving closer.

"I'm fine," she mumbled, pulling the blanket tighter around herself.

"If you'd rather stay and rest tonight, no one would blame you."

She shook her head. "No, I'll be fine. Besides, I don't want to miss it."

From across the room, Martin intervened, "You need to obey the doctor's orders, Miss. We can't have you pushing yourself and disrupting your recovery."

Letting out a huff, Abi hoped to set their minds at ease. "Guys, please. I'm fine. I promise. I'm still a bit sore and tired. That's all." She got comfortable. "Now, go back to what you were doing. I'm gonna go back to sleep."

Unbeknownst to them, while the two continued to work, Abi listened to everything discussed until the chef and Anton announced that dinner was ready. Pretending to have heard him, she rustled around and stretched before going to join everyone gathered around the table.

Oddly muted, the guys limited their interaction over dinner. It made Abi wonder if they knew something she didn't. She took note of Martin making lighthearted attempts to spark conversation as Burton fueled for the event, but nobody took the bait. Thoughts dulling her appetite, unsure what tonight would bring, she ate a small amount of food before looking at the time on her phone and pushing back her chair.

"I'm just going to shower and get dressed," she said. "I'll see you in a bit."

"Take your time," Burton replied. "If you need anything, just yell."

She gave him a thumbs up before heading toward her room, her steps still a little slow. As she was closing the door, she heard Martin's voice.

"You've got to be on high alert tonight, my boy. Don't get caught up in the showboating. We've got a job to do."

Closing it behind her, leaning her back against it, she took a deep breath before making her way into the bathroom and turning on the shower. Exhaling, she hoped the warmth would calm the storm raging in her mind. But it didn't. Images of Burton's Vegas appearance flickered in the way he'd commanded the stage, the crowd alive with his every move. Would tonight carry that same electric energy? Her instincts said something was looming.

Running her fingers through her hair, her chest tightened as her thoughts shifted to Shane. A messy tangle of guilt, anger, and frustration bubbled up. He'd been her rock through some pretty rough days, always supportive, always there. But Sara's bombshell last night had shattered all of that, leaving an ache she couldn't ignore. Before he left, she could see it in Shane's eyes: he no longer believed in their future. He no longer trusted her.

Abi groaned, pressing her palms against her face as the water cascaded over her. "Just a disaster…" She didn't know how to deal with any of it—her relationship with Shane, the feud with Sara, and why her heart kept gravitating to B when her mind wandered.

Trembling with uncertainty, she whispered, "What am I even doing?"

Burton had saved her life again, and now she couldn't deny the feelings surfacing. Another ache twisted painfully in her chest. She hated herself for hurting Shane, for not being the person he needed her to be. Knowing he'd already gone home made her feel even worse. "Maybe it's for the best," she muttered, though the words felt meaningless.

Turning off the faucet and wrapping herself in a towel, she stood before the mirror, staring at her reflection. Disappointment stared back, her choices evident in her tired eyes. When she first arrived in Los Angeles, all she wanted was to blend in, to disappear into the background. Never in her wildest dreams did she think she'd end up here, standing in the ruins of everything she'd built.

Miraculously, amidst the blur of a million thoughts over the next hour, she emerged with her hair curled in soft waves with natural makeup upon her face. Joining the guys in the foyer, she ascended the stairs.

"Wow," Burton said upon seeing her, unable to believe she'd endured such a traumatic ordeal just days ago. "You look great."

"Thank you," she replied with a small smile, slipping on her white coat with a fur collar and wrapping a gray scarf snugly around her neck. Grabbing her hat and mittens from Burton, he smiled while pulling on his parka, his Dark Demon hoodie still visible underneath. Slinging his satchel over one shoulder, laptops tucked safely inside, he turned to everyone standing around and said, "Well, let's get this show on the road."

About to leave, Martin stealthily pulled one of the maids aside and whispered instructions before following the group to the vehicles.

Abi took notice but couldn't hear what was said while approaching the line of sleek BlackLane SUVs and the Bentley idling in the drive-way.

Settling into the bucket seat, she watched curiously as Burton and Martin loaded an impressive amount of gear into the back of the third truck. She had never seen them prepare for an event like this.

Before she knew it, by eight-thirty, they'd piled into the vehicles and were finally en route to the venue.

| 39 |

NIGHTFALL

Friday, December 29 ~ 9:00 pm JST

Andaru Resort, Niseko

Darkness stretched all around while Abi focused forward at the head-lights, carving a path through the night. It wasn't long before they drove through the stone gates of the Andaru Resort, the inflatable dome alive, its lights pulsing in sync with the music. Countless VIPs were arriving in luxury coaches and exotic SUVs, greeted by valets who ushered them along the red carpet and through the crystallized turnstile glass doors.

Their vehicles bypassed the main entrance and headed toward a private one that led backstage, where the team could unload.

"Nervous?" Abi glanced at Burton.

He shook his head with a grin. "No. Why? Do I look it?"

She smirked. "Somehow, you never do."

Andrew knocked on the window, signaling it was time.

"Okay, let's go," he said as the door opened.

Flipping his hood up, Burton stepped out, and Abi followed, tuck-ing herself beneath her white fur-lined hood. She stayed close to Martin and Andrew, feeling the steady presence of the others as they surrounded their boss like a protective shield.

When they got inside, Red Dragon was on stage with his wife, Lelin, standing nearby, music pulsating through their bodies.

Abi's eyes landed on her, and a flicker of surprise crossed her face when she noticed the woman's hands resting on a subtle baby bump. *How did I miss that?* she thought, realizing Lelin must have concealed it beneath her red ball gown at the Osaka event. It made her question whether the woman was capable of anything corrupt. Recalling the Tokuryū's Red Dragon tattooed followers and their recruiting games, Abi hoped all of that wouldn't resurface tonight. Seeing Lelin smiling and cheering on her husband, for a brief moment, the couple looked disarmingly normal, a sharp contrast to the chaos and controversy surrounding them.

Face obscured in the shadows of his hood, Burton leaned in close, shouting above the music, "Stick with Martin and the guys! Don't leave their side! Understood?"

She gave him a thumbs-up while Martin and Andrew did the same, their watchful eyes scanning the room.

As Red Dragon's set came to an end, the crowd erupted in cheers. The energy shifted as Burton's lead-up music took over, his distinct vibe rippling through the air. Instantly, the crowd shouted, their excitement building.

One of Burton's tech guys grabbed his laptops from him before darting on the stage to install his setup. The anticipation in the air was electric, the crowd buzzing with restless energy as they waited for the show to begin. When the lights dimmed, the atmosphere shifted. Burton, now fully embracing his Dark Demon persona, winked at Abi, a flicker of his true self shining through. His transformation complete, he reached for her hand as she took hold. Squeezing it, he let go and climbed the stairs.

The bass hit like a heartbeat, sending vibrations through the floor and into Abi's chest. With it, the holographic display came to life, weaving intricate patterns of neon colors across the massive dome.

Light exploded outward in a kaleidoscope of shapes—spinning galaxies, shimmering waterfalls, and fragments of digital art that morphed into pulsating fractals. The crowd collectively gasped, their awe intense, as if they'd gotten transported to another dimension.

Phones shot up like a forest of white screens, capturing every dazzling second. Some people screamed, while others stood still in stunned silence, mouths open in amazement. The music built, layer by layer, the beats growing faster and more complex.

Burton stepped behind the deck, the crowd erupting in a roar of cheers and applause. With his silhouette, towering against the radiant backdrop, the music intro morphed into his next beat. Hands commanding the controls like a maestro guiding an orchestra, each movement—adjusting sliders, twisting dials—seemed effortless, as if he were one with the music.

Overhead, lasers cut through the air in synchronized bursts, their sharp beams slicing through thick clouds of smoke pumped out by hidden machines. The haze created a dreamlike effect, making the lasers shimmer over the audience.

Amidst it all, Martin donned a headset behind the line of techies, ready to unleash the vault. Suddenly, the clock appeared on the big screen to their right. The countdown had begun.

Peeking over his shoulder at his screens, she watched them single-handedly manage the Nightfall App transactions and monitor the crypto exchanges with ease.

Out of nowhere, the dome's ceiling displayed an otherworldly projection: a dark, stormy sky filled with crackling lightning and constellations swirling beyond the clouds, all moving in time with the music. The air itself seemed charged, every beat resonating in the bones of everyone present.

Dark Demon's music was hypnotic, pulling the crowd into his rhythm. Heavy bass drops sent shockwaves rippling through the place while intricate melodies wove through the layers of sound, giving the performance an almost ghostly quality. Each note seemed to sync perfectly with the visuals—every crescendo marked by a burst of light, every drop accompanied by a shattering effect that made the holograms appear to explode into a thousand pieces before reforming into something even more spectacular.

Peeking in on the crowd, Abi saw a sea of moving bodies lost in the music. That is when she spotted it - strangers dancing together as if they'd known each other forever, their hands raised high, faces lit with euphoria. Others were mesmerized, staring up at the projections like they were watching a celestial event. The collective energy was overwhelming, a tidal wave of sound, light, and emotion.

From where she was beside Martin and Andrew, Abi felt like a privileged observer, witnessing Dark Demon's performance. He wasn't just commanding the room. He had drawn every person into his world. But, here and there, she saw people who didn't fit in with the ravers. With stern expressions, she knew they weren't there for the music and the dancing. These were the crypto users. Some stood out, while others hid in the shadows, lurking along the edges of the dome.

Partway through the first set, he raised a hand in her direction. It felt intimate despite the sea of people. Abi couldn't help but smile, pride swelling as she watched him own the moment. He was unstoppable, a force of nature that the crowd couldn't get enough of.

The music shifted again, darker and grittier, the bass pounding so hard it felt like the ground might crack open. As the holograms changed, morphing into dragons that raced across the dome, their fiery trails lingered in mid-air. Gasps rippled through the audience as the creatures seemed almost alive.

Unable to remember the last time she'd seen something so extraordinary - the energy, the lights, the music—it was all-consuming. For a moment, she let herself get lost in it, the worries of the past days melting away as she got swept up into the fantasy rave.

The strobe lights pulsed as the crowd embraced the beat. In an instant, she saw it. A red dragon tattoo centered amongst a group of guys with silvery hair and perfect complexions.

Focusing in, she muttered, "Wait... Are those the teens from the Consulate?" About to warn Martin, another familiar figure moved toward her with urgency. Before she could process it all, the men parted, allowing him through.

"What are you doing here? I thought you went with Jade and Reg!"

Shane leaned in and shouted near her ear, "I couldn't leave! Not like that!"

"How did you find us?" she shouted, straining to hear over the noise.

He held up his phone. "Andrew gave me the coordinates!"

Knowing the quarterback's unexpected arrival was far from convenient, she tried not to look irritated.

"I needed to see you!" he shouted close to her ear. "Can we go somewhere and talk?" Wanting to pull her away for a minute, her eyes remained locked on the sinister figure behind Shane.

Raising a hand to stop him, she shouted, "One second!" Turning away, she grabbed Martin's arm, drawing his attention.

The gentleman looked down at her and slipped off one side of his noise-canceling headphones, his brow furrowing as she pointed to the nape of her neck and then gestured toward the man in the crowd, but he was no longer there.

"Where did he go?" she shouted. "He was there a second ago!"

"Who, Miss?"

"Red dragon tattoo!"

"Where?" Understanding her warning, Martin nodded and moved quickly, alerting the team. In unison, the men sprang into action, their movements precise and practiced.

The bassline pounded so hard it rattled the floor, lights slicing through the haze of sweat and smoke. Bodies surged in rhythm, hands thrown up, a thousand voices blending with the music's pulse—until a blinding white flash tore through the strobes.

A single, deafening BOOM cracked the night open.

Ground buckling, a violent pop from the speakers, sent people's hands flying to cover their ears. Heat and pressure slammed outward, flinging cups and glass everywhere as the music died.

Darkness engulfed the dome.

"Abs!" Shane shouted, unable to see her. "Where are you?"

The canopy above rippled, then sagged like a punctured lung. Its vast surface began to collapse in slow motion, a suffocating wave of heavy tarp and steel cables descending over the crowd.

Someone shouted, "Get down!" but no one listened. The air filled with chaos—metal screeching, people shoving, crying, stumbling over one another in the dark.

Smoke billowed from the far stage, stinging eyes and burning throats. Red emergency lights flickered to life, painting everything in a hellish glow. The smell of burned circuitry and melted plastic clung to every breath. Clusters of revelers surged toward the exits, but the path was jammed. Someone fell. Another screamed.

Through the haze, a figure cut forward with calm precision.

Burton.

His silhouette was unmistakable—shoulders squared, jaw set, with three laptops clutched tight against his chest. Two of his men flanked him, pushing through the panicked mass, lighting a path through the chaos.

As sparks rained down from a collapsing light rig, his gaze locked on Coppersmith across the wreckage. Eyes narrowing, tension flaring, he turned sharply and found Abi frozen for half a heartbeat beneath the sagging dome, the flashing red light reflected off the fear in her eyes.

"Let's go!" Burton's voice cut through the noise. "This way!"

She didn't hesitate. Abi's hand shot out and found his as he pulled her close, shielding her as another explosion rippled from outside.

Following the men, unable to see, she turned around. "Shane?"

"I'm right here!" he yelled, staying close to her.

Hitting the crash bar with his shoulder, Lorenzo led the group through the emergency exit. The bitter night air hit them heavily while the sounds of distant sirens and the crowd wailing inside added to the terrifying scene unfolding.

The SUVs were waiting, engines revving, but as they reached them, Lorenzo shouted while taking a head count. "Wait! Where's Martin?"

A sickening pause followed. Scanning the area, it became clear—he was nowhere to be seen. He hadn't made it out.

Seeing Red Dragon and Lelin huddled by an SUV blocked in by the fallen support post, Lorenzo guided them over to Burton. "Stay together! I'll go back for him! Don't move!"

In seconds, he disappeared into the smoke. Amidst it all, a sleek luxury Sprinter pulled up.

"Get in!" Sara shouted from behind the wheel. "I'll get you out of here!"

Not thinking twice, DJ Red Dragon and Lelin quickly climbed into the passenger seats when the door slid open. Seeing Burton, Akio waved them over. "Come on! Hurry!" he shouted.

Without hesitation, shielding Abi, Burton pushed forward with Shane right behind them as they piled into the van. When the doors slammed shut, the vehicle peeled away, navigating a rural road to escape the mayhem.

Inside, the tension was suffocating.

Burton checked on her. "Are you hurt?"

"No, I'm okay," Abi replied, visibly shaken.

When she answered him, Shane interjected, his frustration boiling over. "Who did this? Were you the target?"

His mind racing for an explanation, Red Dragon spoke. "Someone sabotaged us, man," he said grimly to Burton. "I've never had anything like that happen before." Holding his wife tightly, face etched with concern, he asked, "Are you good? How's the baby?"

Terrified, Lelin nodded. "We're fine," she whispered, though her hands trembled as they rested on her bump.

Speeding along, the road narrowing quickly, the engine hummed as Abi leaned back, her chest heaving as she tried to process what had just happened. But her thoughts swirled back to Martin. He was still there, somewhere in that collapsing dome, and they had no idea if he was safe. Worse still, there was no security with them—it was just Sara. It felt like they were alone and vulnerable, with danger lurking in the darkness.

"Red Dragons were in the audience," she whispered in Burton's ear, low and shaky.

Overhearing, Lelin turned her head sharply.

Something in her expression stole the air from Abi's lungs. The doubt she'd been trying to suppress came roaring back. Was Lelin involved in this somehow? Abi swallowed hard, unsure of what to think.

The van jolted slightly as the road grew uneven. Up ahead, a single light loomed amongst the dark forest, second only to the moon lofting high above them.

Burton, ever watchful, leaned forward and demanded, "Sara! Where are we going?"

The girl silently glanced in the rearview mirror, now pale and withdrawn. Her mouth opened as if to answer, but before she could speak, a shadow shifted in the passenger seat.

Abi's pulse spiked as a man swung around, his face partially obscured by the dim light. The unmistakable glint of a barrel flashed as he swiveled, aiming the weapon directly at Sara.

"Keep driving," he growled, cold and commanding.

Immediately, DJ Red Dragon shielded Lelin and sat between her and the man. At the same time, Burton instinctively did the same with Abi, his arm bracing her against his body, his presence acting as a barrier.

"What do you want!" Burton barked despite the threat.

The gun shifted slightly, pointing toward them. Tossing a cloth bag their way, he shouted, "Phones! Pass 'em up!" When no one moved, his patience snapped. "Now!"

Heart pounding, Abi clutched her phone, holding the only pictures she had left of her Mother. Her fingers felt like they were made of lead as she finally handed it over, her breath expelling as it disappeared into the bag.

Shane, however, was already one step ahead. He'd sneakily slid his into his sock when the guy wasn't looking and tugged his pant leg down over his boot before raising his hands in mock surrender. When the guy spoke to them, he searched his pockets and lied smoothly, "I must have lost it at the rave. It's not here."

The man said nothing.

When Red Dragon passed the bag back to the guy, Abi noticed Burton's hand twitching subtly toward his concealed carry. Her stomach knotted. With Lelin there, he had no way to act without putting her in danger. He must have realized that because his hand stilled before retreating slowly as he waited for a better opportunity.

"Turn here!" the man yelled, making Sara brake and yank the wheel to veer onto a deserted road. Tight and dark, branches hitting the windows on the way past, there wasn't a car in sight.

"Where are you taking us?" Burton shouted again.

The man twisted in his seat, his focus flickering between Sara and the rest of them, his grip tightening on the weapon. "You'll see soon enough."

| 40 |

Taken

Friday, December 29

Undisclosed Location

A faint light flickered through the trees, barely cutting through the heavy darkness. As the SUV crept closer, a warehouse loomed into view, its metal frame jagged against the night sky. It looked abandoned, but the eerie presence of movement around it told a different story.

Hitting a dead end, they stopped with a jolt.

"Get out!" he ruthlessly shouted at Sara, gun pointed at her. "Don't try anything stupid, or I'll kill you!"

When she opened the door, another man yanked hold of her and dragged her around the vehicle with his gun pressed hard against her temple. Her shaky breaths broke the quiet as she stumbled, fear written all over her face as she cowered.

"Move!" the man barked, harsh enough to make everyone freeze. "Hands where I can see them!"

DJ Red Dragon helped his wife, his hands trembling as he whispered something in her ear and shielded her with his body. "Stay behind me," he said.

About to follow, Shane turned to Burton. "There's gotta be thirty guys out there. Maybe more," he paused. "What's the plan? Whatever you wanna do, I'm in."

Surveying the scene, realizing they were far outnumbered, Burton weighed their options. "We don't have a choice. They'll target Abi if we try anything. Do what they say so no one gets hurt. Got it?"

Nine armed men closed in like a pack of wolves, rifles raised, barking orders. "Hands on your head!"

A man with facial tattoos bellowed, "Take these two back to town!"

Corralling Akio and Lelin toward a waiting truck, Burton realized what the guy had done.

When he moved past him, Akio whispered, "I'm sorry, man. They were gonna kill my wife and kid if I didn't do what they said."

Not saying a word, he watched the two go scot-free.

Roughly shoved forward, the sharp bite of zip ties snapped around their wrists, cutting into their skin.

"Oh, my god..." Abi's voice carried an edge of fear as familiar faces surfaced amongst the gathered men, each bearing red dragon tattoos on the napes of their necks.

"Abs." Assessing the danger, Burton said, "Stay close."

Taken into the warehouse through the large garage door, the air was damp and cold. Just the faint hum of a generator vibrated under their feet.

Without warning, Sara got dragged through a side door, the barrel of the gun still digging into her head as the door slammed shut.

Burton feared for what they'd do to her.

From the shadows, a slow clap broke the silence, followed by a haunting voice dripping with mockery. "So this is him. The famous Burton Lancaster. Or should I say... *Dark Demon.*"

A figure stepped into the dim light, handsome but weathered. The scar along his hairline was hard to miss. He sized Burton up as if he were challenging him to a fight.

"What do you want?" Burton didn't flinch.

The man smirked, his eyes narrowing. "Straight to the point. I respect that. But let's get one thing clear." A snarl darkened his face. "You're not calling the shots here. I am!" he belted.

With a nod, one of the guards grabbed Burton and dragged him forward. Abi attempted to follow, but Burton flashed a look that said, *Don't move.*

Frozen in place, Shane tried to step closer to her but was forcefully shoved back.

The villainous man in charge growled, "So, let's see what the great Dark Demon is really made of. Shall we?"

Two men hit Burton behind the legs with a steel pipe, pummeling him to the floor.

"Stop!!" Abi's screams echoed through the building. "Don't hurt him!"

"Abi, no." On his knees, Burton could barely get the words out while straightening his posture defiantly.

The man released a low, menacing chuckle. "Impressive. You said she was feisty, and he was courageous. You were spot on, my dear." His sight drifted past Burton and fixed on a figure emerging from the shadows. "Right on cue."

A voice, smooth as glass and just as cold, sliced through the air. "Of course, I was right."

The words landed with the weight of betrayal hanging heavy.

Abi's breath caught. Her lips parted, barely able to form the name. "Sara..."

"Oh, shit." The color drained from Shane as reality hit.

Out of the darkness, she stepped forward—blonde hair gleaming under the flickering overhead light, a black pantsuit hugging her frame like armor, crimson-soled stiletto boots poised, predatory, icy, and exquisite.

Sara's eyes met Burton's. Her smirk was like a blade wrapped in silk. "Miss me?" she said before joining the man and facing her ex. "Burton. I don't believe the two of you have met. This is Pavel Korolev..." She paused. "My Father."

Handed a gun, the man racked the slide. Way too comfortable, he pointed it at Burton's head.

With arms crossed over her chest, Sara looked to her right and nodded. "All this time, you've been played," she smirked. "Men are so gullible when it comes to love. So easily manipulated. Aren't they?"

Burton didn't flinch.

A devious chuckle escaped her lips. "Oh, I almost forgot! How did you like my recruiting games? Did you like how my minions terrorized your little friends? Watching on the cameras was entertaining, to say the least."

Peering past Burton, the woman zeroed in on Abi. With a nod and a wave of her hand, two men suddenly grabbed hold of the girl and dragged her forward.

She stumbled but didn't fall.

A surge of rage coursed through Burton as four armed guards pushed down on his shoulders to keep him from standing. "Don't touch her!" He fought against them with every ounce of strength he had, eyes fixed on Abi.

"She invaded our relationship again and again," she hissed to Burton, low and vicious. "You should've known it would come to this. I sent warnings. Signs. I even resorted to black magic and had a local witch take a doll and put a curse on the girl. But you still chose *her* over me every time. That is why my Dragons caused the avalanche."

The news of that sent shockwaves through the place.

"See, where we come from, we don't just dispose of our enemies. We ruin them. We punish the ones they love. It is the old way. The only way," she added grimly.

"What do you want? Money?" Burton yelled. "Just name your price!"

Joining his daughter, Pavel's smirk twisted into something grotesque. "Oh, Mr. Lancaster," he hissed, "I want far more than *that*. Stripping you of every last shred of what you own might begin to balance the scales. Because of you, my brother and nephew are dead.

Their blood is on *your* hands. You thought avenging your parents would cripple us. But every attempt you made was futile."

"Once we bleed your accounts dry, take back the mine, and seize every property deed you thought was safe, our empire will eclipse even my uncle's legacy." Heels clicking like a death toll on stone, Sara added cunningly, "But the real prize is the vault. The heartbeat of your little operation." She stepped closer. "And once we have that…nothing will stop us from becoming the most powerful family in the world." Her eyes flicked toward her Father, almost looking for validation. "Isn't that right, Daddy?"

Growing impatient, he angrily said, "Get on with it!"

Eyes gleaming with something ancient and cruel, Sara focused on Abi, bound and terrified. Approaching her, she laughed in an evil tone, the sound of it more chilling than any scream. "Ready to witness the closing ceremonies of my recruiting games?" Her breath crossed Abi's cheek eerily. "Congratulations," she whispered, slow and venomous, lips faintly touching her ear. "You are the grand finale." Eyes on her tattooed Dragons, she said, "Where's Raff?"

From the shadows, a tall, lean figure emerged: Cold-eyed. Merciless. His presence silenced the room.

"Meet my front-runner." She reached into her coat and pulled out a plaque engraved with crimson characters.

Handed it, Raff stepped forward to accept it before slipping the cord around Abi's neck almost ceremoniously. It hung against her chest like a noose.

Burton's heart pounded so hard he thought his ribs would crack.

"Raff completed every task ruthlessly and without question," Sara addressed the others like a viper preparing to strike. "Now, he has one last task to perform to become your Red Dragon leader and prove his loyalty to us." Shifting from him, she pointed to Abi. "Death to her."

Anger boiling over, Shane shouted, "No!" and tried to break free of the men holding him, but suffered a blunt hit to the head.

When Raff pulled his gun from behind his back, four Dragons dragged a hostage through the back doors. Barely recognizable through the blood and bruises, the man was dropped to the floor, gagged, and bound.

"Lorenzo…" Shane mumbled in a daze, a heavy boot pressing on his spine.

"Welcome, my friend! Glad you could join us!" she addressed her former colleague before turning to Burton. "It seems your valiant right-hand man has failed you," Sara said sharply. "Now, he can witness your demise before his own. But first…" She moved her attention back to Abi.

Raff released the safety on the gun, cold and calculated beneath the flicker of warehouse lights.

Sara and Pavel stepped back, their shadows retreating into the dim edges of the concrete floor, leaving Abi standing alone at the center—isolated and exposed.

Legs trembling beneath her, she tried to lock her knees to steady herself as she watched the barrel slowly point at her. Breaths taken in shallow bursts, ragged and quick, her chest rose, but her lungs couldn't hold enough air. Instinctively hoping to shield herself, to *do something*—she knew there was no way out despite her mind screaming *run, fight, hide*—but her body stayed frozen.

Then, through the haze of terror, she locked on Burton like he was the last light in a collapsing world. His face, twisted in desperation, was the only thing tethering her to the moment. To *life*.

"Haven't you forgotten something?" Burton's voice thundered through the space as the gun in Raff's hand lowered slightly.

Both Pavel's and Sara's attention darted in his direction.

"If you kill her, you'll get *nothing*. No money. No fortune. No vault."

Sara blinked.

"You think I didn't anticipate this?" he snapped, shaking with fury. "I knew you'd betray me!" Drawing Sara's attention away from Abi, he taunted the woman, knowing what would set her off. "I don't just own the vault. I *built* the system that harbors the world's most dangerous secrets. Do you really think I'd leave it unguarded?"

Instantly, when Burton fired back, Pavel converged angrily. With a snarl, he swung the pistol and cracked it against Burton's skull. The impact of metal on bone hit like thunder.

"No!!" Abi's screams ripped through the air as Burton staggered, blood splashing the concrete.

He rose slowly, drips of red trailing down his jaw, eyes locked on them in defiance. "The only way you'll get anything from me," he growled while recovering from the blow, "Is if you let *them* go. I've installed failsafes. If they aren't freed, the vault locks down, and everything disappears."

A silence fell like a shroud. Even the guards tensed.

"You're bluffing." A bitter laugh escaped the woman's lips.

"You, of all people, know I always have a plan B." His tone dropped to a dangerous calm like a blade sliding free of its sheath. "Abi is phase one of the biometric key sequence to this protocol. Coppersmith and Lorenzo are phases three and four."

"I take it Martin is second in line?"

He nodded. "If they die, you lose, and I win."

The room stilled.

Not flinching, he added, "You want the one-point-nine-billion? Release them. They need to return to the States and will be instructed on what to do from there. If you attempt to override or hack my systems without these safeguards disengaged, every backup system triggers a cascading effect. You lose access to the vault. The assets. The encrypted servers. All of it!" He stared straight into Sara's eyes.

Her expression curdled. "Or we can kill you one by one right now and end this."

"And lose the money? The power? What's the fun in that? That's not revenge. It's conceding." He stared her down. "If you want my fortune, let all of them go free." His eyes bored into hers. "Give me proof of life when they land in the States safely at a government facility, and I will make sure you get what you want—then you can kill me."

Hearing him say that, Abi felt her legs buckle, and she collapsed to the floor, sobs wracking her body.

"I suppose knowing she'll *live* this nightmare—*day after day*—is far more satisfying than ending her quickly." Jealousy surfaced as the woman's venom curled around every syllable. Her arms folded like a judge about to deliver a death sentence, then, with a smirk of cruel indulgence, she flicked her wrist. "Fine," she hissed. "Take them."

The order dropped like a guillotine. In a flash, the men with the crimson dragon tattoos surged forward. Black-gloved hands seized Abi, Shane, and Lorenzo. Guns clicked. Aimed. Deadly.

Dragged along, Abi tried to regain her footing. Reality hit her like a gut punch - Burton had traded his life for theirs.

The warehouse's silence was shattered by the rattle of chains and barked commands. At gunpoint, the captives staggered, the cold steel of the barrels pressing into their backs.

Abi's eyes locked onto Burton's through the chaos. She didn't blink. Didn't breathe. Her pulse thundered like a war drum in her ears. "No," she breathed—then *ran*. A scream tore from her throat as she yanked against the guard's grip, wrists bound, legs burning. Her body slammed forward with every ounce of adrenaline she had left. "Burton!" she cried, colliding into his chest. His body sagged against her, blood dripping from a cut along his temple, one eye nearly swollen shut.

Knowing time was of the essence, he rasped urgently. "Find Martin..."

Abi clung to him, her fingers twitching against the ties still biting into her wrists.

"Tell him..." He winced, breath ragged. "*LOCKSTEP*. Repeat it."

She shook her head, heart splintering. "Lockstep," she whispered, the word searing across her tongue.

The ground shook.

Boots thundered against the warehouse floor like an oncoming storm.

"Enough of this!" Pavel's voice thundered.

In slow motion, Abi heard them converging, and in that single heartbeat, Burton looked into her eyes, the depths of him laid bare.

"I love you," he whispered in her ear. Soft. Final.

Those three little words struck like stabs to the heart just as hands ripped her from him.

"No!" she screamed, kicking, thrashing, teeth bared like a wild animal. "Burton!!!"

The guards wrenched her backward. One nudged her shoulder with the butt of a rifle, sending her stumbling. Still, she fought, eyes not leaving his.

Forced to his feet, Shane stood, ready to fight, his face filled with anger. When she got close, she collapsed against him, her screams breaking into gasps and sobs.

"Coppersmith!" Burton shouted, unable to fight off the men holding him. "Get her out of here! KEEP HER SAFE!" His voice echoed like gunfire through the warehouse before Raff shoved his head down and delivered another brutal blow.

Shattered, Abi saw him fall lifeless. "Nooo*!!*" Her scream tore through the air, unanswered.

Manning up, protecting her, Shane did what he had to as the men dragged them through the snow toward a white cargo van that blended in with the snowbanks. The freezing wind ripped past.

Forced inside with Lorenzo, it was pitch black. No windows. No sound but their shallow breaths as the engine kicked to life.

A fit of anger overcame her, causing Abi to slam her feet against the metal walls repeatedly. "No! No! We can't leave him!"

When the van jerked forward, she fell back hard.

Unable to snap the thick restraints, Shane caught her awkwardly and quickly encircled her tight enough to contain her grief above all else. "I got you," he whispered, trembling himself as Lorenzo tried to sit up.

Noticeably having sustained a head injury, the two saw him fall to the floor again.

"Lorenzo..." She bent down next to his shoulder.

Mustering a reply, he whispered, "I'm good, Miss."

Sobs wracked her body. "They're gonna kill him..." Hopelessness overtook her as tears flowed. "Tell me what to do."

Mustering the strength, Lorenzo sat up. His face was bludgeoned. "We need to find Martin, and fast. It's his only hope in hell."

| **41** |

Released

Saturday, December 30 ~ 2:00 am JST

Unknown Location

Tires crackling on the icy road, the van skidded as it made an abrupt left turn. Continuing only a short distance, they felt them slow down and suddenly screech to a stop. Abi barely had time to register the silence before the back doors wrenched open. The two watched in horror as a man climbed in, grabbed Lorenzo by the collar, and yanked him out.

"No—wait!" Abi screamed. "What's happening?"

Shane moved fast, positioning himself in front of her like a shield. But nobody touched her.

In seconds, the doors slammed shut again, and the van peeled off.

Abi broke into sobs. "What did they do to him?"

Witnessing the grim scene, Shane didn't turn around. "There was no shot. They probably just dumped him."

Her body trembled. Every worst-case scenario flooded her mind. Were they next?

Their shoulders brushed in the darkness as Shane shifted closer. "Focus on my voice," he said gently. "I swear I'll keep you safe, Abs."

But they felt the van slowing down again.

She froze.

Preparing for the worst, once again, the QB got ready to fight. "Get behind me," he said as the brakes hit hard, shoving them against the wall. Not wasting time, he planted himself between her and the doors.

They heard the crunching of snow under heavy boots just before the back flew open.

The guy shouted, "OUT! NOW!"

As the two men lunged forward, one grabbed Shane. He fought, grunted, and tried to twist away, but they dragged him out.

Screams escaped her as she watched the other man approach. Grabbed, her heart slammed into her ribs as she kicked and flailed, but suddenly, her feet hit the ground.

Without warning, the villains backed off, eyes flicking nervously down the road before they got in and drove off.

Tires screaming, Abi and Shane saw the brake lights dim before the white van disappeared into the night.

Left in the darkness, bodies shivering, the cold bit through them.

Fear settled in. "Are you hurt?" she asked Shane as he struggled to his feet, wrists still bound.

"No. You?"

"I'm okay."

Dumped at a random location, not knowing where they were, Shane finally twisted his wrists, snapped the zip ties, and pulled out his phone hidden in his sock.

"Call Martin!" Her mind raced, replaying Burton's instructions over and over. "He said...to tell him... Lockstep. Burton said Lockstep."

Confused, Shane asked, "What does that even mean?" as he searched for Martin's WhatsApp. He could see that the tears on Abi's face had begun to freeze.

When the phone rang, someone answered.

"Martin? Martin!"

Hearing Shane say his name, Abi listened in as he put it on speaker.

"Andrew? Where's Martin?"

Abi interjected, "Is he there? Is he okay?"

"Yeah, we've got him," the security guard stated.

Martin got handed the phone. "Are you alright?" he said in desperation.

"Abs and I are good. They dumped Lorenzo somewhere..." He stopped and couldn't finish the sentence.

"And Master B?"

Shane didn't know what to say.

"They've got him, Martin!" Abi shouted.

"Who?"

"Sara and Korolev's brother," the QB interjected.

"Pavel is her father!" Abi divulged before adding, "We need to save B!"

All business, Martin's tone lowered. "Where are you?"

"I've dropped a pin," Shane stated. "We're near a field, on a sideroad, somewhere."

"Martin! Burton said to tell you, Lockstep!" Abi screamed.

Martin's calm demeanor came through the phone. "Understood," he said briskly before shifting into action. "Hold tight. We're on our way."

Shoving his phone in his pocket to keep it warm and prevent the battery from draining, Shane freed Abi and grabbed hold of her. Tucking her head inside her hood, he zipped her up as her teeth chattered and she shivered.

"We need to keep you warm," he said while holding her tightly and rubbing her arms. He could see, with the light of the moon, the red and white blotches developing on her cheeks.

"Hang on," Shane whispered. "They're coming for us."

The minutes dragged on, seemingly lasting what felt like hours, each second an eternity, as Abi and Shane huddled together against the merciless cold. The wind howled through the skeletal trees, cutting through their clothes. Snow swirled in the air, stinging their faces as if nature itself were conspiring against them.

Shaking uncontrollably in Shane's arms, Abi felt her body going numb. Sobs muffled against his chest. Each one echoed in his ears, a haunting reminder of her fragile state. He tightened his hold on her, his body acting as a shield against the elements, though he could barely feel his own fingers anymore. His toes were frozen, and the frost creeping into his veins made his legs stiff and unresponsive.

As Abi went limp in his arms. The blue tinge on her lips and the vacant glaze creeping into her eyes were all too familiar. He could not forget how she looked in the hospital two days ago. It had taken hours to bring her back, and now, here she was, teetering on the brink once more.

Determined not to lose her, he shrugged out of his jacket despite his seizing muscles, desperate to keep it. The cold immediately bit into his skin, but he ignored it and wrapped the coat around Abi's frail frame, tucking it tightly to trap whatever warmth remained.

"No, Shane," she protested weakly. Her hands reached up to push the jacket off, but she lacked the strength to do so. "You can't..."

He caught her hands gently, his grip firm but careful as he brought them back to her lap. His eyes locked with hers, fierce and unyielding. "You need it more than me," he stated.

Tears welled in her eyes as she shook her head. "But you'll freeze..."

"I'll be fine," he assured her, though the truth was far less certain. He crouched closer, his body curling around hers like a protective co-coon. "Focus on me." Staying positive, he cupped her icy cheeks, his thumbs brushing over her skin.

Abi tried to respond, but her teeth chattered so violently that her words were lost.

When her head lolled against his chest, a fresh wave of panic surged through him as he flipped his hoodie hood over his head. The cold seeped deeper into his bones, but Shane refused to give in. Every instinct screamed at him to fight, to protect her, to endure just long enough for help to come.

As the darkness pressed in, Shane whispered promises into her ear, each a lifeline against the encroaching void. "We're going to make it, Abs. Just hold on. I've got you."

Then, through the darkness, headlights finally appeared over the hill.

Abi's heart raced as the beams drew closer, illuminating the frozen ground. "Who…" Her teeth chattered. "Is…it?"

"I don't know." Shane stayed with her, his body tense and ready for anything.

Two black SUVs came to a halt a few feet away. The second the doors swung open, Martin raced over with a mixture of relief and urgency on his face. His coat flaring in the wind, he barked, "Rob, get the parkas from the back!"

Quickly gathering the coats, Matt amped up the heat in the vehicle.

"Come on. We're getting you out of here." Scooping her up in his arms, Shane rushed past Martin to the truck. Setting her in the seat, he closed the door and put on the coat the man gave him before jumping in on the opposite side.

As they drove away, unable to contain her trembling, Abi asked Martin. "What is…Lockstep?" she gasped, teeth chattering wildly. "What…does it…mean?"

He glanced back at her, his expression flat. "I'm sorry, Miss. That's classified."

Eyes filled with tears, she got her bearings and said, "We must…go back! We need…to find…him! He can't…be far…"

To her surprise, Matt kept driving, and Martin stayed silent.

"What is…going on?" A tinge of panic set in while Shane rubbed her arms to keep her warm.

Staring straight ahead, her legal guardian divulged regretfully, "We've been given orders to leave the country."

"What? No! We…can't! Please!" she pleaded. "How can…you do that…to him?" She took a breath. "No! I'm…begging you! Please… Go…back!" Trying to open the side doors, she realized they were safety-locked. Yanking on the handle repeatedly to no avail, she had a flashback to being kidnapped by Black Lyon as he whisked her away from Reggie's party.

"I'm sorry, Miss. My job now is to get you both to safety, and that is what I intend to do."

"So we…just leave him…to die?" Her face flared with anger.

Shane could see it.

Flailing her fists, targeting the man, Shane held her down. "No, Abs. Don't," he said while restraining her as she cried hysterically.

"He would never…give up…on us! Never! How…can you…do this!" About to explode, she suddenly yelled at the top of her lungs. The shrill of it made Matt cower in his seat slightly as he continued driving into the night.

Doing his best, Shane tried to console her, but she wasn't having it.

"Leave…me…alone!" she shouted. "Don't…touch me!" Body heaving as she sobbed and shivered, Abi recalled his last words. *I love you,* she heard him repeat in her mind and realized, amidst the chaos, she hadn't said it back.

| 42 |

Escape

Saturday, December 30

En Route to Chitose Airport

With no headlights, the caravan sped along the narrow road, hugging the base of Mount Yotei as it loomed ghost-like in the bright moonlight. Just the steady growl of the engine was heard as they pushed through the brutal winter landscape. Snowdrifts bordered the pavement, untouched and gleaming.

Matt's breath fogged the inside of the windshield. His gloved hand wiped it clear. No one spoke. Not even the radios crackled.

Then, a darkened shape crested the hill ahead.

The SUV stopped on a dime.

Staggering towards them, somewhat dazed, Lorenzo paused, unsure who was there. With shoulders hunched, his lips blue, Abi watched Rob run and grab him beneath his arms to help him to the second truck. Soon, he was safe inside.

Quickly getting back on the road, the engines rumbled as the snow swept across the asphalt in thin ribbons. They could feel the force of the crosswinds hitting the truck as they drove further and further from Niseko.

"Will he be waiting for us at the airport?" Abi asked with a glimmer of hope.

Measured and calm, Martin answered, "It's out of our hands now."

Frustration bubbling over, she questioned, "Is that what it means? Lockstep? That he be left behind? Is that it?"

Silence followed her outburst, stretching until she slammed her hand against the seat. "Say something!"

A deep breath preceded Matt's reply. "Sometimes…it's better not to know, Miss."

The crypticness shattered what composure she had left. Tears streamed down her face as she struggled to breathe, her sobs coming in uneven gasps. Feeling arms wrapping around her tightly, holding her as her grief poured out unchecked, Shane did not let go.

With a hint of morning light starting to paint the horizon, they merged off the highway and slipped through the tolling station before bypassing the main terminal. Arriving on the other side, Matt veered left and headed toward the small Chitose FBO building.

Holding out hope, Abi sat up in her seat and leaned left, then right, desperate to see him waiting for them at the plane. But he wasn't there.

Briefly glancing at her, Martin gathered his things and got out of the front seat to meet the pilot.

"Come on, Abs. We gotta go," Shane said upon opening his door.

When she slid over and saw Matt carrying all her bags to the plane, she froze. "Where is it?" Martin! Please tell me you packed…"

Before she could say it, Martin opened his briefcase and handed her the photo album Burton had given her for Christmas. Taking hold of it, pressing it tightly against her chest, she felt forceful hands guide her up the steps, her movements mechanical as though she were a shell. The cabin was warm, a stark contrast to the icy air outside, but it brought little comfort.

Numb, boarding the aircraft in a zombie-like state, Abi found a seat in the back room beside the bed. It wasn't long before she slid the pocket door closed with a loud smack, cutting her off from the rest of the group.

Seeing this, Shane took a seat on the opposite side of the wall and settled in, hearing Abi sobbing. As her chest heaved, he felt her pain along with his own. They had both lost someone today, it seemed. To him, a piece of Abi had died too.

The engines roared as the private jet prepared for departure just before five that morning.

From their seats, the muffled sound of sobbing spread about the cabin. None of them spoke as the sorrow of the past few hours pressed down on everyone.

"I've gotta do something," Shane muttered to Martin under his breath. "Can't I just be with her?"

The man shook his head and rested a hand on his shoulder. "No, it's best to give her space."

Soon, with everyone buckled in their seats, the plane raced down the runway as the lights of Japan disappeared beneath the clouds.

Hour after hour, the flight dragged on. Every so often, the sound of Abi's cries pierced through the barrier separating them, a haunting reminder of what had happened. But no one dared to disturb her.

Feeling for the young woman, Martin stated, "In times like these, some burdens are best carried alone."

| 43 |

Transpacific Flight

Saturday, December 30

Over the Pacific Ocean

The plane cut smoothly through the skies while Martin reclined in his seat, his arms crossed as his attention drifted to Shane, who sat stiffly, earbuds in but clearly not listening to anything. They could no longer hear Abi's muffled sobs and assumed she'd fallen asleep.

Now in the air for two hours, Martin looked across to Shane.

Seeing his eyes on him, the big QB leaned forward and ran a hand over his face. "I knew she loved him," he said quietly, the thought hitting harder than he expected. "I just didn't realize how much until now."

Surprised by his statement, Martin studied him for a moment. "I know you love her, and we are eternally grateful for that, but…"

"You think I didn't see it?" The QB clenched his fists in defeat. "Every look they shared, every moment they figured no one was watching—well, I did. I just… I thought if I loved her enough, it wouldn't matter."

"You were there when she needed someone the most," Martin replied gently.

He sat back, staring at the ceiling. "So, what now?"

"We return to the States and wait for news." Needing to bottom line things, Martin said firmly, "No matter what you hear or read in the coming days, you must not tell anyone what happened. If you do, it will put her at risk."

Without hesitation, Shane nodded in silent agreement.

"Sara will not quit. Unless they've gotten to her and disposed of her already, I feel that evil woman will hunt her down for sport."

"What do you mean, gotten to her - disposed of her?"

"It's not something you need to concern yourself with."

Shane knew what that meant. "What about Abi?"

Her guardian's eyes softened. "She is coming with us. Hopefully, while keeping her safe, her heart will heal in the process. It'll take time, but we'll help her get through this," he paused. "And don't worry. We will have eyes on you for a while. You will be protected until this thing ends."

"How long will that take?"

"Not longer than a month, possibly two."

"And, Burton?"

"I haven't heard and may never hear what happened..."

Missing Abi already, even though she was mere feet away, Shane said, "So, there's no point in fighting for her anymore, is there?"

"I'm sorry, my boy. I truly am."

| 44 |

Home

Friday, December 29 ~ 10 pm PST

Van Nuys, Los Angeles

After crossing the Pacific, the plane cruised over Santa Barbara, heading south to Van Nuys. Slowly beginning its descent, Shane gathered his things. A looming goodbye weighed heavily upon his shoulders.

Needing to check on her, Martin knocked on the door.

"Leave me alone..." is all she said.

"We are landing, dear. Buckle up, please." Martin returned to his seat.

The landing was smooth as they touched down in Los Angeles. When they taxied over to the main hub, the jet soon came to a halt, and the engines cut.

Not seeing anyone packing their things, Shane was confused. "Aren't you disembarking?" he asked.

Martin shook his head. "No, but you are. We're heading to another undisclosed location. It's not safe for us here."

Hearing this, Shane dropped his backpack on the seat. "Can I talk to her? Please. I need to know where things stand. If this is it, I believe we both need closure."

Understanding his position, the gentleman nodded and had everyone leave to give them a moment alone. "Don't push her too hard," he warned.

Once they'd gone, he approached the pocket door and knocked gently. Not getting a response, he slid it open and stepped inside. There, he found Abi lying on the bed, curled up with her knees tucked to her chest, hugging a blanket, noticeably grieving.

"Abs?" he said quietly as not to startle her.

She didn't flinch.

Sitting down, he said, "I need to leave now." Upon hearing that, she slowly rolled over. That is when he saw her eyes, red, swollen, and distant. They reflected no warmth, no fight—just exhaustion and pain.

"I...umm..." Shane continued. "I just need to know..."

Interrupting him, Abi sat up slowly, her body dragging as if gravity had tripled. She pulled in a fractured breath, her voice low and brittle. "Guess you're secretly happy he's gone."

Shocked, Shane flinched. "Is that what you think?" he asked quietly, the pain in his voice no match for the depth of hers. Realizing the vindictiveness was sparked by grief, her words still cut deep. Her tone wasn't just cold. It was hollow. Shattered.

Not answering him, he watched her trembling hand move to her finger as his ring slid off without resistance. Staring at it in her palm, like it was a relic from another life, she set it gently on the bed between them. It was a final offering. A silent goodbye.

Upon seeing this, his breath caught. "Abi... please. Don't do this. Don't throw what we have away."

And just like that, she turned and curled back into the ball with her back to him. Shoulders trembling, she broke down. The sound of her sobbing—raw, guttural, unrestrained—as it echoed off the walls. It was the kind of grief that carved a person from the inside out.

Helpless, Shane sat there for a long moment before reaching for the ring and threading it onto his chain for safekeeping. Eyes burning, he blinked back tears repeatedly and knew that no amount of love or pleading could reach her now, not when she was drowning in sorrow and loss. Burton was gone, and she was consumed by it.

Standing at the edge of the bed, he looked down at the girl he still loved, unraveling before his eyes. "This goes without saying," he whispered, his voice catching, "but if you ever need me… please… I'll do everything in my power to get to you. I wouldn't think twice."

She didn't respond. All he got in return was a barely-there nod, shaky and small.

Knowing there was nothing he could do or say to change things between them, he reached for her hand one last time, but she pulled away upon feeling his touch. "I love you, Abs. Nothing will ever change that."

Stoic, the shell of her stayed silent as the tears flowed.

"Take care of yourself." Ducking under the door, he lingered there a second, the shock of everything hitting him. Leaning forward, he rested his hands on the seats and tried to breathe while fighting the pressure building in his chest before his emotions got the better of him. Scrubbing his hand down his face, a tear drifted down his cheek. Eyes squeezed shut, he clenched his jaw and both fists to gain control once again, determined to hold it together. But his heart was breaking, and there was nothing he could do about it.

Composing himself, Shane grabbed his backpack from the seat and flung it onto his shoulder before walking down the aisle. Each step felt heavier than the next, the further he got from her.

Stepping off the plane, he went to the SUV waiting.

The men watched him. Each offered a farewell nod, assuming what had happened.

Looking back, part of him was hoping she'd come after him, and they'd leave together to start their life in Huntington Beach. Focused on the doorway, he waited, but she never came.

Inside the plane, Abi heard the truck door close. Her heart was a tangled mess of emotions while the plane refueled. Moments later, she heard the men return on board. Hearing someone walk in and sit beside her, she suddenly felt Martin's hand on her shoulder.

Caught off guard, he saw her roll over and reach for him. Arms encircling his neck, she clung tightly in desperation as the pain overtook her.

Lost for words, he did not know how to comfort her. "There, there, Miss," he said gingerly, completely out of his element.

Amidst her tears, body heaving, she took whatever solace he could offer, knowing she'd lost everything she'd ever loved all in one day.

As the plane began to move, Martin whispered, "I'm sorry, but we will be taking off shortly. You need to buckle into a seat."

Guiding her to the one just across from the bed, he sat her down and belted her in as she grasped the blanket and held it tight to her chest.

"I will be right back. One moment."

When Martin returned, he handed her one of Burton's Dark Demon hoodies. "I thought he'd want you to have this. Perhaps it will give you solace."

Taking it, she looked up, sorrow reflected in her tear-filled eyes. Burying her face in it, she sobbed but could feel him. Smell him.

"If you need me, I'll be right outside the door."

"Where are we going?" she muttered, chest still heaving.

"Some place safe, Miss."

At the end of the runway, the engines roared to life, and soon, the plane lifted off the ground. Not knowing where they were headed, she felt numb while flying high above the city of Angels. Memories of her past life went with her. But never again would she see her friends. Never again would she see her Father or visit her Mother's grave. It had all become a piece of the past.

Catching a glimpse of Burton's Carbon Beach Terrace house on the Malibu hillside, the plane veered East. Seeing the illuminated white structure with pool lights sparkling, she already missed the beautiful view from her room and all the memories of him it housed. Placing her hand over her heart, she prayed he'd come back to her, even if it were only in her dreams.

| 45 |

Hideaway

Saturday, December 30 ~ 1:10 am MDT

Somewhere over Colorado

Flying over the dim, snow-capped mountains, the plane circled a dark forested valley and landed on a deserted runway surrounded by white, grassy fields. Pulling into a large steel hangar, the jet came to a stop. Beside them were two black SUVs and a group of security agents, mostly men, but this time, she noticed a few women.

"It's time to go, my dear. We are not far. Just a ten-minute drive," Martin divulged, shocked to see the level of devastation on her face.

Wearing the Dark Demon hoodie, she went through the motions. Clutching the photo album, Abi left the plane with help from Martin before he got her settled in the truck. Unable to keep her head up, she bunched her coat up against the window and rested her head as the man looked at his iPad.

When they pulled away, she noticed the scenery on either side of them. "Where are we?" she mumbled quietly, unable to see anything.

"We are in Aspen, Colorado, dear. I think you will like it here."

Incapable of answering, she just watched the world go by.

In minutes, they turned off the highway and onto a county road. Veering left into a private, gated community, five-foot snow banks lining the sides, they maneuvered many winding turns before slowing down and pulling into an uplit modern house blending into its surroundings. Built amongst the trees with light wood, stacked stone, and steel, the driver went around back and stopped at the front door.

Not saying much when a strange man opened her side, she took her things and walked with Matt when he met her partway.

Stepping through the threshold, the large pivot door was held open by Martin.

"Welcome home, Miss Abi."

Her gaze swept over her new surroundings. The silence hit her first—a heavy, echoing emptiness that seemed to swallow every sound.

The foyer stretched upward, its twenty-five-foot ceilings drawing her eyes to the stark, angular lines of the architecture. Only darkness poured through the expansive windows. Her heart clenched as she imagined Burton's voice filling this vast space, a laugh bouncing off the walls that would never come.

The gleam of steel railings lining the staircase boasted clean, modern edges almost too perfect. It was all so sleek, so grand, and utterly designed to reflect Burton's taste, right down to the contemporary furniture, which was painfully pristine—neutral tones of cream and charcoal with soft lines. She could picture him sprawled across the couch, teasing her about some small, insignificant thing, his voice a soothing sound she desperately missed.

She closed her eyes for a moment, her hand tightening around the strap of her bag. When she opened them again, the space seemed even larger, more hollow. Abi whispered into the stillness, "Where is my room?"

"Right this way, Miss."

Taking her to the main level primary suite, Abi stopped midway down the hall. "I need to be on the second floor, or I won't sleep."

Martin stopped and said, "Very well. Follow me."

Climbing the stairs, they walked along the railing overlooking the windows in the living room. Martin opened the door and said, "Will this do?"

Seeing the space, with a king-sized bed and an ensuite, she walked over to the glass. Nodding her head, the man did the same.

"If you need me, I am just at the end of the hall on the opposite side of the house.

Cold and lifeless, she said nothing in return.

When he left, he closed the door behind him. Abi dropped her bags and curled up in bed. Slipping under the covers, she fell asleep, unsure if she'd ever wake up from the nightmare she was living.

| 46 |

Three Weeks Later

Friday, January 19

Aspen, Colorado

Time passed, but the ache in Abi's chest remained raw. She'd buried herself under the weight of her grief. Barely eating. Barely speaking. Barely existing. Her days blurred into nights as she clung to the faint hope that maybe—just maybe—it was all a mistake. But deep down, she knew the truth. Burton wasn't coming back.

But this morning, something felt different when she sat up in bed and stared out the frosted glass in her chilly room. Pulling her knees to her chest, the icy pellets from yet another winter storm hit the window in rhythmic bursts while she thought of him.

"He would hate seeing me like this," she mumbled.

Her mind swirled with memories of him: the quiet confidence, the way he took on the world without flinching, and most of all, the way he looked at her. His sacrifice was still incomprehensible, but one thing she knew for certain, he gave everything so she could live. She couldn't let that be in vain.

Taking a deep breath, Abi swung her legs over the side of the bed. The cold floor sent a shiver up her spine, but she ignored it. Today, she had to start again. For him.

After brushing her hair and putting a little gloss on her lips, she got dressed and headed downstairs. The comforting scents of coffee and waffles filled the air, along with the clattering of dishes and low murmurs. Stepping into the kitchen, Abi saw eyes gravitate her way.

Shocked, everyone's conversations stopped. For a moment, the room froze.

Hesitating, she quietly addressed everyone for the first time in weeks. "Good morning, gentlemen."

"Morning, Miss," the men said almost in unison.

Anton was at the stove, his apron dusted with flour as he flipped another batch of waffles and scrambled some eggs. "Miss Abi! Morning! You join us today? So, very happy to see you. So, so happy."

She nodded her head timidly.

"I make your favorite. Okay?" he said energetically.

"That would be wonderful. Thank you."

Sitting with his teapot and a steaming cup in front of him, Martin sat with Andrew and Matt, each with a coffee mug in hand.

The gentleman's expression brightened when she sat down. "Glad you joined us this morning, Miss," he said gently, not sure what to expect.

"Figured I'd return to the land of the living," Abi replied quietly while Anton set her plate of freshly made waffles and fruit in front of her. Head low, she poured syrup over her breakfast and asked, "Can you help me get caught up on school today?" Her eyes remained fixed on her fork.

For a moment, Martin didn't respond. But then a small smile broke through. "Absolutely, Miss. I have everything prepared for you," he said, thankful to see her come around finally.

She nodded once, not meeting his gaze. "Okay," she murmured, taking her first bite of breakfast.

The men smiled as their eyebrows raised. For weeks, they had watched her retreat into herself, her light dimmed by the weight of her loss. But this—this was a glimmer of the Abi they knew, a spark of the girl who had always been stronger than she realized.

As the storm raged on outside, Abi sat at the table, eating. She wasn't okay—not yet—but she was trying. And for now, that was enough.

| **47** |

Two Months

Friday, March 22

Aspen, Colorado

Keeping a structured routine, day after day, she never imagined her senior year would look like this. Confined to a secluded house, this is what her life had reduced to, and she needed to accept it.

Thankful that Martin had stepped in as her teacher, Abi thought of him as one of the threads tethering her to the life she once knew. Somehow, with him around, her time with Burton didn't feel like a dream. He kept it real despite her still being in disbelief some days.

Meticulous about her studies, ensuring she stayed on track to graduate, Abi couldn't shake the growing ache of isolation. Every morning felt the same - each with a question burning in her soul.

Curious as to what the outside world knew of Dark Demon now, after the whirlwind of attention he once commanded, Abi decided to finally venture down that path after avoiding it for so long. Grabbing her laptop, she opened it. Hands hovering over the keyboard, her mind racing, she hoped to find answers but wasn't holding her breath.

Typing the words DJ Dark Demon, her pinky finger hesitated over the enter key, a tremble running through her hand. Finally, she tapped it. The search loaded, and the screen filled with headlines that hit like daggers.

Famous DJ Dies in Niseko Avalanche.

Celebrity DJ, Dark Demon, Succumbs to Injuries After Being Buried in Avalanche.

Avalanche Claims Life of International Music Icon, DJ Dark Demon.

Mystery Surrounds Death of Reclusive DJ in Japan.

Fans Mourn the Loss of a Legend: Inside Dark Demon's Life and Death.

Conspiracy Theories Arise Over DJ Dark Demon's Sudden Passing.

Reading the seemingly endless list, Abi felt her heart sink deeper. The words blurred together, an ocean of fake narratives and glossy fabrications. None of it was real. None of it came close to the truth. What Burton did that day was heroic, and not one person outside their circle knew it.

"It was all planted—covered up..." she muttered under her breath, her eyes scanning another headline that twisted the story even further. A bitter laugh escaped her lips, humorless and hollow. The media had painted a tragic portrait, but the reality was far more complex and devastating.

Reading through a few articles, she typed in Japan Avalanche. December 27th.

A list surfaced again. This time, upon reading the contents, she discovered that a number of people did not survive, including an American girl from California, who was not named.

Checking her social media, not having seen her friends' posts in quite some time, she stopped, knowing Martin had warned her to stay off every platform. Creating a fictitious account, she immediately looked up her friends, knowing theirs were public. Searching for posts dated from December to early January, she discovered the first R.I.P. Abi Acardi post on Laney's feed.

"What is this..." she muttered, staring angrily in disbelief.

Scrolling through everyone else's Instagram, she found countless tributes. Feeling almost faint, like she could fall through the floor, it seemed she was having some sort of out-of-body experience. Shaking her head, she closed the laptop with a decisive snap and pushed back her chair before marching out of the room. There was only one man who had answers, and she was done sitting in the dark. It was time to confront Martin.

As she shuffled into the kitchen, her slippers brushed against the floor.

The man was already seated in his usual spot with a steaming cup of tea and a stack of papers. When she entered the room, he looked at her atop his reading glasses.

Laptop in hand, she stood before him. "So when were you gonna tell me?" she asked point-blank as Martin closed his iPad.

Not expecting her accusation, he knew what was coming next. "I might need a little more information, Miss?" He leaned back in his chair.

In an instant, what they both said sparked Andrew's attention.

"I'm dead." Setting her laptop on the table in front of him, she showed him the headlines she'd found. "So, is this some sort of cover-up?"

"I'm not at liberty to say."

"Bullshit!" Abi's emotions boiled over.

The men's eyebrows shot up before every one of them swiftly vacated the kitchen. Anton included.

"My God, Martin! Don't you think I should have been told this bit of information, like weeks ago?"

"Apologize, but we were going to reveal this when the time was right."

"Does this mean I've lost my acceptance to Harvard?"

"On the contrary, my dear. My people have digitally scrubbed all traces of your old identity. Everything has been erased, suppressed, or overwritten using classified clearance. Even hard copies have been replaced by our cyber team and internal connections. Nobody will be the wiser. Everything is fine."

She flipped the tab to the headlines about Burton's death. "What about B? It says Dark Demon died in the avalanche."

He sighed deeply, setting down his glasses on the table. Leaning back, he folded his arms in front of his chest. Hesitation, louder than words, Abi waited for his answer. "Master B was on the mountain with you that day when the avalanche happened. It seemed the most plausible story to run with. We couldn't very well tell the world he died at the hands of the Korolev family. Now, could we?"

Hearing that, the air expelled from her lungs. Simmering down, she collapsed in the chair across from him, feeling her world tilt beneath her.

Martin lowered his gaze.

The silence cut her more than any answer could.

All she could say was, "I'm sorry for yelling."

"It's quite alright, Miss." He took in a breath. "I know this transition has not been easy for you. I'm sorry you found this out before I could explain."

Processing it all, she replied, "Fair enough," before slowly rising to her feet. Her chair scraped slightly against the floor as she pushed it back.

"There will be no lessons today." Martin tread carefully. "I think it's best we discuss a few details, primarily your new name and how you can attend school in the fall. Some decisions need to be made sooner rather than later."

With slight hesitation, Abi nodded. "Fine," she mumbled, feeling it was all too much too soon. Grabbing a plate of food from Anton as he sheepishly returned to the kitchen, she stayed at the table and ate in silence.

Thoughts of Burton took over. He was supposed to be invincible. Abi held back her tears, but the heartbreak remained raw and unrelenting. For the first time, she wished the story told to her was a lie, but deep down, she knew it wasn't. The truth had finally come out of the shadows, and sadly, it shattered what little progress she'd made.

| 48 |

Graduation Day

Thursday, June 20

Aspen, Colorado

Still, miles from California, the bitterly cold winter gave way to the greenness of spring and soon, the warmth of summer. Remarkably, the air didn't seem as cold, and the world was less dark.

Trying to concentrate on her studies, Abi used it as a distraction more than anything. Hoping to graduate despite the setbacks, she submitted her last assignment and instantly felt a million times lighter.

"Well, that's it," she said, leaning back in her chair.

Staring out the window, the view of the mountains was pretty, but they held a sadness that would not leave. Burton's absence haunted her daily, and it was hard to think of anything else. She missed him so much it hurt.

Moving to her bed, with her computer on her lap, she typed in DJ Dark Demon in the search bar. This had become a daily ritual. Finding pieces of him brought back memories. It helped keep him alive in her mind.

Coming across a few leaked videos from his raves and a rare interview with his face obscured under his hood, she scrolled down and suddenly found a reel from the Vegas event at Caesar's Forum. Watching it, she saw the pictures from Tahoe fading in and out on the screens behind him and waited to see him point at the audience. When he did, she said fondly, "That was for me," remembering the feeling it gave her.

Realizing he was gone, suddenly, grief hit in waves. With it, an unwelcome thought surfaced - Sara. Hating herself for telling him to give the girl a chance, she mumbled through the tears. "Why did you interfere? You should've stayed out of it..." Burying herself in the pillows, she rubbed both eyes with her hands in frustration. "So stupid." She stood up and tried to shake it off, her heart aching. "You've gotta stop this."

Planting more positive thoughts, knowing that anything else would be detrimental, she looked back on the last six months. Through the sorrow and the nightmares, the outbursts and the dreaded silence, she thought of Martin, Anton, and the guys. Each had given up everything to keep her safe and help her through this difficult time.

"It wasn't easy for them, either," she said, realizing today was not only graduation day for her but also a celebration of those who'd gotten her there.

So thankful to have made it to this point, she opened social media, curiosity pulling her toward updates from old friends. Shawn and Laney had posted about their acceptance letters and their new roles within their family's business empires. Allie and Alan were set to graduate with honors and had already lined up leadership internships. Ben and Ming were heading overseas to expand their family's global reach, while Adrian and Mei shared snapshots from their campus visits and corporate life. As she scrolled through their posts, she felt nostalgic and missed them all terribly, knowing that, unlike her, they'd be walking across a stage this week to receive their diplomas.

Letting out a sigh, she muttered, "What I'd give to be with them."

Switching gears, she checked on the newlyweds. Making headlines in the AI Technology market, the new CEO and President of the Wilson Corporation, along with his wife and their partners, including his ex-fiancée and her husband, successfully took control of their family's conglomerates and achieved their goals. Ousting their fathers from power and generating millions in revenue since then, Abi found an article about the two couples rumored for a possible Forbes' Top 30 Under 30 nomination this year.

Knowing there was only one more person to search up, she slowly typed the name Shane Coppersmith. Reading the latest article on him, she read aloud, "Shane Coppersmith, the quarterback sensation on everyone's radar, has captured headlines and dominated the sports scene as the top recruit nationwide. Praised as a leader both on and off the field, Coppersmith has earned the respect of his teammates by coming off a powerhouse season with 224 completed passes, 41 touchdowns, and an impressive 3,001 yards passing. Coppersmith's on-field command is a force to be reckoned with. Having signed with the University of Alabama, it seems Coppersmith's path to the NFL is all but paved, with scouts already projecting him as a future standout in the pros. His skill, leadership, and relentless drive position him as a top contender for the league, promising a bright future for this rising star." Abi paused and managed to smile. "You've accomplished what you said you were going to do," she whispered, recalling how they'd left things. Flipping through his social media, she wondered if she should message him under her unnamed account. Opting against it since Martin was not in favor, she reluctantly continued to follow the rules set out to keep her safe, but couldn't help clicking on the videos. His most recent in-person interview revealed a stronger, more confident Shane—a testament to his commitment to the game. At the end of it, the sports commentator stated, *Yet, there's an unmistakable depth behind his focus, a hint of sadness that leaves analysts wondering what challenges this star athlete might be privately facing.*

Abi knew what that meant. Not recalling much from their abrupt departure, given the emotional blur she was in, she knew they'd parted ways with a lot left unsaid. Analyzing him on the screen, she could tell by his eyes that something was missing and figured, to some extent, she was to blame.

Popping over to his Instagram account, she found a number of pictures with unfamiliar faces, both guys and girls. "I guess these are his new friends from the Huntington Beach school," she said with a sigh, missing their Gilderson group. A part of her felt a little jealous. Some of the girls he was pictured with were really pretty, and one girl seemed to be posted a few times on his feed. Strangely, she resembled her. That is when she noticed something. Zooming in, she found her ring hanging from the chain around his neck. Maybe he hasn't forgotten me…" she mumbled before clicking on his latest post. It was a picture of him peering out the window of an airplane. The caption read, *Heading East to see a close friend.* Below, the comments had blown up, with several girls questioning where he was headed, but he did not post a reply. That is when the thought crossed her mind – was he coming to see her?

Lonely on so many levels, she plopped herself back amongst her pillows. Peering out at the mountains, feeling lost and without direction, she whispered, "Don't worry. In six weeks, you'll be in familiar territory. It'll be good to be back in Boston."

No stranger to integrating into a new environment, she looked forward to attending Harvard but knew she would have to do so incognito as much as possible. Thinking of it as a fresh start, she was nervous and anxious about introducing herself as Abby Townsend versus Acardi. A strange but necessary change, she knew Martin was doing what was in her best interest, given everything that had happened.

Scooching off the bed, she took a breath, happy that high school would soon be behind her and the college phase of life was about to begin. Martin had successfully helped her reach graduation, but he'd also guided her through the grief of losing Burton and had gone above and beyond in the past six months to provide her with stability despite their extenuating circumstances.

As the heavenly smell of breakfast rose to the second floor, she headed downstairs to see what Anton was cooking. Barefoot, she padded toward the kitchen, drawn by the promise of coffee.

Anton looked up from the stove with a glimmer in his eye. "Morning, Miss. Sleep well?"

"Same as always..." Catching a few covered smiles and the guys refusing to make eye contact, she squinted.

He handed her a coffee. "It's a big day today. Excited?"

"That's debatable," she said, surveilling the odd tension in the room.

At the table, the men—Matt, Andrew, and Lorenzo—pretended to be absorbed in their breakfast. Amongst them, Martin sat comfortably, teacup in hand, legs crossed like nothing was out of the ordinary.

"Okay, what's going on?" Abi asked slowly, her instincts firing off. "You're all acting...weird."

Martin gently set his cup down. "Don't be alarmed, but we planned a little something for you. Graduation day should not go uncelebrated."

She stilled. "You didn't have to do that... I don't need anything."

"You deserve *something*," Martin said warmly. "We know the past six months have been—"

"Hell?" she offered with a hint of humor.

Martin stared her down.

Hands up in defense, she said, "Okay! Okay. That was a little extreme."

"As I was saying. Since you couldn't graduate with your peers," he gave a knowing nod, "We thought we'd bring the celebration to you. A small surprise."

Her heart snagged at the word *surprise*. Shane. That post. *Heading east to visit a close friend.* Her mind reeled. He was the only person who knew she was still alive. Swallowing, she felt a knot in her throat.

"That's really kind. Honestly. But just having the space to breathe is enough."

The guys all grinned. Almost too much. Then, one by one, they left without a word.

Only Martin remained. He rose, adjusted his blazer, and motioned with his hand. "Follow me."

"Martin, what is happening?"

"Outside, dear."

The foyer was silent as the men stood waiting in the wings.

Following him to the massive front door, he opened it slowly. A cool breeze swept in, laced with the sharp scent of pine, just as a distant peel of thunder rumbled in the distance. Stepping out on the porch, she watched the clouds, dark and heavy, rolling over the mountains like a slow tide.

"In honor of your graduation," Martin announced, "You have a visitor."

"A visitor?"

Before he could reply, the low purr of an engine grew louder—closer. Her pulse spiked. A black SUV curved around the driveway and rolled to a stop at the front entrance.

Her feet were cemented in place.

Rain began to fall in quiet taps on the stone. Each drop, a beat louder than the last.

"Oh, my…" she mumbled under her breath, not ready to deal with everything attached to seeing Shane again.

As Lorenzo stepped out of the house, he opened an umbrella in his hand as he moved to the far side of the SUV. The engine hummed low, the vehicle still idling against the gray drizzle that had gotten heavier, blurring the landscape.

Abi squinted through the downpour, her breath catching as Lorenzo opened the rear passenger door. As the figure gathered their things behind the tinted glass, she could only make out the shape: tall, broad-shouldered. Somewhat familiar.

Martin stood beside her, and though he said nothing, she felt his hand hover just behind her back—ready.

Hearing her heart pounding inside her skull, Abi waited for Shane to round the corner. When the hooded figure appeared, athletic with perfect posture, she tried to see his hidden face.

Her knees buckled, but the weakness lasted only a moment.

Standing still, eyes on her, his chest rose and fell with every heavy breath. The moment he peeled back his hood, a sudden burst of life propelled her forward, and she sprinted through the storm, the rain soaking her hair and clothes in seconds. Finally feeling something for the first time in months, a surge of excitement flowed through her. Arms lifting before her mind had even caught up, she launched, colliding into his chest. Feeling his tight embrace, it was as though he'd been waiting his whole life to catch her.

Blinking against the droplets, she tried to speak—tried to make sense of everything.

His warmth wrapped around her. The scent of him. The feel.

"Say something," he whispered with tears in his eyes.

She froze.

"Aww, Abs," he said, softer now. "I've missed you."

Her breath stuttered. "Oh, Burton…" she said, trying to take in a small bit of air as the tears fell. "But, how…" Trembling inside and out, hands shaking profusely, a flood of emotions overwhelmed her.

"It's a long story," he said softly, his lips brushing her ear. "The important thing is, I'm here."

She pulled back just enough to look up at him, her hands framing his jawline as her eyes frantically searched him. "Are you okay?" Her gaze roamed over him, scanning for scars, injuries, and any sign of what he might have endured.

Steady hands cupping her cheeks, his thumbs brushed away the rain and tears. "Yes," he assured her. "Are you?"

She didn't answer. Instead, she buried herself in him again, holding him so tightly she feared he'd disappear if she loosened her grip. Cradling her, one hand rested gently on the back of her head as she trembled against him.

"Martin said you were gone..." Hearing his heart beating, she knew he was real. It wasn't a dream. "I can't believe it's you."

"There is so much I need to say..."

Spotting Martin, still standing in the doorway, quietly observing the reunion, Burton knew that despite his stoic demeanor, the slight quirk of his lips and the shimmer in his eyes said he was happy to see him. "Sorry, Abs. Can I just...?"

Abi smiled. "Of course."

Turning his attention to the fatherly gentleman, without hesitation, he extended his arms. When he did, the man broke a smile as they embraced in a firm, manly hug that spoke volumes.

"Good to see you, my boy," Martin said gruffly. "You made it."

Thick with gratitude, Burton nodded. "Yes, thanks to you."

The older man's lips trembled for a moment.

"How have you been?"

He slid his hands into his suit pockets with regal ease. "Good, Sir. We missed you around here," he replied, noticeably elated.

"Well, I'm happy to be back." He hugged him a second time and patted his shoulder as Martin did the same.

Hearing another vehicle pull up, Burton said, "By the way, I brought someone with me."

Head tilting slightly, Abi was curious as to who this was.

A much smaller figure stepped out of a Mercedes sedan. While the rain slid off a wide umbrella held by Andrew, he shielded them from the storm.

When the woman stepped forward, it didn't take long to recognize her as she got closer. With each step, the same warm eyes and graceful demeanor shone brightly. It was someone Abi hadn't seen in years.

"Sorry, give me one minute." With a smile, he released her and walked toward the woman. Offering her his arm, Burton guided her over. "Abs? You remember my Mom?"

"I certainly do."

"Hello, my dear."

"Hi..." Abi replied, still stunned, her arms instinctively wrapping around the woman. Peering past her, she stared at Burton. "She's alive?"

To Abi's surprise, his Mom placed a hand on her cheek. "I know you probably have a million questions."

Burton spoke up. "I've had her in hiding all this time, hoping that one day, it would be safe enough for her to come out of the shadows. Everything I've done over the past three years has been for her. I did what was necessary so she could live a somewhat normal life."

With a mix of emotions, Abi's heart swelled. "And your father?" A pang of sadness settled in her chest when she asked.

The weight of that answer hit hard as Burton confirmed, "They took him from us. But I avenged his death and protected her in the process. Now, that part of my life is closed."

The finality of his words hung in the air, a moment of silent understanding between them all. The journey they had walked together, the darkness they had fought through, was now behind them.

The woman's gaze slid past Abi and spotted Martin standing not far away. "Well, I need to get out of the rain," she said point-blank, eager to meet the refined gentleman waiting in the threshold.

As the three of them approached the doorway, Burton stretched out his free arm to Abi, who instinctively nestled under it, his hand curling protectively around her shoulder.

"Martin, meet my Mother, Ms. Mary Sullivan." Inching her forward, he said, "Mom, this is Martin."

With an air of quiet poise, she extended her hand.

Almost entranced by her grace, Martin took it gently. "A pleasure to meet you, Madam," he said with a respectful bow of his head.

A warm, pleasant smile appeared, her eyes glistening with unshed tears. "Well, Martin," she said. "We finally meet." Her gratitude spilled over. "How can we ever thank you for helping us?"

"No need to thank me, Madam." Clearly touched by her words, he shifted the conversation. "You must be parched after your long journey. May I brew you a cup of tea?" he asked, offering his arm regally.

Met by a gracious nod, she took hold. "That would be wonderful. Lead the way."

As they walked off together, Abi turned to Burton in shock. "Now, this all makes sense. Your determination. The fearlessness. You were doing it all for her."

"And you," he added.

She didn't know what to say as the two walked toward the kitchen and rounded the corner, leaving Burton and Abi alone.

Taking the opportunity, he asked, "Is there somewhere we can go and talk?" Abi nodded. "Sure. Follow me."

She led him up the spiral staircase. When they entered her room, the storm outside was already beginning to subside, faint rays of sunlight fighting to break through the heavy clouds.

Abi walked to the chair by the window, sinking into it, unsure of what he would say.

Burton closed the door behind them, his presence filling the room. He approached, his eyes never leaving hers. The weight of her pain and confusion was evident, and it broke his heart.

"I have so many questions," she said, her mind reeling.

He nodded, heavy with regret. "I know. There's much to explain."

For a moment, silence stretched between them, filled only by the soft patter of rain and the distant rumble of thunder. Sitting beside her, he leaned forward, his elbows resting on his knees as he stared at the floor, searching for the right words. Finally, he turned, his voice thick with emotion. "I'm sorry I did this to you. I didn't have a choice. It had to be this way."

Her eyes filled with tears as she waited for the answers she desperately needed. "Why didn't Martin tell me the truth?"

He exhaled slowly, his jaw tightening. "Because I am what he said. Burton Lancaster doesn't exist anymore. Neither does Burton Baxter nor Dark Demon. They're all gone."

Upon hearing that, her heart sank. "And now?" she asked cautiously. "Who are you?"

He leaned back in the chair, a faint smirk tugging at the corner of his lips. "Dean Anderson," he said with a touch of humor, clearly testing how the name rolled off his tongue.

Abi tilted her head, her brows knitting in mild amusement. "Dean, huh? You don't look like a Dean."

He chuckled, the sound warming the space between them. "Yeah, I don't think so either, but..."

Her face brightened when she countered, "Well, mine's Abby—A-B-B-Y—Townsend."

"I like it," he said warmly, clearly relieved she had kept her first name.

A beat of silence passed.

"Can you tell me more about how your Mom fits into all this?"

"The agency shielded Mom after she submitted testimony against Alexei Korolev. Her statement provided them with sufficient evidence to proceed with the sting operation while we were in Tahoe. But when it all went sideways..." He didn't answer right away. It was as if he were having flashbacks as a shadow crossed his face. "They kept her safe while Martin and I got tasked with taking down the people responsible for my Father's death."

She reached out, her hand resting lightly on his arm. "What happened to you after we left the warehouse?"

He studied her hand as he caressed it. "That's not important. All you need to know is that I did what I had to. The objective was to shut down the Korolev family's operations, and we did that. In the process, I became a ghost."

Emotions swirling, she said, "I thought I'd lost you forever."

He shifted closer, his hand moving to rest on her shoulder. "You couldn't lose me, Abs. I've been fighting to get back to you. Every single day."

Tears streaming, she whispered, "I'm just so glad you're here."

Holding her as if to shield her from the torment and pain, Burton whispered, "Hey, don't cry. I'm back, and I promise I'll never leave you. Well, unless you ask me to." He chuckled.

Hugging him, she said, "Never."

The sun came out from behind the clouds. Shining through the windows, he skimmed the mountain view.

A knock came to the door.

Getting up, he opened it and found Lorenzo with his bags. Taking them from him, he left them just inside the room. "Thanks. Appreciate that, man."

The guy nodded and left them again.

Returning to Abi, staring outside, he said, "So, Martin tells me you invested well the past few months. The stocks made a killing."

"I bought into Bitcoin when it plummeted. Most thought it would tank, but I knew otherwise. Now, it's over $105K."

"Impressive. Are you sure you want to go into medicine and not finance?"

Reminded of her Father's profession, she said, "Speaking of which. Did you see the news a few months ago?"

"No, I didn't."

"In February, Jenna filed for divorce. But that's not all. She told the medical board that he was having relations with another coworker after they were married. She wasn't surprised by this and reported that the two of them had an affair while my Mom was in palliative care. She resigned from her position, but Dad was put on leave pending an investigation. Thank God I wasn't there." She thought for a minute. "Long story short, he was dismissed from his position, and she took him for every last penny he had. Now, he will likely never practice medicine again. Guess there is such a thing as karma."

"I think it was more Sara...than Karma."

"What do you mean?" she asked.

"Abi, Sara hired that woman, Jenna, to kill your Mom and destroy your Dad. It was meant to hurt and maim those around me – to make you suffer for what I was doing. She's the one who left the black rose in her hospital room. Not Eastwood, despite him using the flowers as a psycho way to stalk you. The girl copied what her cousin did, so he would take the blame if things went bad. Strangely enough, after hearing through the grapevine that your Mother had died, he took credit for it. Guess he wanted to score brownie points within the family."

Shifting in her chair, having been hit by that blow, somehow she knew Jenna was up to no good – but never this.

Burton opened his duffel bag and pulled out a dry shirt. Peeling off his damp hoodie, he quickly changed as Abi looked away. "Do you mind if I use your shower?"

"No problem. It's right through there," she pointed.

"I won't be long. Don't go anywhere."

As he disappeared into the bathroom, she heard the rhythmic sound of water hitting the tile. Soon after, the faucet shut off.

When he emerged, fully dressed, his hair was partially dry. Unsure how to break the ice again, he admired the mountains. "That's quite the view."

"It's the only thing I've seen for six months."

"Can we step away from the heavy for a bit?"

She could tell he was overwhelmed.

"What do you do for fun around here?"

"Nothing," she answered with a subtle sigh. "I eat, sleep, and study. Haven't done much else."

"Do you want to go somewhere with me?"

She stared at him blankly.

"What..." he chuckled. "Did I say something wrong?"

Tears in her eyes, she said, "I still can't believe you're here. It's like I'm dreaming." With open arms, she stood up as they wrapped around her.

Feeling the urge to kiss him, she nervously refrained.

"So?" he questioned, feeling the newfound tension building between them. "Want to head out?"

"Umm, sure."

"Good. Follow me," he said, taking hold of her hand.

She eyed him up while walking along the upper railing to the stairs. "I have a sneaky suspicion you're up to something."

He flashed a mischievous grin. "Aren't I always?" Making it to the lower level, seeing his Mother and Martin getting acquainted, Burton politely interrupted and asked, "Excuse me, Martin. Did you get those things I requested?"

The man silently peered over his reading glasses.

"Are they in the garage?"

"Yes, Master B."

"What did you do?" Abi was confused.

"You'll see." Reaching out to her, he said, "Come with me."

Leading her through the mud room, he opened the interior door and let her go first.

There, she found two RZRs parked in the third bay along with a few rather expensive mountain bikes propped against the wall at the far end.

"So? What do you want to do first? Bikes or an ATV ride?"

She wasn't sure what to choose.

"With the unsettled weather, we should take the ATVs." Walking over to one, he opened the small door. "Care to join me for a tour up the mountain?"

Unable to say no, she nodded and said, "Sure," knowing they still had so much to catch up on. She figured this was his way of addressing the rest, so she went along with it.

He handed her a helmet. "You're gonna need this." Helping her put it on her head, he secured the strap and smiled. "Is that good?"

She nodded. "Yep."

Securing his own, he opened the garage door with a push of the remote. As it retracted, Abi got settled in her seat while he got behind the wheel. This was completely out of her element.

The machine had an LCD screen and resembled a car. Belting in, he started the ignition. In an instant, the RZR came to life with a soft purr.

"Ready?" he asked, seeing her grab the bar in front of her.

"No going fast," she stated nervously, having never been in one of these before.

"Don't worry. You're safe with me," he reassured.

Leaving the garage, Abi noticed Lorenzo and Rob in another machine. Not paying them any mind, they veered left at the end of the driveway and continued down the road.

With one hand on the steering wheel and the other on the gear shift, Abi noticed how comfortable he was. Suddenly, he touched the gas and sped up on the straight stretch.

"Hey!" she shouted, hanging on tightly.

He slowed back down again and said with a smirk, "You're okay."

Amidst the tall, slender white birch trees blowing in the wind, they approached a parking lot before leaving the paved path and going off-road.

A smile crept across his face while maneuvering the rugged trail.

Seeing the motionless chairlift to their right, she realized they were driving up the ski hill.

Upon reaching the summit, finding two lift canopies and a restaurant called the Cliffhouse, Burton steered away from the mountain bikers gathered outside the eatery and drove behind the ski patrol building to a picnic table hidden from sight. Lorenzo and Rob kept their distance but remained alert as Burton got out, opened her side door, and removed his helmet before helping Abi with hers.

Getting her bearings, she appreciated the vast valley between the two peaks. It was a long way down.

Taking a blanket handed to him by Lorenzo, Burton spread it over the table.

"After you," he said, offering his hand to help her have a seat. Sitting beside her, he tilted his head to the sky and soaked up the sun's warmth as it peeked through the clouds.

"Wow, this is stunning."

He said, "Yeah, it's an amazing spot."

With his arms resting upon his legs, Abi noticed Burton rubbing his palms together, almost as if he was building up the courage to say something. Staying quiet, waiting for him to speak, she heard him clear his throat.

Focused forward, he stared at the view. "I hope you know…I thought about you every day."

She threaded her arms around his before tightening her grip and resting her head upon his shoulder. "You never answered my question."

"What's that?"

"Why didn't Martin tell me the truth?"

"He only found out yesterday. It wasn't his fault. It had to be this way." He peered down at her. "I'm sorry. I know I caused you a lot of pain, but…"

"It doesn't matter now. What's important is that you're here." She clung to him, unsure what he'd endured all this time. "What happened after I left?"

"Because you gave Martin the code word, he checked my location and sent a team in to extract me. He wasn't privy to the outcome." Holding up his wrist, he said, "By the way, your watch came in handy. Martin had synced it with his iPad. That's how they got my location."

Processing this, she asked, "I saw them hit you…"

Unwilling to divulge all the gruesome details, he replied, "Let's just say they weren't kind. If you know what I mean."

Staring at him, his hair much shorter than normal, he seemed different. Thinner.

"So, Sara got everything she wanted?" Hating the thought of her, she added, "Did she get away? Is that why I'm here?"

He shook his head. "No, on all accounts. See, the code word I gave you tipped off Martin to lock everything down. I had a fail-safe in place in case of this scenario, and it worked. She got nothing. Well, except for what she had coming. I promise Sara will never bother us ever again."

Scared to ask what that meant, she simply let it go, not wanting to know the rest.

"I don't want to rehash it all. The main thing is you are safe, and I am, too."

"And your Mom."

"Yes," he nodded. "Her too."

She smiled.

"That said, I want you to know that was my last job. I'm out…"

"For good?"

"Yeah. I promise."

Nodding her head hesitantly, she remained silent.

To lighten the mood, his face brightened. "So, Martin tells me it's Graduation Day. I'm sorry you couldn't be with your friends."

"It's probably for the best."

"What do you mean?"

"When we returned to the States, Shane and I, we…umm… broke it off." Abi's voice wavered. For some reason, she couldn't bring herself to look at him.

"Is that right?" He tried to be sympathetic. "I'm sorry to hear."

"Are you?" Abi got up off the table and walked toward the edge, the wind teasing strands of her hair. Arms folded in front of her, she watched the sun spill a flood of gold over the jagged peaks, darkening the gully below. Behind her, she heard the soft crunch of feet on gravel and didn't need to turn around to know it was him. "Leaving you behind that night shattered my heart into a million pieces," she admitted without hesitation.

He inched closer.

"That's when he knew my heart no longer belonged to him."

Standing behind her, arms crossed, he asked, "And, do you still feel that way?"

The moment she turned around, his eyes searched hers with an intensity that left her breathless. "Did you mean it…" She fidgeted with the cuff on her sleeve. "When you said you loved me?" Afraid to hear the answer, she once again put her back to him. Waiting for his reply, she finally heard him say, "I meant every word."

She gasped.

Feeling his arms cautiously slip around her waist, mindful of her boundaries, he pulled her close, resting his cheek along her temple.

She tearfully clung to him. Drawing her back against his chest with a quiet kind of certainty, it sent a shiver through her. Soon, his fingers laced with hers.

He leaned down, his lips grazing the shell of her ear. "My heart has always been yours," he whispered.

A sob tore free, breaking down the last of her walls. She turned in his arms, pressing her palms against his chest, as his warmth filled the void she'd been carrying for months. "I hate that I didn't say it."

"What do you mean?"

"When you told me you loved me, with everything happening, I realized I didn't say it back." Tilting her head, the tears flowed as she tried to speak. "All these months..." she whimpered, "It's haunted me."

"Hey... Don't cry." He cradled her cheeks in his hands. "I knew. You didn't have to say it."

"But how?"

"It was the way you looked at me. That's all I needed. Nothing more," he reassured.

Heart bursting, she squeaked out, "I do love you," as every syllable tumbled.

With unrivaled gentleness, he reached up and tucked a piece of hair behind her ear. Delicately lifting her chin with his finger, coaxing her eyes to meet his, he caressed the curve of her lips before resting his forehead against hers. "I don't think you realize just how much I missed you."

Those words came quietly, but the meaning behind them meant everything.

Leaning in partway, staying mindful, he waited until she moved ever so slightly in his direction. "So, if I wanted to kiss you now, would you object?"

When she tearfully shook her head, his lips brushed hers, the tenderness suddenly sparking a surge of urgency. Wrapping his arms around her neck, feeling hers encircling his waist, a multitude of kisses followed. No hesitation, no lingering doubts—only the two of them and the love that burned brighter with each passing moment. Her soul ignited. He'd set it ablaze.

"So, what now?" she questioned with happiness etched upon her face.

"Don't worry. We've got lots of time to figure that out."

Lifting her feet off the ground, he swung her around as she giggled. Hearing applause nearby, they found the guys clapping. Lowering her, bringing her back down to Earth after their walk amongst the clouds, they stood together on the cliffside, with nothing but the mountains and sky bearing witness to their new beginning.

"We should probably head back," he said in a husky tone, glancing at the dark clouds rolling over the range to their right. "We don't want to get caught in the rain."

A nod was her only response as she stepped away from the edge.

His hand reached out, and when she took it, his fingers closed around hers, warm and firm. Folding the blanket, they began walking together down the rocky path toward the RZR. The world felt quiet, almost surreal.

From a distance, Lorenzo and Rob stood near their machine, their eyes carefully tracking every step the pair took. The security guards exchanged a quick, telling glance, a silent understanding passing between them as they noticed Burton's protective stance and the way his hand never left hers.

Rob took his wallet from his pocket and pulled a hundred-dollar bill. Handing it to Lorenzo, the guy laughed and said, "Pleasure doing business with you," knowing he had won their bet. Happy for his boss, he shoved the guy and taunted, "Told you so."

As they neared the machine, Burton let go and stepped ahead, moving to the passenger side. The wind had picked up, tugging at the hem of his shirt while ruffling his hair. Packing the blanket in the back, he grabbed her helmet from the seat and turned to her, holding it out.

"Here. Let me help you."

Carefully, he slipped it over her head, his fingers brushing against her cheek as he adjusted the strap under her chin. The small movements sent a warmth through her, and for a second, it felt like time had slowed.

"All good?"

She gave a thumbs-up as she peered through the visor.

He stepped back, gave a quick nod of approval, and helped her before closing the door when she'd gotten settled.

Rounding the machine to the driver's side, his stride unhurried, she noticed his every move exuding a quiet confidence. Grabbing his helmet, he pulled it on, the sharp angle of his jaw catching the fading sunlight as he snapped the buckle into place. With one last glance toward the horizon, he slid into the driver's seat and started the engine, the low rumble cutting through the stillness.

Without warning, the storm converged upon them as the RZR rumbled along the grassy hillside. Raindrops splattered against the windshield, and the tires hissed against the slick, wet roadway as they passed the parking lot.

By the time they reached the house, the drops were falling intensely and drumming the garage roof as they parked inside. Both of them were drenched.

The guys stopped beside them and quickly vacated the area to give them privacy.

Burton switched off the engine and removed their helmets. Holding them on their laps, they just sat there, the only sound the soft ticking of the cooling machine and the steady rhythm of the rain.

"Guess we got a bit wet," Burton chuckled with a smirk.

"Yes, just a little."

Opening the door, leaving his helmet on the seat, he swung around to her side and opened hers. Upon offering his hand, she stood on the edge of the machine to wrap her arms around his neck. Now, at eye level, she boldly kissed him as he pulled her close. Arms on her waist, he lowered her down and locked his hands with hers.

"A wise man once told me to be patient. That love would be worth the wait." His face brightened beneath his tough exterior. "You were."

"There you go again, always saying the right thing."

Closing the garage bay, their clothes, chilling their skin, Burton opened the mudroom door and had Abi enter first. He reached for her hand. Water dripping from them, they ignored everyone's curiosity and walked through the house in silence, the hum of voices and distant clatter of dishes echoing as they climbed the stairs. Wet footprints marked their path, but neither paid attention. Once inside her room, they closed the door.

Briefly disappearing into the bathroom, she soon returned with two hand towels. Giving him one, they stood there, drying their faces and wiping away the rain.

When she lowered her towel, her eyes met his. They were so blue.

The look he gave her sent a flutter through her chest. Slowly reaching for her hand, his fingers brushed against hers before curling around them. With the rain outside providing tranquil sounds, he inched backward until she eventually reached the bed. As they fell into it together, their wet clothes clinging to their skin, he wrapped her in his arms, eliminating the space between them. Their lips met, a kiss that started slow but quickly escalated.

But as fast as it came on, Burton suddenly stopped.

Mindful of her innocence, his hands stilled. Lips parting from hers, he pulled back slightly, breath uneven. The hesitation in his eyes was enough to make her sit up.

"What is it?" she asked, scared to know. "Did I do something wrong?"

Shaking his head, a faint smile erupted. "No, not a thing," he said quietly, carrying a level of devotion she didn't fully understand but felt nonetheless.

Silence stretched longer than she'd liked while the rain tapped the windows. When he ran one hand through his damp hair and shifted, he tapped her knee with the other and said, "I'm gonna let you get changed into dry clothes."

She nodded, folding her towel in her lap. "Okay..."

He could tell his restraint had confused her by the way she bit her lip and tilted her head. Stopping, he looked into her eyes.

In that moment, Abi saw it—the depth of love that was there.

To ease her doubts, he leaned in slowly, brushing his lips over hers. The kiss was gentle and reassuring, saying more than words ever could.

Pulling away, he caught her hand and held it as he rose. While moving toward the door, his fingers remained linked with hers until the distance forced him to let go. Pausing, he turned and glanced back. "Meet me in the hall when you're done," he said happily. "I want to show you something."

Curiosity lit her face, dousing any trace of uncertainty. "Okay," she whispered. "I'll see you shortly."

He nodded once before stepping into the hall.

As the door closed behind him, she sat there for a moment, heart pounding, with fingers pressed to her lips, wondering how he always managed to leave her breathless. She didn't know what he planned to show her, but one thing was certain - whatever it was, Abi knew her heart fully belonged to the man who'd just walked out that door.

| 49 |

The Promise

Thursday, June 20

Aspen, Colorado

Minutes later, Abi left her room to find the sun breaking through the clouds, scattering light across the damp earth below.

Finding Burton leaning forward, his arms resting casually on the second-floor railing, his silhouette was framed by the brightness of the large cathedral window beyond him. A duffel bag sat on the floor, containing two Featherlite-down jackets, hats, and mitts.

Her brow lifted. "What do we need those for? It's summer."

Before he could respond, the rhythmic whirl of a machine reached her ears.

A knowing smile flashed across his face as he extended his hand. "Follow me."

They descended the stairs together, his steps calm and measured, hers filled with quiet anticipation as his Mother, Martin, and the others looked on curiously, their presence fading into the background.

Lorenzo followed them out the front doors to a sleek helicopter nestled on the grass.

A soft laugh escaped her. "Oh, no. Not again."

His confidence was unwavering, his eyes locked on hers. "You'll be fine. I promise. Come with me."

Rushing across the field hand in hand, they ducked their heads on approach. The helicopter's cabin was snug, its interior humming with life as they climbed in. He leaned over to secure her seatbelt, his fingers brushing lightly against her arm before adjusting her headphones with care. Every motion was purposeful, his focus entirely on her. When the machine lifted off, they leaned into each other, just as the world fell away beneath them.

Flying northeast, the expanse of Gray's Peak revealed itself in majestic detail. Mountains stretched endlessly before them, each summit sharp against the brilliant sky. Remnants of snow adorned the ridges, glinting like scattered diamonds, while the valleys dipped into shadows of deep green forests. Rivers coiled through the landscape like silver threads, their surfaces reflecting the light of the retreating storm.

"This view…" she whispered. "Is beautiful."

As the helicopter descended, he glanced her way. "We're going to land for a minute," he said, a quiet intensity in his voice. Reaching for the jackets, he handed her one, along with a hat. "You're gonna need these."

Hovering steadily, the skids touched down.

Ensuring she'd bundled up, he opened the side door and stepped out, offering his hand. Together, ducking their heads, careful of the rubble beneath their feet, they moved toward the cliffside, the gusts of cool air brushing against them.

Below, the Earth dropped sharply, revealing a panorama of unspoiled wilderness. The wind was fresh and cool as the faint hum of the helicopter's rotors floated away.

"What do you think?" His arm slipped across her shoulders, pulling her close as another breeze swept past.

"This is absolutely amazing," she said, nuzzling into him for warmth.

Turning to her, he reached for her hands. Despite his calm demeanor, a slight tremble in his fingers betrayed his nerves. "Over the past six months, I've had a lot of time to think. For a guy like me, it was an opportunity to reevaluate things and gain clarity. Being away from you all this time has been the hardest thing I've ever had to do. That's when I realized my life only has meaning if you're in it. Having had a brush with death, it makes you truly understand what's important—and that is, life is short."

The words hung in the air as he sank to one knee, the movement sturdy and sure, his eyes never leaving hers.

Her free hand flew to her mouth, heart pounding as realization dawned.

Reaching into his pocket, he pulled out a small box. Opening it, presenting a ring that sparkled in the sunlight, he explained, "This is the very first diamond my Father unearthed. With it, he told me to give it to the one I love – the woman I can't live life without."

She cried upon hearing this.

"I know this may feel sudden, but I promised myself, if I ever found you again, I would not waste another minute."

Gasping, she lovingly tilted her head.

"Whenever I've thought of this moment, it was always you by my side," he said in a quiet tone. "You know I don't make promises I don't intend to keep. So, here's mine — I swear to protect you from harm, to love you with all my heart, and to make sure there's never a day that goes by that you don't know how much you mean to me." He looked up at her, the sincerity in his eyes stark against the strength he carried. "Abs...will you do me the greatest honor of becoming my wife?"

Tears streaming freely down her cheeks, she nodded and quietly whispered, "Yes."

Rising to his feet, he cupped her face in his hands and kissed her tenderly, his lips warm against hers despite the chill in the air.

The helicopter circled above them while Lorenzo recorded the entire thing.

He slipped the ring onto her finger. "I want to be with you—body and soul." What he said spoke volumes. His feelings shone through stronger than anything he could ever describe. "I love you, Abi Acardi."

Unable to contain herself, she gushed, "I love you, too, Burton Lancaster."

The mountains stood silent, bearing witness to the joining of two hearts that had endured a number of turbulent storms, distance, and time. In that sacred space, with the vast expanse of Gray's Peak as their backdrop, forever truly began.

| 50 |

Romance in the Air

Thursday, June 20

Aspen, Colorado

As the helicopter touched down gently on the sprawling estate grounds, Abi and Burton stepped out into the cool evening air, their fingers intertwined. The sound of the rotors faded into the distance as the pilot lifted off again, leaving them standing together on the lawn.

When they reached the front door, Burton waited a minute, his hand gripping the handle. "Are you ready to share the news with them?" he asked, searching for any sign of hesitation.

Bubbling over with excitement, Abi grinned, her eyes sparkling. "Yes. Absolutely."

Happy to hear it, he nodded and opened the door. The hum of conversation drifted out as they entered, hand in hand. Inside, the dining room was alive with warmth and laughter, the table set for dinner. Everyone had gathered around, chatting and pouring drinks, when Burton and Abi's presence caught them by surprise.

"Can I have your attention for one second?" Burton called out amongst the chatter. The room quieted, heads turning toward the couple.

Abi could feel her heart pounding as his Mother stepped away from her conversation with Martin, her curious gaze landing on them.

"We have some news," Burton said, smiling.

As Abi held out her left hand, the light from the chandelier made the diamond ring sparkle like a tiny star. For a moment, there was a collective intake of breath and gasps before the room erupted in joyful shouts and applause. Their friends surged toward them, offering hugs, handshakes, and congratulations.

Mary approached them with open arms, her face bright. Resting her hand on Burton's cheek, she said, "Oh, my boy. I am so happy for you both." She embraced Abi tightly, the warmth of her love clear. "Finally," she said, joy radiating from her. "I have a daughter."

Hugging her back, Abi felt a surprising wave of emotion as she realized how much this moment reminded her of her own Mother. It was as if, somehow, her angelic presence was also there, enveloping her in a heavenly embrace.

Anton popped the cork on a bottle of champagne as Martin stepped forward, lifting his glass. The room quieted once again, everyone turning their attention to the man who had been a steady presence through all of Burton and Abi's trials.

"Months ago," Martin began, filled with affection, "A young lady by the name of Abi Acardi caught the eye of Master B most unconventionally, I must say. It was a meeting none of us could have predicted, but one that, looking back, was clearly fate. Burton, being the man he is, couldn't help but step in, saving her from harm. Each time, I watched him grow more protective, more in awe of her. His love was undeniable, but their timing - well, that was not quite right." A knowing smile spread across Martin's face as he glanced at Burton and Abi, who stood arm in arm. "But as life often does, it tested them, challenged them, and made them stronger. Through trials and tribulations, they have proven that their love is not fleeting or fragile. It's resilient. It's enduring. And now, the two of them have found their way back to each other, where they belong."

Feeling a lump rising in her throat as Martin's words washed over them, she turned to Burton with tears in her eyes as he hugged her tightly.

"I'm sure I speak for everyone here when I say—it's about time," Martin said with a chuckle, eliciting laughter and cheers from the room. "So, let's raise a glass to Burton and Abi, the happy couple. We know their love will last a lifetime because they've already weathered storms that would have broken others. To Abi and Burton—may your future be as bright and beautiful as the love you share today."

"To Abi and Burton!" the room echoed as champagne flutes clinked and cheers erupted once more.

Unable to resist, Burton leaned down and kissed Abi's lips before she nuzzled against him. For the first time in a long time, everything felt right.

| 51 |

That Night

Thursday, June 20

Aspen, Colorado

After the celebration had wound down and the house grew quiet, everyone retired to their respective corners for the night. Burton, carrying the weight of the day's joy and exhaustion, wandered through the hallway in search of a room. It wasn't long before he realized there wasn't one available. His mother had claimed the primary suite on the lower level, and every other space was taken.

Noticing his hesitation, she smiled. "You can share with me," she said, her tone both warm and confident. "Besides, you should get used to it," she giggled lightheartedly.

Appreciating her cheekiness, he stopped. "If you're sure," he said, earning a playful eye roll in response.

"Come on," she urged, leading the way upstairs.

He followed her, their steps light.

As she closed the door behind them, the reality of the day sank in deeper. Abi turned to him, brushing a strand of hair behind her ear. "I'm just going to have a shower."

"Okay," he said quietly.

As the sound of running water filled the room, Burton sat on the edge of the bed. In the quiet moment alone, clarity came to him. He knew in his heart what he wanted for Abi—for both of them. Their relationship was not what most would expect, given his past, but being with her made him want to be more. Focused forward, he intended to be a supportive husband who loved his wife through good times and bad, a man who would welcome children without reservation and build a family and a home they could be proud of. Almost in disbelief, recalling the milestones achieved that day, he knew it all happened fast, but his heart wouldn't have had it any other way.

When Abi returned, her hair damp and curling at the ends, she gave him a gentle smile before slipping under the covers.

He got up, grabbed his toothbrush from his bag, and disappeared into the bathroom.

While he was gone, Abi lay there, her head resting lightly against the pillow as the bedside lamp illuminated the room. She listened to the faint sounds of Burton brushing his teeth, the rhythmic splash of water, and the muffled hum of activity, yet her mind was anything but calm.

She ran her fingers along the edge of the blanket and dreamily studied the beamed pattern on the ceiling. Thoughts of the day swirled like a whirlwind, refusing to settle. The engagement still didn't feel real. Every time she looked at the diamond sparkling on her finger, a wave of emotions washed over her: joy, excitement, and an overwhelming love she didn't know was possible.

Her hand found its way to her heart, the weight of the ring grounding her as much as it thrilled her. This was real life. Burton was her best friend. It was hard to believe he'd returned, and now, she was about to spend forever with the man who had seen every part of her—the good, the bad, and the broken—and still chose her, loved her, and cherished her.

But as her heart soared, a quiet question lingered in the corners of her mind: *Am I ready for everything tonight might hold?*

Abi closed her eyes and exhaled slowly. She knew she loved Burton with every fiber of her being. She trusted him more than anyone in the world. But the possibility of taking that next step—the most intimate one—was both exhilarating and scary.

Her cheeks flushed at the thought of it fully registering. This wasn't a decision she had taken lightly. *Will this change things?* She asked herself. *Will it make our bond stronger, or will I lose a piece of myself?*

The sound of the faucet turning off brought her back for a moment, but the question stayed with her, lingering. Palms pressed to her flushed cheeks, Abi tried to calm the fluttering in her chest. Her thoughts swirled with anticipation, longing, and a twinge of uncertainty. But as her hand rested again on the blanket, a steadying realization swept over her.

Yes, I'm ready, she thought.

Being with Burton felt as natural as breathing. There was no one else she'd ever want, and the thought of giving herself to him felt like the final thread tying their souls together.

The sound of footsteps approaching snapped her out of her reverie. When Burton appeared in the doorway, his presence filling the room with an ease she couldn't quite describe, and for a moment, she wondered if he could see everything she was thinking - if he somehow knew the silent battle she'd just fought and the quiet victory she'd found. As their eyes met, she saw nothing but love in his, and that alone solidified it.

Seeing her hair cascading over her pillow, the sight of it made his chest tighten with affection. Switching off the light, he walked around to his side of the bed and slipped under the covers. Leaning over, he kissed her cheek. "Goodnight, Abs." Inching away, he rested one hand behind his head and the other lightly on his chest. "Sweet dreams."

The room went quiet except for the faint rustle of sheets. Then, Burton felt her hand rest on his arm. Glancing down at it, he turned to her.

"Is something wrong?" she asked, her innocence shining through.

He smiled and rolled onto his side. Running his fingertips along her brow, he said, "No, not at all. You've made me the happiest man alive today. I can hardly wait to call you my wife."

The brightness of her smile cut through the dimness surrounding them, warming him to the core. Without thinking, he leaned closer, and her lips met his in a loving kiss. The connection, electric yet gentle, was a reflection of the bond they shared.

Tempted beyond measure, Burton felt things escalate before he once again pulled back. "As much as I want to make love to you tonight," he began, his voice low, "I think it's important to honor your Mother's wishes."

Abi blinked, her expression curious.

"You once told me the two of you talked about waiting until you were married," he explained, brushing a kiss against her forehead. "I want that for you."

Backing away, she flashed an awestruck smile. "You're okay to wait?"

"Of course." To lighten the moment, Burton grinned, adding, "But that's not to say we can't cuddle until then."

Offering his arm, he waited as Abi nuzzled closer, resting her head against his chest. The warmth and strength of his body enveloping her caused a contented sigh to escape.

"How's that?" he asked, intermittently tightening his grip on her.

"Perfect." Drowsy with happiness, she exhaled.

As the house fell into a peaceful silence, the two of them lay entwined, the promise of their future quietly taking shape in the stillness of the night. Without a doubt, Abi knew with unwavering certainty that this man was her forever.

| 52 |

Here Comes the Bride

Saturday, July 13

Aspen, Colorado

In the days that followed, Burton and Abi slowly found their rhythm again, reacquainting themselves after the long, aching stretch of six months apart. They kept a low profile, spending their days mountain biking through the secluded trails of Aspen, stopping often to take in the sweeping views and simply enjoying their time together—no schedules, no pressure. They laughed more, talked deeply, and rediscovered the ease that had always lived between them. Away from the noise of the world, their bond deepened, growing steadier and more certain with each passing day.

Meanwhile, Martin worked tirelessly to put together the most beautiful wedding despite the quick turnaround, securing flowers, a flawless dress, and a reception that felt intimate yet unforgettable for their small circle of well-wishers. Every detail fell into place as if it had been waiting for them all along.

When Abi woke that morning, a soft light filtered through the sheers, a hush in the room reminding her she was alone. The bed beside her was empty—just as they'd agreed. Bad luck, they said, to see each other before the wedding. So Burton had taken the couch downstairs, no complaints, just that familiar, reassuring smile as he kissed her forehead the night before.

I'll see you tomorrow. Look for me. I will be waiting. The words echoed through her mind again and again.

A soft knock interrupted those fleeting thoughts.

She padded to the door, robe wrapped around her loosely as she opened it a crack and peeked into the hallway. There stood Burton's Mother, graceful as always, holding a small tray with a steaming cup of tea and a delicate plate of toast and fruit.

"May I come in, dear?" she asked gently in a motherly tone.

Stepping back, she swung the door wide. "Yes, please."

Entering quietly, she placed the tray carefully on the side table, adjusting the cup so the handle faced just right, and then settled into the chair beside the window. Her presence brought comfort, like something familiar in the nerves and flutter of the day.

"I thought you might need a little something to calm the butterflies," she said with a smile.

Abi glanced at the tea, then back at her. "Thank you. I didn't even realize how much I needed this."

Mary nodded, her eyes kind, taking in the girl her son had chosen. "Today is a big day. I wanted to share a few family traditions." Mary leaned forward and took the box resting on the tray, then handed her the small, elegantly wrapped gift. "Because all I have now are a few cherished pieces of my past, there a two things I wish to pass along to you. You're something borrowed and something blue," she said gently. "But first, you're something new. This is from Burton."

Gently peeling away the white paper, Abi unveiled a delicate silver bracelet. Her eyes immediately fell on the charm dangling from it—his Black Lyon pin from his hoodie, the night he saved her. With the bracelet was a card that read, *I will always love and protect you for the rest of my life.*

The gift was a symbol of the trust they had cultivated. Her heart soared as her fingers brushed over the charm, touched by its meaning.

Tears stung her eyes again, but this time, they were the happy kind—the kind that came from knowing her life was about to change in the most beautiful way.

"Now for your something borrowed and blue," the woman said with a smile. "This was my grandmother's. She wore it on her wedding day, and I wore it on mine." Mary carefully handed over a vintage cameo pin, its delicate carving of a lady set into a pale, tan conch shell. The cameo's intricate details, framed in fourteen-carat gold, were a timeless piece that held the weight of generations of love and tradition.

Taking it from her, Abi knew what it represented. "It's so beautiful," she whispered with a flood of emotion. "I... I don't know what to say. This means so much to me." She gently pressed the pin to her chest. "Thank you."

"I was never blessed with a daughter until now. So, it is yours, my dear," Mary shared. "Welcome to the family. Take care of my boy. He has a big heart."

Chest tightening, Abi's eyes welled with tears at the depth of Mary's words - the raw sincerity and love in the statement hitting her like a wave. Without thinking, she stepped forward and wrapped her arms around her soon-to-be mother-in-law, unable to hold back. "Thank you. I will cherish it, always," she said. "And, I want you to know how much I love Burton... I wish I could put it into words."

Realizing that being unable to describe it spoke volumes, she tilted her head. "If what you share is indescribable, then, to me, that means you've found forever." Fidgeting, the woman removed something from the layers of tissue paper. "On a lighter note, I also wore this something blue for my wedding and thought it would be fitting," Mary said with a lighthearted chuckle, presenting her with a baby blue garter. She giggled, adding, "I hope that's not too corny."

A smile broke upon Abi's face. "No, not at all."

"Thank you for loving my son." Tears began to flow freely, making Mary embrace her. "I didn't get an opportunity to extend my condolences to you on your Mother's passing. I am so sorry..." The woman's heart went out to her new daughter-in-law. Holding the girl tightly, she tried to impart all the consolation she could. After a moment, she pulled away and dabbed her eyes before tilting her head towards the ceiling to stop the flood. "She will be here today in spirit. Never doubt that." Emotions running high, she added, "Well, on that note, I will leave you to get ready. Holler if you need me, my dear," the woman said before walking out the door.

"I will. Thank you."

Alone again, tasked with getting ready on her own, Abi started with a shower before proceeding to do her hair and makeup. Turning every so often to see the pretty wedding dress hanging from the door frame, she loved the intricate lace that edged the bodice, along with the plunging back and free-flowing silk skirt that shimmered in the light.

"In less than an hour, I will be Mrs. Burton Lancaster." She stopped. "Wait... Or will I be Mrs. Dean Anderson?" Never having discussed it, she whispered to herself, "What is important is that I will be Burton's wife." The thought of it made her gasp, sending chills down her spine. Grateful for her life, she suddenly felt so grown up. "Yes, his wife," she repeated while putting the finishing touches on her hair and makeup.

Ready to put on the dress, she carefully slipped into it and zipped up the side before putting on her dainty shoes. Pinning the cameo to her bustier, she clasped Burton's bracelet and slid the soft blue garter up her leg under her skirt.

"There," she said, looking in the mirror. "I think that's it."

A gentle knock came on the door. Walking over, mindful of her dress, Abi opened it to find Mary in a navy blue gown with a brightness upon her face. Feeling nervous excitement, the woman's sights settled on her.

"Oh! My dear, you look absolutely beautiful," she exclaimed with a gasp, fluttering her hands to stop herself from crying.

"Thank you," Abi said, peering down at the dress. "Do you like it?"

Clutching her heart, she replied, "Oh, it's perfect."

Nodding nervously, Abi squeaked the word, "Yes, I think so too."

"Are you ready?" she asked.

Butterflies taking flight, she took a breath. "I think so."

Leaving the room, the two women made their way toward the grand staircase. Their footsteps were light and rhythmic on the polished hardwood floor. Abi's heart pounded in her chest. The gown flowed around her as she took each step carefully, knowing this was it. Her wedding day.

Mary remained steady and calm, her arm linked with Motherly affection.

As they reached the top, the bride glanced down. Almost unable to breathe, she saw Martin standing at the bottom, looking effortlessly handsome in a designer suit, his eyes full of pride as they found her. Strains of the song *Can't Help Falling in Love with You* by Kina Grannis played faintly in the background, filling the air with the romantic, timeless melody she loved.

Ascending the stairs to escort the two safely down the steps, Martin handed the bride her bouquet when they reached the bottom.

As they approached the flower-lined path, Abi spotted Burton waiting at the far end. Moving toward him, a vision in white, his Mother to her left and Martin to her right, she smiled through the tears.

Standing tall, forever brave, and selfless with his hands formally clasped in front of him, he beamed. The best man, Lorenzo, was by his side while the other men turned around in their seats as she made her way down the aisle.

His expression softening the closer she got, Burton met them a few feet away and offered his hand so they could move forward together. Guiding her, arm and arm, his eyes on hers—intense and unguarded, she could see a flicker of joy while Martin ushered Mary to her seat and stepped behind the podium before them.

The instrumental music chosen continued to play in the background as Martin began:

"Dearly beloved. We are gathered here today to witness the union of Burton and Abi in holy matrimony."

Hearing pieces of his opening address, Abi nervously recalled the vows she'd written.

"This is the moment where love becomes a promise. Burton and Abi, your vows are the bridge between your past and your future—the sacred words that will bind your hearts and your lives from this day forward." Martin paused. "Burton, please recite your vows to Abi."

With a deep breath, he faced her and held both of her hands. "Abi," he said, "It's no secret that I've always been very protective of you. Looking back, when we were young, I think a part of me loved you even then. But when we found each other again, our friendship slowly grew into something deeper, and before I knew it, you had my heart. We've faced fear, loss, and danger, and through it all, we survived, together. You've stood beside me when the world felt impossible, and reminded me what it means to fight, to hope, and to love. You've seen me at my strongest and my weakest, yet you never gave up on me. Instead, you spoke words of encouragement that kept me going. Today, I promise to protect you, to listen, and to make you feel safe no matter what life brings our way. I'll hold you close, hear you when you speak, and always be your safe place in this chaotic world. I vow to love you not just for who you are today, but for all the incredible things you'll become in the years ahead." He paused, his thumbs gently brushing the tops of her hands as he looked into her eyes. "I will proudly walk beside you, hand in hand, through every joy and every challenge, knowing you are the greatest gift I will ever receive in life."

As his words sank in, Abi gasped and barely heard Martin prompt her to go next.

"Burton..." she said, "From the very beginning, you've been my best friend and my protector. This steady and quiet presence, watching over me like it was second nature. And maybe for you, it always was. You've given of yourself—your time, your heart, your whole being, and did it while carrying more than most ever see without complaint." She paused to gather her thoughts. "You've given me a home when I had nowhere to go. Gave me fairytale moments despite the darkness falling upon my life. Through it all, you held me together when I was breaking apart. You believed in me when I lost faith in myself. And now, you love me with an ease I didn't know was possible- a love that has been there all this time. Today, in front of everyone, I promise you this: To never take you for granted. To honor you with loyalty, with patience, and devotion. I promise to laugh with you, to grow with you, and to stand by you through every season life gives us." She tightened her grip on him. "I promise to honor your dreams as if they were my own, to stand beside you when the world feels heavy, and to celebrate every victory, no matter how small. I vow to love you not just for who you are today but for who you aspire to be. You are my greatest love, and the partner I will choose every single day." She took a deep breath, holding back her tears.

With that said, Martin requested the rings, which Lorenzo handed over willingly.

Resting them in the middle of his Bible, he raised it between them. These rings, though simple in form, are rich in meaning. They are a symbol of the sacred promise Abi and Burton have made to one another today—a promise of love, loyalty, and forever. Let these rings always remind you of this moment—of the vows spoken, the quiet strength between you, and the deep love that brought you here. May they be a circle unbroken, just like the bond you share. May they carry the memory of every hand held, every challenge faced, and every joy celebrated together. And when the days are easy, may they shine as reminders of gratitude. When the days are hard, may they serve as anchors, drawing you back to one another. These rings are not just worn—they are lived. May they be a constant whisper of your promise: *Always.*"

The wind shifted, sending a soft breeze through the garden, and for a brief moment, time felt suspended. Burton reached for her hand, his grip unwavering, his love eternal, as he slid the ring onto her finger. She did the same for him, solidifying the promise made between them.

"Since Burton and Abi have declared their love before us today, I now have the greatest pleasure of introducing them as husband and wife. You may now kiss the bride," Martin said joyfully.

Burton didn't hesitate. He leaned in, his lips finding hers in a kiss that sealed not only their vows but everything they'd survived—the narrow escapes, the months of looking over their shoulders, every brush with danger tied to the names Black Lyon, Dark Demon, and Red Dragon. Those shadows no longer held power over them. They had stood face to face with some of the world's darkest forces and come out stronger. Now, surrounded by flowers and the loyal few who had become their family, they were ready. Whatever came next, they knew they would survive it—together.

| 53 |

Sneaky Lane

Saturday, July 13

Aspen, Colorado

The evening air was cool, carrying the faint scent of flowers from the garden where they had pledged their love to each other forever. The stars above sparkled brightly as though the universe itself was celebrating their union.

At their fairy tale reception, adorned with towering tabletop trees filled with blossoms, white flowers, and flickering candlelight, the celebration was filled with laughter, heartfelt toasts, and the warmth of family. Sadly, just before eleven, it all came to an end.

Bidding goodnight to half of the staff, the newlyweds took a moment to honor his Mother and Martin before the guys took their bags and packed them in the SUV waiting outside. Burton shrugged out of his suit jacket and wrapped it around Abi's shoulders as they walked hand in hand toward the truck, the night air brushing against their skin. She leaned into him, the gesture small but full of affection.

"So... Where are we going?" she asked, curiosity flickering.

A mischievous smile appeared on his face. "I've got a, umm, *sneaky* surprise for you."

She raised an eyebrow. "Sneaky, huh?"

"Yep."

Wondering what he'd planned, her heart fluttered.

Offering his hand to help her into the truck, he gathered the train of her dress and got her settled before getting in beside her. About to depart, the two stole one last look at Martin and Mary in the doorway. Hands lifted in a silent goodbye, it felt meaningful somehow, like they were leaving one life and embarking on the next.

As they eased through the gates and merged onto the highway, they left the city lights shimmering in the distance. With so much change on the horizon, Abi realized she was entering an adult world, one with responsibilities and expectations. Unafraid, she snuggled in closer to Burton and brushed her cheek against his shoulder. "You're really not going to give me a hint?" she asked, veering away from her heavy thoughts.

Tight-lipped, he wrapped his arm around her, fingers caressing her arm. "Nope. You'll see."

Crossing a wide bridge, the subtle gleam of the moonlight reflected off the black river below. When they left the highway and curved through a quiet roundabout, the truck veered onto a narrow lane. The world outside grew quiet, more still, until they saw a stately uplit wooden sign at the edge of the tree line. As the headlights passed over it, she read: *Welcome to Sneaky Lane.*

Abi blinked, and a soft laugh escaped her. "Oh, so it's the name of the house?"

His eyes brightened with affection. "Yes. It is."

Loving this newfound playful, thoughtful side of him, she knew this was a memory she'd forever cherish.

Entering the gates, winding through tall pines, they reached the hidden home. A modern house of stone and wood, tucked quaintly amongst the trees like a secret kept by nature. Softly lit from within, it looked like something out of a dream. Its black tin roof gleamed under the stars, and expansive windows illuminated like lanterns.

Peering out the window, Abi's eyes sparkled.

Seeing how happy she was, he didn't have to ask, but did anyway. "So, will this do?"

She grasped his hand. "Oh, Burton. It's perfect."

Giving their boss a knowing nod, Lorenzo and Andrew continued with their duties and efficiently unloaded the bags before disappearing inside a nearby guesthouse to leave the newlyweds in peace.

"They'll be close but will remain out of sight," Burton divulged, guiding Abi to the front entry. "We've got this place all to ourselves."

He opened the large pivot door but paused before letting her walk in. There was something in his expression. "I think the tradition is to carry you over the threshold."

Before she could protest, he whisked her into his arms.

"Oooh, Mr. Anderson!" Her whimsical laugh was infectious.

How she said it caught him off guard, but in a good way. Spirited and sexy, it only increased his attraction as he held her tightly while her laughter spilled into the night. The joy on her face mirrored the relaxed grin on his - a rare gleam appearing in his eyes.

Inside, Burton set her down gently.

The interior welcomed them with clean lines, light wood, and linen textures that made the place feel like a sanctuary. Floor-to-ceiling windows invited the forest in, along with the babbling brook visible from every room.

Closing the door and locking the bolt, Burton watched Abi explore their surroundings. The scene almost had a magical quality as her fingertips trailed over the curve of a leather armchair, the marble counter, and the smooth grain of the table as he followed her from room to room.

When she reached the end of the lower level, they stumbled upon a stunning primary bedroom with walls of glass framing the river and towering trees like living artwork. The bed was made up of white linens, soft pillows, and cozy throw blankets along the footboard.

Burton came up behind her, his warm hands set gently on her waist.

"Do you like it?" he asked, having placed their bags on the nearby bench.

She turned to him. "It feels like the Malibu house."

"I thought so, too."

Wanting to change out of her wedding dress, she removed her heels. "I'll be right back," she said, clutching her overnight bag as she stepped into the bathroom.

Anxiety surfaced the moment she closed the door, and without warning, nervous energy coursed through her veins. Looking in the mirror, she knew she would be forever changed after tonight. Body infused with butterflies and anticipation, she gathered her hair in a messy bun and stepped into the shower. Thoughts of loving him appeared, but not from experience. She just relied on her imagination, taking from what she'd heard and read. There wasn't an ounce of fear or doubt. Everything they'd been through, everything they'd waited for. It all led to this.

Not wanting to keep him waiting, she dried off and brushed her hair so it cascaded freely over her shoulders before slipping on her white silk nightgown. Ready to walk out, the fabric floating around her like mist, she paused, her hand resting on the door handle. Taking a deep breath, she quietly opened it. About to turn off the light, she stopped.

The room had changed.

Warm candlelight now filled the space, and rose petals were spread over the bed. A floral bouquet of roses sat on the nightstand while music caressed the air. It was beyond beautiful.

There, she found Burton freshly showered and standing near the window. Hands buried in his pajama bottom pockets, she opted to watch him for a moment. It was hard to believe he was now her husband. A white, fitted t-shirt clung to his chest. His posture appeared relaxed. But beneath the surface, Abi could see he was deep in thought while staring out over the rapids.

She didn't speak right away. Just watched him, her heart full. The boy she once knew had become the man who was now her partner for life, and he'd planned every detail tonight not for show but to make her feel loved.

Turning off the light, she asked quietly, "Penny for your thoughts?" hoping she wouldn't startle him.

When he swiveled around, the look on his face made her knees go weak. His smile, slow and warm, greeted her like her presence alone was all he needed.

The nightgown she wore shimmered faintly in the candlelight. With its delicate spaghetti straps looped over her shoulders, she crossed the room and stepped into his waiting arms before resting her head against his chest.

For a moment, neither spoke.

Then, quietly, she asked, "Everything okay?"

Burton drew in a breath, needing to voice his thoughts. "I know how special this night is," he said sincerely. "And it isn't lost on me. I hope you know that."

She nodded, making him hold her a little closer, the warmth of his body grounding her.

"And if you wanted to wait," he continued gently. "If you're not ready—"

She lifted her hand and pressed a single finger over his lips, stopping him mid-sentence. "No," she said. "I am right where I want to be. Fully and completely—as your wife."

When she said that, it sparked something strong inside him. "My wife," he said, wrapping his heart around it.

Abi rose on her tiptoes as her lips delicately touched his. "That's right. I'm yours. Always and forever."

His hands found her cheeks, framing her face with aching tenderness. Then, with one strong, fluid motion, Burton scooped her into his arms. Sweeping her off her feet, he clutched her against his chest.

Caught off guard, Abi gasped and clung to his shoulders, her laughter echoing through the house. "You really do like carrying me around," she whispered.

"You'd better get used to it, Mrs. Townsend-Anderson."

She kissed him. "No, Mrs. Anderson will suffice."

Full of admiration, he smiled and said, "Good to know."

They crossed the room slowly, his steps silent but sure. The world outside was hushed—just moonlight pouring through the window and the quiet rhythm of their breathing.

Reaching the bed, Burton knelt on one knee and laid her gently on the cool sheets. Precious and fragile, he gazed upon her, not with lust but love.

As he inched closer and hovered, she felt his fingers graze her arm delicately.

"I love you," he whispered.

As his strength and protective nature surfaced, she looked into his eyes. "I love you, too."

Showering her with kisses, each slow and meaningful, his lips brushed her shoulder to jawline as his eyes fell upon hers periodically, reading her like he was asking permission for every movement.

Fingers curling into the fabric of his shirt, her heart fluttered as she ran her hands along his chest before peeling it off his body. Never having done this before, she traced his muscles with her fingertips while exploring him, immersed in every ounce of the moment.

She felt the soft press of his forehead against hers as he breathed her in.

"Are you still…" he whispered, his tone low.

She nodded, but that wasn't enough. She wanted him to know, beyond words, that she was truly okay. Taking his hand and placing it over her heart, she let him feel how it raced only for him.

Fingers hidden behind her ears, his thumb caressed her cheek. This newfound trust meant everything. Sliding his hand down the curve of her neck, memorizing her with his touch, he kissed the hollow beneath her ear. Each was unhurried. Light.

When his fingers reached the delicate straps of her nightgown, he paused, eyes on hers, waiting for quiet reassurance.

Lovingly, she whispered, "It's okay."

Mindful as the white satin eased down her shoulders, he felt as though he were unveiling something sacred. Stepping back, he stood before her and pulled the drawstring on his pajama bottoms. As they fell away, she got her first look at him before the two converged in the most vulnerable way.

"You are so beautiful," he said as they sank into the pillows.

Making sure not to overwhelm her, he left a little space between them before nestling her body with his own. His weight was comforting, his arms strong yet gentle. They lay bare, their skin touching in quiet communion.

Exhaling slowly, Abi's fingers curled against his chest, and for the very first time, the world outside faded away.

Just the two of them, emotions rising fast, Abi trembled unexpectedly.

Sensing it, his eyes searched hers. "Hey..." he whispered faintly. "We can stop..."

"No." She shook her head. "It's not that." Looking up at him, something in his eyes—calm and loving—made it easier to breathe. "I'm feeling so many things...all at once."

Time seemed to stretch and bend, no longer moving in minutes or seconds but in the rise and fall of breath. Only devotion and love unfolded. Two people learning how to be close in a way that went far beyond anything she'd known.

What followed was like time standing still. Every movement, every kiss, every sigh, and whisper was a conversation between them—a promise sealed in the commitment they'd made. When she reached for him, he stilled to make her feel safe, the kind of closeness that could never be explained—only felt.

And when they finally came together, it felt like every love song suddenly made sense. Wrapped in the white sheets amidst the flicker of candlelight, they finally gave in as the rhythm between them built slowly. As his groan met her lips through every wave, each breath, and tremble, he remained a steady presence, guiding and loving her in a way she never expected. The heat that curled low in her belly was unfamiliar, but not frightening. With him, it felt right. Safe.

Subtle gasps escaped her. Arching into him, lips parting, she emitted pleasured sounds, unable to hold back. Left breathless, clinging to each other, he wrapped her in his arms, chest heaving. He stayed right there, arms tight around her. Kissing her temple, his breathing was ragged against her skin.

"Are you..." He whispered, his gaze fixed on her.

Heart full, knowing what he wanted to ask, she offered a contented grin and nodded, utterly undone. "I love you," she said.

His hand slid up her back, pulling her even closer. "I love you, too," he replied and kissed her like it was the most natural thing in the world.

Heartbeats stabilizing in the darkness, they stayed tangled up in each other, the silence deep and peaceful. Embraced fully, Abi rested her head upon his chest. Listening to the steady beat beneath her ear as it slowed, she lay in the arms of her best friend, the one who used to watch out for her on ski trips and hold her hand when she was scared—the man who had now become far more. And in that quiet, flickering moment between sleep and stars, she knew all of it was worth the wait.

Unable to fall asleep, she listened to Burton breathing while he drifted off. Tucked alongside him with one arm around her, he lay on his back with the other behind his head.

It was so quiet.

All she could hear was the peeping of frogs outside and the babbling brook. Above the water, she could see a number of fireflies clearly visible against the dark forest backdrop.

With legs willingly tangled beneath the sheets, she was immersed in the sheer bliss of the experience that night. Marveling at how he'd barely moved the last hour, she recalled in flashes how he loved her so attentively as she traced her finger across his chest. Cheek pressed against his shoulder, unable to ignore the fire igniting inside her, she whispered, "Burton? Are you asleep?"

He shifted slightly, humming groggily, "Hmm?"

Nervousness flowed through her because she wasn't sure how to ask. "I was just…wondering…if we could…"

His head turned toward her slowly. One eye opened. Then the other. "If we could…?" he asked, not knowing what she needed.

Her hand moved down his body and continued south.

Getting the hint, he rolled onto his side and propped himself on an elbow. Inches from her, he kissed her lips and caught her eye before saying in a sultry voice, "How can I be of service, Mrs. Anderson?"

In a sexy tone, she shrugged and said, "I don't know. Surprise me."

"Hmmm," he growled. "Are you sure?"

"Positive," she answered playfully.

This time when their lips met, his kisses felt different – more daring, less cautious. His hand trailed her body before his muscles flexed and pulled her closer and closer. Melded together, he kissed the hollow of her neck and whispered, "Were you looking for something like this?"

A blissful sound escaped her.

Feeling his cheek brushing against hers, she leaned into him as her body tingled. Then, in a sensual tone, he asked, "Maybe more of this?"

She mumbled, "Oooh… I think so…"

With every confident touch and caress, he explored what lovingly belonged to him now.

"Just so you know, for future reference, I will never be too tired to love you."

She smiled. "I sure hope so."

Lacing their fingers together, he said, "Good, because I plan to love you like this forever."

| 54 |

Nine Weeks Later

Tuesday, September 10

Harvard University, Boston, Massachusetts

When Lorenzo pulled up in front of Adams House - an old collegiate building on a one-way street surrounded by Harvard history, Burton turned to Abi and said, "Be safe. Have a good day."

"Thanks. Don't miss me too much."

"I'll try not to." Burton saw the guys get out of the truck and survey their surroundings. Before she got out, he said, "I love you," hating the idea of her being out of his sight.

"Love you, too." Leaning over, she kissed him.

With no choice in the matter, Burton reluctantly let go of her as Andrew opened her door.

Waving to him with the guys a few steps behind, she continued toward the historic building, prepared to face the day.

Making it through registration and her first orientation, the guys followed her to the lecture hall. As she took a seat along the outside edge, many of the students around her wondered who the goons were. Through it all, Abi kept to herself as people whispered.

Amidst her first lecture, the professor stepped to the front of the class.

"Welcome! As you will learn in the coming months, I like to get straight to the point. I was a high-achieving honors student and valedictorian during my high school years. Figured that would pave the way for me. It was fine and all, but I'm here to tell you that academic achievements alone won't shape your journey here. When you decide to pursue medicine – especially at this institution – you'll need to navigate a bit with your head and a bit with your heart." The professor smiled, pausing for a moment. "I know that might sound a little sentimental, but it's the truth. And if my years of teaching have taught me anything, it's that the students who thrive here are the ones who balance both. Sure, there are brilliant minds among you. Some of you may already have accolades that put you at the top of your class, maybe even your field. But the thing that stands out the most about the students here isn't just their intellect – it's their purpose. Those who succeed are those who care deeply about something bigger than themselves. They believe in the power to change the world, not because it's easy but because they know it's possible. As you embark on this journey, I challenge you to consider what you want to create and the lasting impact you aim to leave. Medicine is malleable. The world is malleable. And you-you're the sculptor. Let's see what you can create." He paused and scanned the room. "Now, I want you to take a moment—look to your left, then to your right," he said calmly. "Each one of you earned your seat here. You're brilliant, driven, and likely used to being the best. And many of you came with the goal of helping others, of changing lives. That's noble. It matters." He let the weight of his words settle before continuing. "But let me be clear. Talent got you in—but it won't be what gets you through. This program will test your endurance, your discipline, and your ability to stay grounded when the pressure is suffocating. If you don't fully commit—if you don't show up every day ready to grow, to fail, and to keep going anyway—there is no guarantee you will graduate. Not because you aren't capable, but because medicine demands more than potential. It demands sacrifice, humility, and relentlessness to survive under pressure. That's what it takes here."

The weight of his words hung in the air, a challenge and a call to rise.

"If you're willing to meet those demands, then you'll not only graduate–you'll become the kind of person who truly makes a difference. Question is. Are you ready?"

Abi looked around the lecture hall. The people sitting beside her were beyond stressed—bent over textbooks, highlighters in hand, caffeine in veins. And in that moment, she wasn't sure if she wanted to spend the next twelve years—give or take—chasing a life that no longer felt like hers.

The rest of the day, she went through the motions. Class. Notes. Numbness. By that afternoon, she slipped into the flow of students heading toward the street. The moment she stepped outside, the air felt heavier. She wasn't sure why—that is when she heard it.

"Hey, you?"

The voice stopped her cold as she glanced over her shoulder.

There he was. Shane Coppersmith, standing between two buildings in his red Alabama cap, with that familiar grin catching the light.

For a moment, she forgot how to breathe.

"What are you doing here?" she asked, stunned, her words clumsy with nerves.

"I, umm… I asked my cousin for help. She goes here. Figured this was the only way to see you." He took notice of the black SUVs and the discreet security team standing by. "I see Martin's still got the guys with you."

"Yes…umm… can't be too careful."

"How have you been? How's Martin?"

Abi looked down at her shoes. "Good. He's… good. He moved here with me."

The sun broke through the clouds, making Abi unknowingly raise her hand to shield her eyes from the brightness. It was then that Shane spotted the diamond sparkling on her finger.

"What's with the ring?"

She followed his gaze, startled. "Umm…"

His face dropped. "Abs… is that an engagement ring?" His voice cracked, despite the effort to keep it casual. He shifted on his feet, heart visibly unraveling.

"Married, actually."

He blinked. Once. Twice. The punch hit slowly. "To whom?" He knew, even before he asked, as his eyes drifted toward the line of SUVs. "He's alive? Is he here?"

She glanced at Andrew and Lorenzo, who immediately began to approach. "Umm, Shane… I need to go," she said before turning to leave.

"No, Abi! Wait!"

She froze.

"Just tell me one thing."

Glancing over her shoulder, she asked, her voice soft. "What's that?"

His gentle eyes searched hers with the weight of the world upon his shoulders. "Are you happy?"

Without hesitation, she smiled with quiet certainty. "Yes. Very much so. How about you?"

Shane swallowed hard. "I'm…okay. I might've met someone, too."

Her arms crossed over her chest without thinking. "Really? That's good. I'm happy to hear that."

Unsure what this was, she wondered if he was seeking peace? Closure, perhaps? Did he want permission to move on with his life? Had he come in hopes of reconnecting?

"I've been watching your NCAA progress," she said, avoiding the drama. "And the promise of making the NFL. You're living your dream, Shane. Keep striving for that. I'm so proud of you and wish you all the best."

She stepped forward and hugged him.

In his arms, she felt like a memory. Shane held her tight, not ready to let go. But he could feel it—something had changed. She wasn't the same girl he used to love. She seemed stronger, wiser.

"Is it okay if I call you sometime? You know, check in, see how you're doing? Not sure if you got a new phone after yours got taken in Japan." Shane pulled his from his pocket.

She immediately saw the picture of him with the Huntington Beach girl on his home screen. "Umm, I did get a new phone."

Standing there, he waited to see what she would do.

"Given my life now and the secret I'm keeping, I think it's best we, umm..."

Realizing every one of their friends believed she was gone, he slowly nodded, understanding her position.

"Nobody can know that I'm really..."

"I won't tell anyone. I give you my word."

"Thank you." When Andrew signaled to her, she abruptly backed away. "I'm sorry. I need to go now. Take care of yourself, okay? It was good seeing you." Turning, she met up with the guys and walked toward the street.

The further she got, Shane recalled Orientation Day at Gilderson. He remembered stepping into the foyer, the noise of excited students all around him. That is when he saw her, a flash of long brown hair amidst a sea of blonde. She wasn't trying to stand out. She just did. Beautiful in a way that didn't beg for attention—but claimed it anyway. The girl who could talk football – nicknamed New England, the girl who had stopped him in his tracks inside the parking garage. The girl he was determined to be with. The one who made him believe in things like fate and timing, and even love at first sight. But now, that once-in-a-lifetime opportunity was gone. Not just walking away...but taken. Sadly, she'd found a future with someone else. Breaking from those memories, he watched her cross the street with the guys flanking either side.

Little did he know, but Burton was watching their every move.

The guy had told himself he was just giving his wife space — letting her handle the unexpected. But when Shane rounded the corner, something primal erupted in him. Motionless, hidden behind the fortress of tinted glass, every shift in Abi's expression was seared into his memory.

She didn't run. Didn't flinch. She also didn't refrain from hugging the QB and didn't push him away either. And that did something to him. He trusted her. But trust didn't erase history - theirs or hers. Watching her speak with her first love rekindled the competitiveness between them. The way Shane looked at her, it was as though he still had a right to that kind of closeness. The scene immediately stirred something dark inside.

As Abi neared the vehicle, Andrew opened the rear door for her.

That is when Coppersmith zeroed in on him. Sitting in the back like a ghost pulled from the past, for a moment, he couldn't move. Couldn't blink. Couldn't breathe.

Instinctively, moving toward the convoy, Shane watched as the doors shut, tires rolled, and within seconds, both trucks vanished around the corner.

When they drove off, inside the vehicle, Abi lowered her head. Exhaling slowly, her fingers trembled as she pressed them to her lap.

"Well," Burton said quietly, "That was unexpected."

She stared straight ahead. "Understatement of the year." Panicking a little at the long pause between them, she heard him say, "What did he want?"

"He wanted to see me and check in but wasn't expecting..." She looked down at the rings on her left hand.

Looking out the window, he asked point-blank, "Do you still love him?"

Startled by his words, she turned and found him bracing for the answer.

Her voice was gentle, but honest. "Like every first love, they will always have a piece of your past." Instantly, she reached for his hand, threading her fingers through his. "But with you... I'm my best self.

What we have is rare, and it's everything to me. You are my husband, and will forever have my heart and soul."

He turned, eyes finally meeting hers as she kissed him lovingly.

Needing a distraction from what just happened, her voice gained strength. "You know, I've had a lot of time to think today, believe it or not..."

"Is that right?"

"My professor basically told us we'd be lucky to matter—after spending twelve years, give or take, sacrificing everything."

He nodded slowly. "And?"

She leaned closer, fire returning to her eyes. "And I don't want to wait twelve years to make a difference in this world."

A grin played on his lips. "I was kind of hoping you'd say that."

She tilted her head, half-teasing. "How much are we worth again?"

Always humble, he replied, "A lot."

"So, would you say we have the means to change the world. Like, right now?"

"Yes." Intrigued, his body relaxed in his seat. "What do you have in mind?"

She inhaled deeply, her voice thick with emotion. "How easy would it be to go back to Japan?"

"It'll be dangerous." His smile faded into something more serious. "But, if it's what you want, we'll make it happen."

Her eyes shimmered. "Good. Because I can't stop thinking about those children, and I want us to be their Mom and Dad. I want to give them the love of a family."

Burton blinked once, absorbing her words. Then he nodded, slowly. "You want to be a Mom? Not a doctor?"

She leaned into him, curling into the safety of his arms. "Is it too soon?"

"No," he said without hesitation. "Truthfully, I haven't stopped thinking about them either." He kissed her temple.

"So... is that a yes?" she asked.

His answer touched something deeper. "I think that can be arranged."

Arms wrapped around his neck, she held him close. "Thank you," she whispered as he pulled her in tight.

"And that is why I love you, Abs."

She tilted her head and kissed him slowly.

"Let's go home and pack," she said.

"Guess I need to tell Martin we are in the market for a rather monstrous house?" he laughed.

She shook her head. "No. Not just a house." A motherly expression flashed upon her face. "A home."

The End

<u>TWO YEARS LATER</u>

Where are ABI and BURTON now?

Visit my website at www.EAStarkBooks.com

and click on BOOKS –> RED DRAGON.

Scroll to BONUS Chapters.

** CLICK and ENTER THE PASSWORD **

<u>**Burton&Abi**</u>

Watch for

Shane Coppersmith's

Continuing Story!